DINOSAUR HOUR!

VOL. 1

Story and Art by
Hitoshi Shioya

DINOSAUR HOUR!

Vol. 1

Story & Art by Hitoshi Shioya

Translation/ Katherine Schilling
English Adaptation/Hope Donovan
Touch-up Art & Lettering/John Hunt
Additional Lettering/Brian Papp
Cover & Book Design/Frances O. Liddell
Editor/Carol Fox

Editor in Chief, Books/Alvin Lu
Editor in Chief, Magazines/Marc Weidenbaum
VP, Publishing Licensing/Rika Inouye
VP, Sales & Product Marketing/Gonzalo Ferreyra
VP, Creative/ Linda Espinosa
Publisher/Hyoe Narita

Kyoryu no Jikan © Hitoshi Shioya 2004
All rights reserved. Original Japanese edition published by
POPLAR Publishing Co., Ltd., Tokyo. English translation rights
directly arranged with POPLAR Publishing Co., Ltd., Tokyo.
The stories, characters and incidents mentioned in this
publication are entirely fictional.

Printed in the U.S.A.

Published by VIZ Media, LLC
P.O. Box 77010
San Francisco, CA 94107

10 9 8 7 6 5 4 3 2 1
First printing, April 2009

www.vizkids.com

store.viz.com

www.viz.com

ARCHAEOLOGIST'S DIG

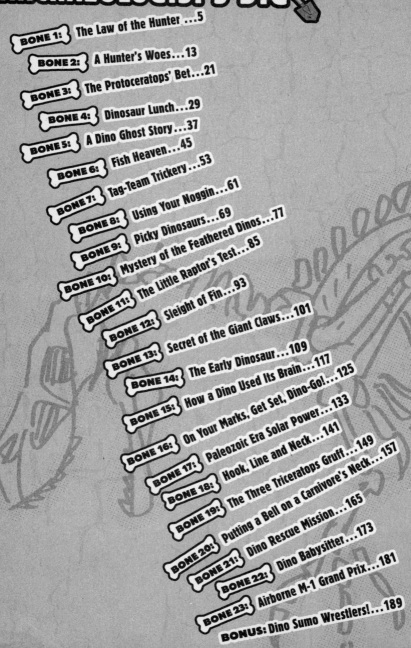

DINO-PEDIA

RAAAARR!

The world of dinosaurs is too dangerous to travel alone! Take along these HANDY FACTS and you'll be ready for anything—even a fierce T-Rex like me!

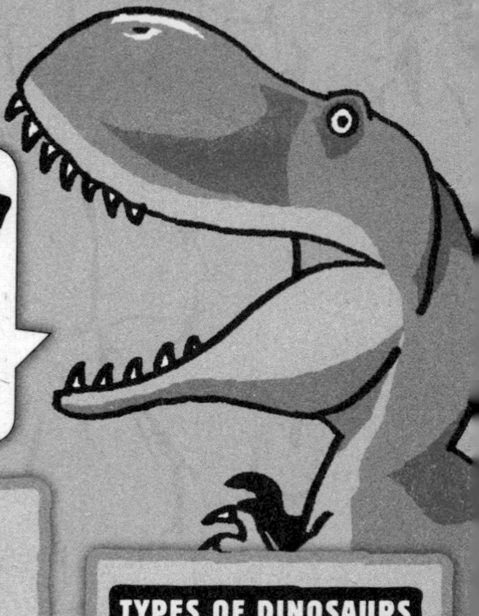

DINO TIMELINE

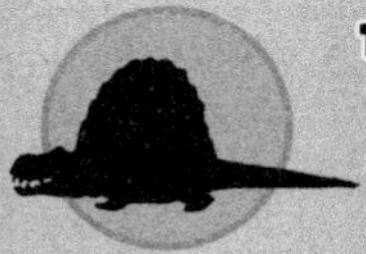

THE PERMIAN PERIOD

About 570 million to 250 million years ago, when *dinosaurs had not yet appeared.*

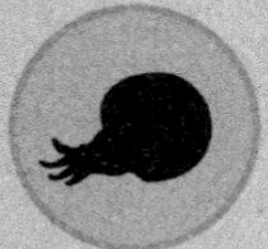

THE TRIASSIC PERIOD

About 250 million to 212 million years ago, when *reptiles ruled the earth.*

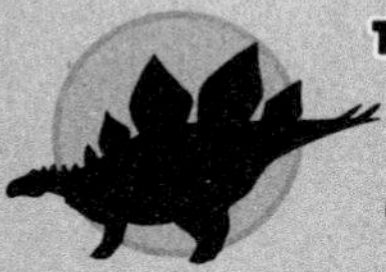

THE JURASSIC PERIOD

About 212 million to 143 million years ago, when *dinosaurs ruled the earth!*

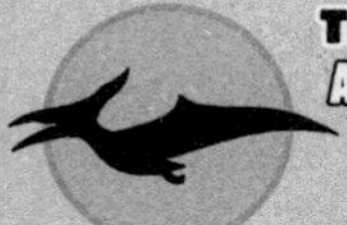

THE CRETACEOUS PERIOD

About 143 million to 65 million years ago, when *dinosaurs STILL ruled the earth!*

TYPES OF DINOSAURS

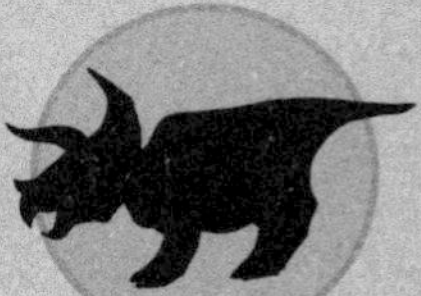

HERBIVORES

Plant-eaters. Despite their fierce reputation, most dinosaurs were actually herbivores.

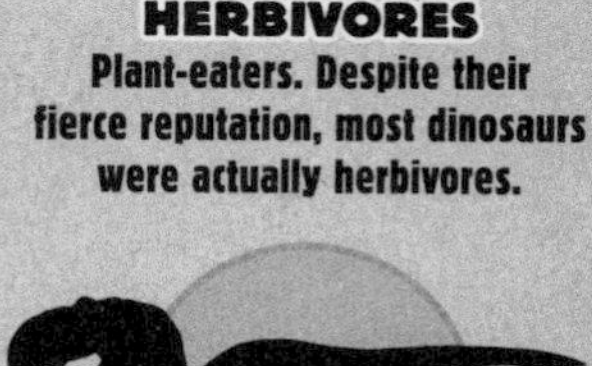

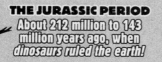

CARNIVORES

Meat-eaters. These dinosaurs ate other animals—including, sometimes, other dinosaurs!

BONE 1

The Law of the Hunter

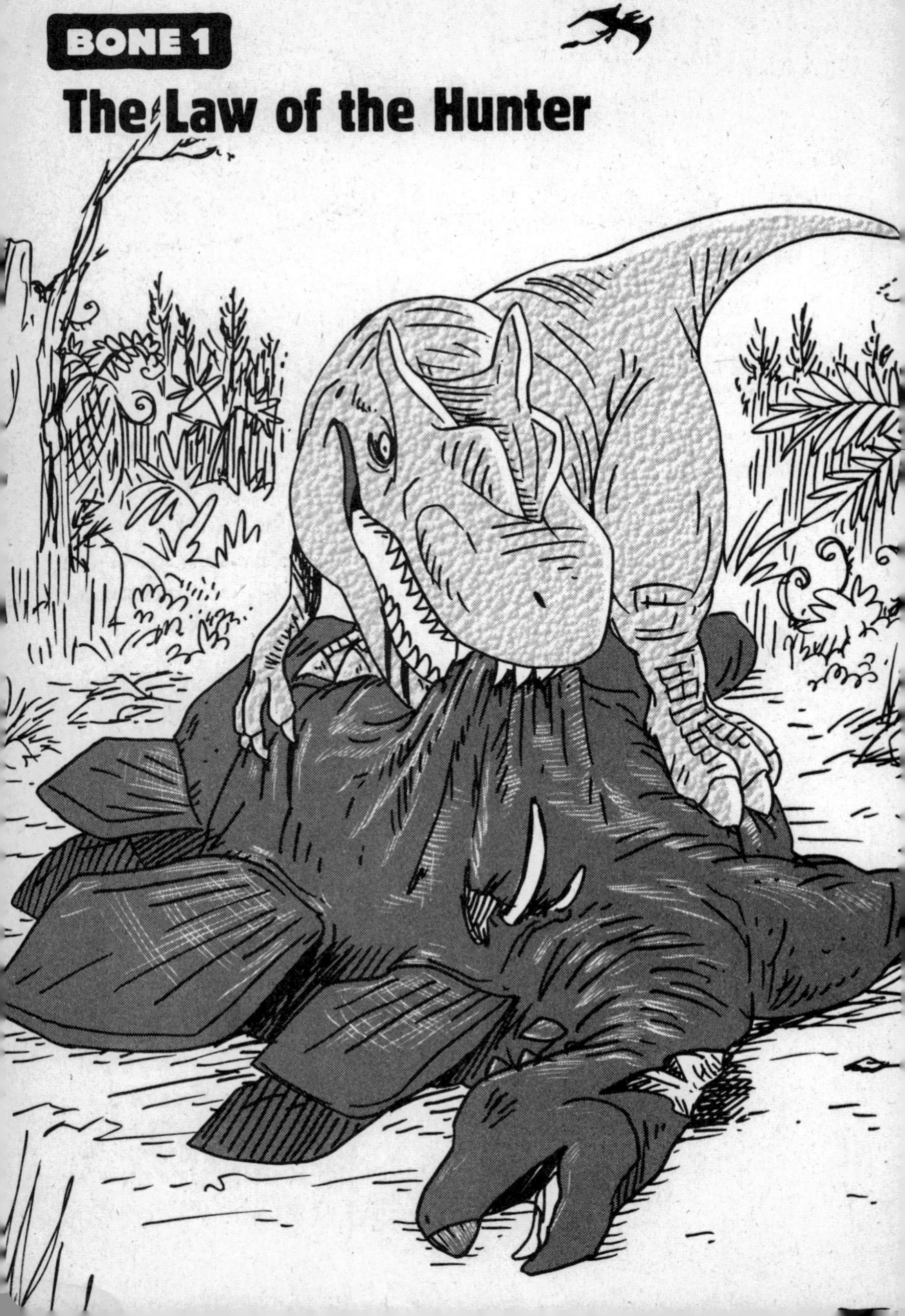

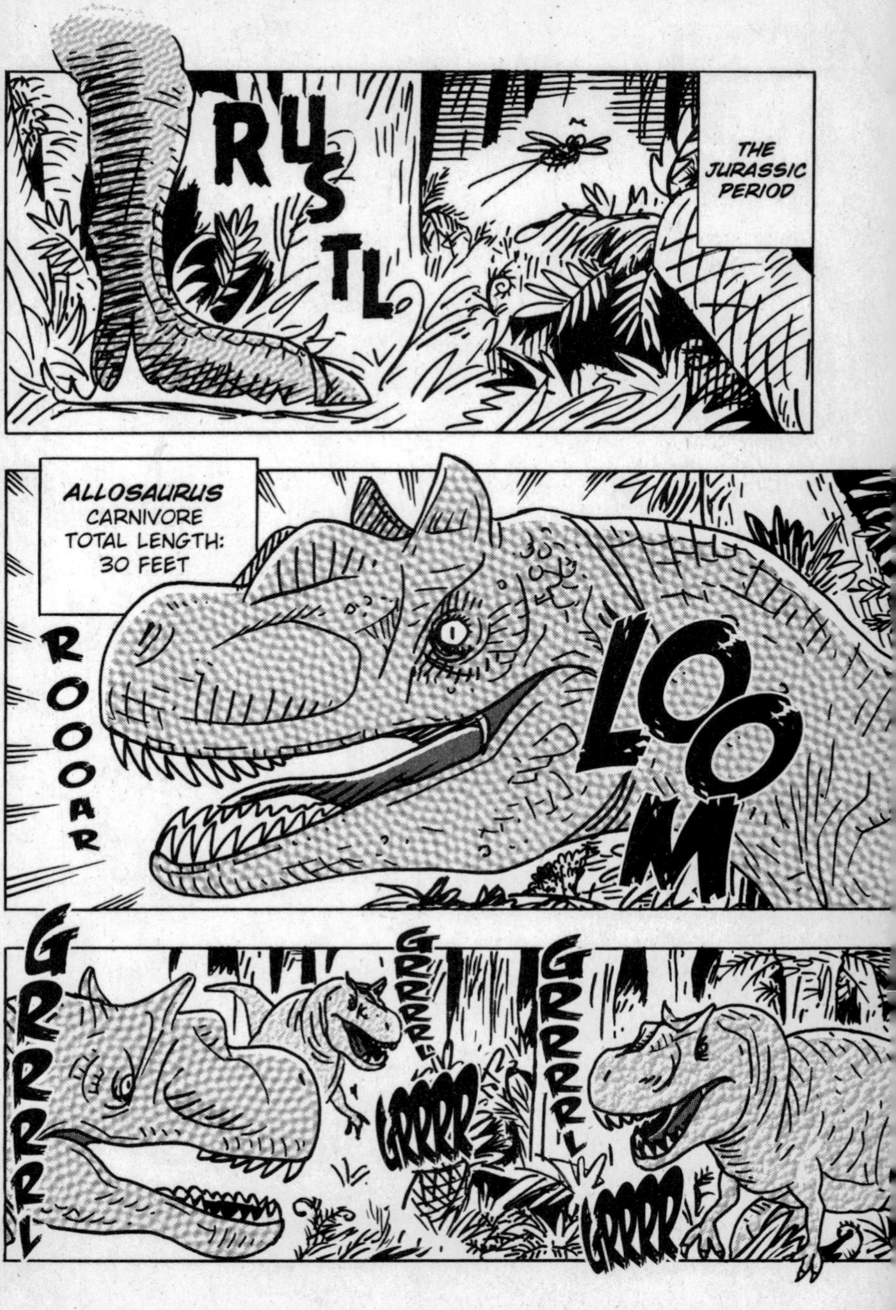
THE JURASSIC PERIOD
RUSTL
LOOM
ALLOSAURUS
CARNIVORE
TOTAL LENGTH: 30 FEET
ROOOOAR
GRRRRRL
GRRRR
GRRRRRL
GRRRR
GRRRRRL

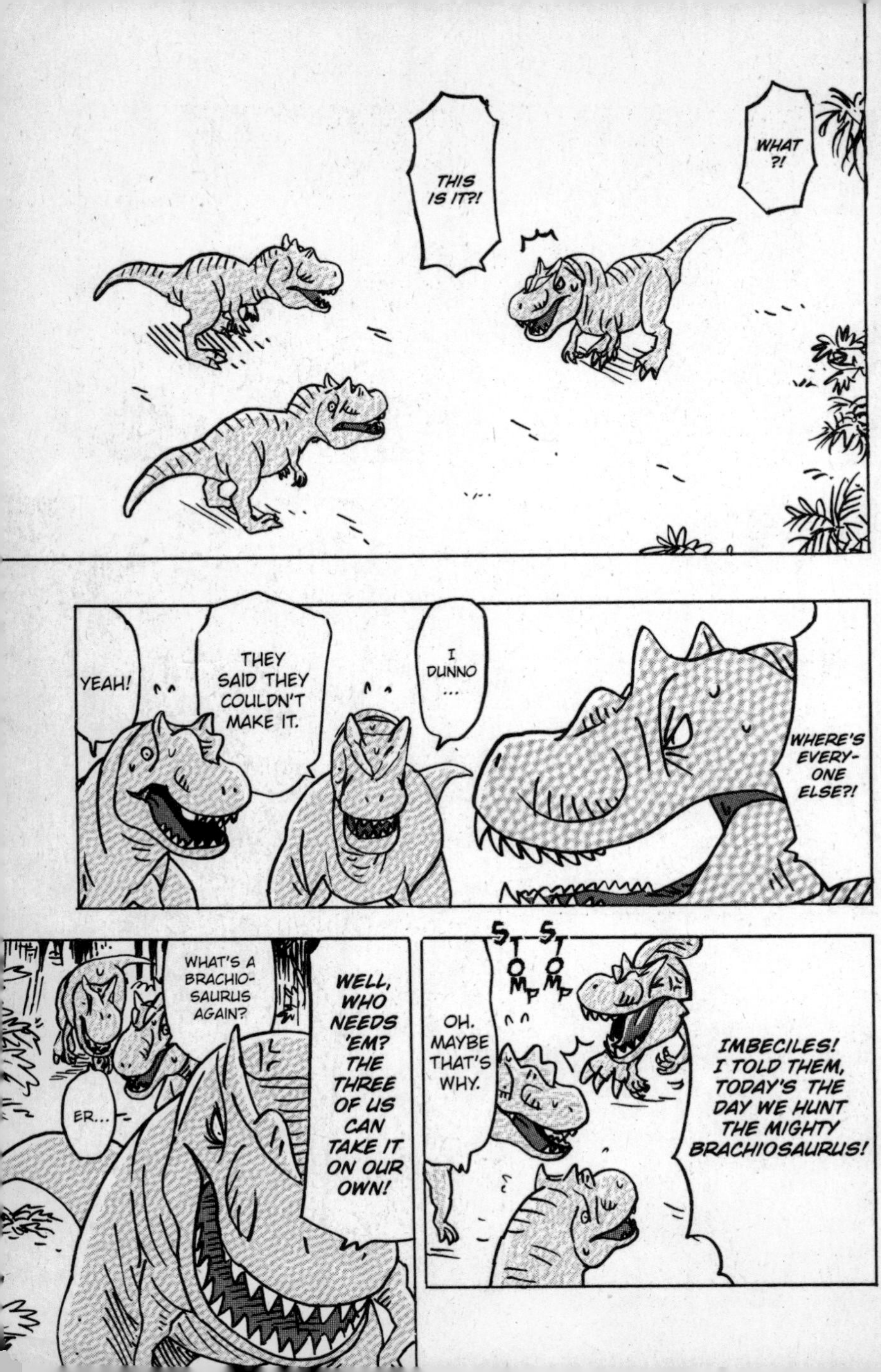
WHAT ?!
THIS IS IT?!
WHERE'S EVERY-ONE ELSE?!
I DUNNO ...
THEY SAID THEY COULDN'T MAKE IT.
YEAH!
IMBECILES! I TOLD THEM, TODAY'S THE DAY WE HUNT THE MIGHTY BRACHIOSAURUS!
STOMP STOMP
OH. MAYBE THAT'S WHY.
WELL, WHO NEEDS 'EM? THE THREE OF US CAN TAKE IT ON OUR OWN!
WHAT'S A BRACHIO-SAURUS AGAIN?
ER...

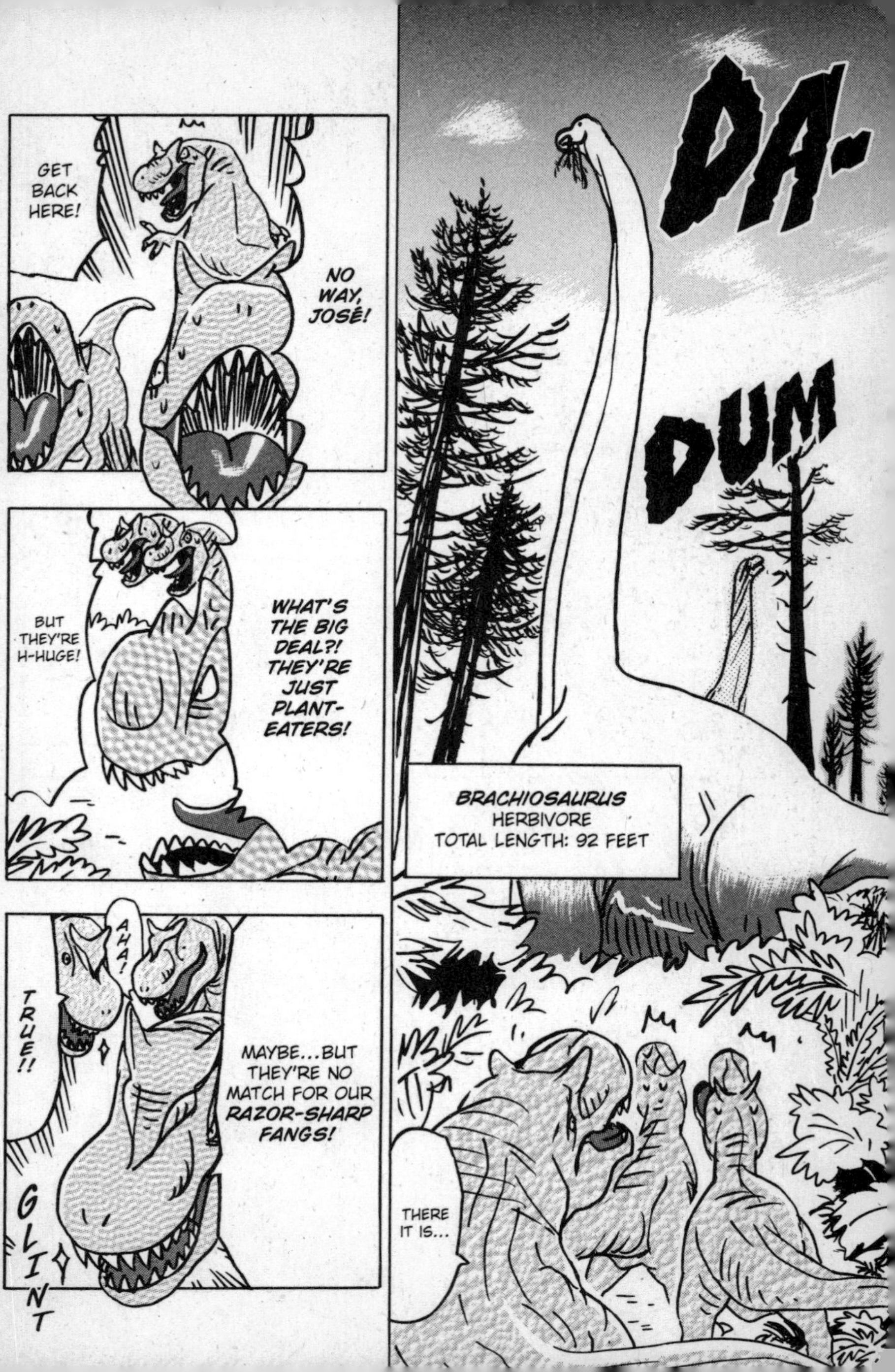
DA-
DUM
BRACHIOSAURUS
HERBIVORE
TOTAL LENGTH: 92 FEET
THERE IT IS...
NO WAY, JOSÉ!
GET BACK HERE!
WHAT'S THE BIG DEAL?! THEY'RE JUST PLANT-EATERS!
BUT THEY'RE H-HUGE!
MAYBE...BUT THEY'RE NO MATCH FOR OUR RAZOR-SHARP FANGS!
AHA!
TRUE!!
GLINT

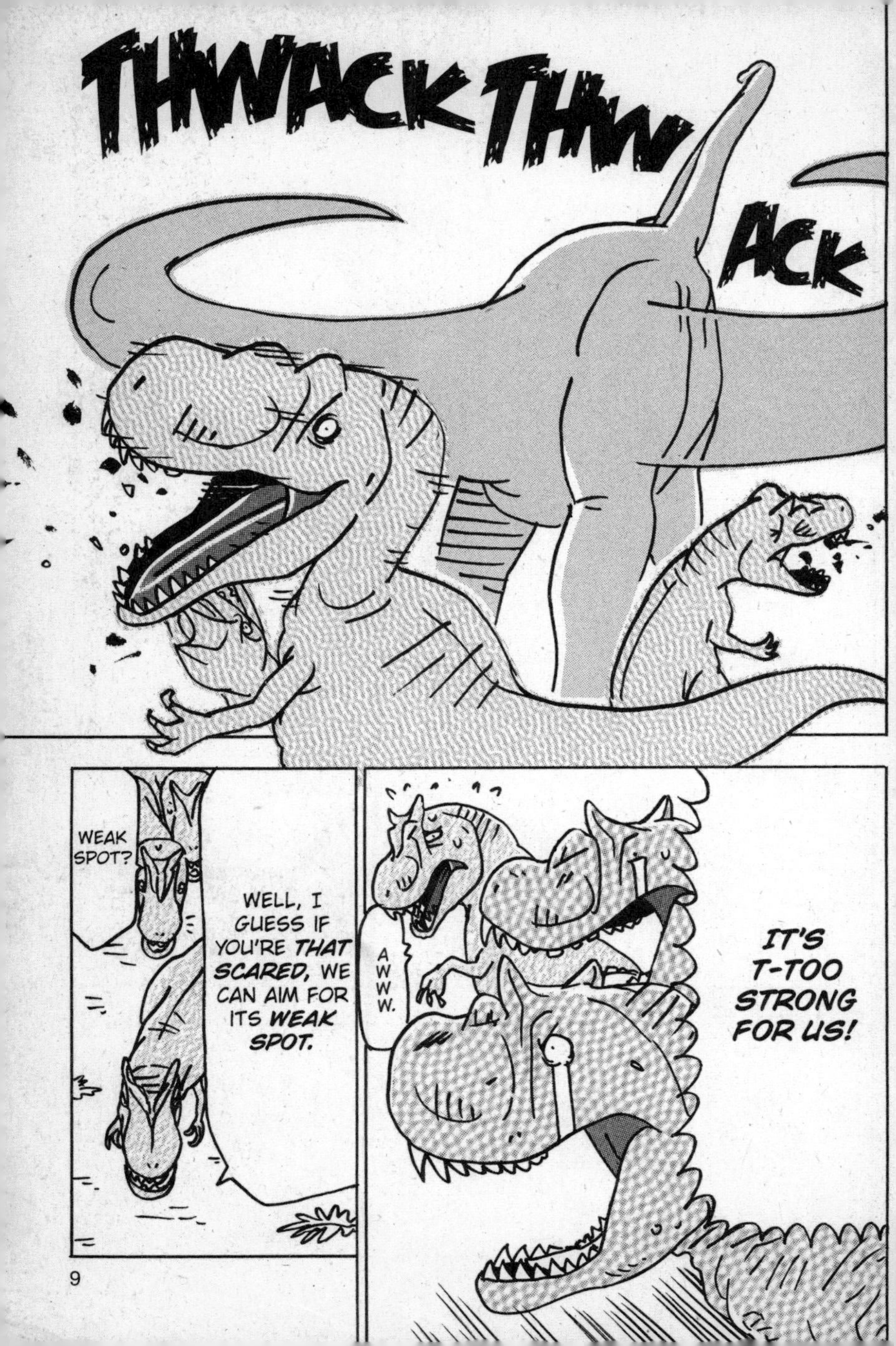
THWACK THWACK
IT'S T-TOO STRONG FOR US!
AWWW.
WEAK SPOT?
WELL, I GUESS IF YOU'RE THAT SCARED, WE CAN AIM FOR ITS WEAK SPOT.

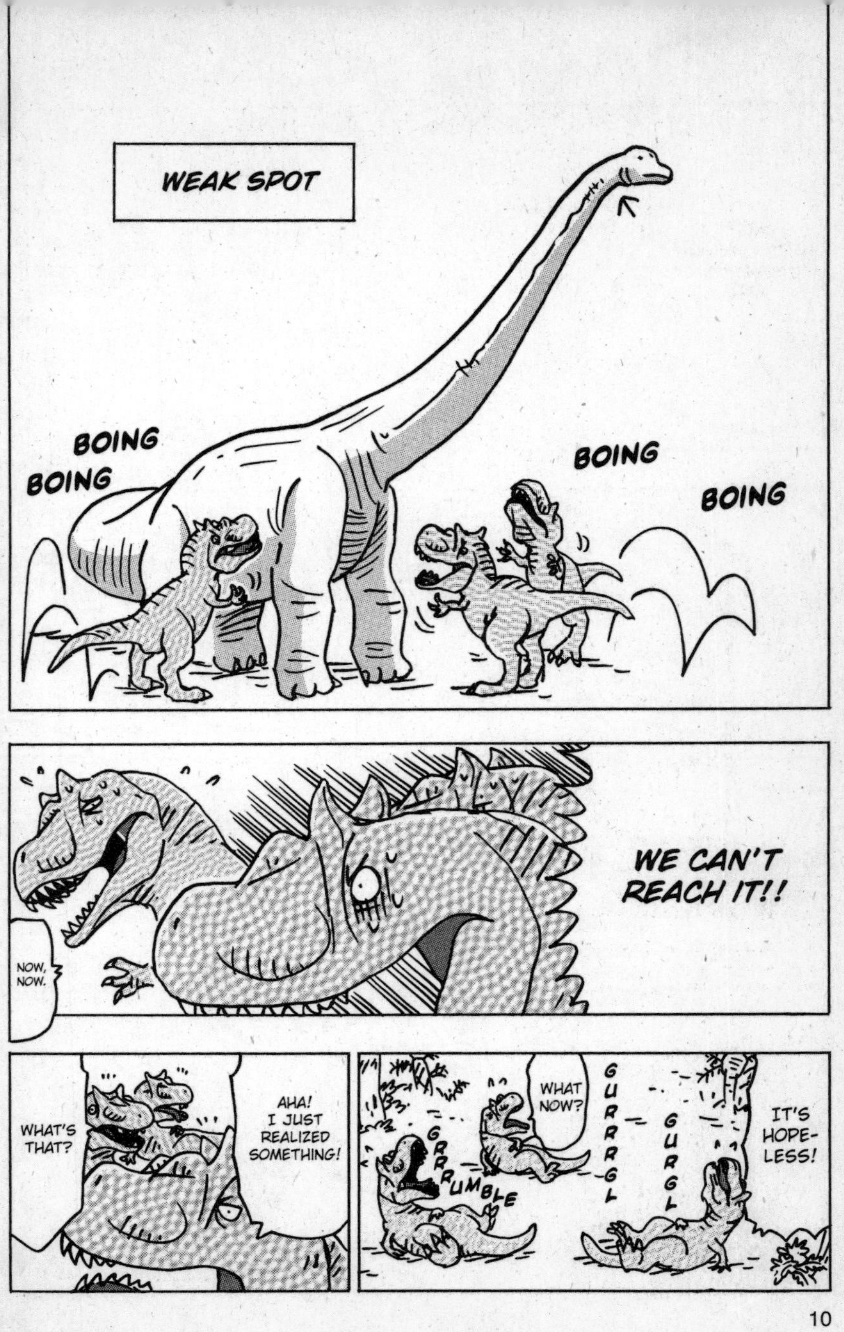
WEAK SPOT
BOING
BOING
BOING
BOING
WE CAN'T REACH IT!!
NOW, NOW.
IT'S HOPE-LESS!
GURGL
GURRRGL
WHAT NOW?
GRRUMBLE
AHA! I JUST REALIZED SOMETHING!
WHAT'S THAT?

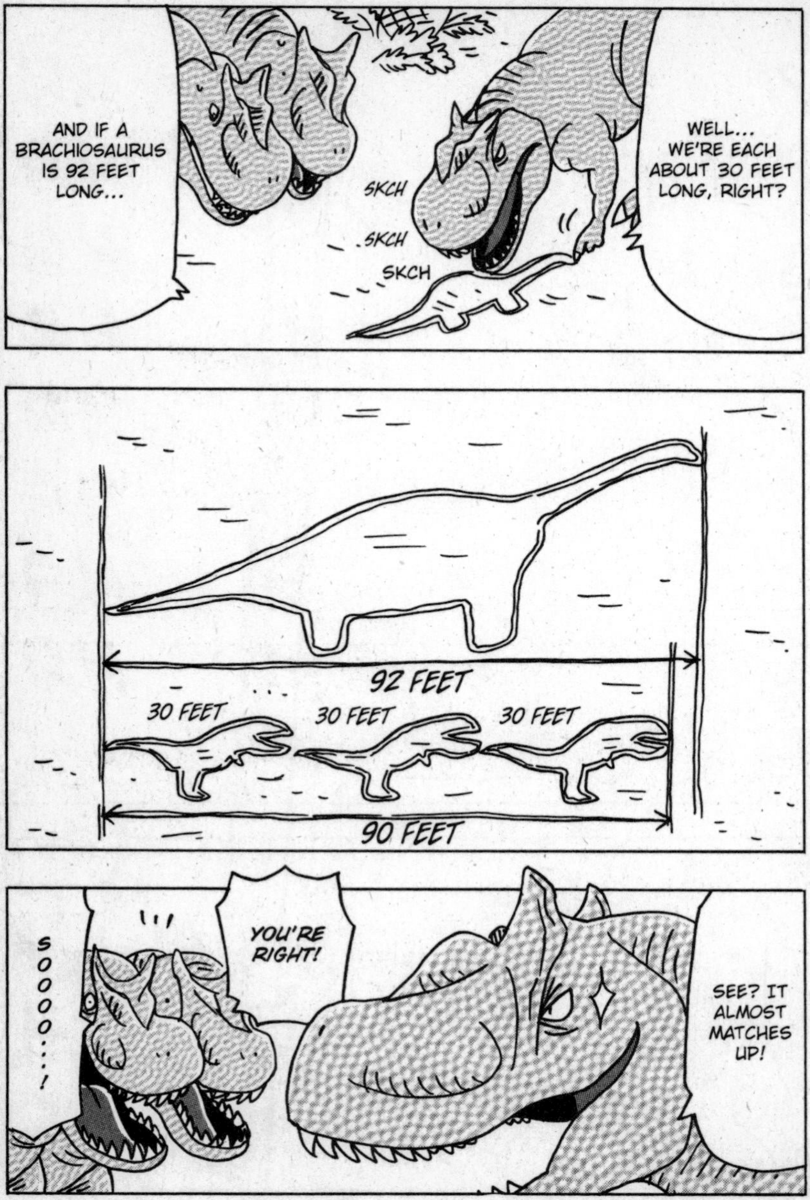
WELL... WE'RE EACH ABOUT 30 FEET LONG, RIGHT?
SKCH
SKCH
SKCH
AND IF A BRACHIOSAURUS IS 92 FEET LONG...
92 FEET
...
30 FEET
30 FEET
30 FEET
90 FEET
SEE? IT ALMOST MATCHES UP!
YOU'RE RIGHT!
SOOOO...!

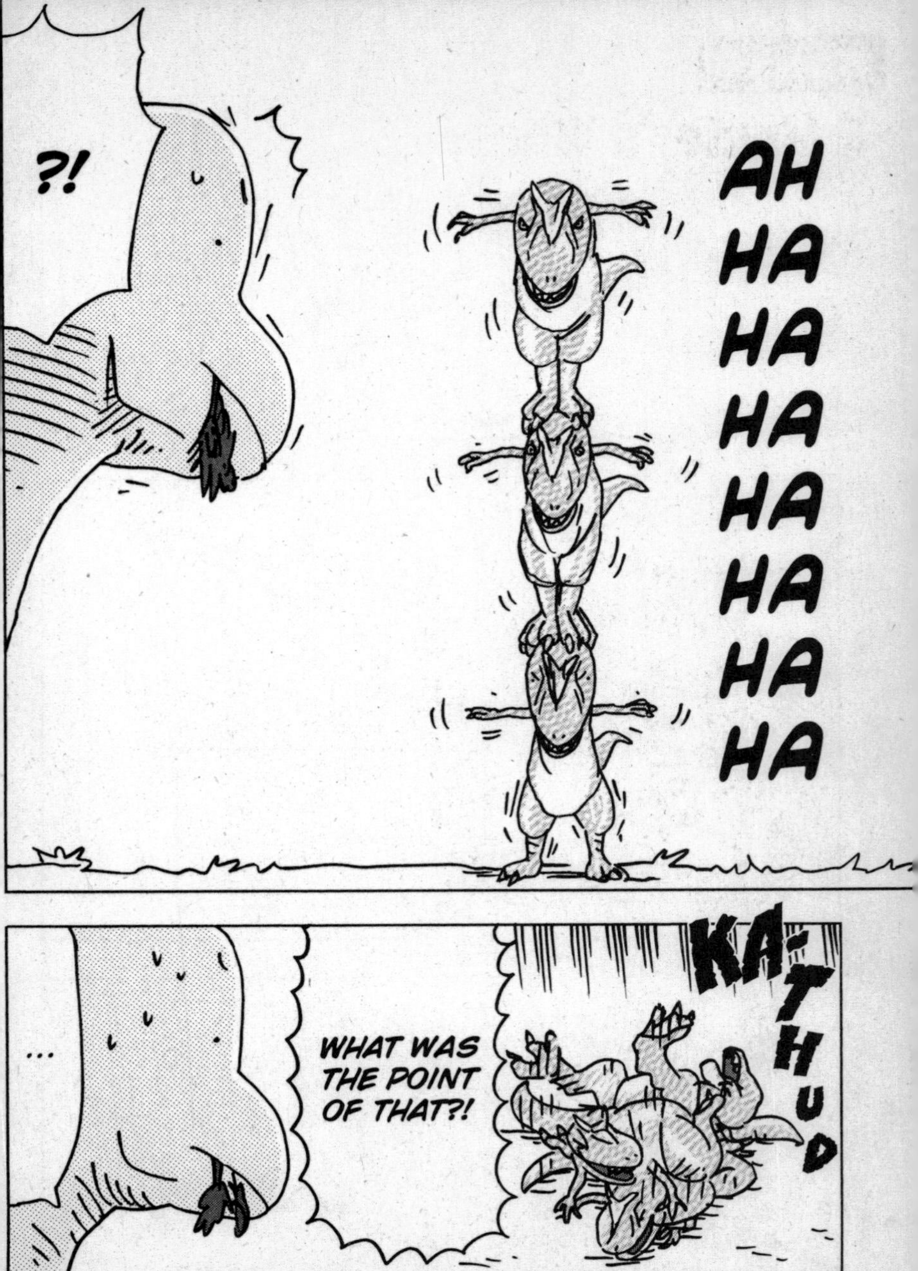
AH HA HA HA HA HA HA HA
?!
KA-THUD
WHAT WAS THE POINT OF THAT?!
...

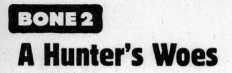

BONE 2

A Hunter's Woes

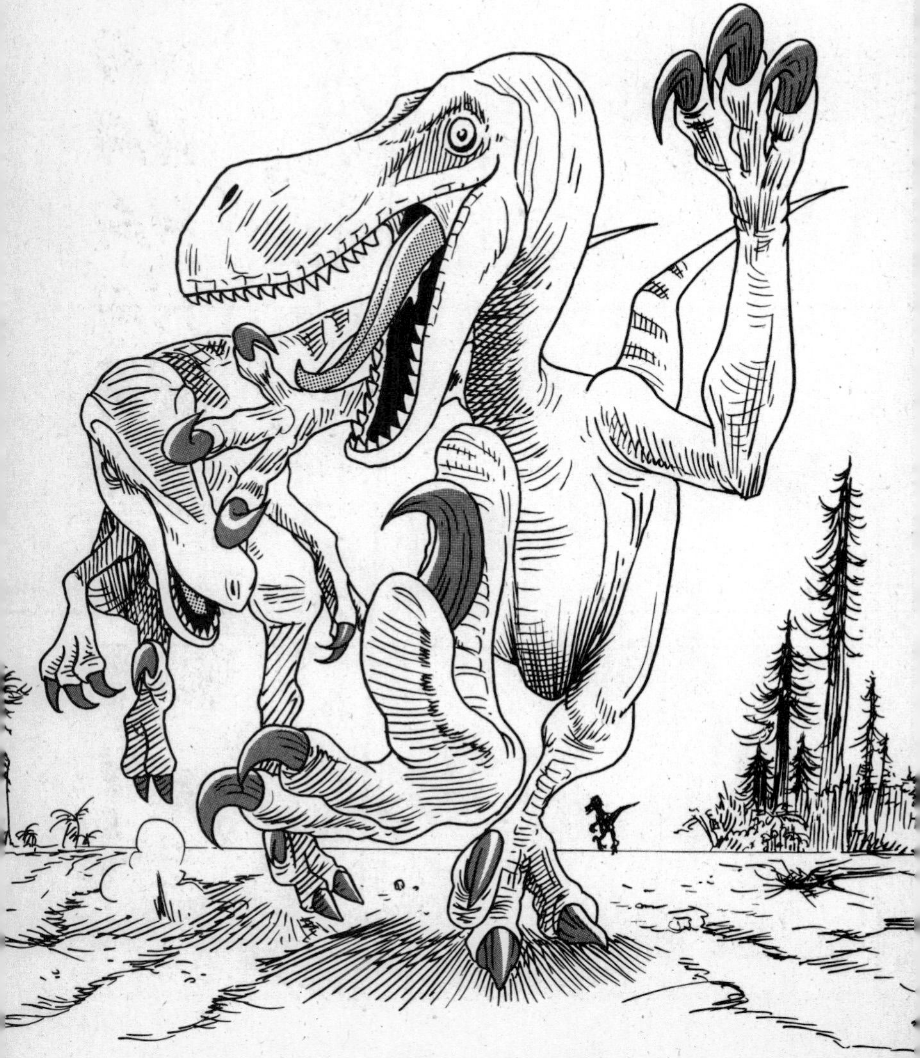

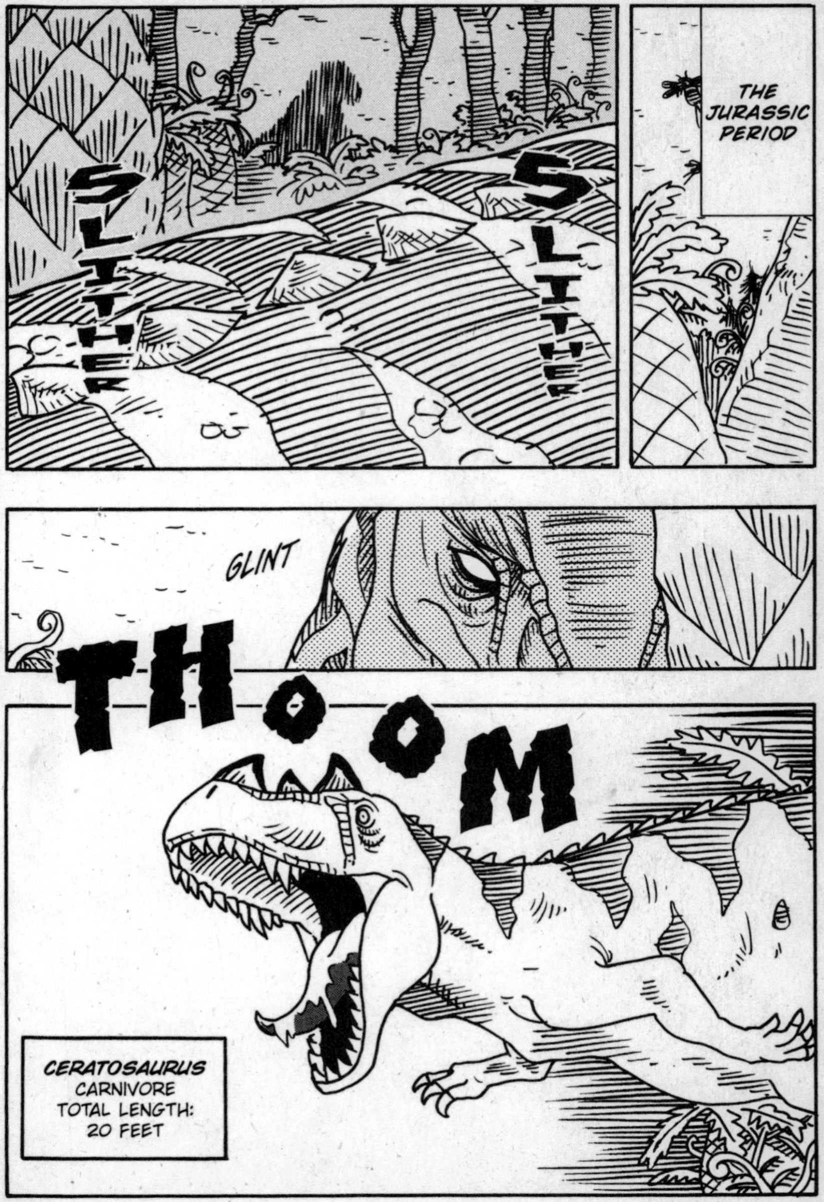
THE JURASSIC PERIOD
SLITHER
SLITHER
GLINT
THOOM
CERATOSAURUS
CARNIVORE
TOTAL LENGTH:
20 FEET

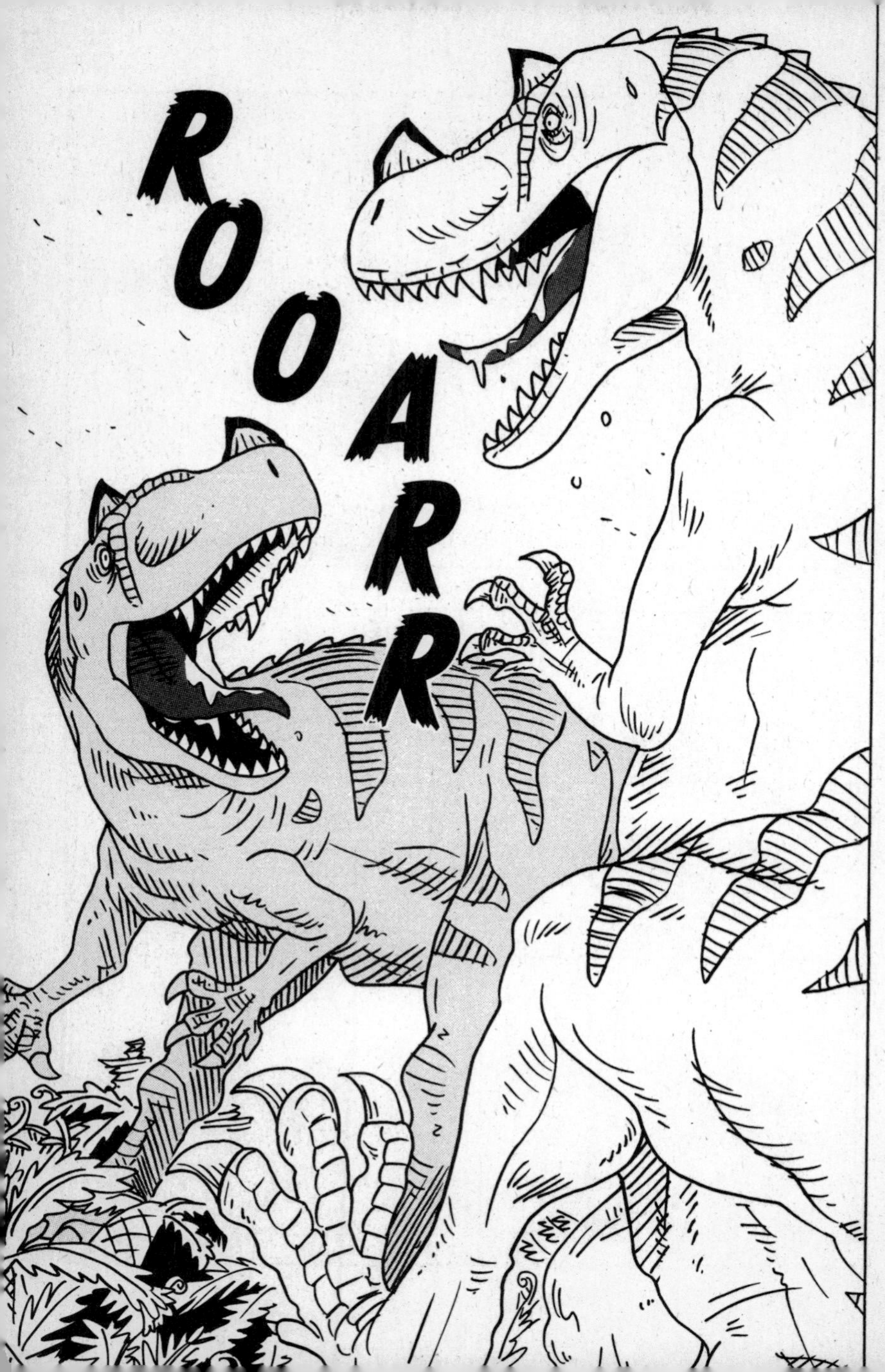
ROOARR

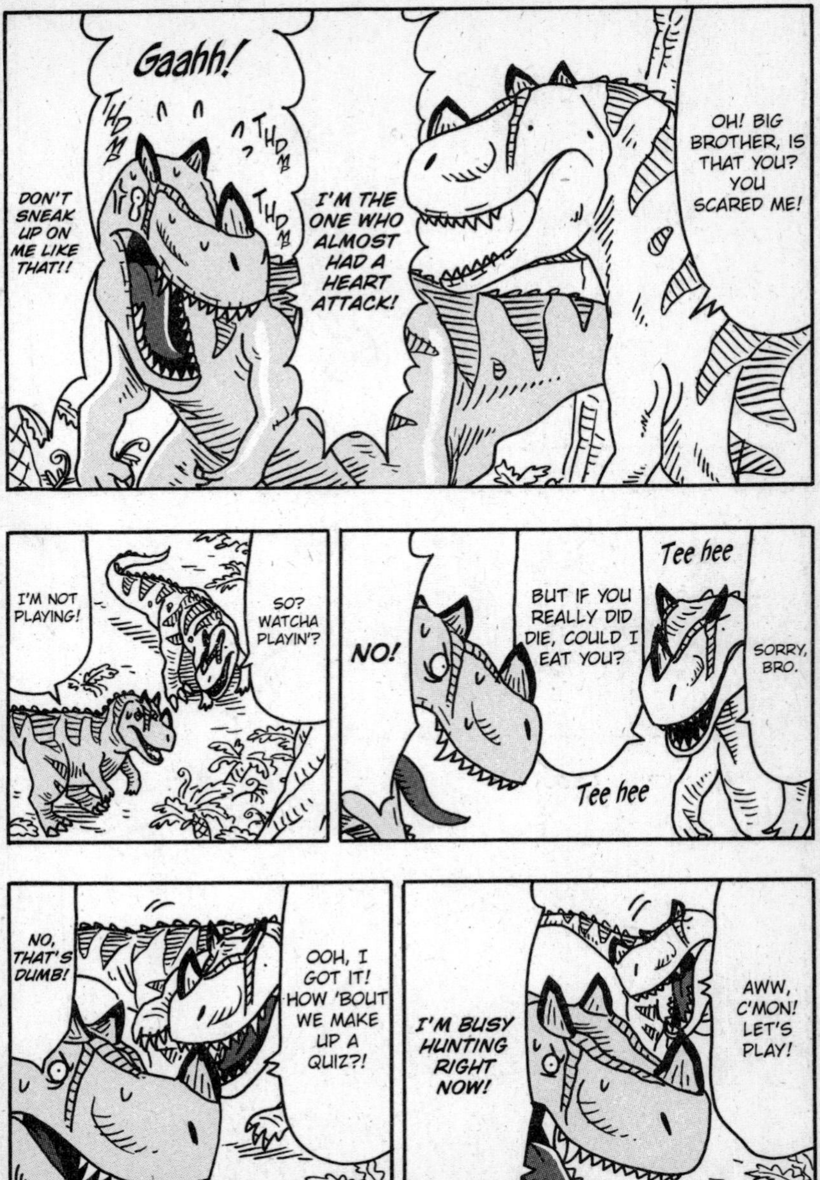
Gaahh!
THDMP THDMP THDMP
DON'T SNEAK UP ON ME LIKE THAT!!
I'M THE ONE WHO ALMOST HAD A HEART ATTACK!
OH! BIG BROTHER, IS THAT YOU? YOU SCARED ME!
SO? WATCHA PLAYIN'?
I'M NOT PLAYING!
Tee hee
BUT IF YOU REALLY DID DIE, COULD I EAT YOU?
NO!
SORRY, BRO.
Tee hee
OOH, I GOT IT! HOW 'BOUT WE MAKE UP A QUIZ?!
NO, THAT'S DUMB!
AWW, C'MON! LET'S PLAY!
I'M BUSY HUNTING RIGHT NOW!

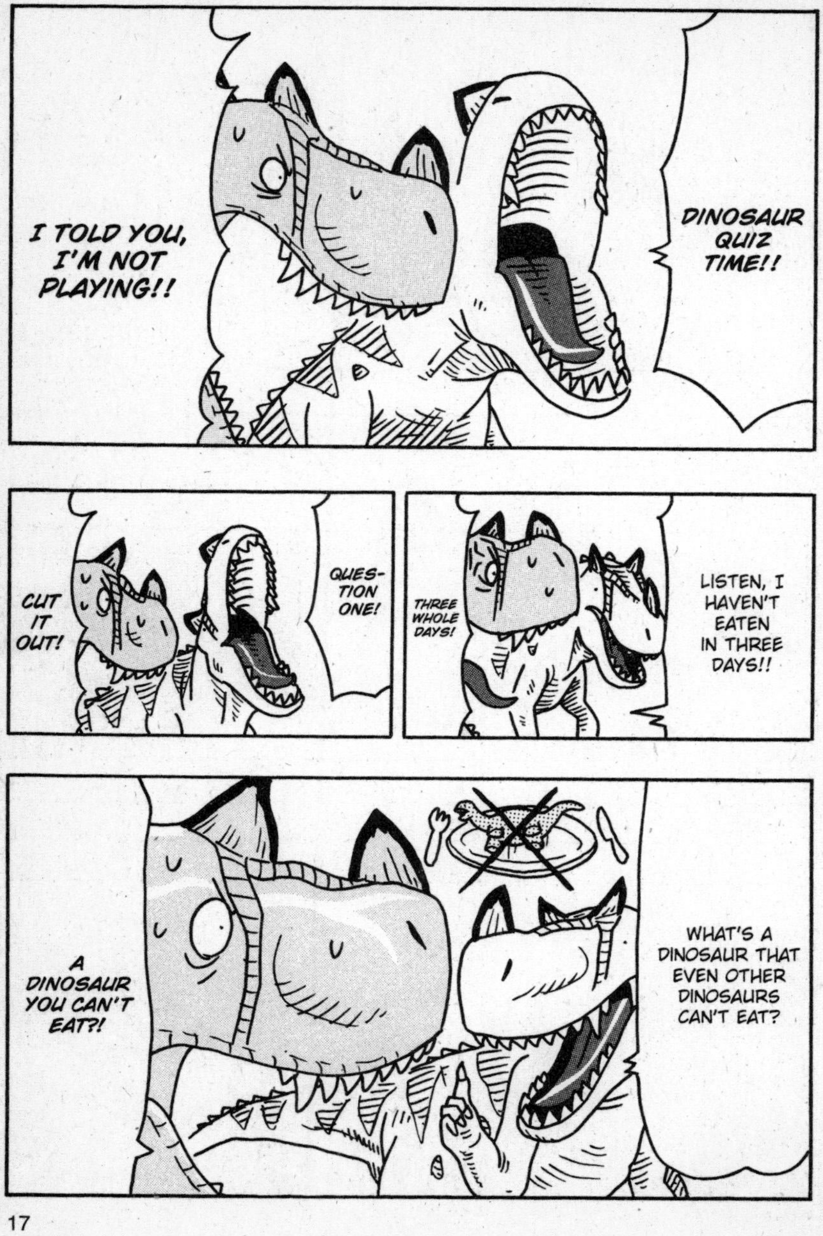
DINOSAUR QUIZ TIME!!
I TOLD YOU, I'M NOT PLAYING!!
LISTEN, I HAVEN'T EATEN IN THREE DAYS!!
THREE WHOLE DAYS!
QUES-TION ONE!
CUT IT OUT!
WHAT'S A DINOSAUR THAT EVEN OTHER DINOSAURS CAN'T EAT?
A DINOSAUR YOU CAN'T EAT?!

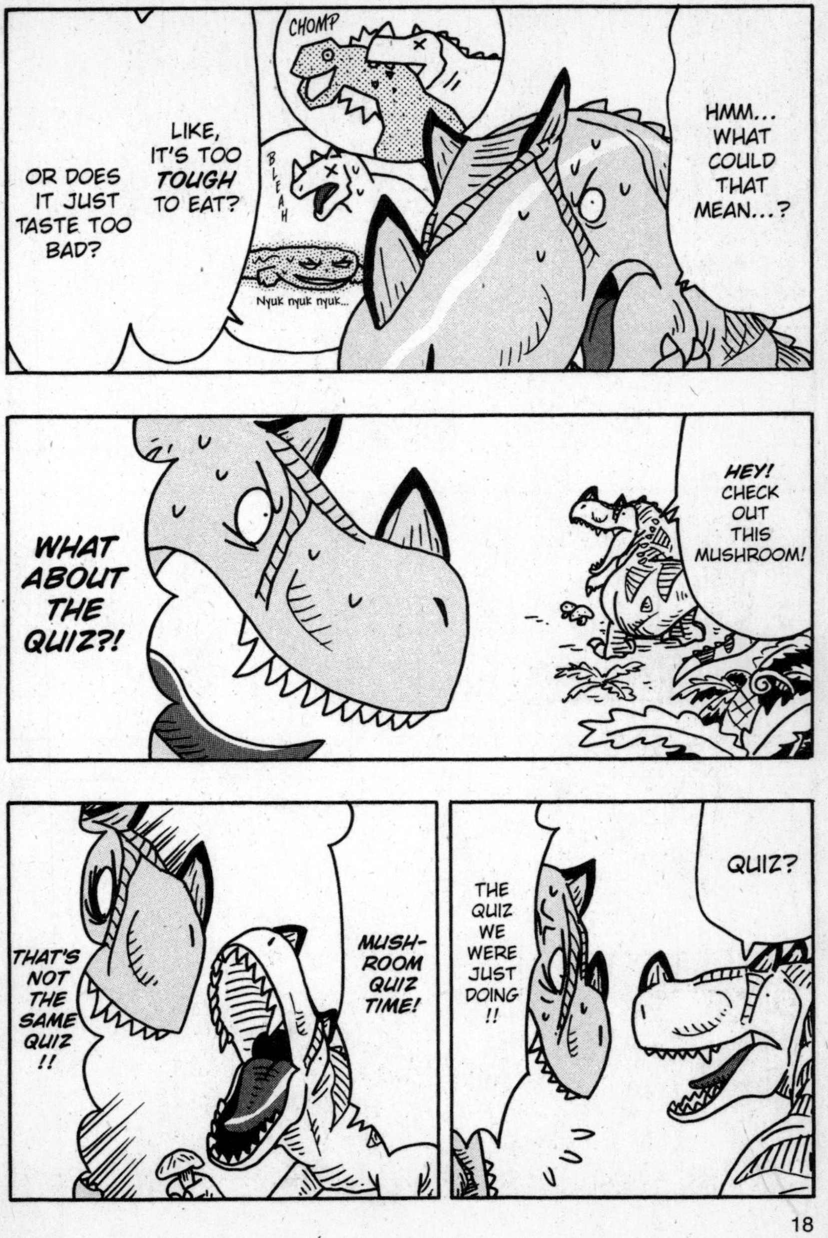
HMM... WHAT COULD THAT MEAN...?
CHOMP
BLEAH
Nyuk nyuk nyuk...
LIKE, IT'S TOO TOUGH TO EAT?
OR DOES IT JUST TASTE TOO BAD?
HEY! CHECK OUT THIS MUSHROOM!
WHAT ABOUT THE QUIZ?!
QUIZ?
THE QUIZ WE WERE JUST DOING!!
MUSH-ROOM QUIZ TIME!
THAT'S NOT THE SAME QUIZ!!

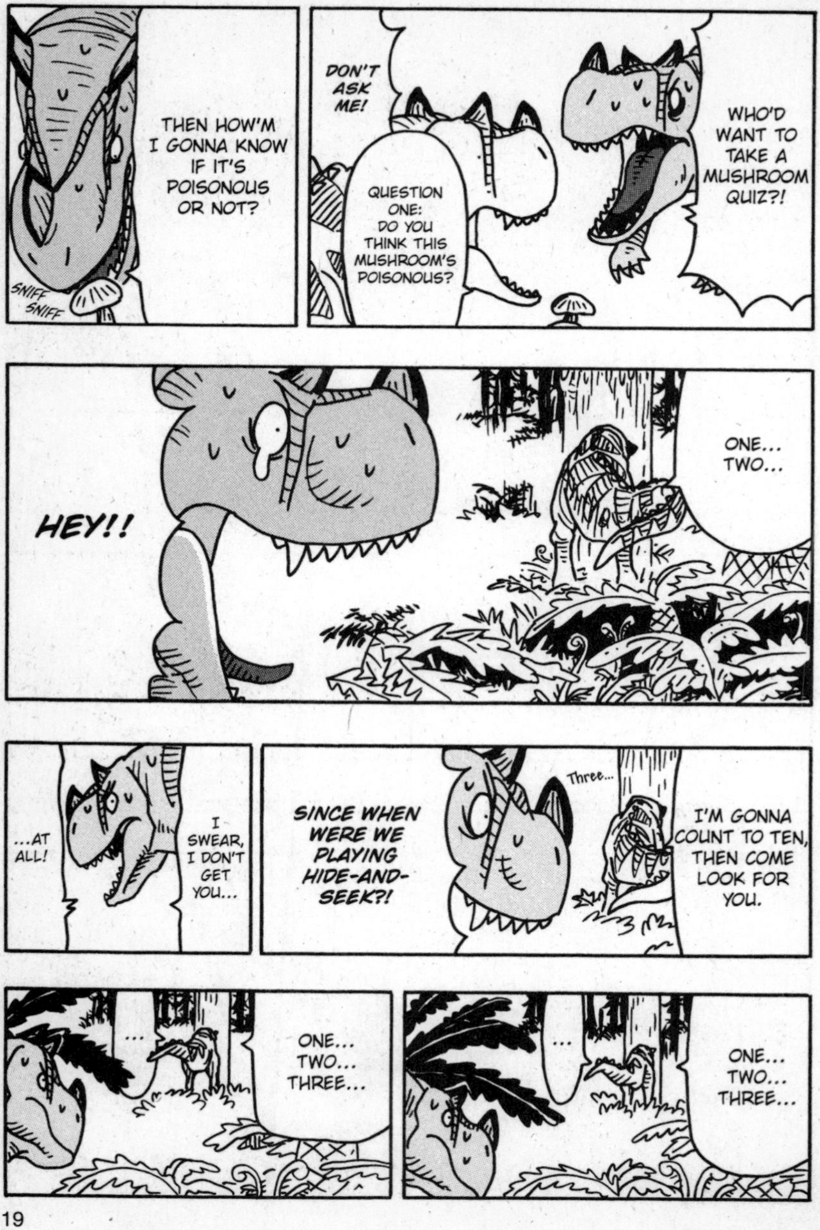
WHO'D WANT TO TAKE A MUSHROOM QUIZ?!
DON'T ASK ME!
QUESTION ONE: DO YOU THINK THIS MUSHROOM'S POISONOUS?
THEN HOW'M I GONNA KNOW IF IT'S POISONOUS OR NOT?
SNIFF SNIFF
ONE... TWO...
HEY!!
I'M GONNA COUNT TO TEN, THEN COME LOOK FOR YOU.
Three...
SINCE WHEN WERE WE PLAYING HIDE-AND-SEEK?!
I SWEAR, I DON'T GET YOU...
...AT ALL!
ONE... TWO... THREE...
...
ONE... TWO... THREE...
...

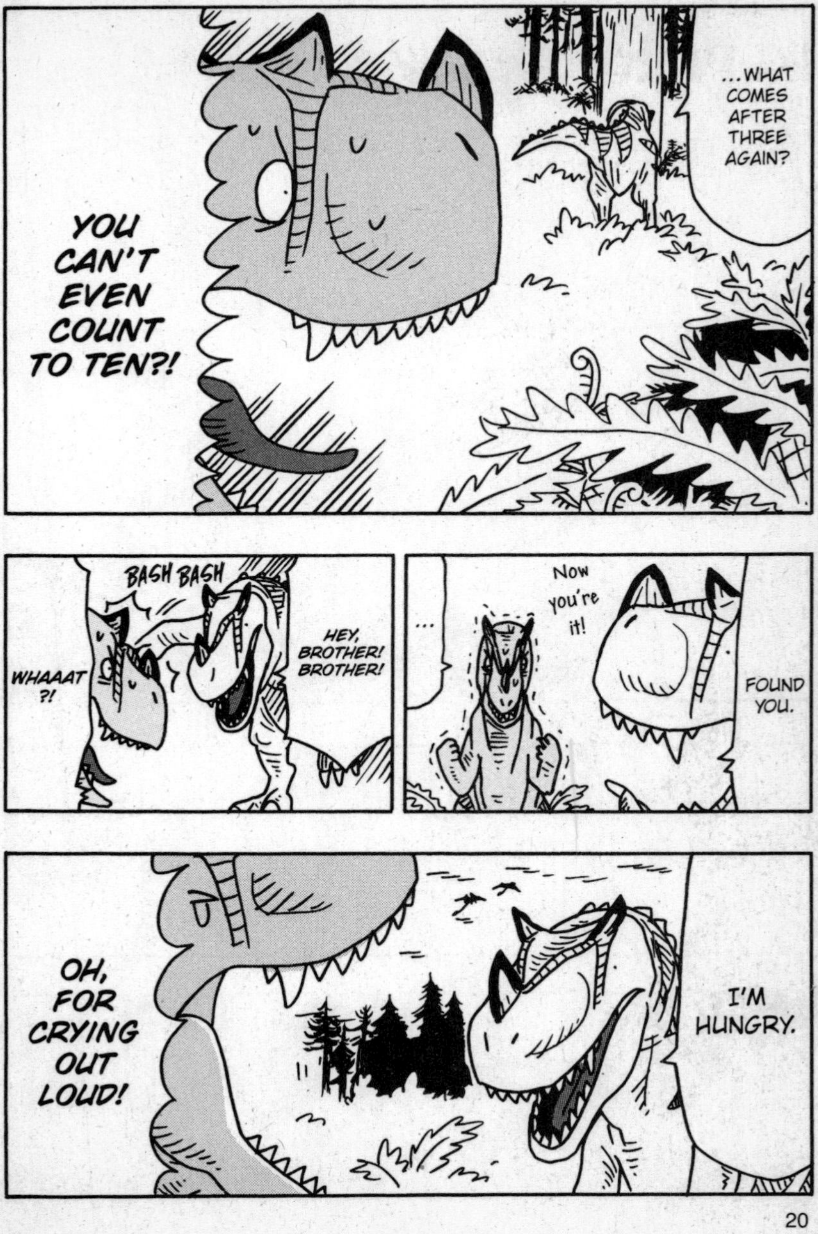
...WHAT COMES AFTER THREE AGAIN?
YOU CAN'T EVEN COUNT TO TEN?!
FOUND YOU.
Now you're it!
...
HEY, BROTHER! BROTHER!
BASH BASH
WHAAAT?!
I'M HUNGRY.
OH, FOR CRYING OUT LOUD!

BONE 3

The Protoceratops' Bet

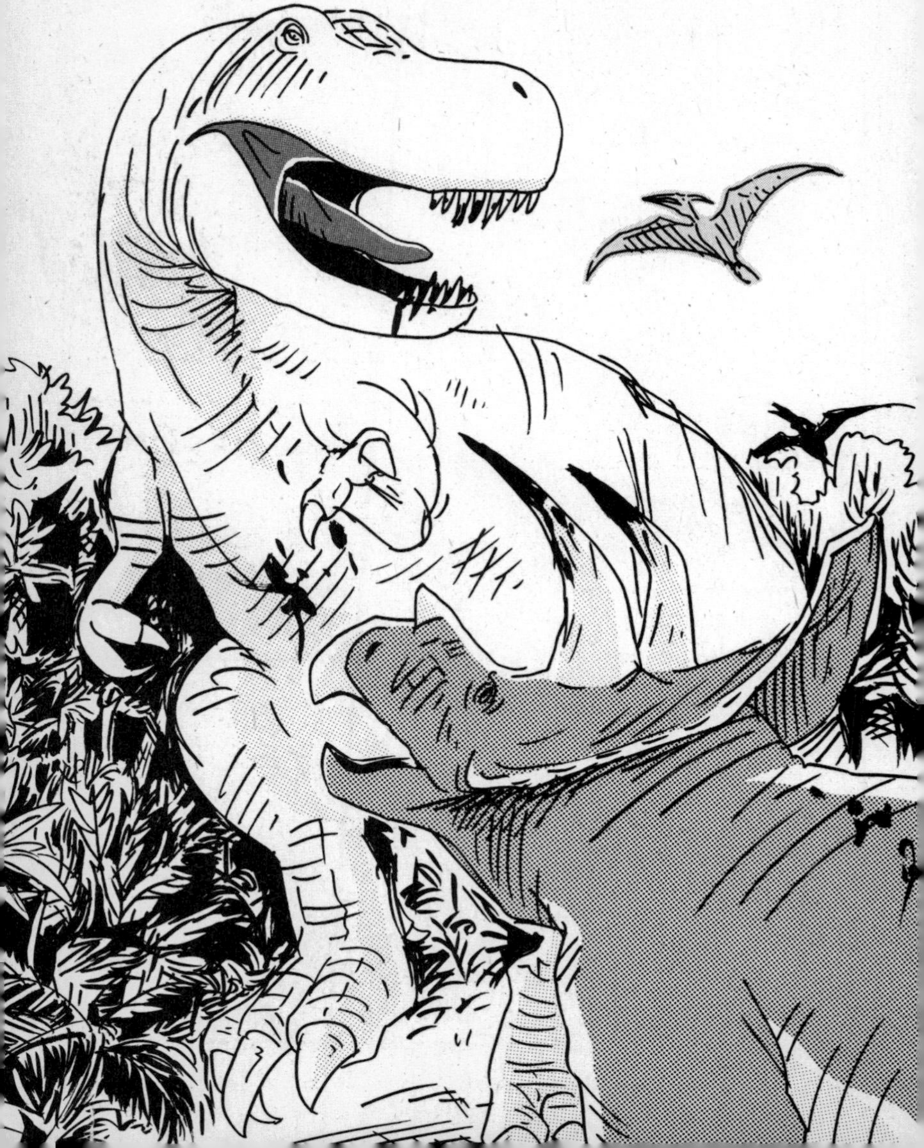

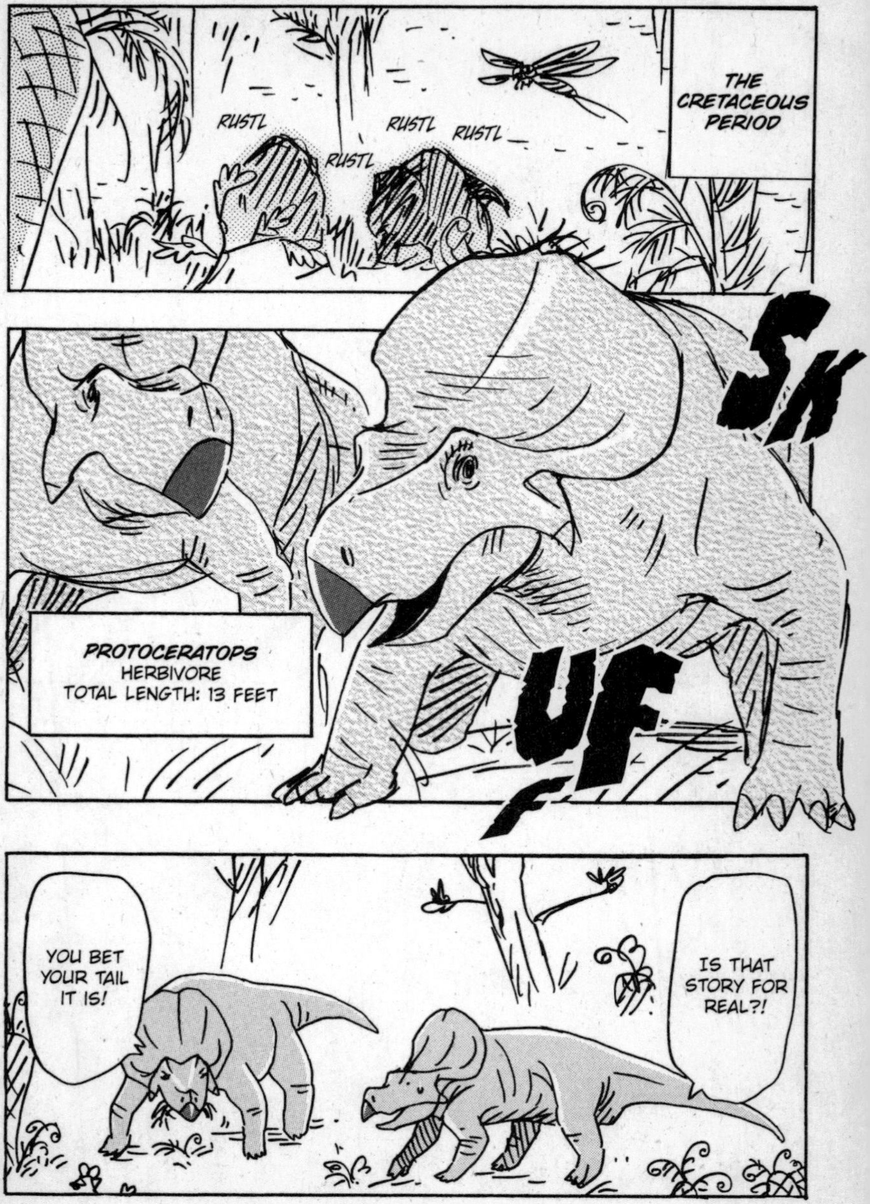
THE CRETACEOUS PERIOD
RUSTL
RUSTL
RUSTL
RUSTL
SKUFF
PROTOCERATOPS
HERBIVORE
TOTAL LENGTH: 13 FEET
IS THAT STORY FOR REAL?!
YOU BET YOUR TAIL IT IS!

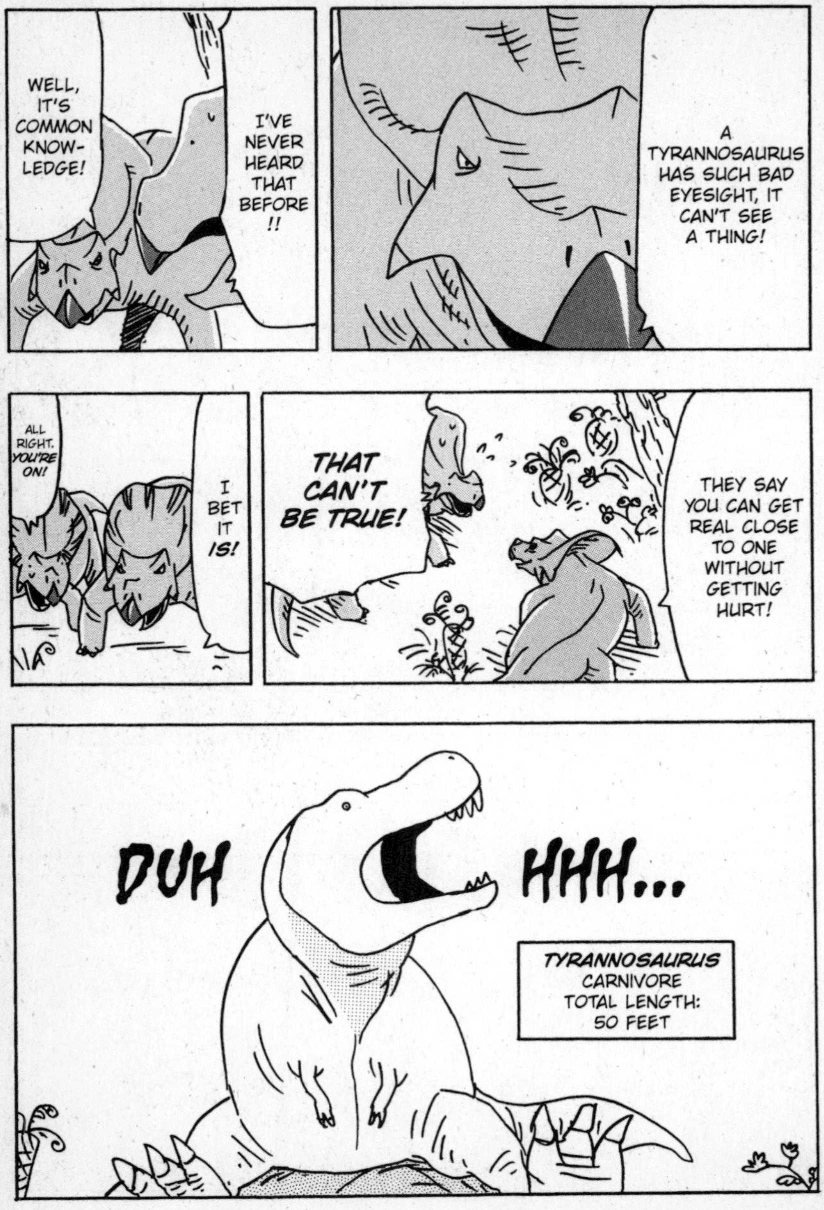
A TYRANNOSAURUS HAS SUCH BAD EYESIGHT, IT CAN'T SEE A THING!
I'VE NEVER HEARD THAT BEFORE!!
WELL, IT'S COMMON KNOW-LEDGE!
THEY SAY YOU CAN GET REAL CLOSE TO ONE WITHOUT GETTING HURT!
THAT CAN'T BE TRUE!
I BET IT IS!
ALL RIGHT. YOU'RE ON!
DUH HHH...
TYRANNOSAURUS
CARNIVORE
TOTAL LENGTH:
50 FEET

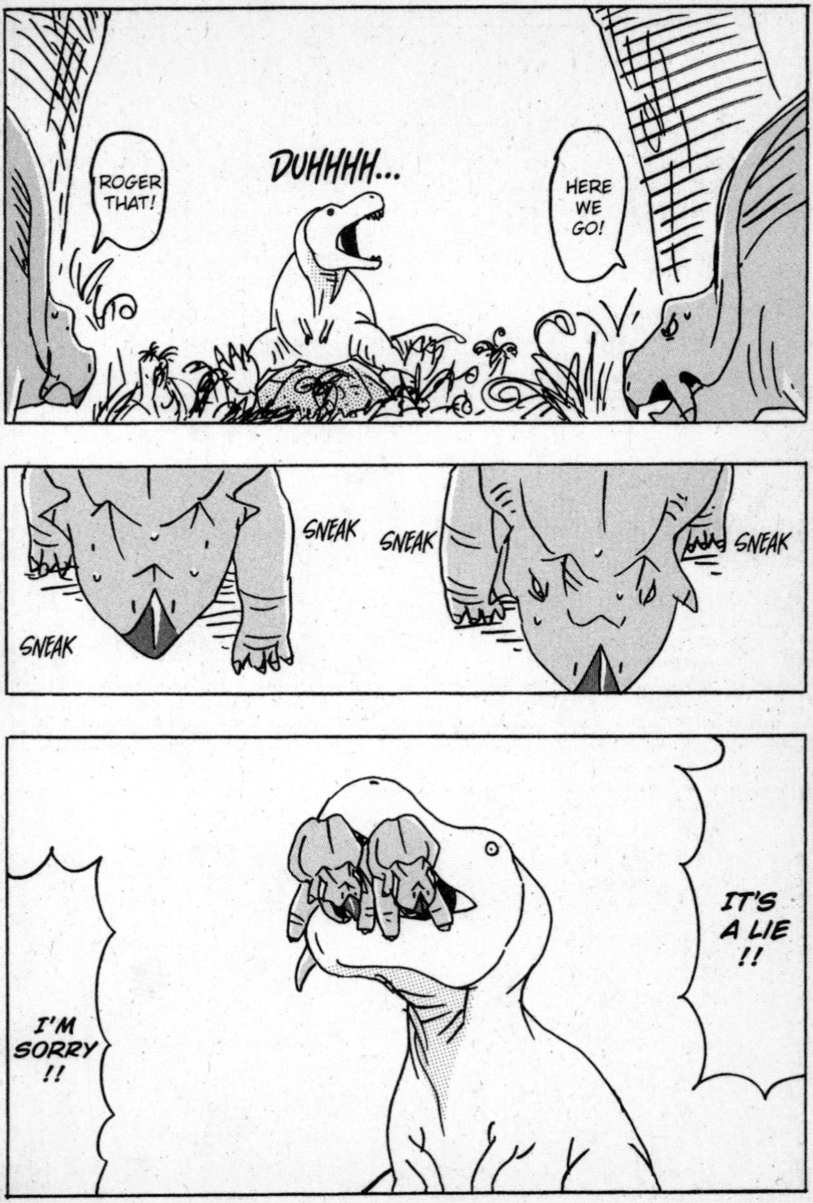
HERE WE GO!
DUHHHH...
ROGER THAT!
SNEAK
SNEAK
SNEAK
SNEAK
IT'S A LIE !!
I'M SORRY !!

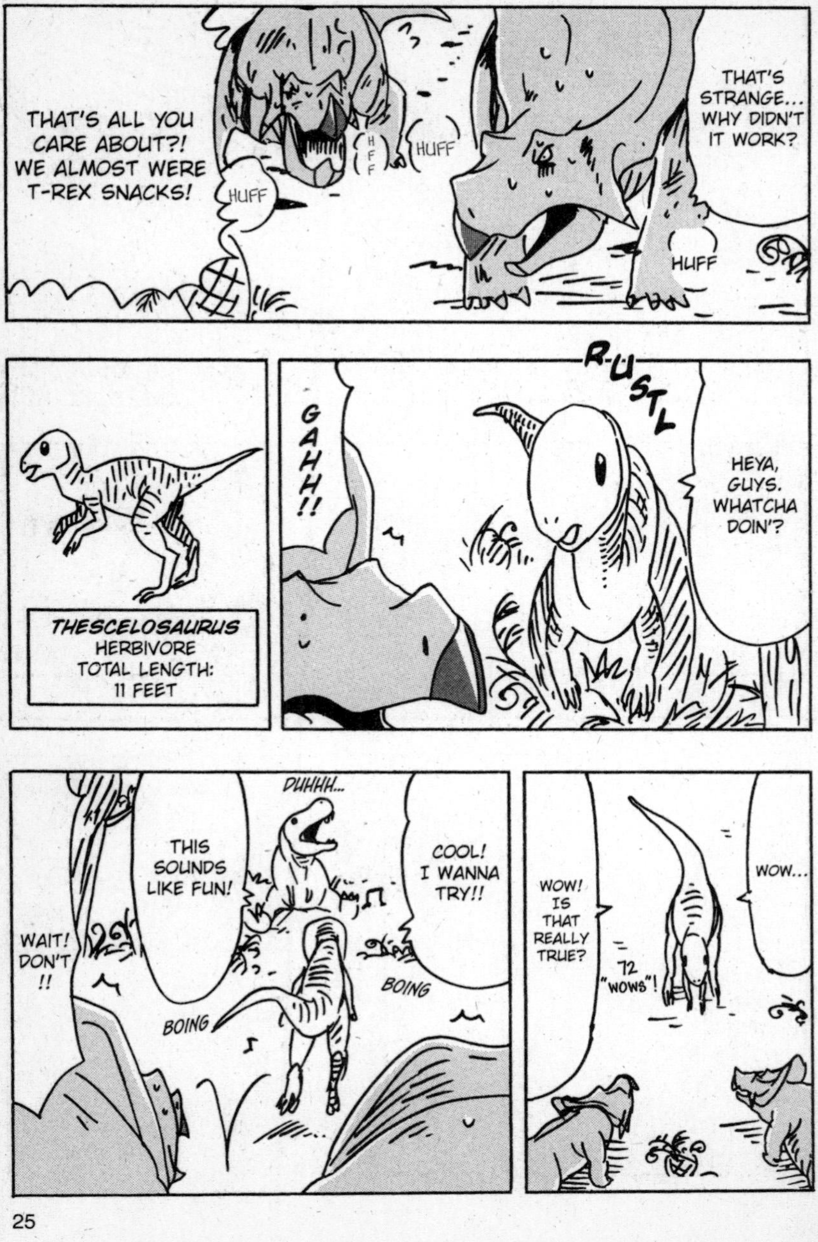
THAT'S STRANGE... WHY DIDN'T IT WORK?
HUFF
HUFF
HFF
THAT'S ALL YOU CARE ABOUT?! WE ALMOST WERE T-REX SNACKS!
HUFF
RUSTL
HEYA, GUYS. WHATCHA DOIN'?
GAHH!!
THESCELOSAURUS
HERBIVORE
TOTAL LENGTH: 11 FEET
WOW...
WOW! IS THAT REALLY TRUE?
72 "WOWS"!
COOL! I WANNA TRY!!
DUHHH...
THIS SOUNDS LIKE FUN!
BOING
BOING
WAIT! DON'T !!

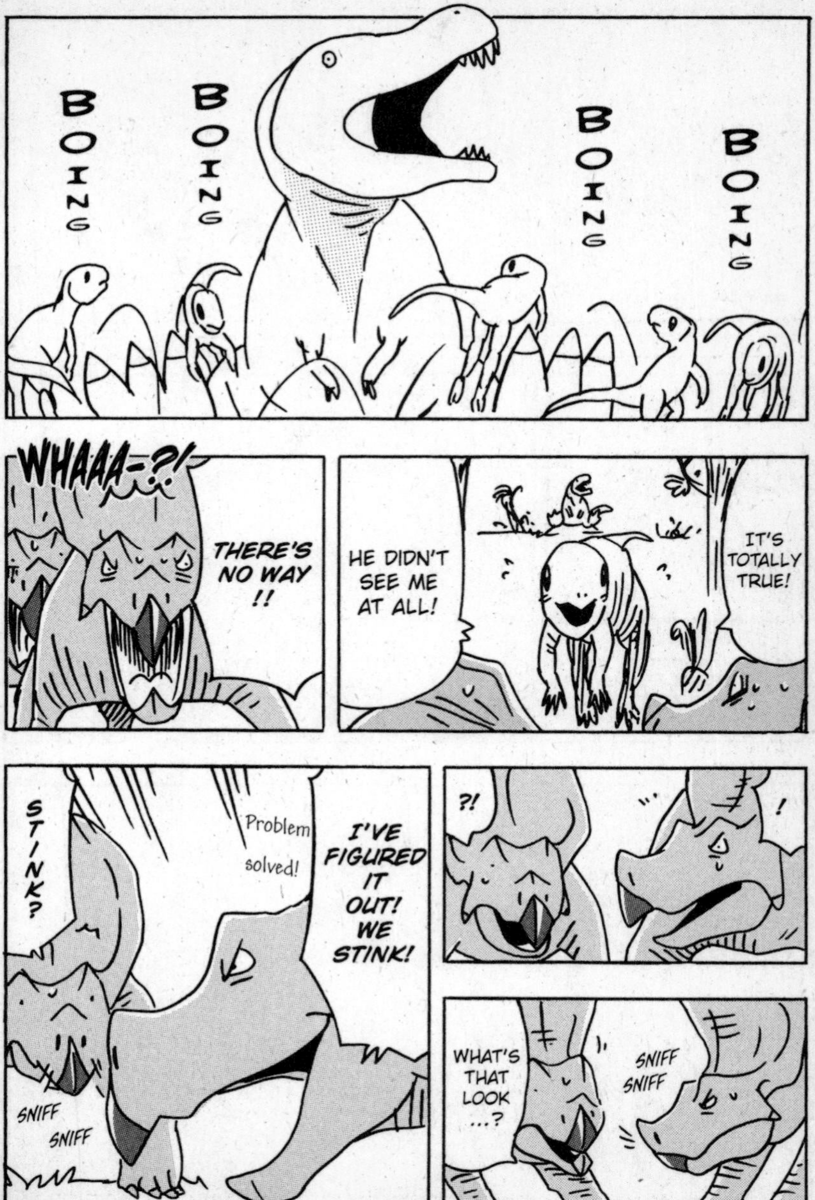
BOING
BOING
BOING
BOING
IT'S TOTALLY TRUE!
HE DIDN'T SEE ME AT ALL!
WHAAA-?!
THERE'S NO WAY !!
!
?!
SNIFF SNIFF
WHAT'S THAT LOOK ...?
I'VE FIGURED IT OUT! WE STINK!
Problem solved!
STINK?
SNIFF SNIFF

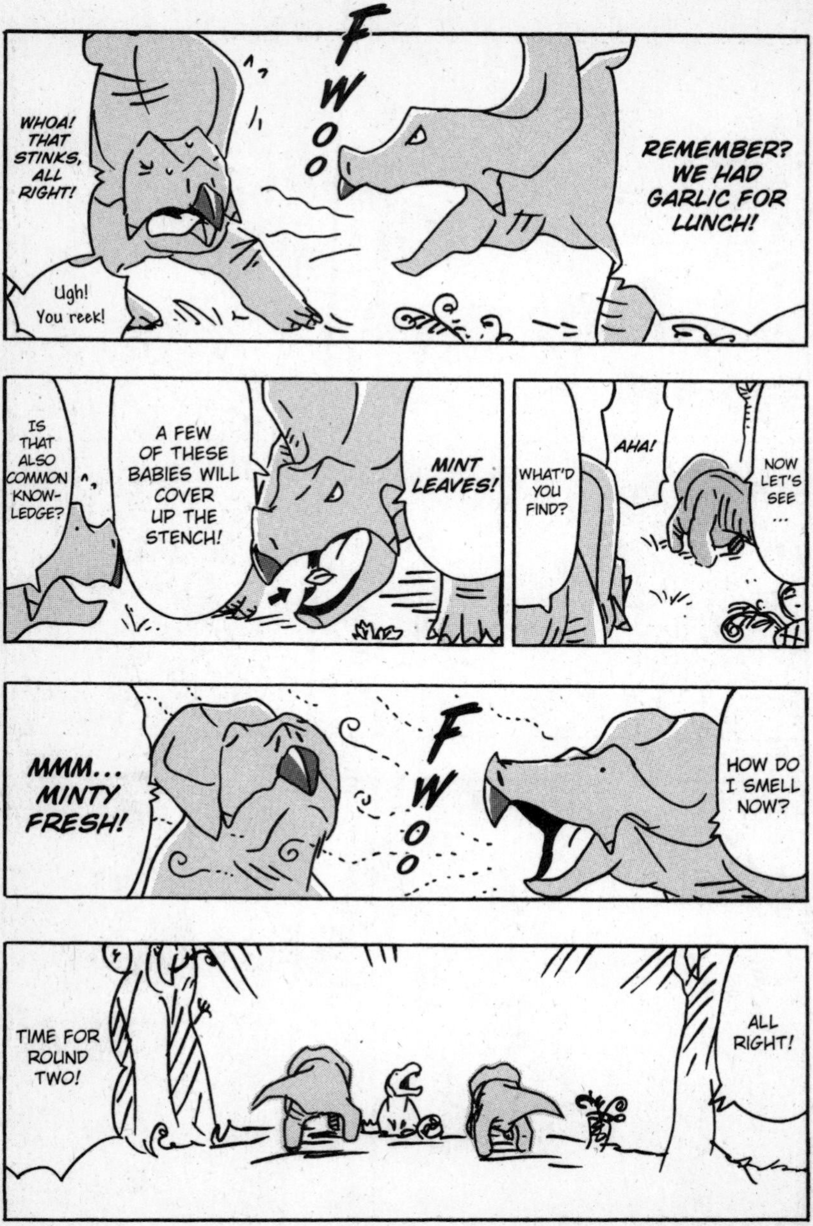
REMEMBER? WE HAD GARLIC FOR LUNCH!
FWOO
WHOA! THAT STINKS, ALL RIGHT!
Ugh! You reek!
NOW LET'S SEE ...
AHA!
WHAT'D YOU FIND?
MINT LEAVES!
A FEW OF THESE BABIES WILL COVER UP THE STENCH!
IS THAT ALSO COMMON KNOWLEDGE?
HOW DO I SMELL NOW?
FWOO
MMM... MINTY FRESH!
ALL RIGHT!
TIME FOR ROUND TWO!

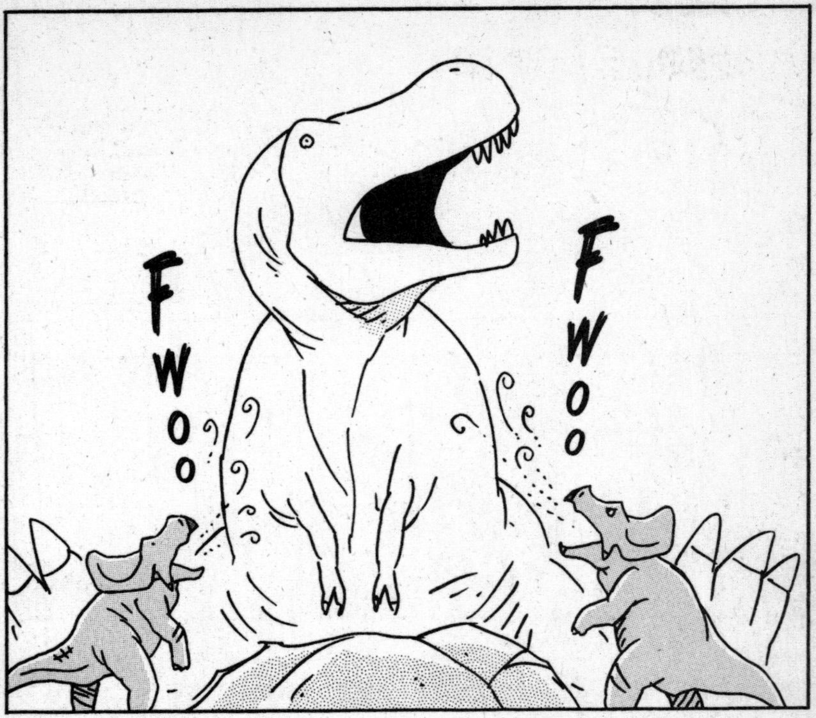
FWOO
FWOO

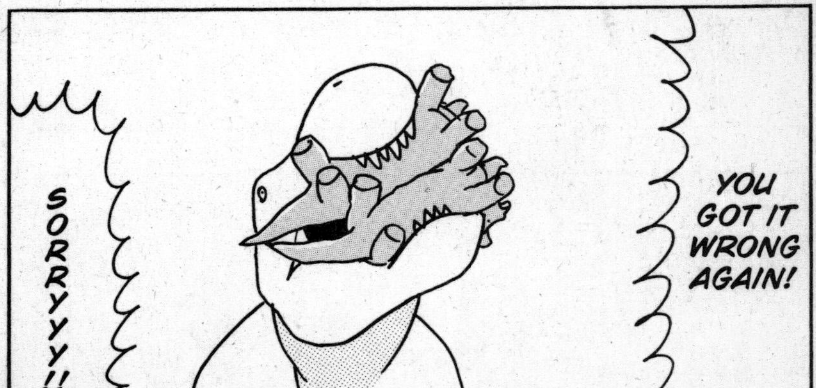
YOU GOT IT WRONG AGAIN!
SORRYYY!!

BONE 4
Dinosaur Lunch

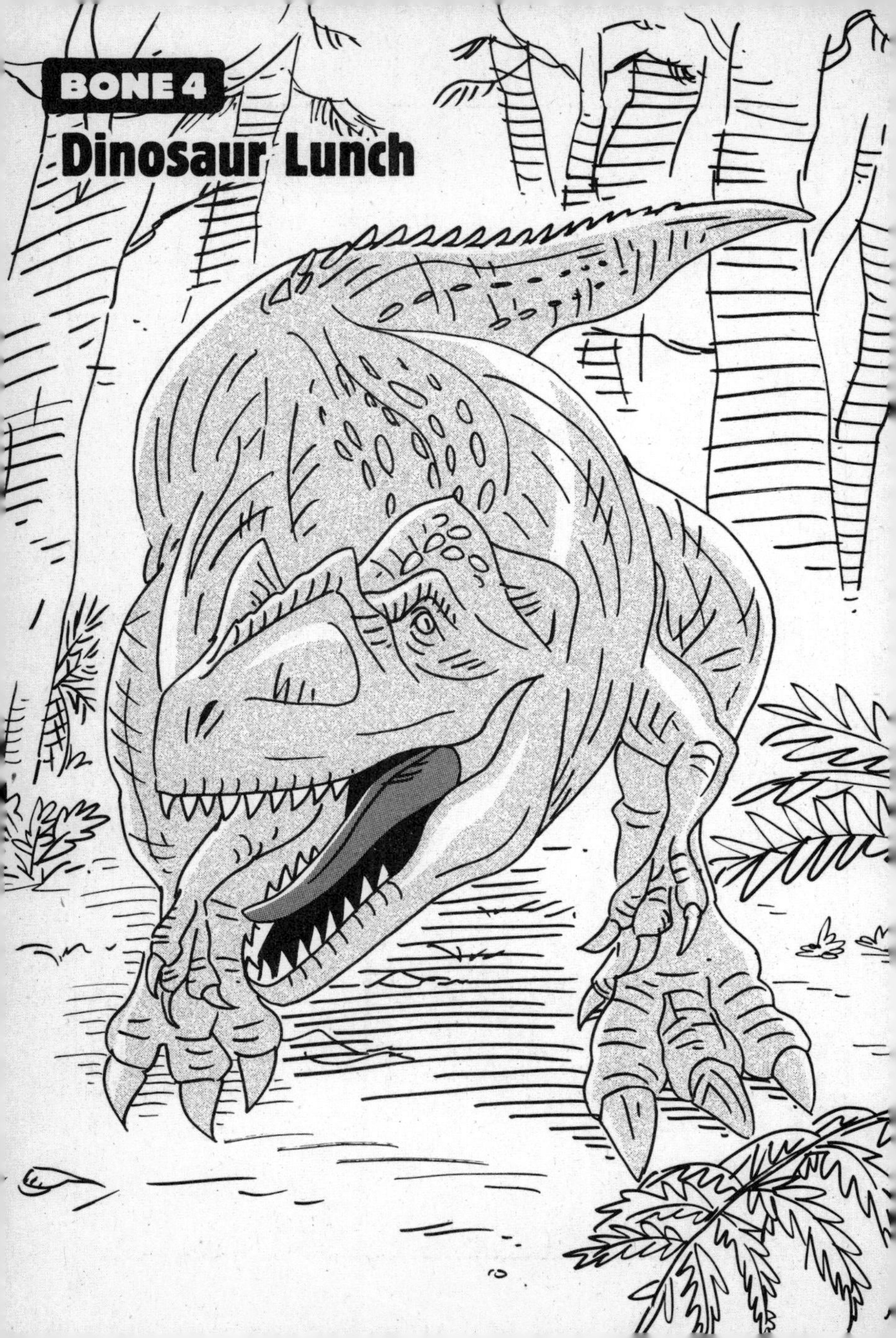

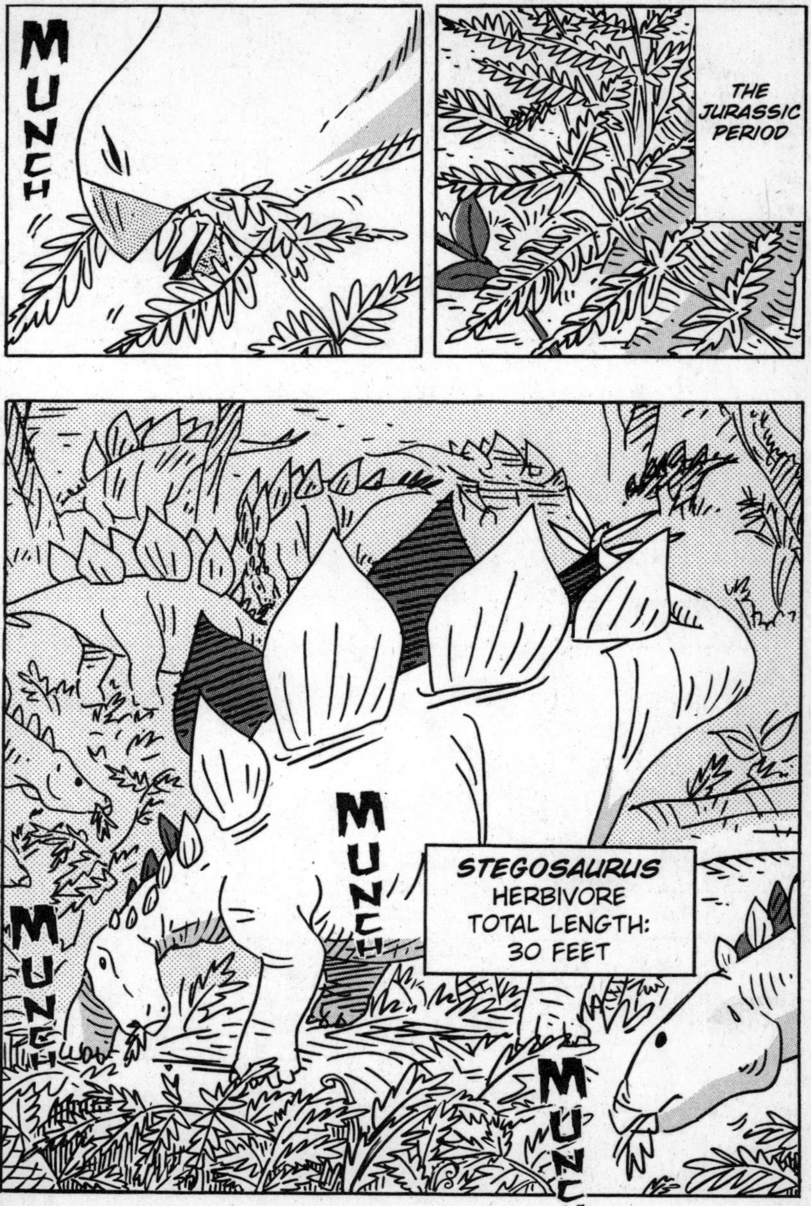
THE JURASSIC PERIOD
MUNCH
STEGOSAURUS
HERBIVORE
TOTAL LENGTH:
30 FEET
MUNCH
MUNCH
MUNCH

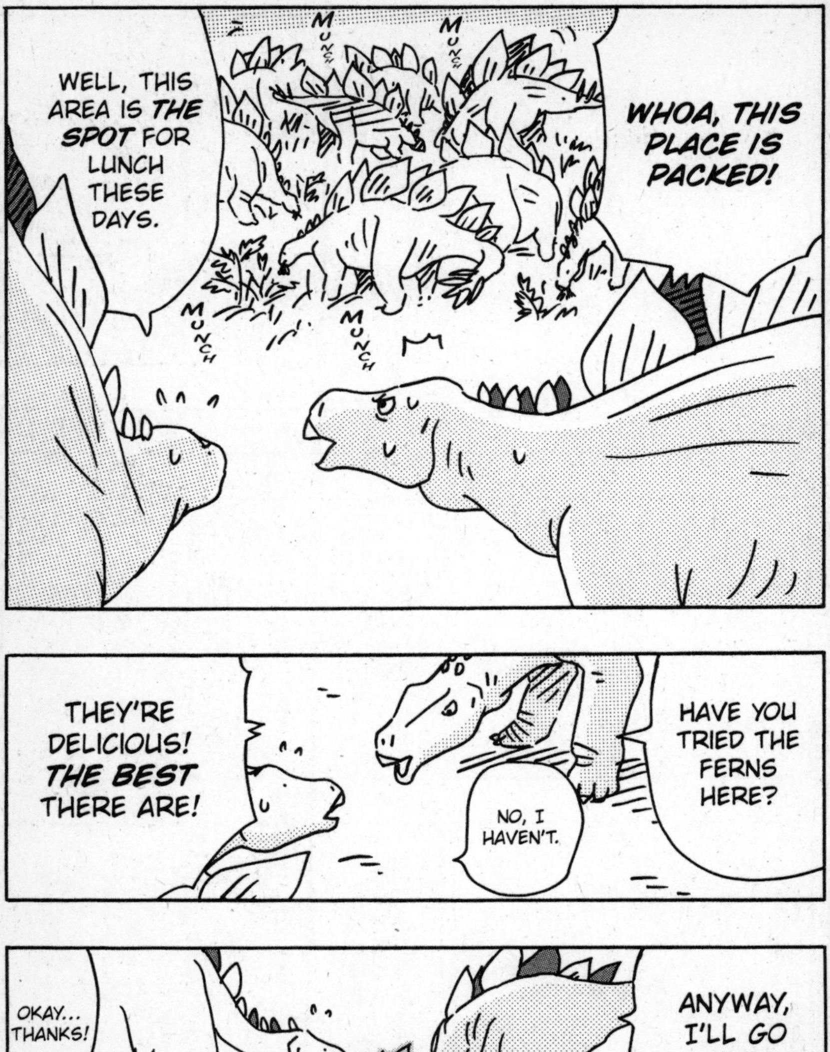
MUNCH
MUNCH
WHOA, THIS PLACE IS PACKED!
WELL, THIS AREA IS THE SPOT FOR LUNCH THESE DAYS.
MUNCH
MUNCH
HAVE YOU TRIED THE FERNS HERE?
NO, I HAVEN'T.
THEY'RE DELICIOUS! THE BEST THERE ARE!
ANYWAY, I'LL GO ASK HOW LONG THE LINE IS.
OKAY... THANKS!

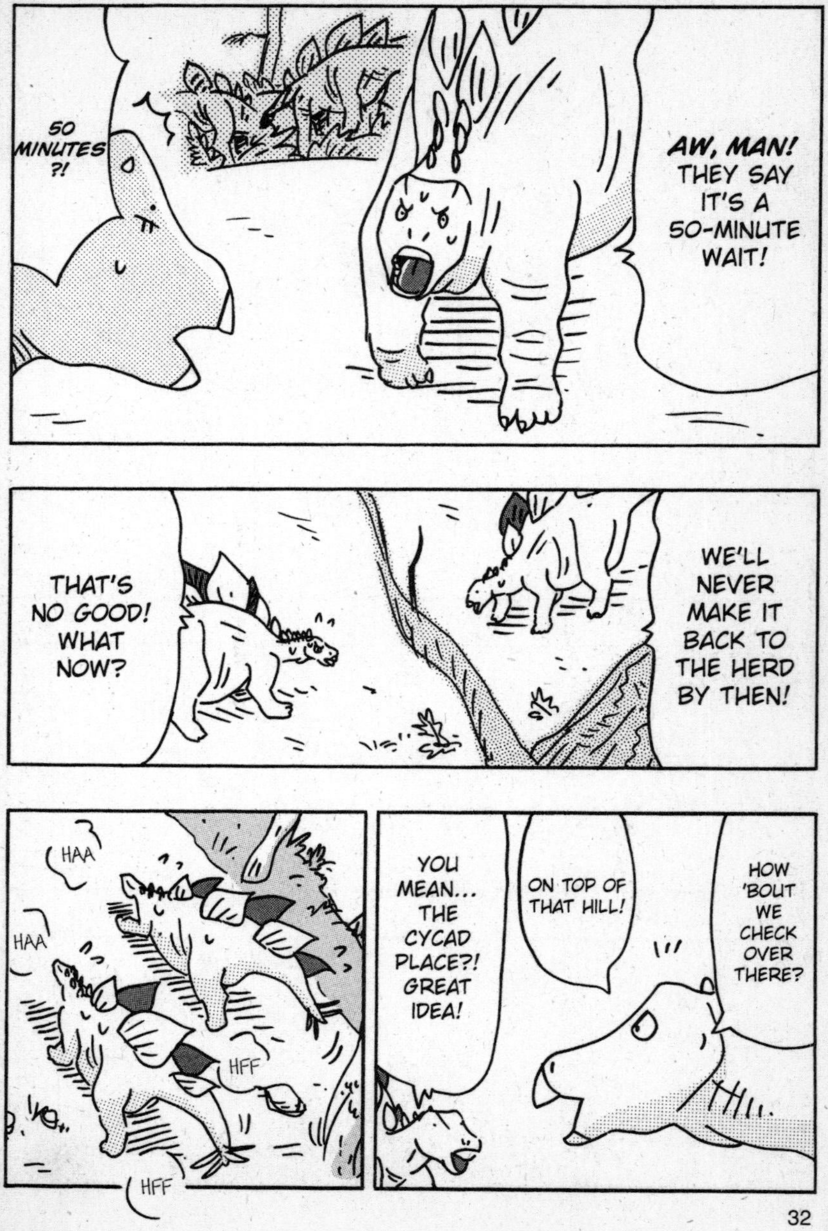
AW, MAN! THEY SAY IT'S A 50-MINUTE WAIT!
50 MINUTES ?!
WE'LL NEVER MAKE IT BACK TO THE HERD BY THEN!
THAT'S NO GOOD! WHAT NOW?
HOW 'BOUT WE CHECK OVER THERE?
ON TOP OF THAT HILL!
YOU MEAN... THE CYCAD PLACE?! GREAT IDEA!
HAA
HAA
HFF
HFF

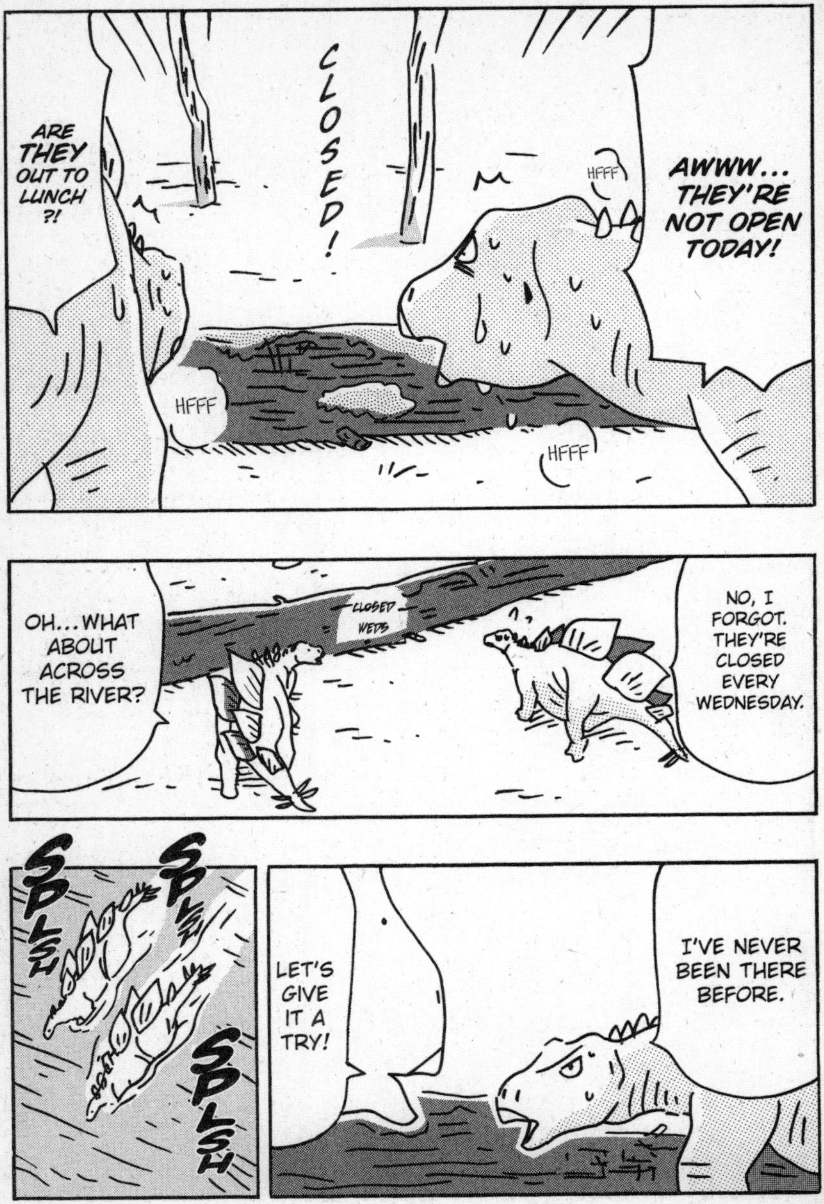
AWWW... THEY'RE NOT OPEN TODAY!
HFFF
CLOSED!
ARE THEY OUT TO LUNCH?!
HFFF
HFFF
NO, I FORGOT. THEY'RE CLOSED EVERY WEDNESDAY.
CLOSED WEDS
OH...WHAT ABOUT ACROSS THE RIVER?
I'VE NEVER BEEN THERE BEFORE.
LET'S GIVE IT A TRY!
SPLSH
SPLSH
SPLSH

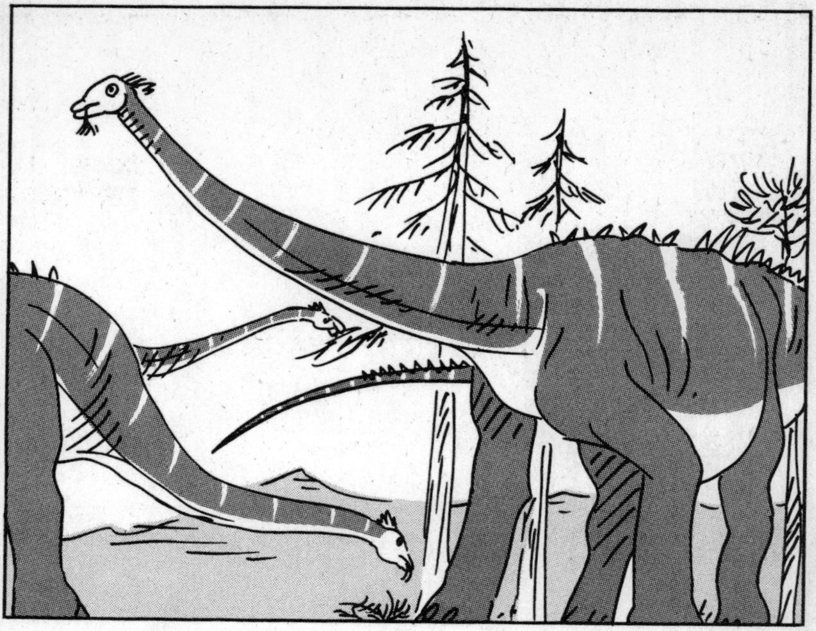

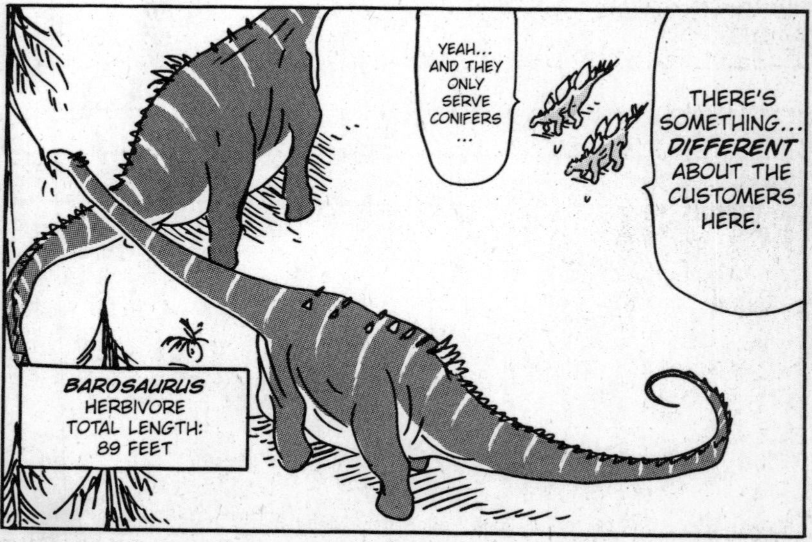

THERE'S SOMETHING... *DIFFERENT* ABOUT THE CUSTOMERS HERE.
YEAH... AND THEY ONLY SERVE CONIFERS ...
BAROSAURUS HERBIVORE TOTAL LENGTH: 89 FEET

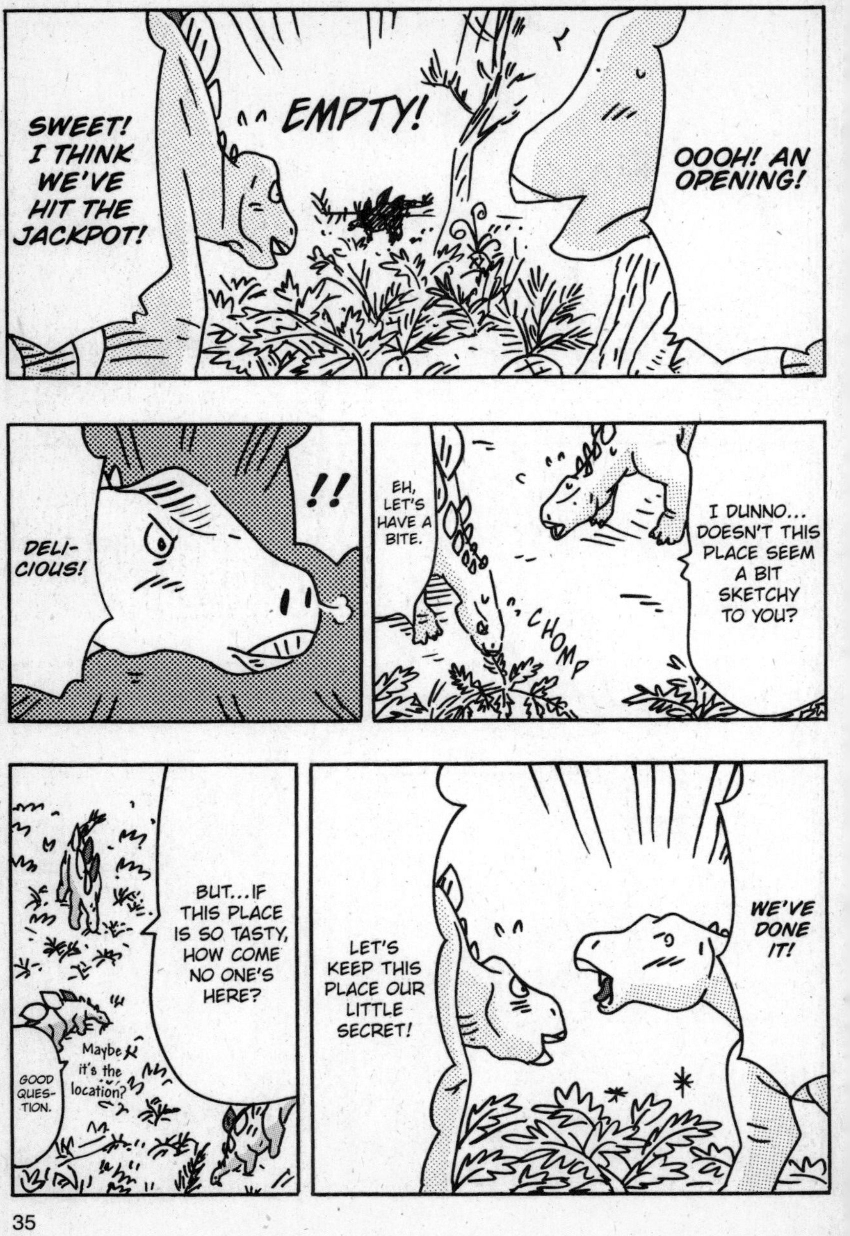
OOOH! AN OPENING!
EMPTY!
SWEET! I THINK WE'VE HIT THE JACKPOT!
I DUNNO... DOESN'T THIS PLACE SEEM A BIT SKETCHY TO YOU?
EH, LET'S HAVE A BITE.
CHOMP
!!
DELI-CIOUS!
WE'VE DONE IT!
LET'S KEEP THIS PLACE OUR LITTLE SECRET!
BUT...IF THIS PLACE IS SO TASTY, HOW COME NO ONE'S HERE?
Maybe it's the location?
GOOD QUES-TION.

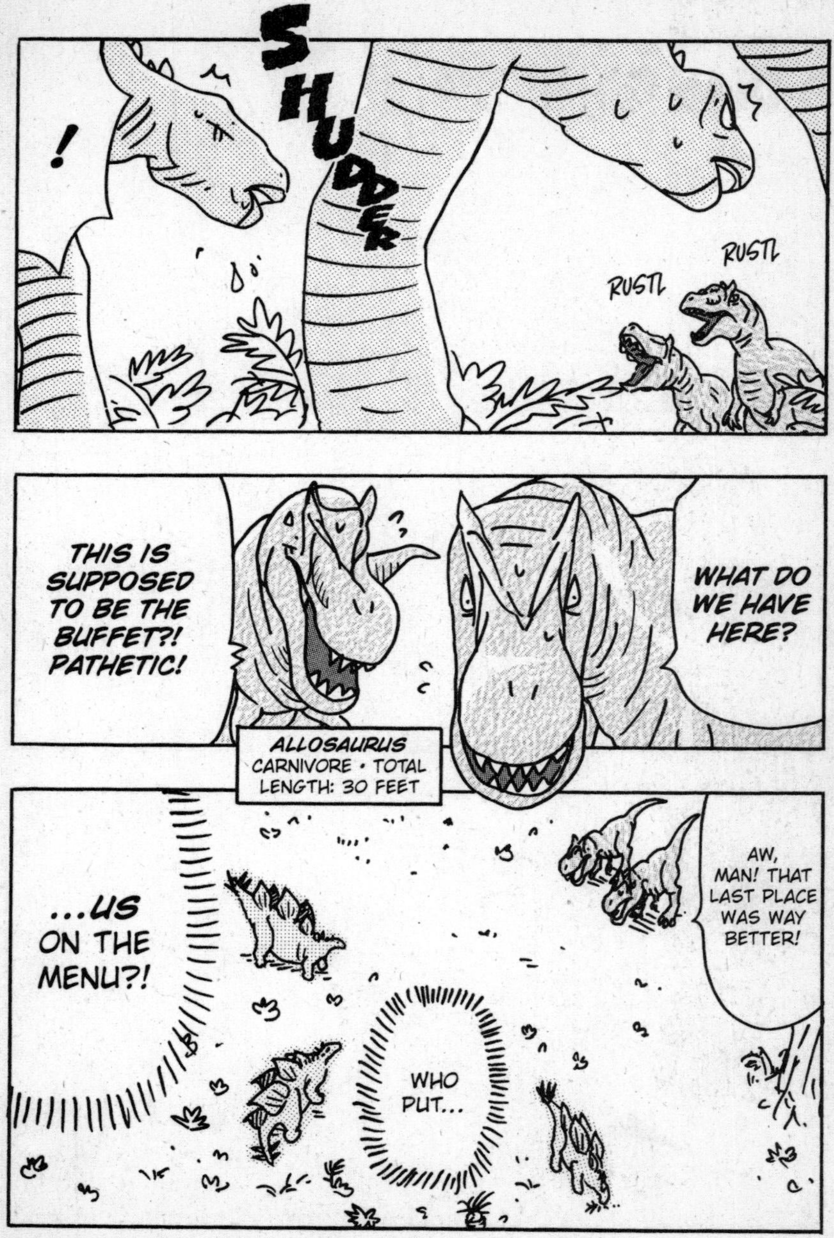
RUSTL
RUSTL
SHUDDER
!
WHAT DO WE HAVE HERE?
THIS IS SUPPOSED TO BE THE BUFFET?! PATHETIC!
ALLOSAURUS
CARNIVORE • TOTAL LENGTH: 30 FEET
AW, MAN! THAT LAST PLACE WAS WAY BETTER!
WHO PUT...
...US ON THE MENU?!

BONE 5

A Dino Ghost Story

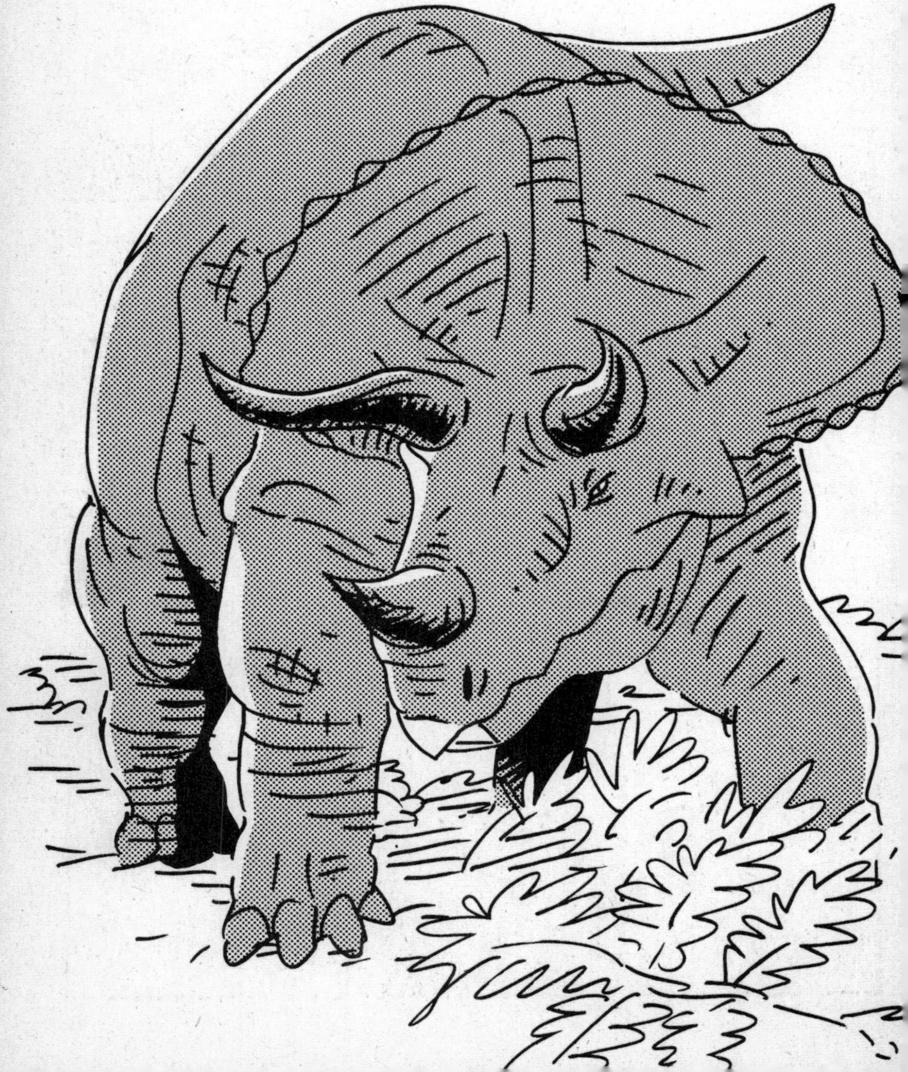

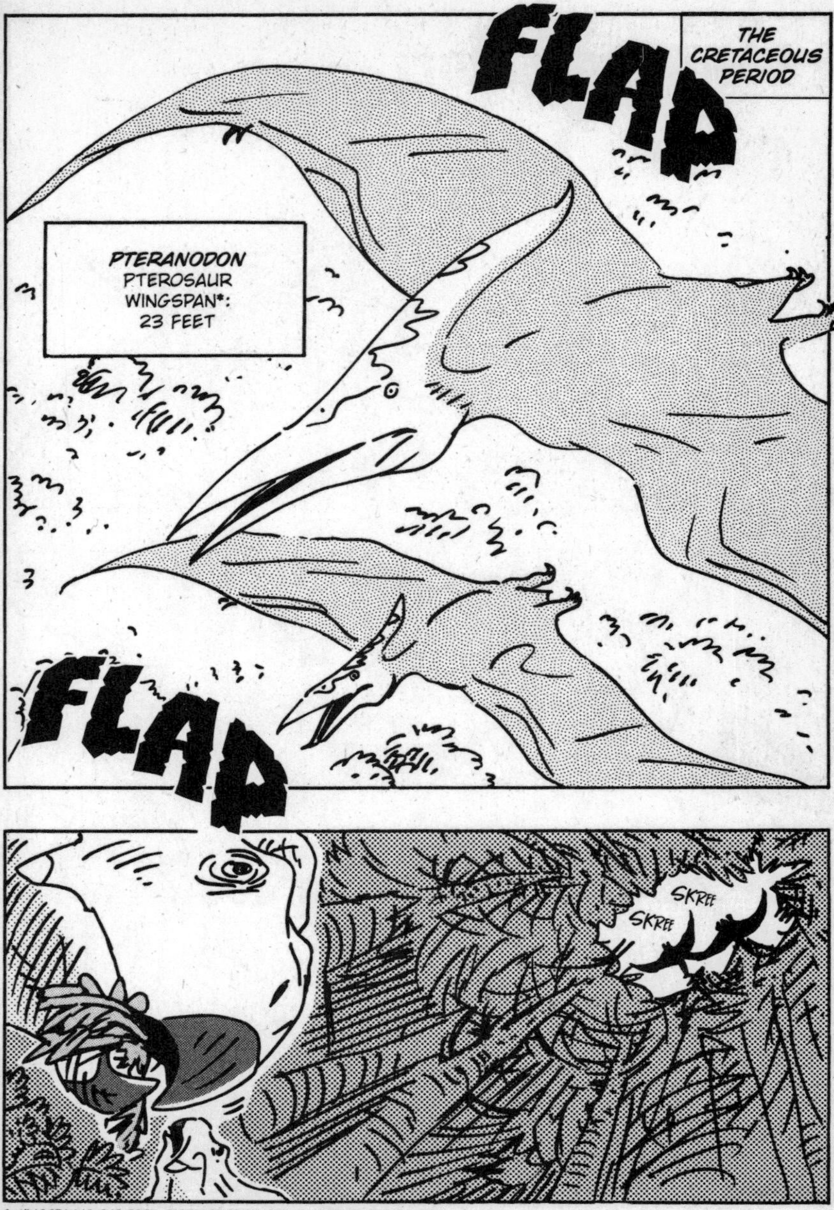
THE CRETACEOUS PERIOD
FLAP
PTERANODON
PTEROSAUR
WINGSPAN*:
23 FEET
FLAP
SKREE
SKREE

* WINGSPAN IS THE TOTAL DISTANCE FROM ONE WINGTIP TO THE OTHER.

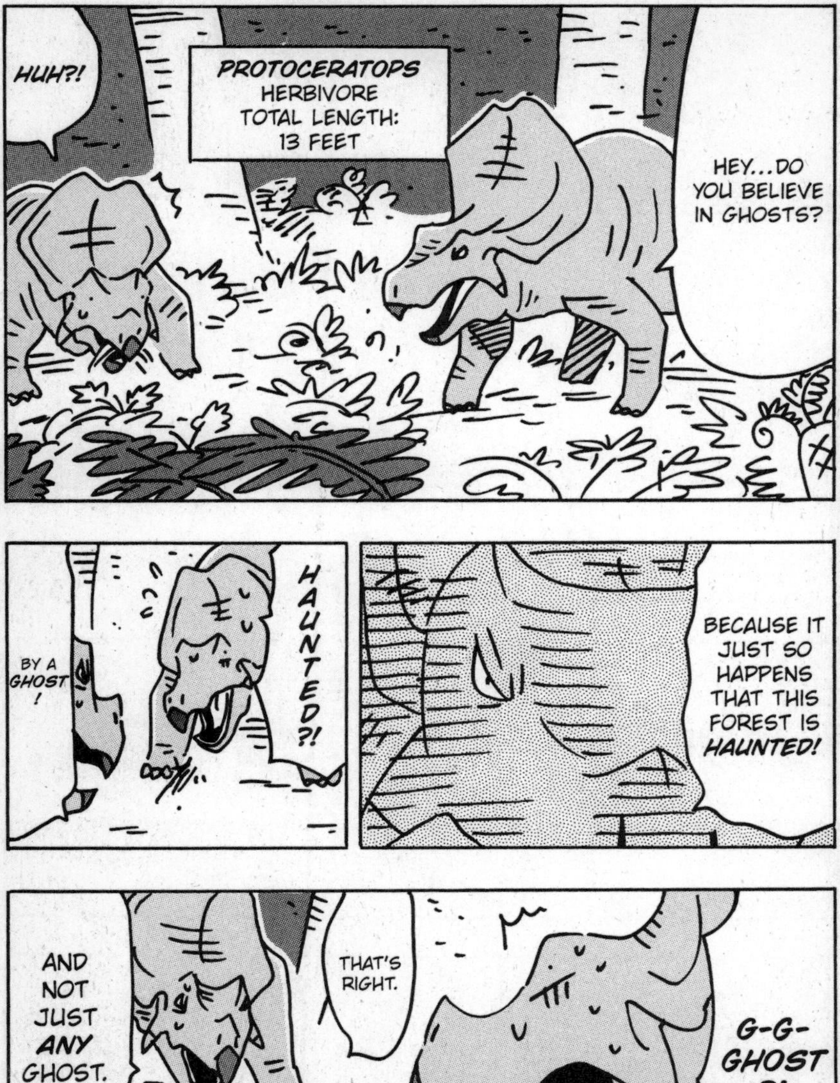
PROTOCERATOPS HERBIVORE TOTAL LENGTH: 13 FEET
HEY...DO YOU BELIEVE IN GHOSTS?
HUH?!
BECAUSE IT JUST SO HAPPENS THAT THIS FOREST IS HAUNTED!
HAUNTED?!
BY A GHOST!
G-G-GHOST?!
THAT'S RIGHT.
AND NOT JUST ANY GHOST.

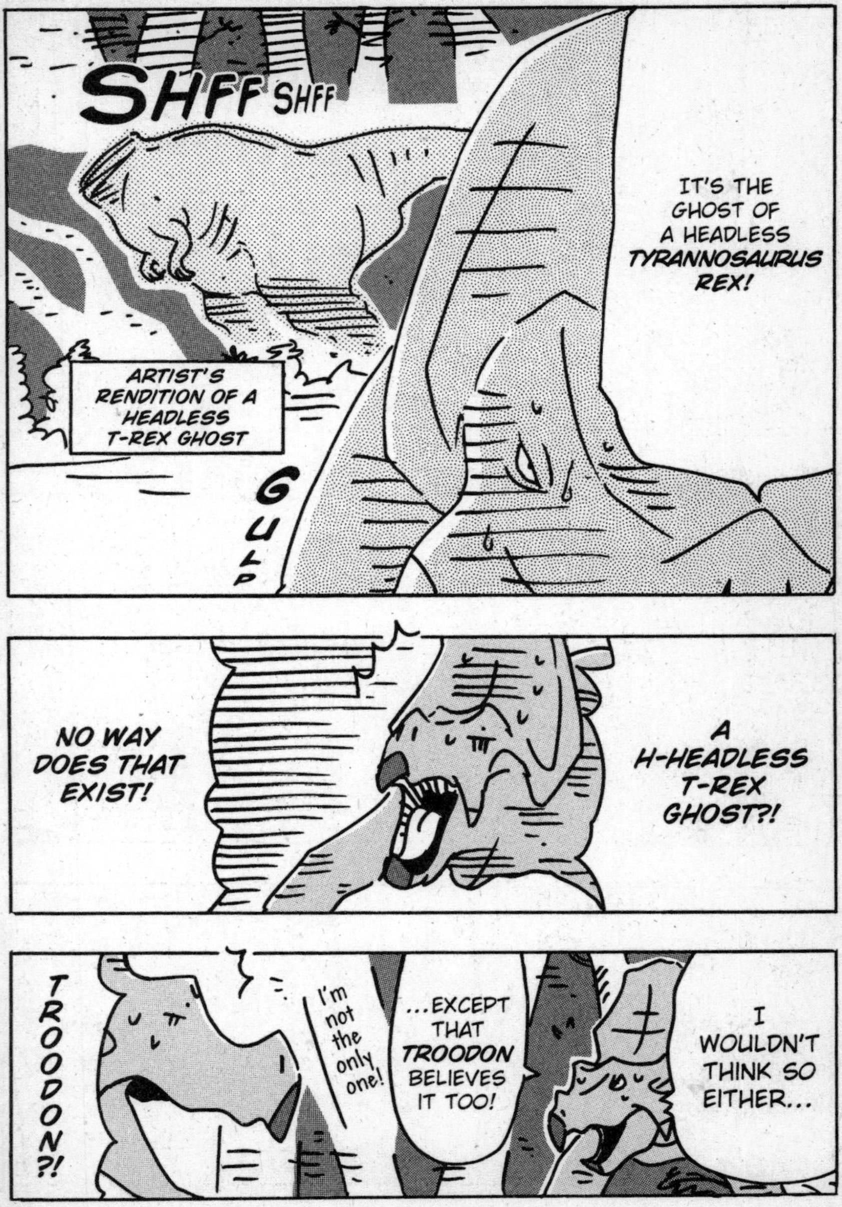
IT'S THE GHOST OF A HEADLESS *TYRANNOSAURUS REX!*
SHFF SHFF
ARTIST'S RENDITION OF A HEADLESS T-REX GHOST
GULP
A H-HEADLESS T-REX GHOST?!
NO WAY DOES THAT EXIST!
I WOULDN'T THINK SO EITHER...
...EXCEPT THAT *TROODON* BELIEVES IT TOO!
I'm not the only one!
TROODON?!

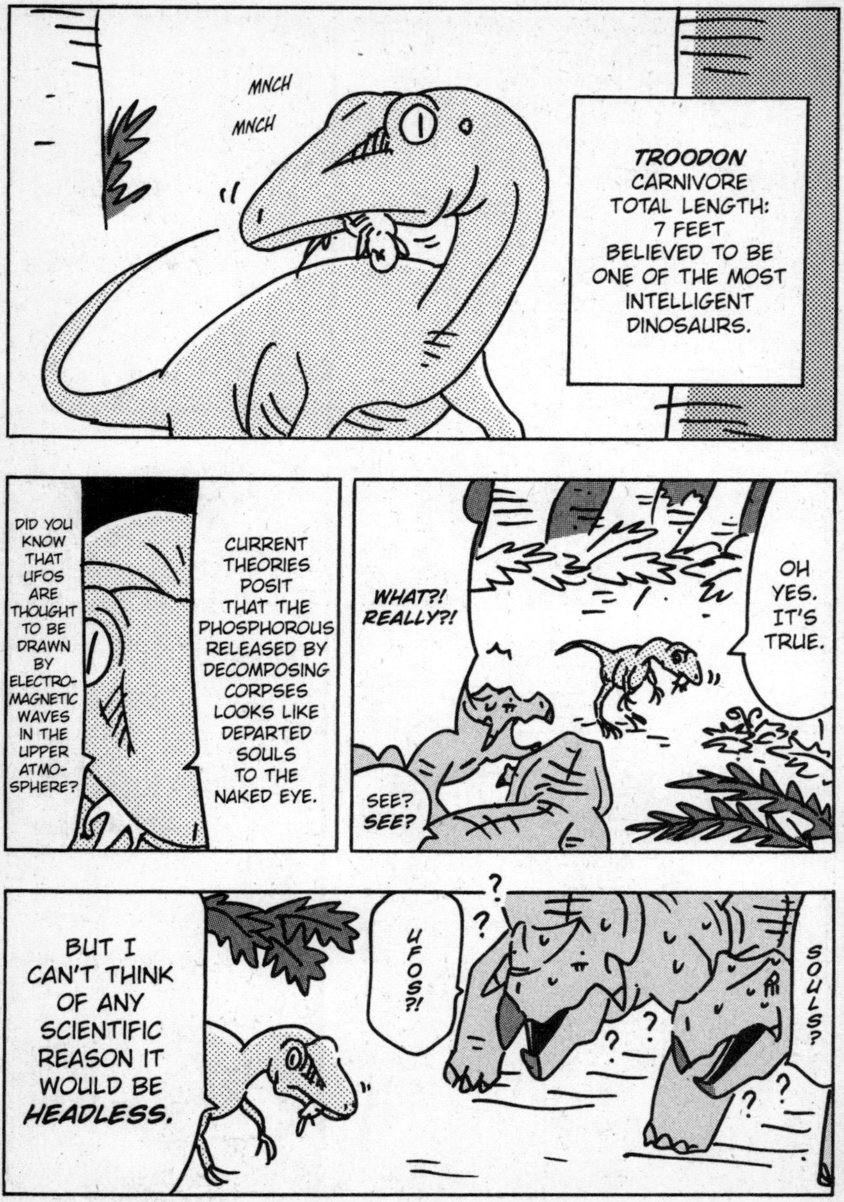
MNCH
MNCH
TROODON CARNIVORE TOTAL LENGTH: 7 FEET BELIEVED TO BE ONE OF THE MOST INTELLIGENT DINOSAURS.
OH YES. IT'S TRUE.
WHAT?! REALLY?!
SEE? **SEE?**
DID YOU KNOW THAT UFOS ARE THOUGHT TO BE DRAWN BY ELECTRO-MAGNETIC WAVES IN THE UPPER ATMO-SPHERE?
CURRENT THEORIES POSIT THAT THE PHOSPHOROUS RELEASED BY DECOMPOSING CORPSES LOOKS LIKE DEPARTED SOULS TO THE NAKED EYE.
SOULS?
UFOS?!
BUT I CAN'T THINK OF ANY SCIENTIFIC REASON IT WOULD BE **HEADLESS.**

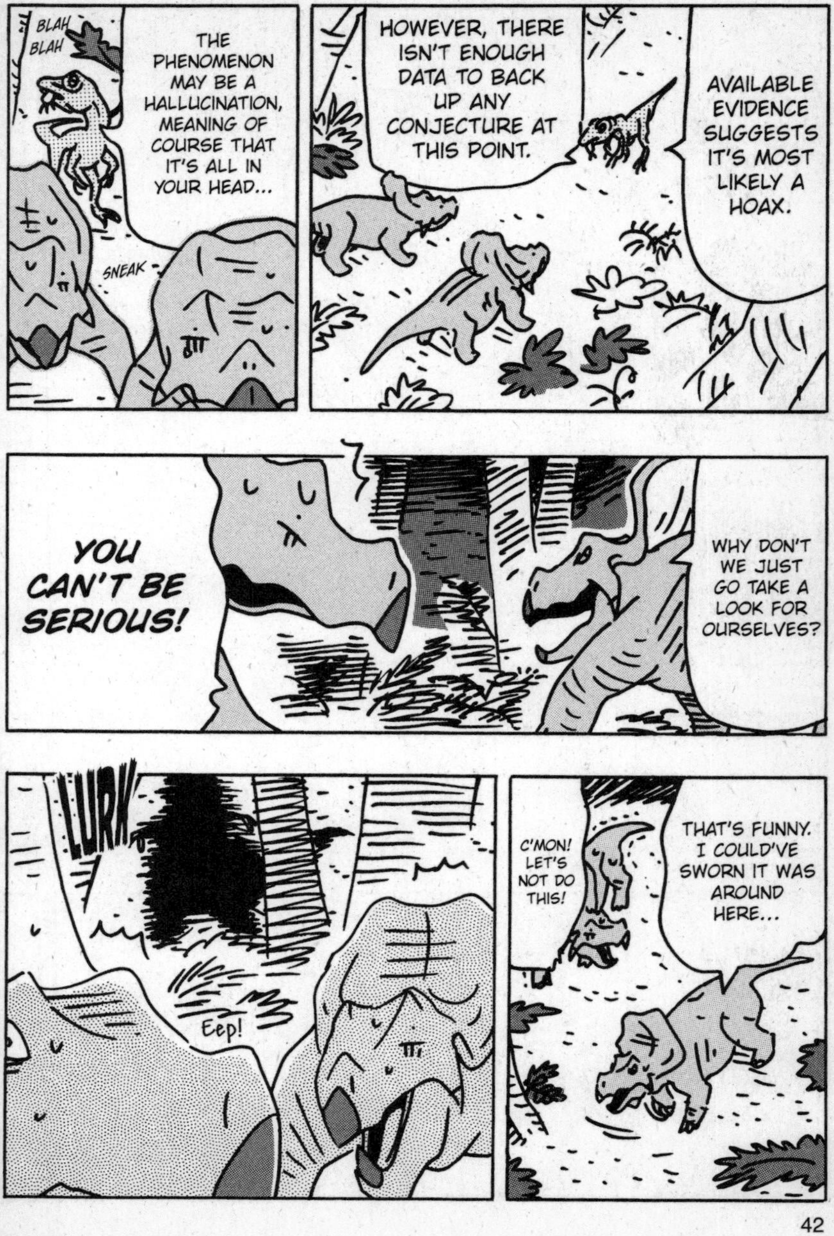
HOWEVER, THERE ISN'T ENOUGH DATA TO BACK UP ANY CONJECTURE AT THIS POINT.
AVAILABLE EVIDENCE SUGGESTS IT'S MOST LIKELY A HOAX.
BLAH BLAH
THE PHENOMENON MAY BE A HALLUCINATION, MEANING OF COURSE THAT IT'S ALL IN YOUR HEAD...
SNEAK
WHY DON'T WE JUST GO TAKE A LOOK FOR OURSELVES?
YOU CAN'T BE SERIOUS!
THAT'S FUNNY. I COULD'VE SWORN IT WAS AROUND HERE...
C'MON! LET'S NOT DO THIS!
LURK
Eep!

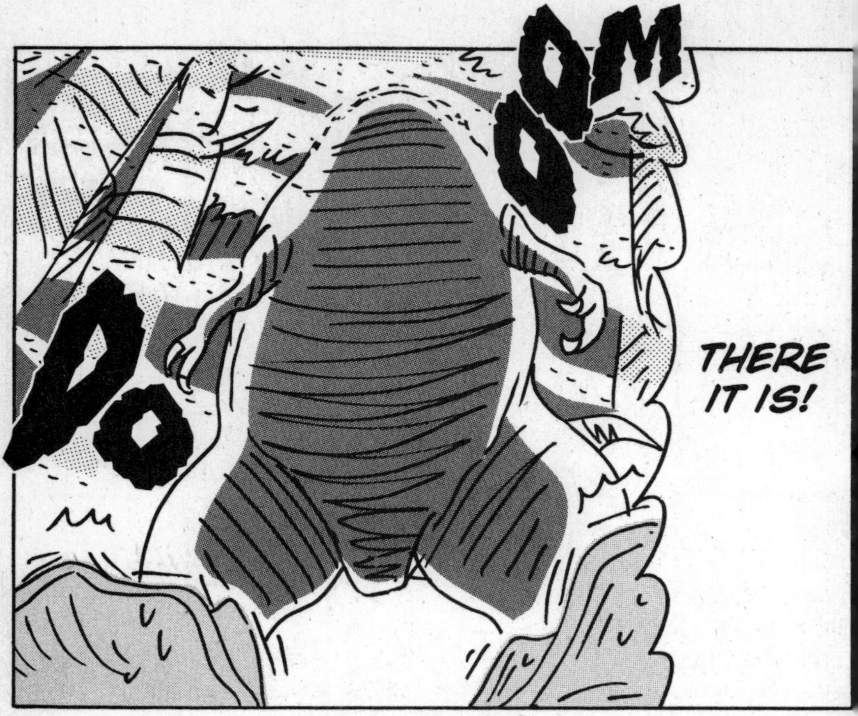
THERE IT IS!
DO
OOM

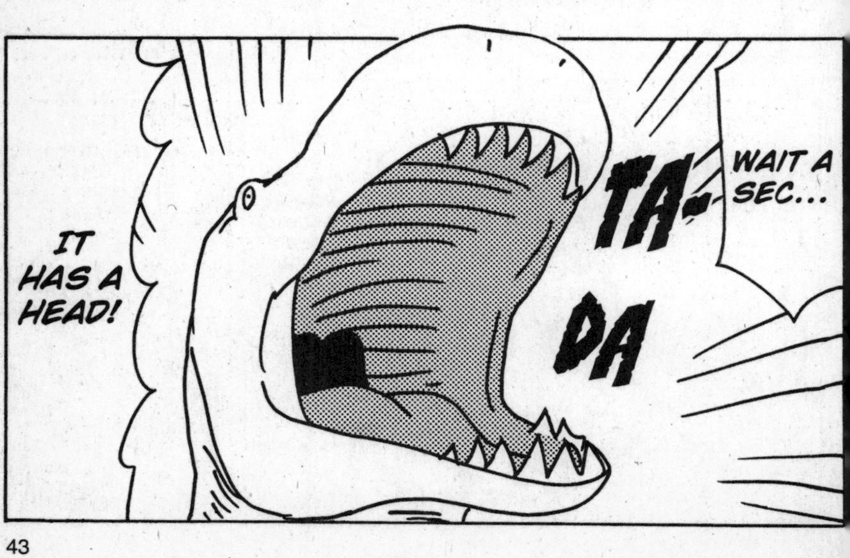
WAIT A SEC...
TA-DA
IT HAS A HEAD!

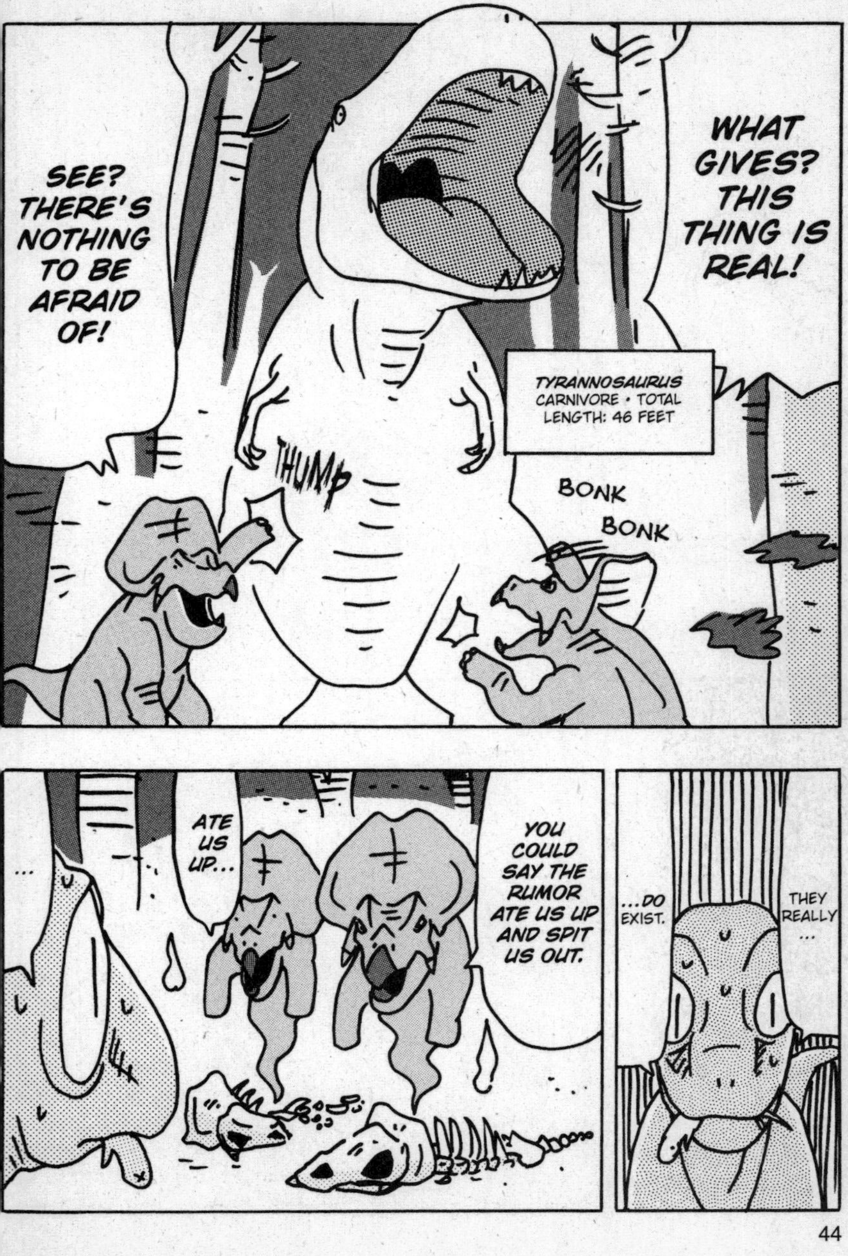
WHAT GIVES? THIS THING IS REAL!
SEE? THERE'S NOTHING TO BE AFRAID OF!
TYRANNOSAURUS CARNIVORE • TOTAL LENGTH: 46 FEET
BONK BONK
THUMP
THEY REALLY ...
...DO EXIST.
YOU COULD SAY THE RUMOR ATE US UP AND SPIT US OUT.
ATE US UP...
...

BONE 6 Fish Heaven

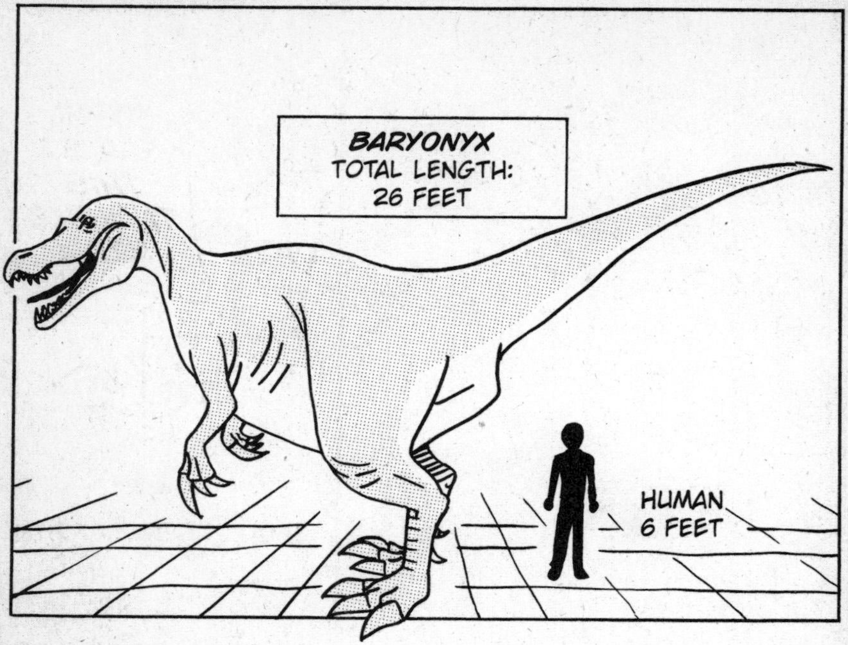
BARYONYX
TOTAL LENGTH:
26 FEET
HUMAN
6 FEET

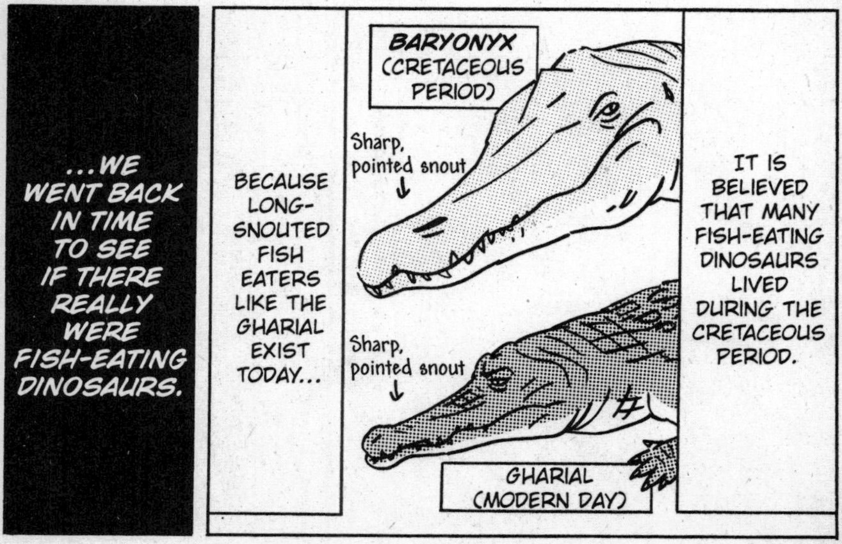
IT IS BELIEVED THAT MANY FISH-EATING DINOSAURS LIVED DURING THE CRETACEOUS PERIOD.
BARYONYX (CRETACEOUS PERIOD)
Sharp, pointed snout
Sharp, pointed snout
GHARIAL (MODERN DAY)
BECAUSE LONG-SNOUTED FISH EATERS LIKE THE GHARIAL EXIST TODAY...
...WE WENT BACK IN TIME TO SEE IF THERE REALLY WERE FISH-EATING DINOSAURS.

BONE 6
Fish Heaven

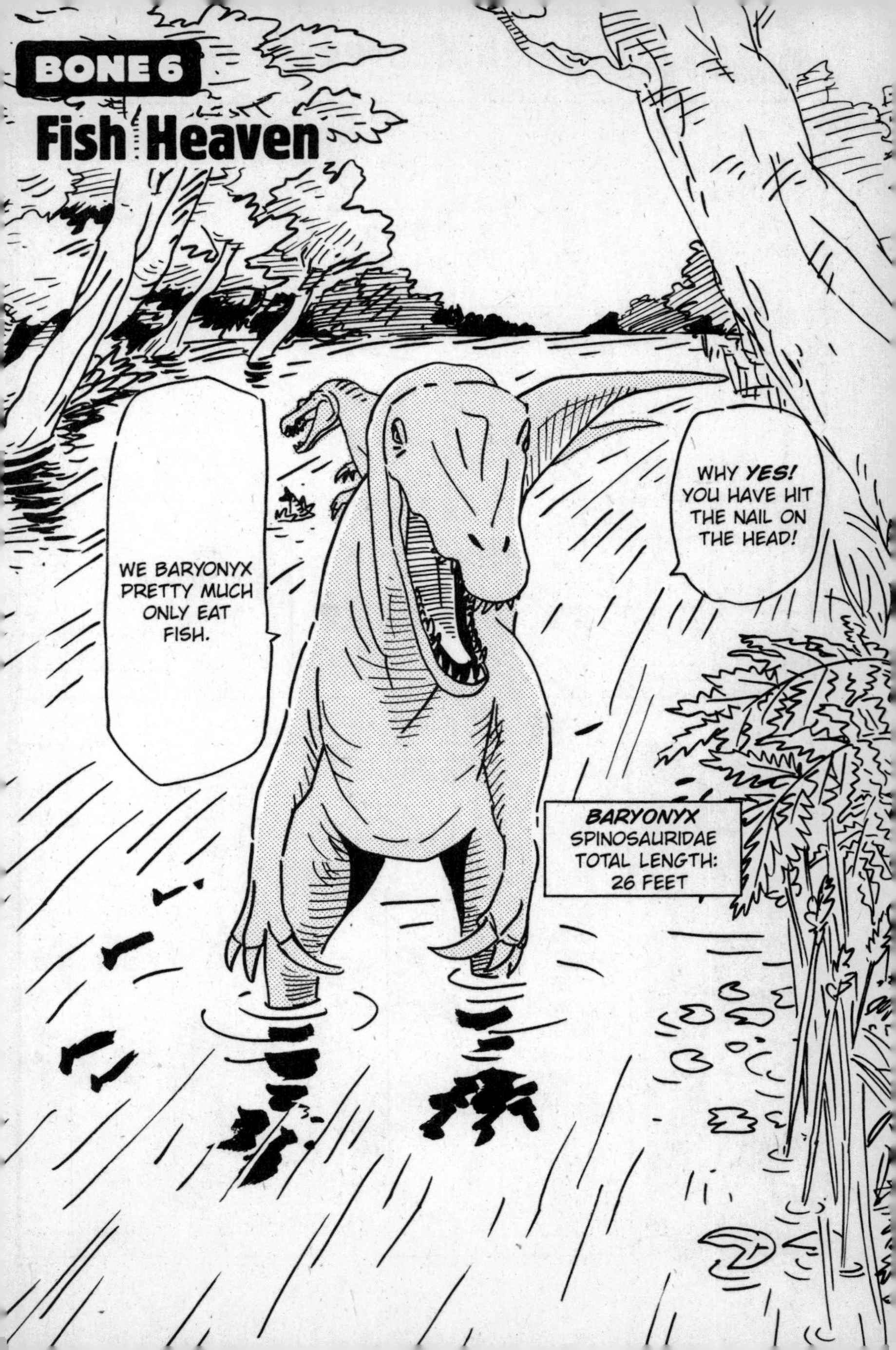
WHY *YES!* YOU HAVE HIT THE NAIL ON THE HEAD!
WE BARYONYX PRETTY MUCH ONLY EAT FISH.
BARYONYX SPINOSAURIDAE TOTAL LENGTH: 26 FEET

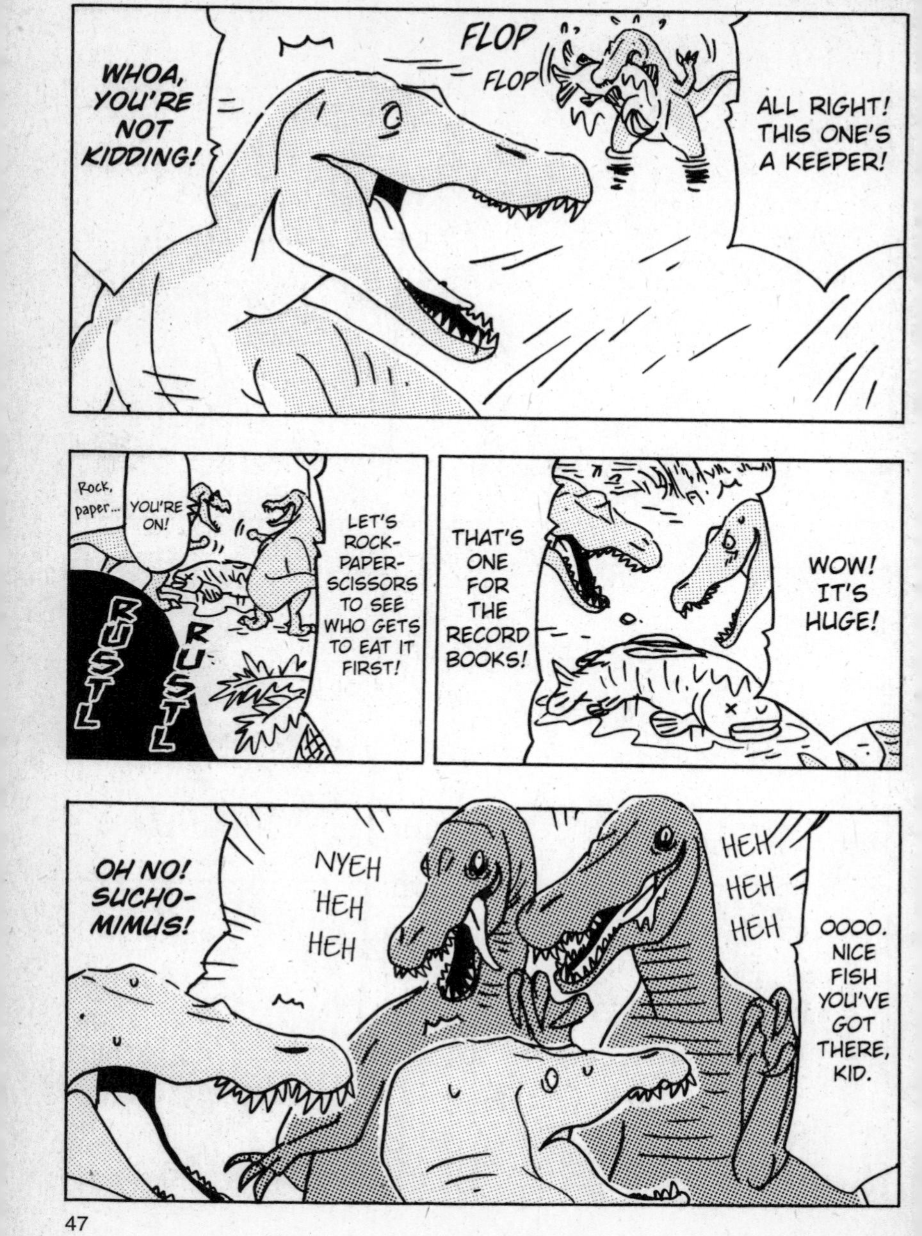
ALL RIGHT! THIS ONE'S A KEEPER!
FLOP
FLOP
WHOA, YOU'RE NOT KIDDING!
WOW! IT'S HUGE!
THAT'S ONE FOR THE RECORD BOOKS!
LET'S ROCK-PAPER-SCISSORS TO SEE WHO GETS TO EAT IT FIRST!
YOU'RE ON!
Rock, paper...
RUSTL
RUSTL
OOOO. NICE FISH YOU'VE GOT THERE, KID.
HEH HEH HEH
NYEH HEH HEH
OH NO! SUCHOMIMUS!

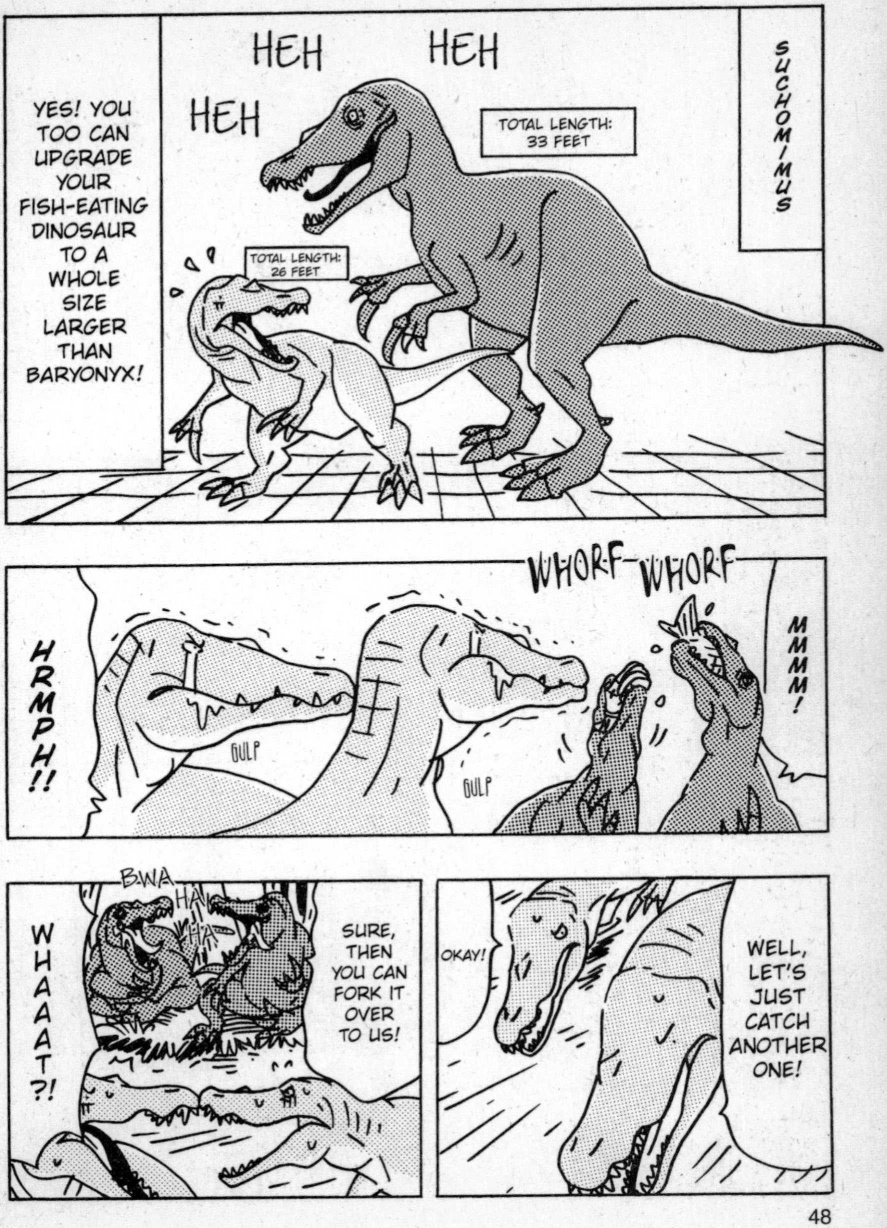

SUCHOMIMUS
HEH HEH
HEH
TOTAL LENGTH: 33 FEET
TOTAL LENGTH: 26 FEET
YES! YOU TOO CAN UPGRADE YOUR FISH-EATING DINOSAUR TO A WHOLE SIZE LARGER THAN BARYONYX!
WHORF WHORF
MMMM!
GULP
GULP
HRMPH!!
WELL, LET'S JUST CATCH ANOTHER ONE!
OKAY!
SURE, THEN YOU CAN FORK IT OVER TO US!
BWA HA HA
WHAAAAT?!

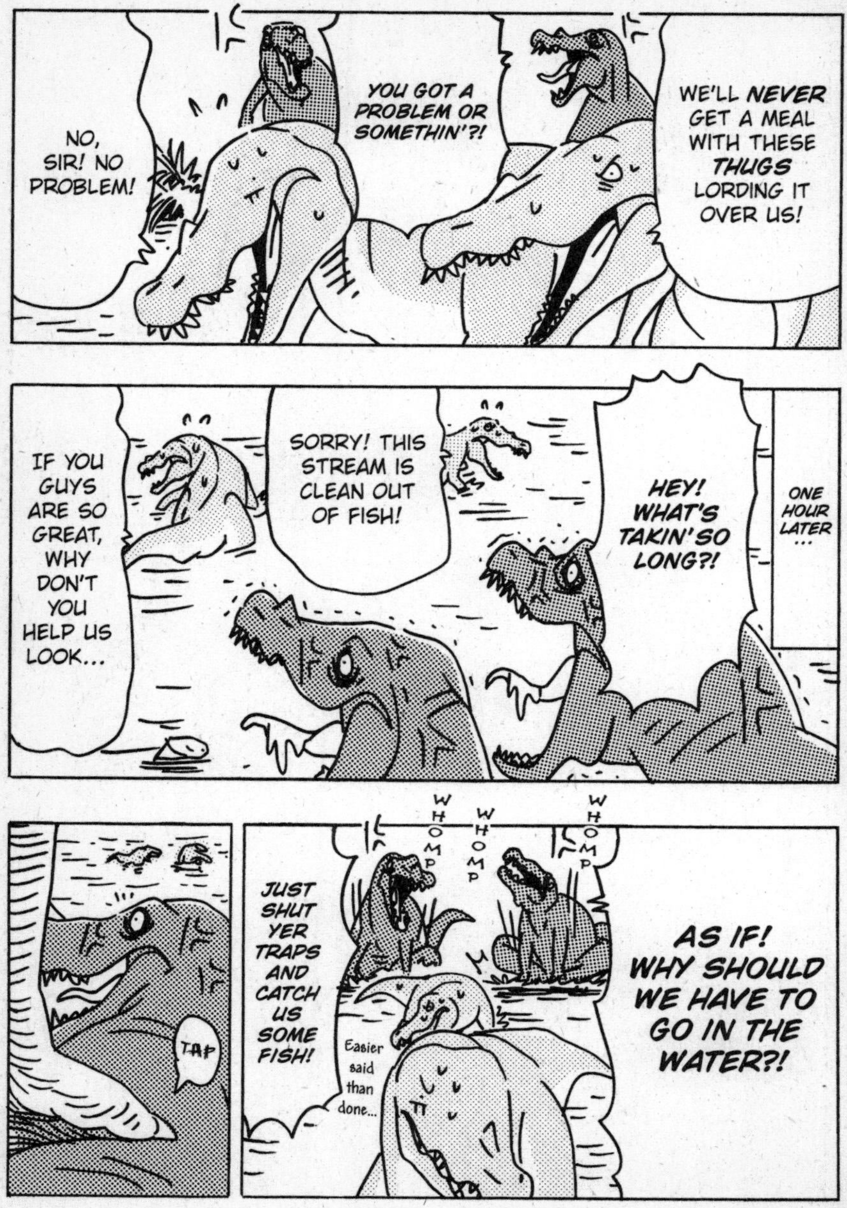
WE'LL NEVER GET A MEAL WITH THESE THUGS LORDING IT OVER US!
YOU GOT A PROBLEM OR SOMETHIN'?!
NO, SIR! NO PROBLEM!
ONE HOUR LATER...
HEY! WHAT'S TAKIN' SO LONG?!
SORRY! THIS STREAM IS CLEAN OUT OF FISH!
IF YOU GUYS ARE SO GREAT, WHY DON'T YOU HELP US LOOK...
AS IF! WHY SHOULD WE HAVE TO GO IN THE WATER?!
WHOMP
WHOMP
WHOMP
JUST SHUT YER TRAPS AND CATCH US SOME FISH!
Easier said than done...
TAP

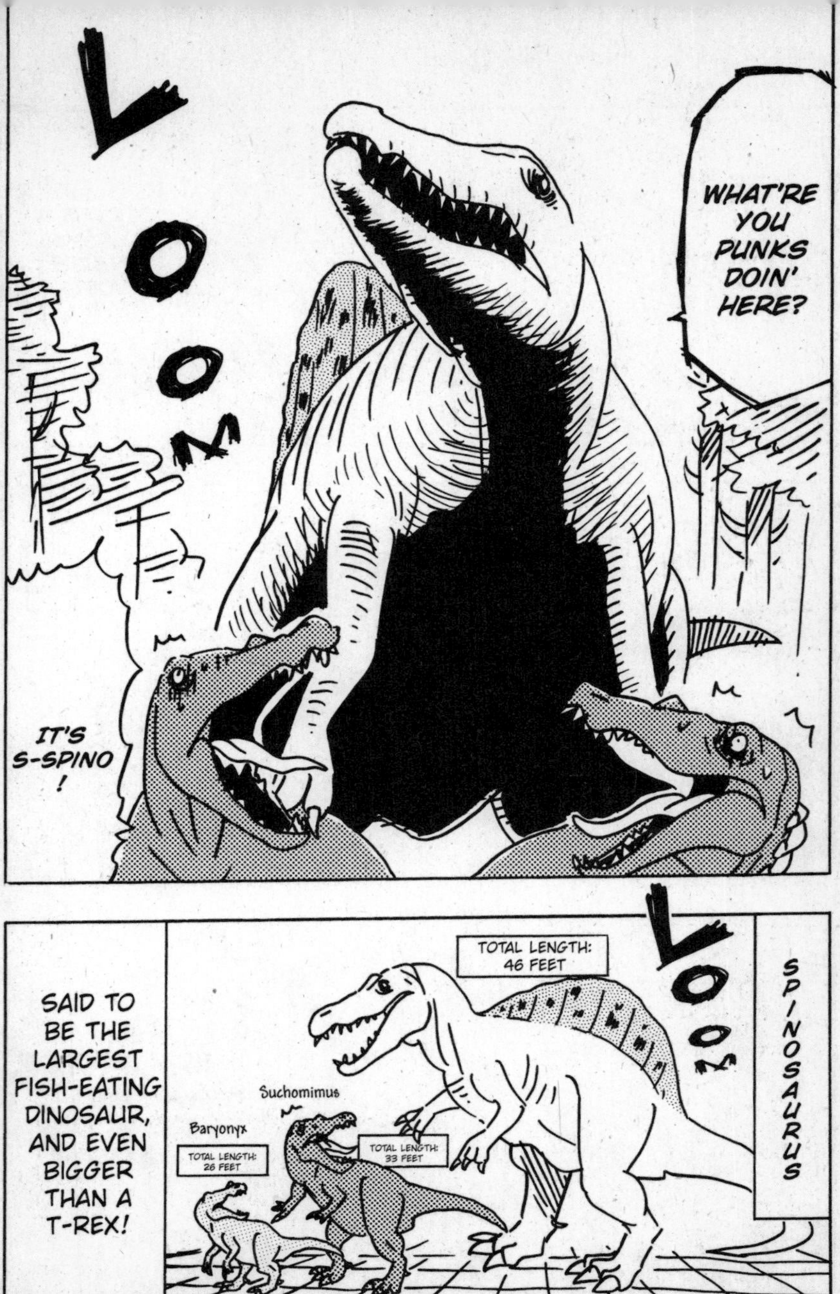
WHAT'RE YOU PUNKS DOIN' HERE?
VOOM
IT'S S-SPINO!
SPINOSAURUS
VOOM
TOTAL LENGTH: 46 FEET
Suchomimus
TOTAL LENGTH: 33 FEET
Baryonyx
TOTAL LENGTH: 26 FEET
SAID TO BE THE LARGEST FISH-EATING DINOSAUR, AND EVEN BIGGER THAN A T-REX!

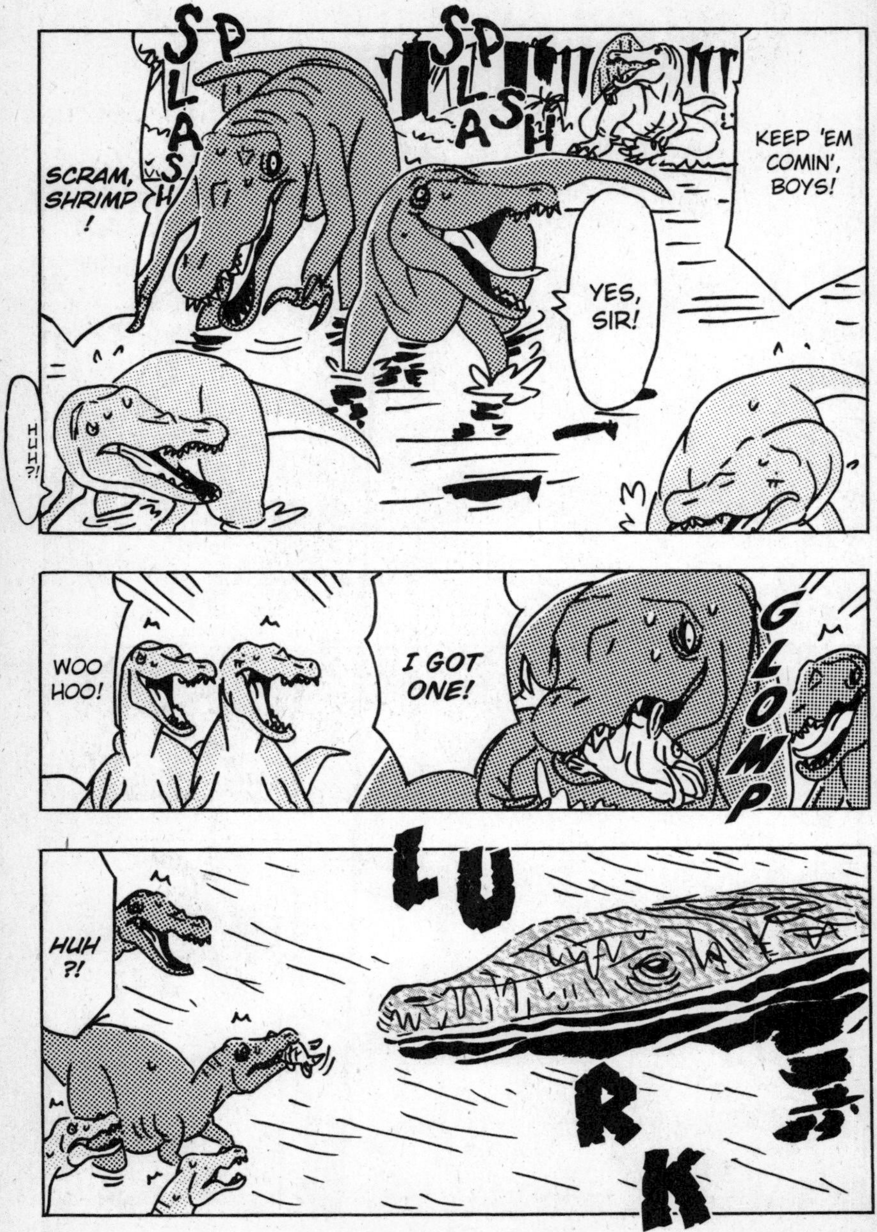
KEEP 'EM COMIN', BOYS!
SPLASH
YES, SIR!
SPLASH
SCRAM, SHRIMP!
HUH?!
GLOMP
I GOT ONE!
WOO HOO!
LURK
HUH?!

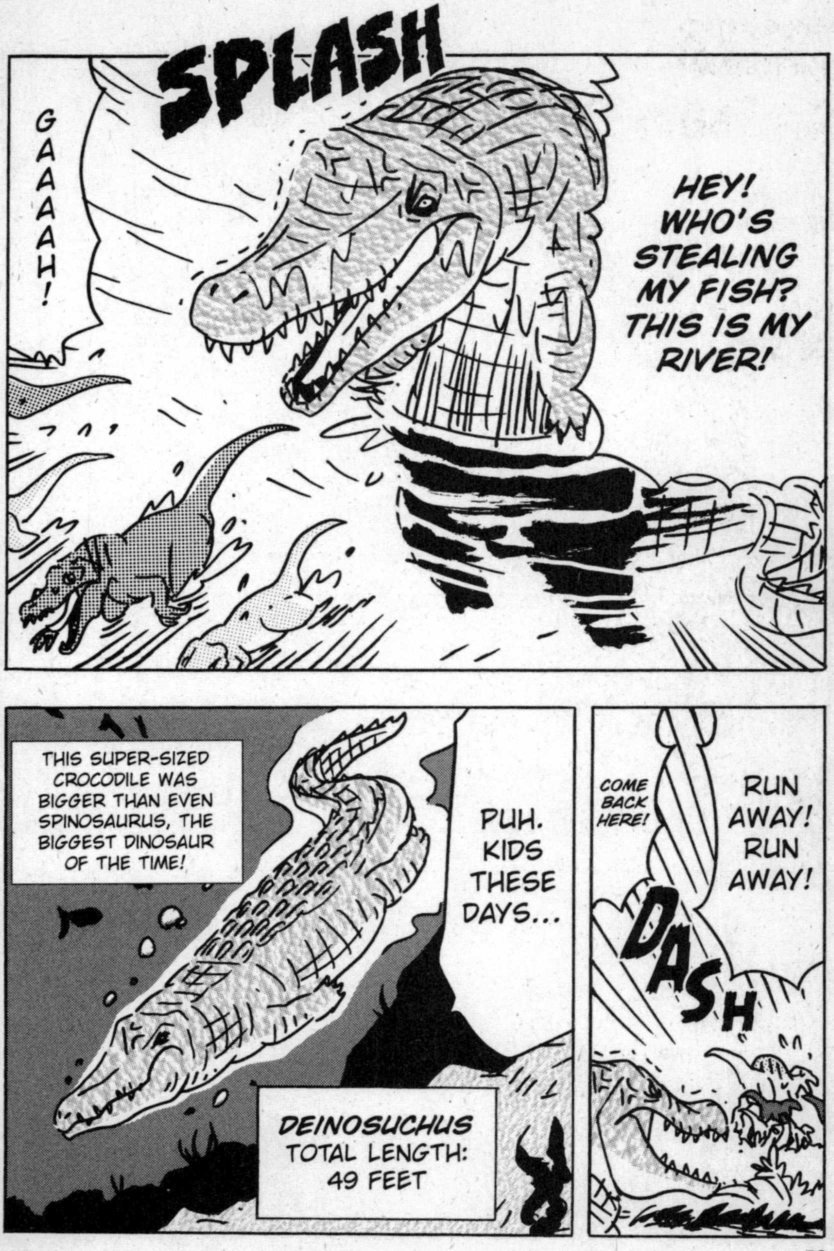
SPLASH
HEY! WHO'S STEALING MY FISH? THIS IS MY RIVER!
GAAAAAH!
RUN AWAY! RUN AWAY!
COME BACK HERE!
DASH
PUH. KIDS THESE DAYS...
THIS SUPER-SIZED CROCODILE WAS BIGGER THAN EVEN SPINOSAURUS, THE BIGGEST DINOSAUR OF THE TIME!
DEINOSUCHUS
TOTAL LENGTH: 49 FEET

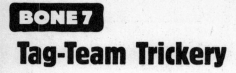

BONE 7
Tag-Team Trickery

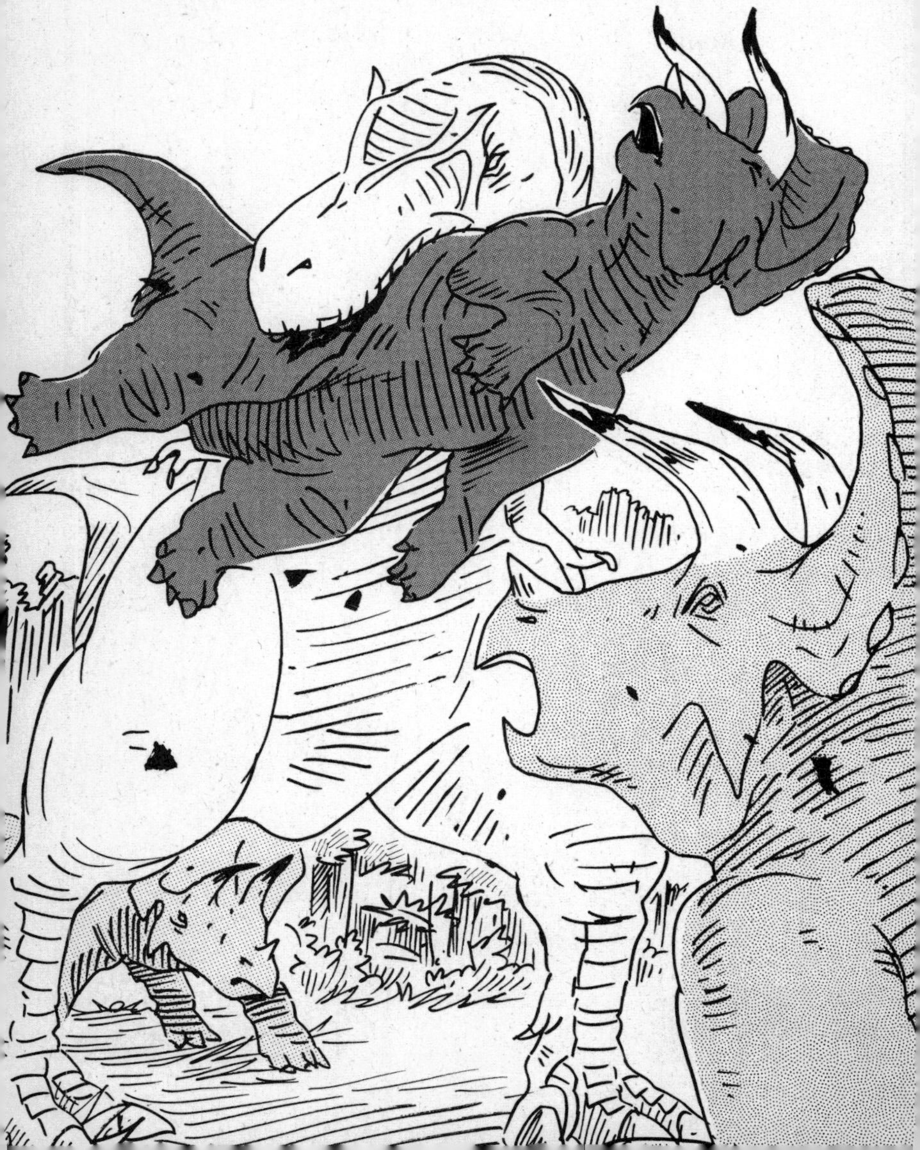

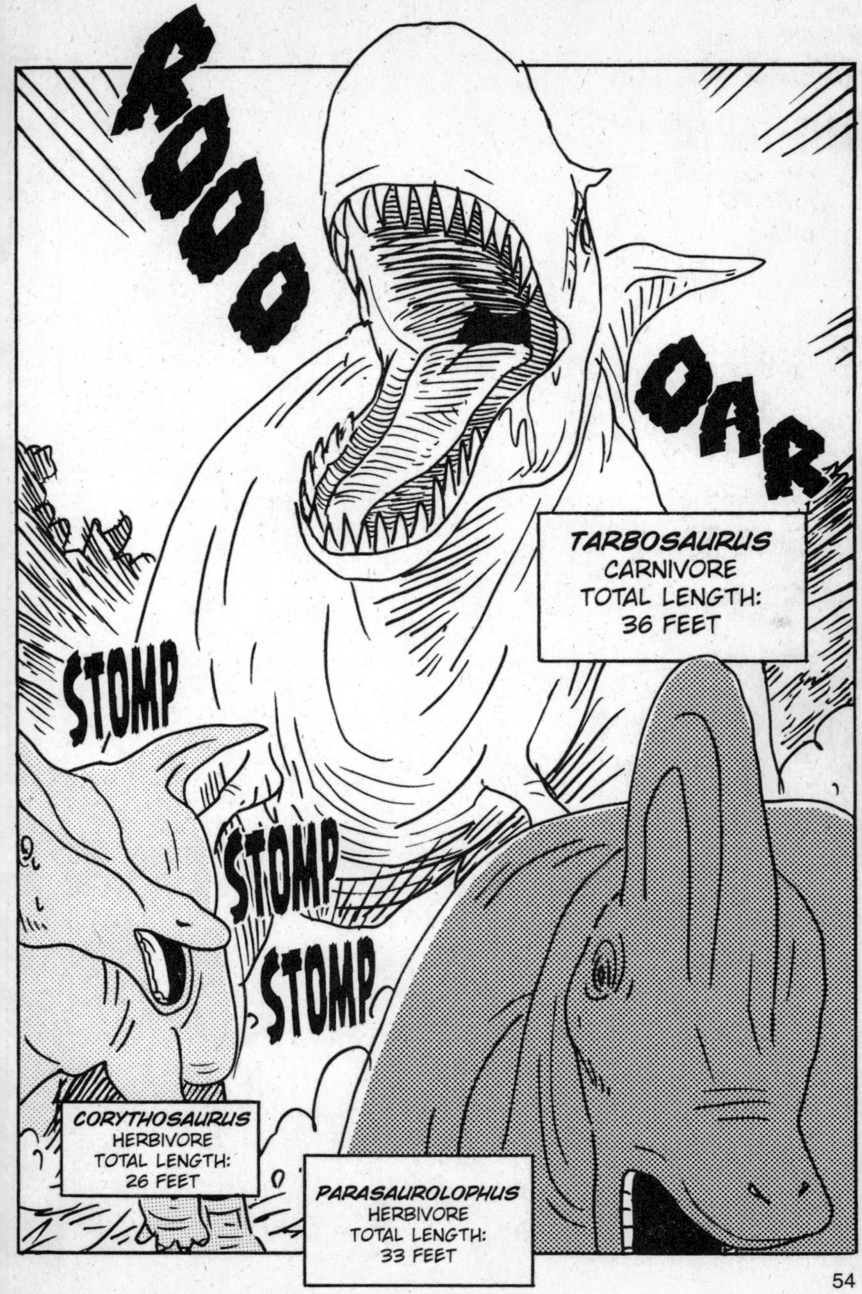
ROOO
OAR
TARBOSAURUS
CARNIVORE
TOTAL LENGTH:
36 FEET
STOMP
STOMP
STOMP
CORYTHOSAURUS
HERBIVORE
TOTAL LENGTH:
26 FEET
PARASAUROLOPHUS
HERBIVORE
TOTAL LENGTH:
33 FEET

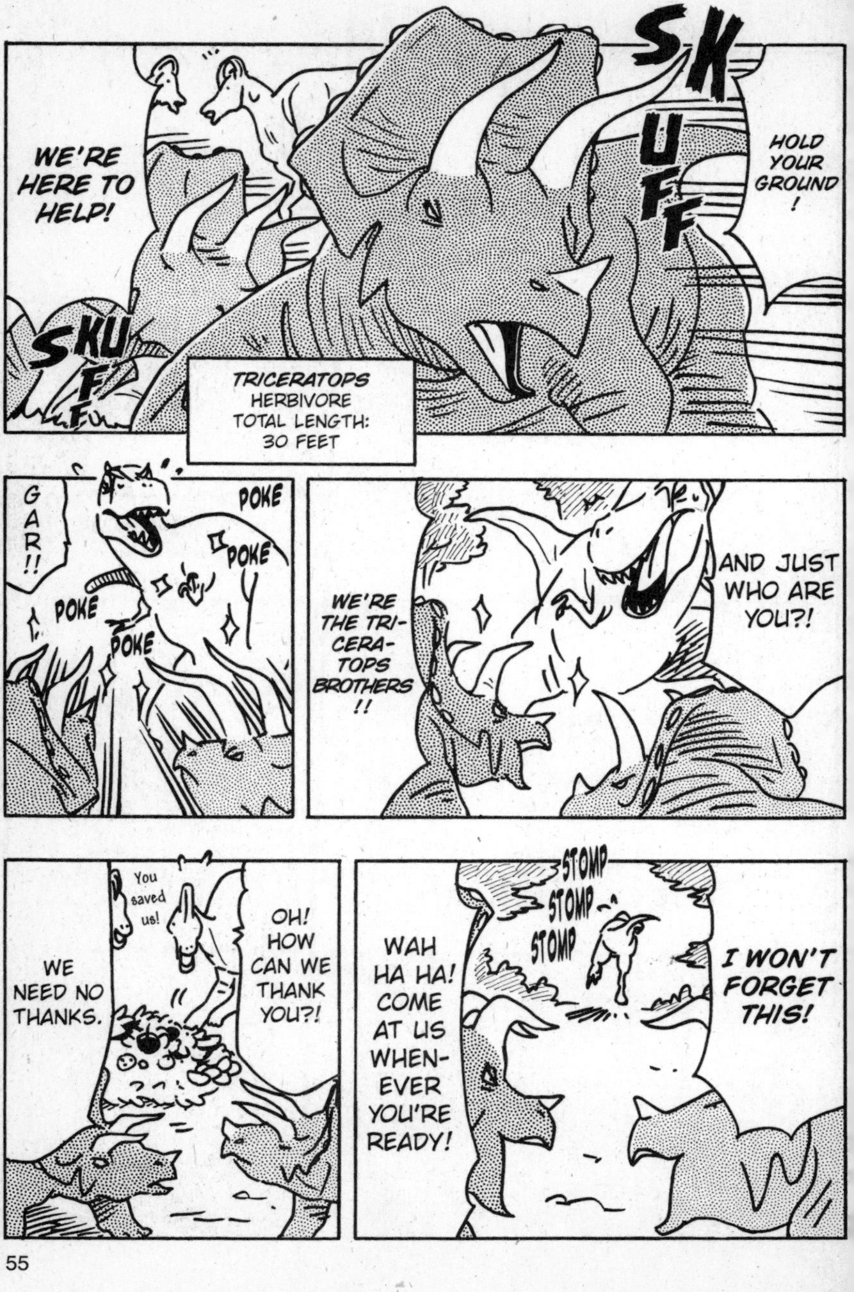
SKUFF
HOLD YOUR GROUND!
WE'RE HERE TO HELP!
SKUFF
TRICERATOPS
HERBIVORE
TOTAL LENGTH: 30 FEET
AND JUST WHO ARE YOU?!
WE'RE THE TRICERATOPS BROTHERS!!
POKE
POKE
GAR!!
POKE
POKE
I WON'T FORGET THIS!
STOMP STOMP STOMP
WAH HA HA! COME AT US WHENEVER YOU'RE READY!
OH! HOW CAN WE THANK YOU?!
You saved us!
WE NEED NO THANKS.

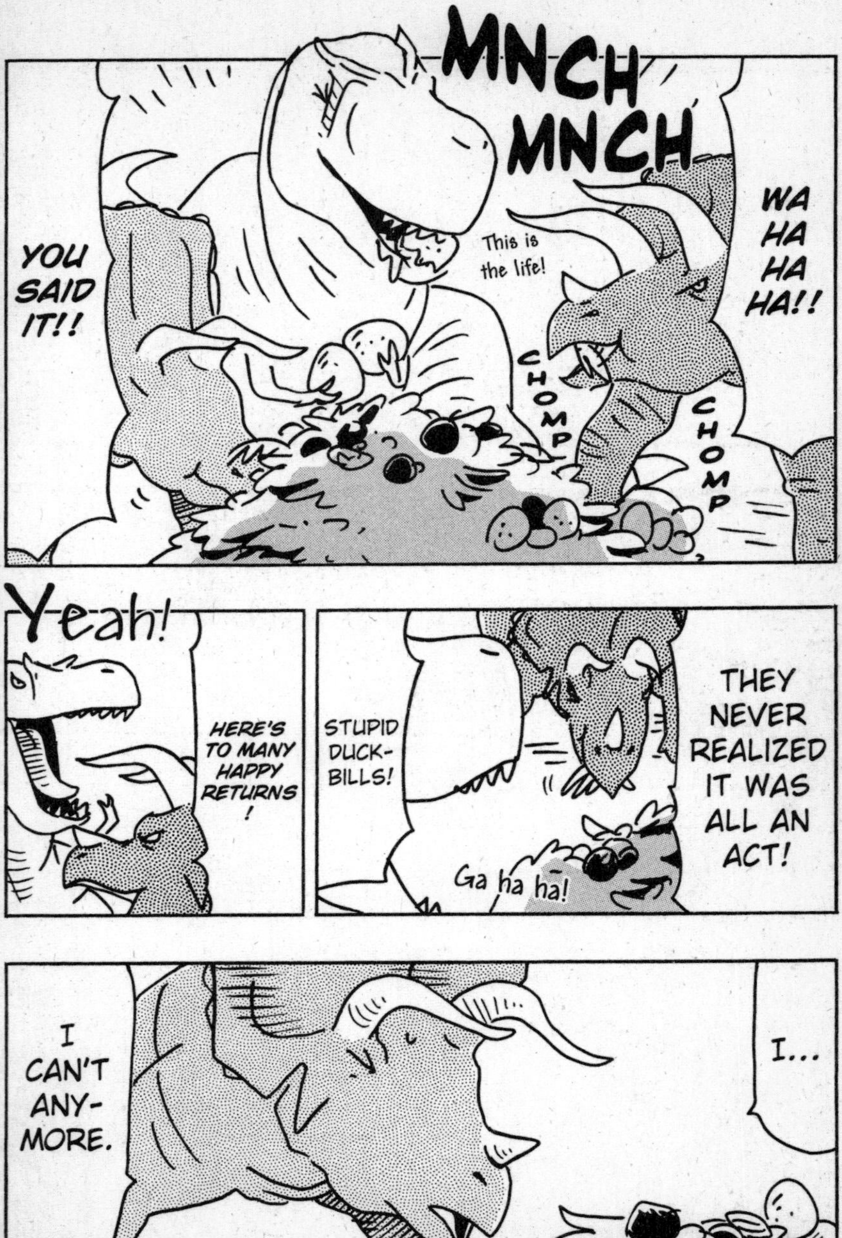
MNCH MNCH
WA HA HA HA!!
This is the life!
CHOMP
CHOMP
YOU SAID IT!!
THEY NEVER REALIZED IT WAS ALL AN ACT!
Ga ha ha!
STUPID DUCK-BILLS!
HERE'S TO MANY HAPPY RETURNS!
Yeah!
I...
I CAN'T ANYMORE.

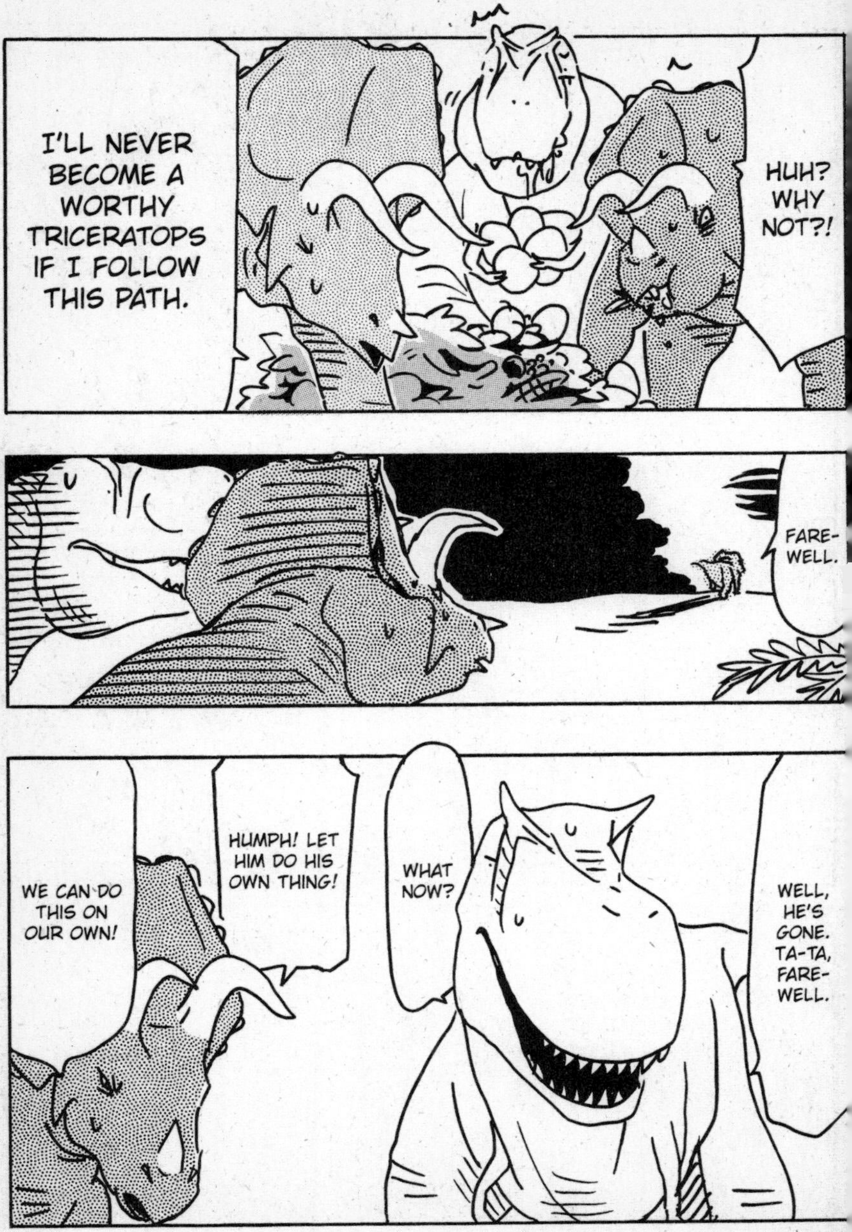
HUH? WHY NOT?!
I'LL NEVER BECOME A WORTHY TRICERATOPS IF I FOLLOW THIS PATH.
FARE-WELL.
WELL, HE'S GONE. TA-TA, FARE-WELL.
WHAT NOW?
HUMPH! LET HIM DO HIS OWN THING!
WE CAN DO THIS ON OUR OWN!

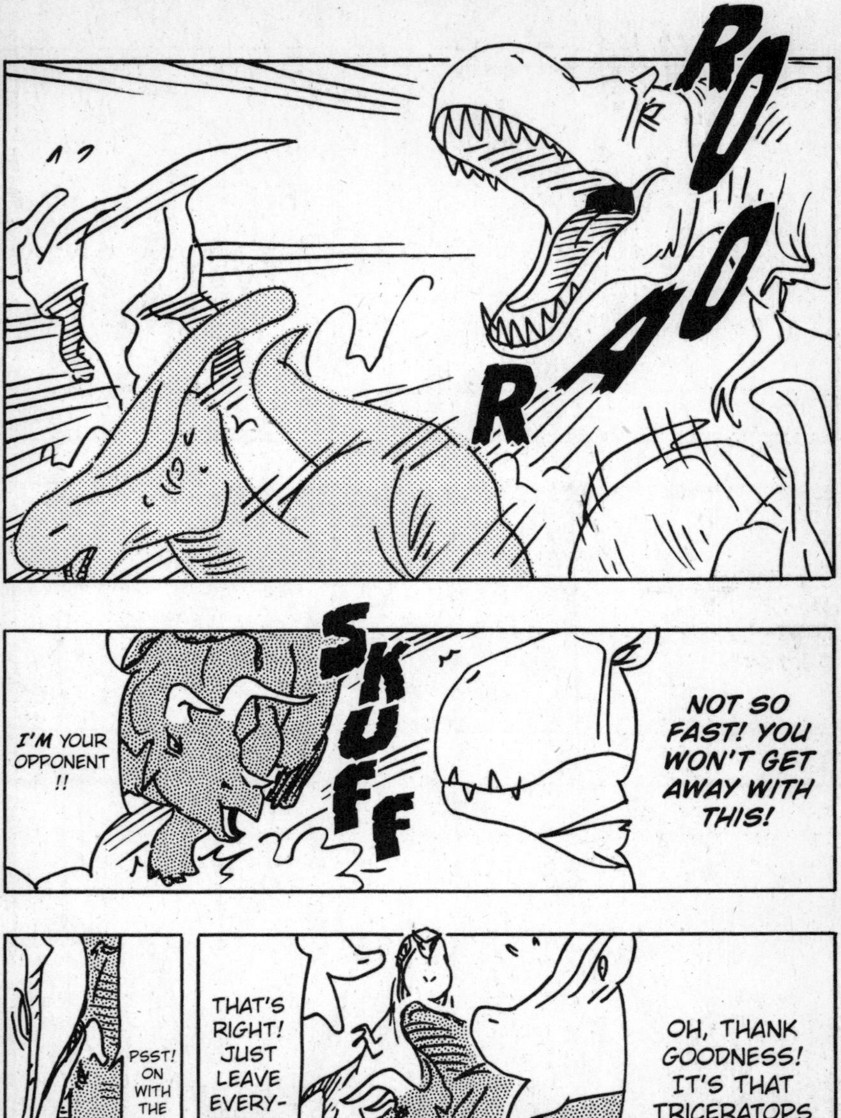
ROOAR
NOT SO FAST! YOU WON'T GET AWAY WITH THIS!
SKUFF
I'M YOUR OPPONENT !!
OH, THANK GOODNESS! IT'S THAT TRICERATOPS FROM BEFORE!
THAT'S RIGHT! JUST LEAVE EVERY-THING TO ME!
PSST! ON WITH THE SHOW ?

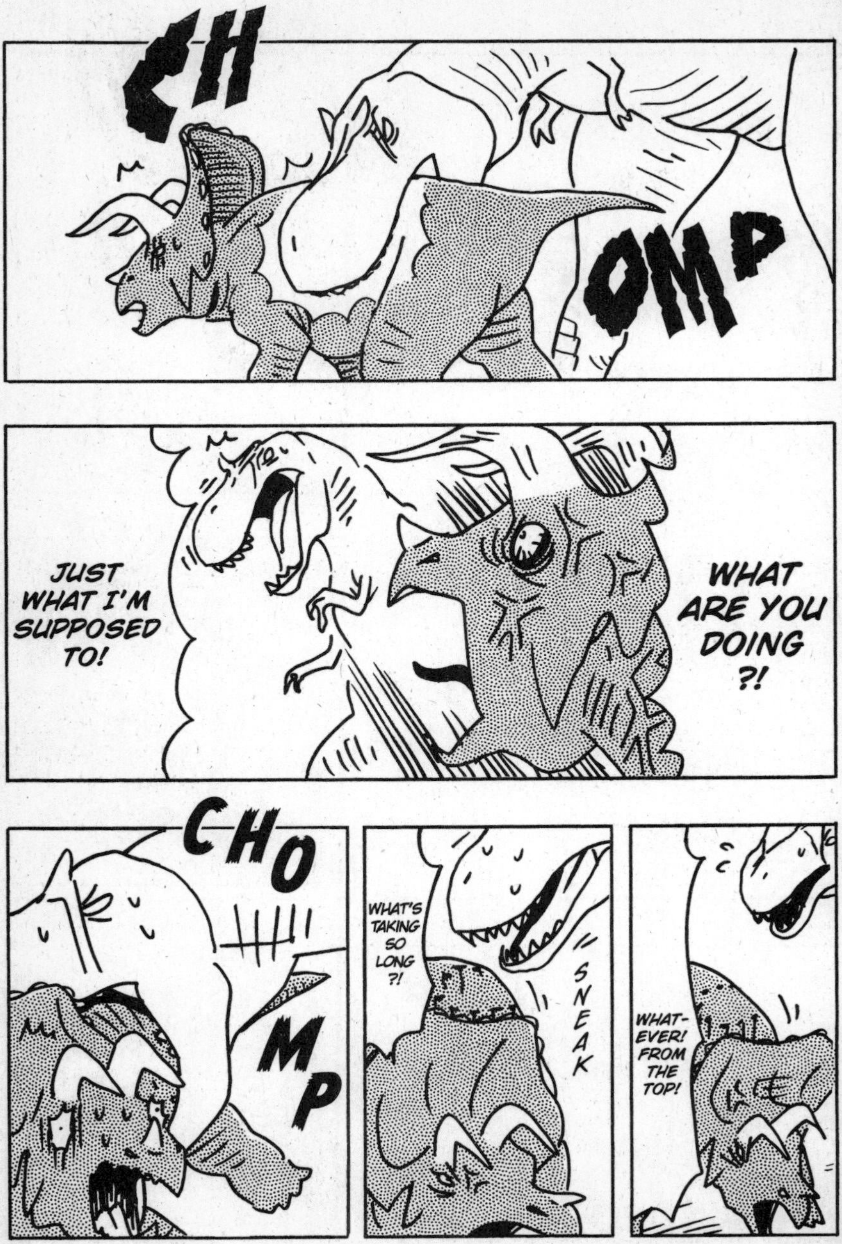
CH
OMP
WHAT ARE YOU DOING ?!
JUST WHAT I'M SUPPOSED TO!
WHAT-EVER! FROM THE TOP!
WHAT'S TAKING SO LONG ?!
SNEAK
CHO
MP

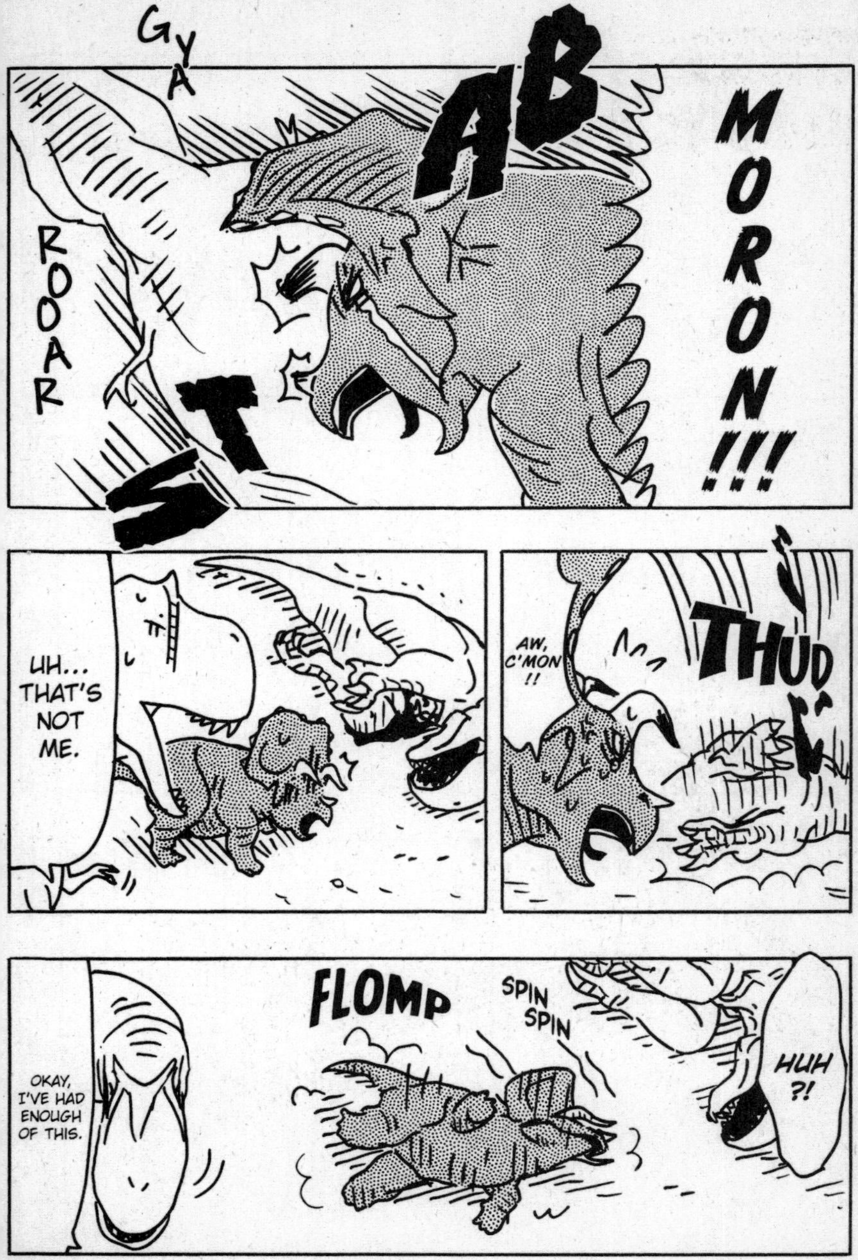
MORON!!!
AB
GYA
ROOAR
ST
THUD
AW, C'MON!!
UH... THAT'S NOT ME.
HUH?!
SPIN SPIN
FLOMP
OKAY, I'VE HAD ENOUGH OF THIS.

BONE 8

Using Your Noggin

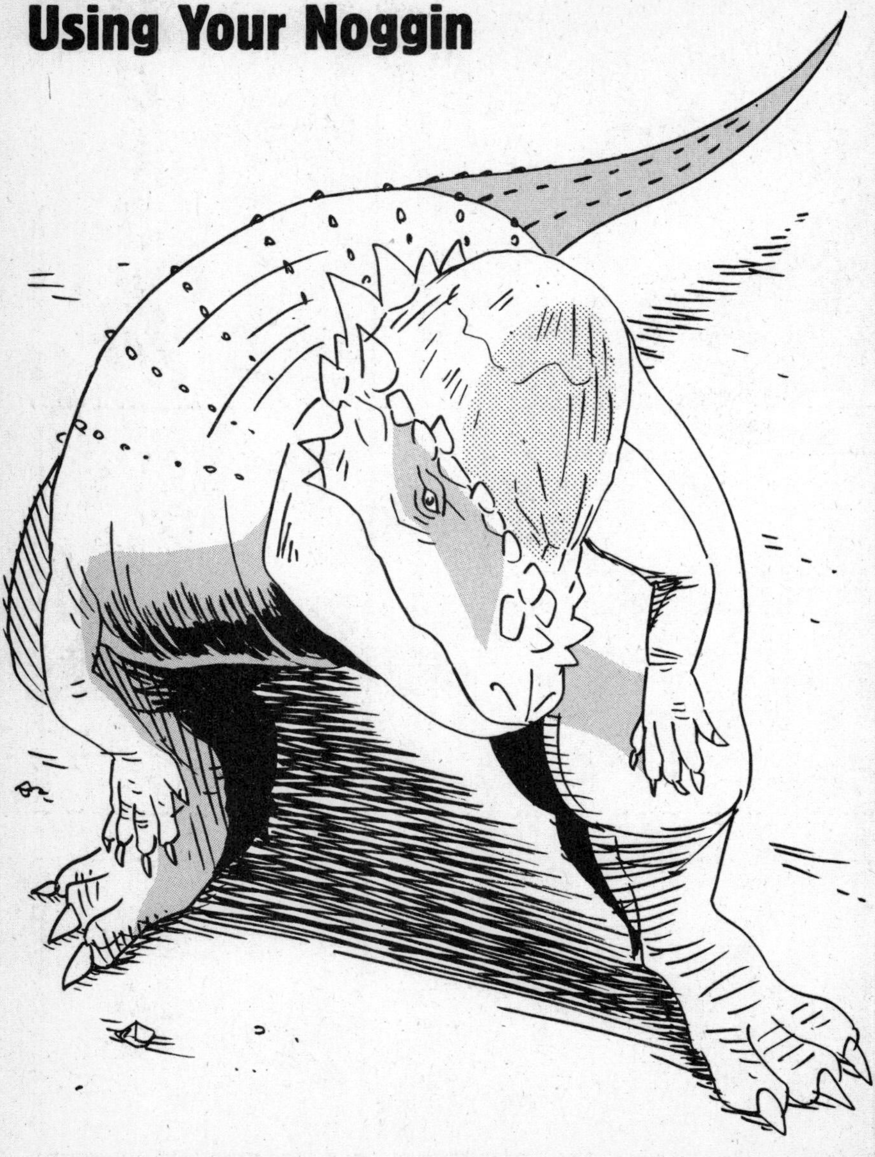

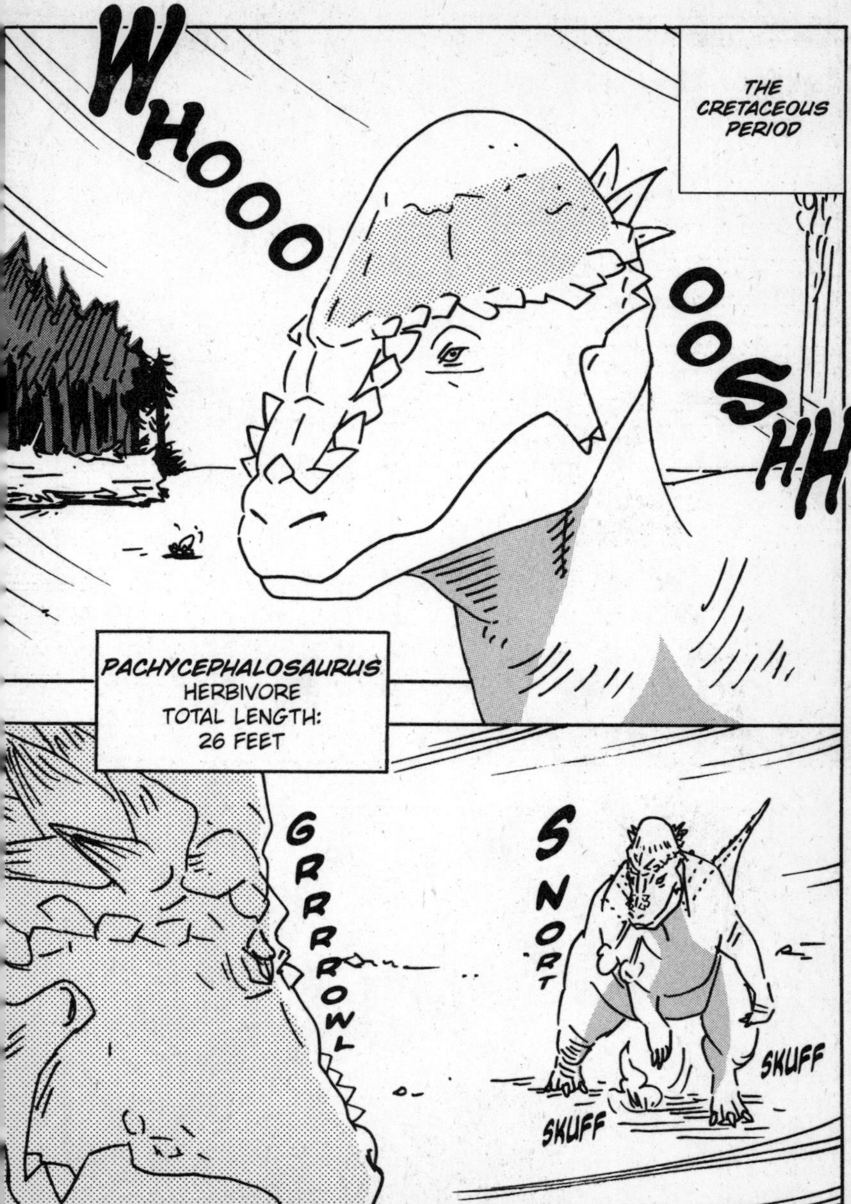
THE CRETACEOUS PERIOD
WHOOOOOOSHH
PACHYCEPHALOSAURUS
HERBIVORE
TOTAL LENGTH:
26 FEET
SNORT
SKUFF
SKUFF
GRRRROWL

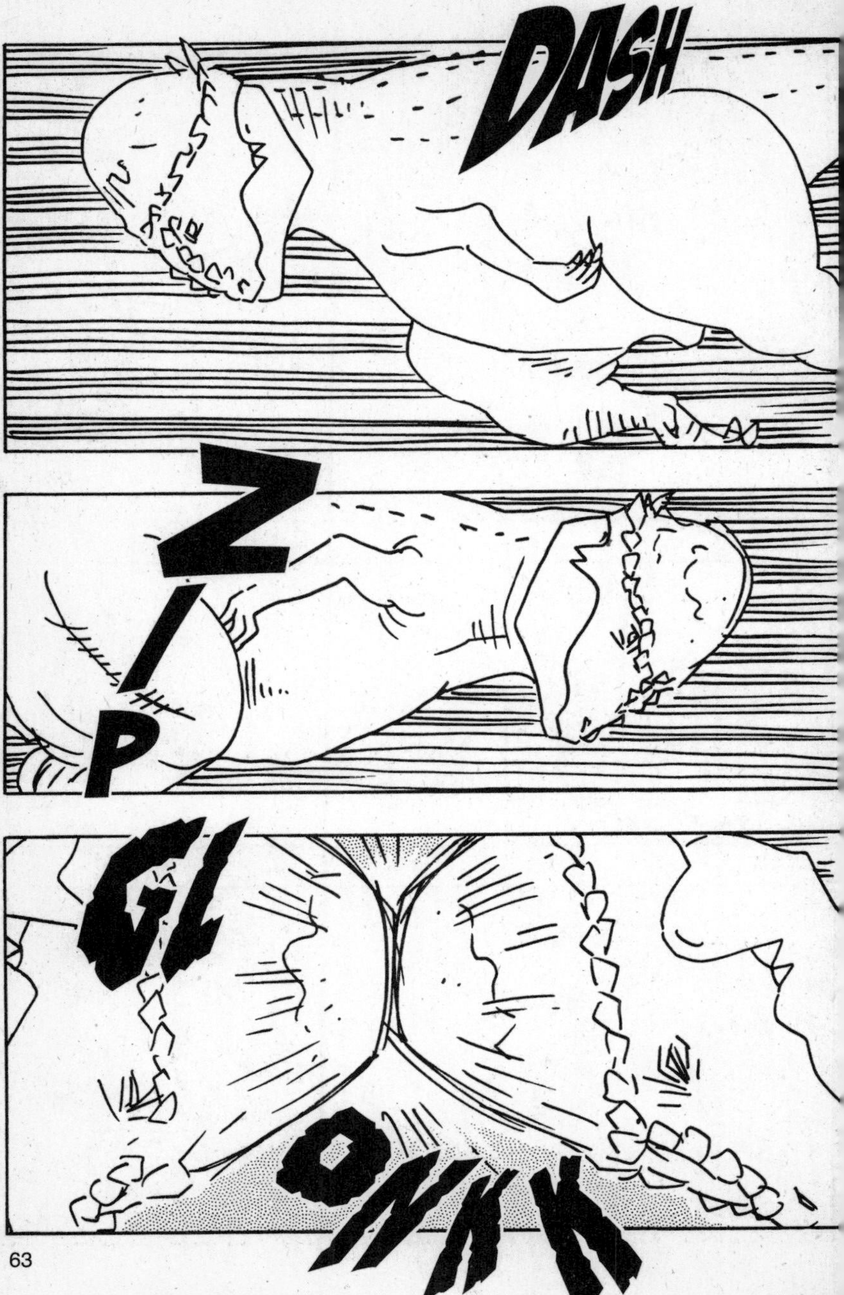
DASH
ZIP
GI
ONKK

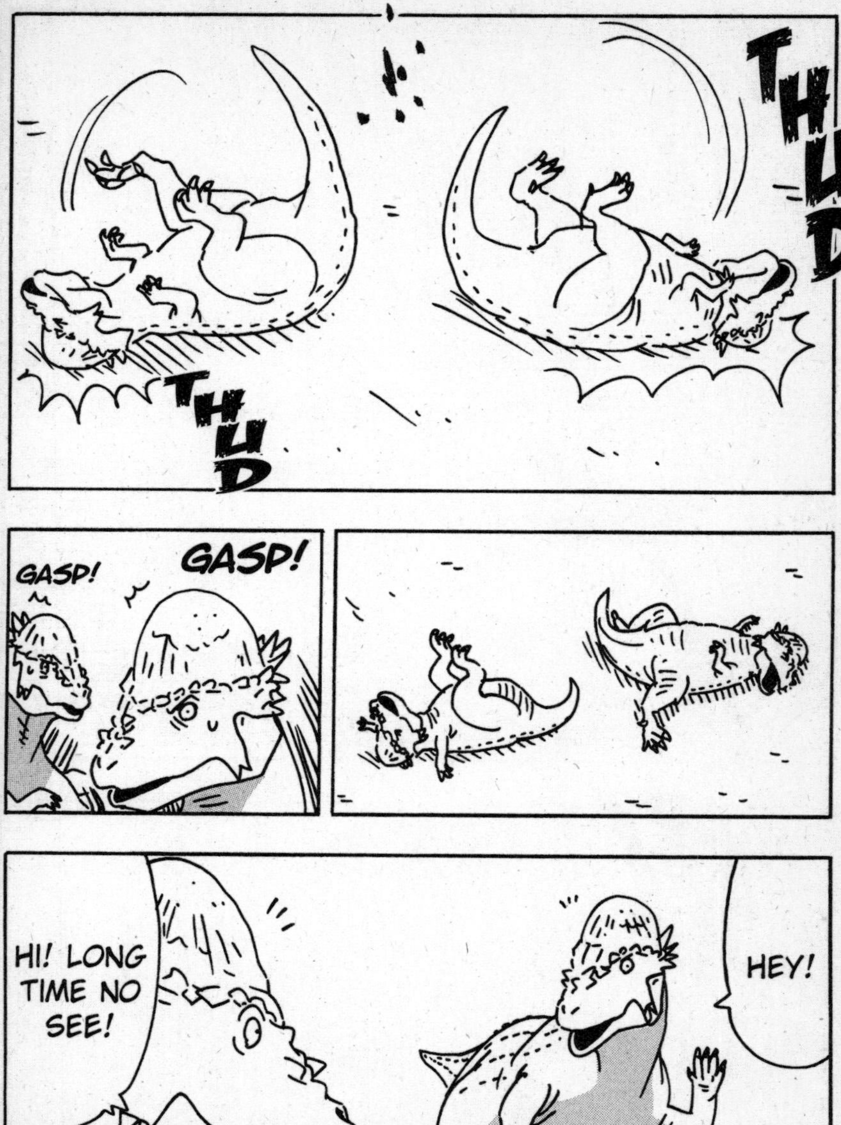
THUD
THUD
GASP!
GASP!
HEY!
HI! LONG TIME NO SEE!

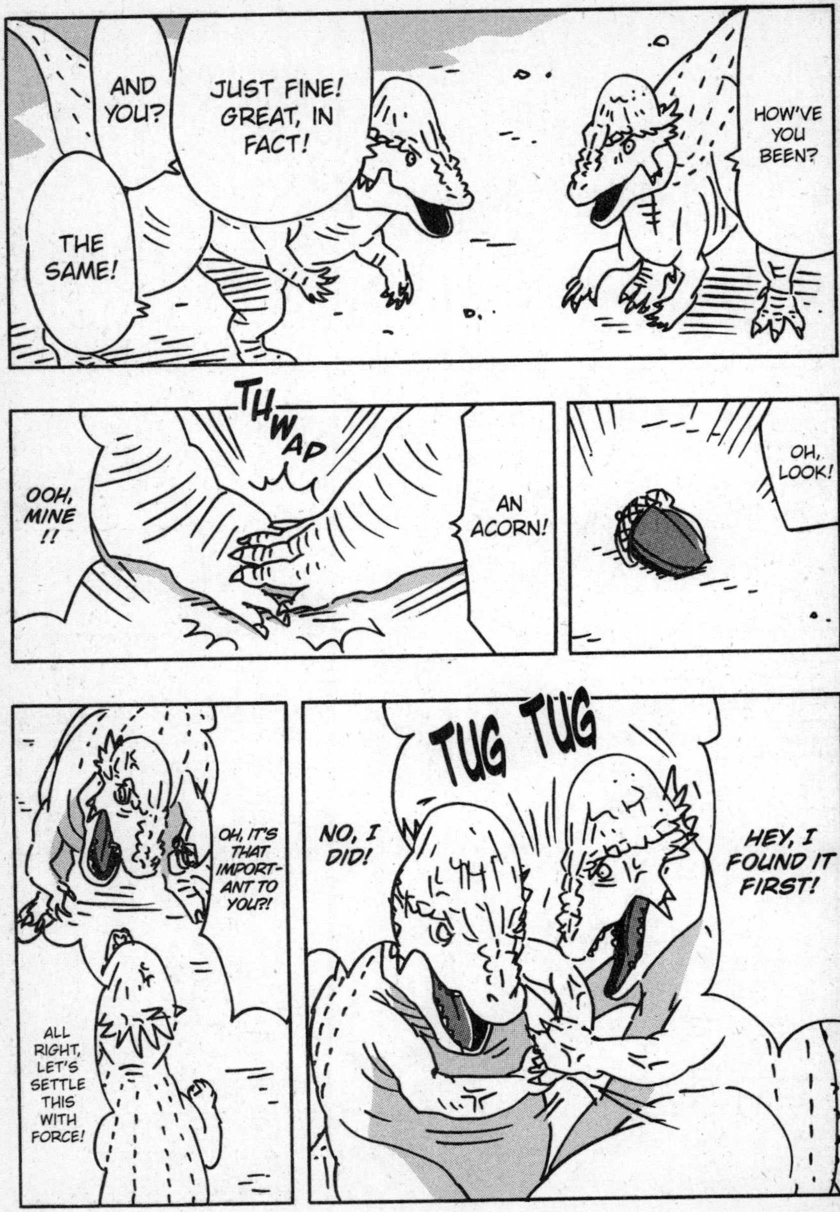
HOW'VE YOU BEEN?
JUST FINE! GREAT, IN FACT!
AND YOU?
THE SAME!
OH, LOOK!
AN ACORN!
THWAP
OOH, MINE !!
TUG TUG
HEY, I FOUND IT FIRST!
NO, I DID!
OH, IT'S THAT IMPORTANT TO YOU?!
ALL RIGHT, LET'S SETTLE THIS WITH FORCE!

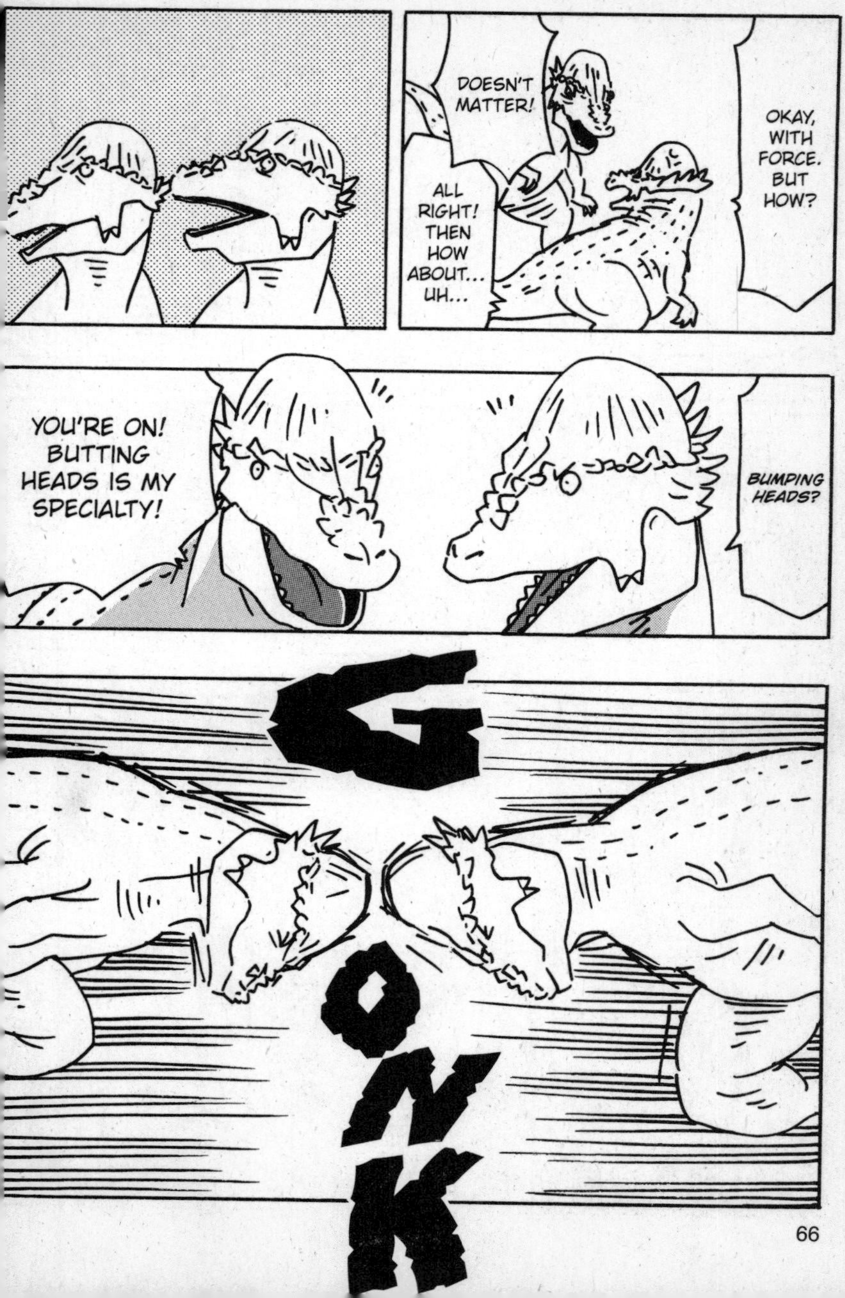
OKAY, WITH FORCE. BUT HOW?
DOESN'T MATTER!
ALL RIGHT! THEN HOW ABOUT... UH...
BUMPING HEADS?
YOU'RE ON! BUTTING HEADS IS MY SPECIALTY!
GONK

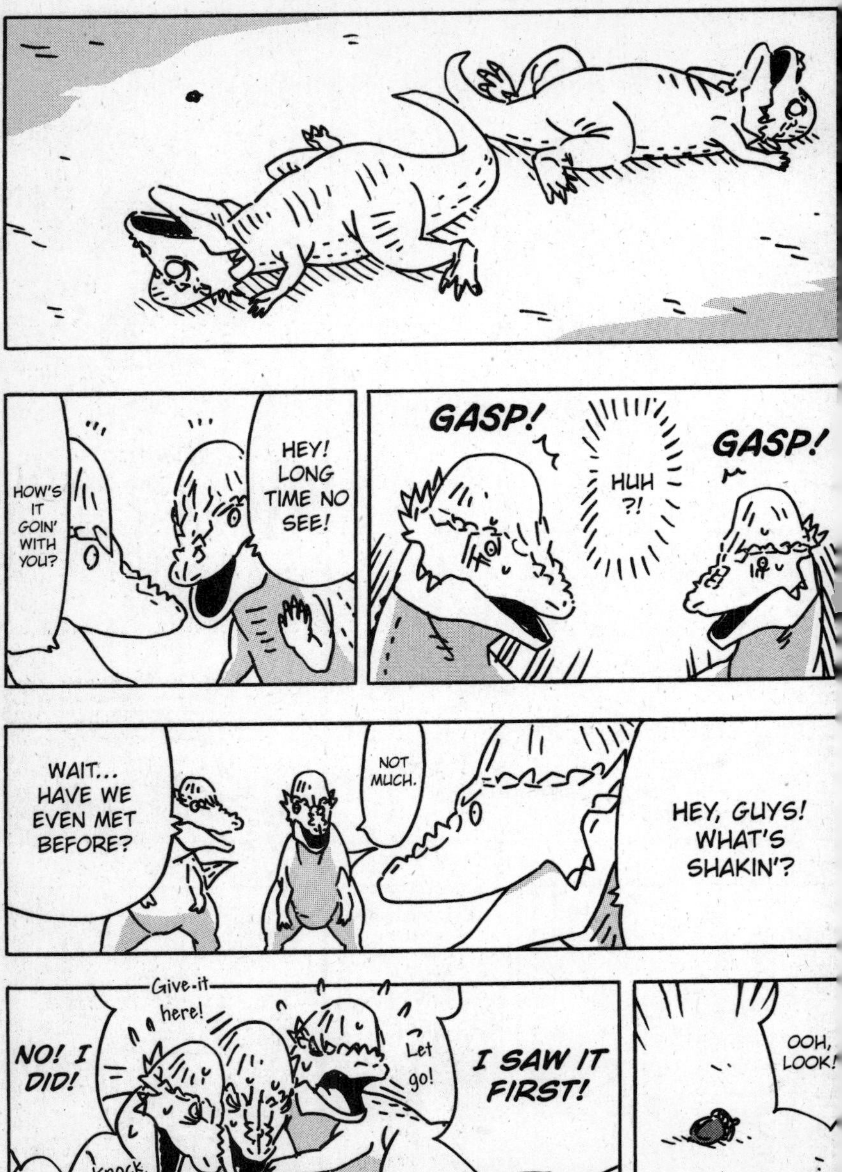
GASP!
HUH ?!
GASP!
HEY! LONG TIME NO SEE!
HOW'S IT GOIN' WITH YOU?
HEY, GUYS! WHAT'S SHAKIN'?
NOT MUCH.
WAIT... HAVE WE EVEN MET BEFORE?
OOH, LOOK!
I SAW IT FIRST!
Let go!
Give it here!
NO! I DID!
Knock it off!

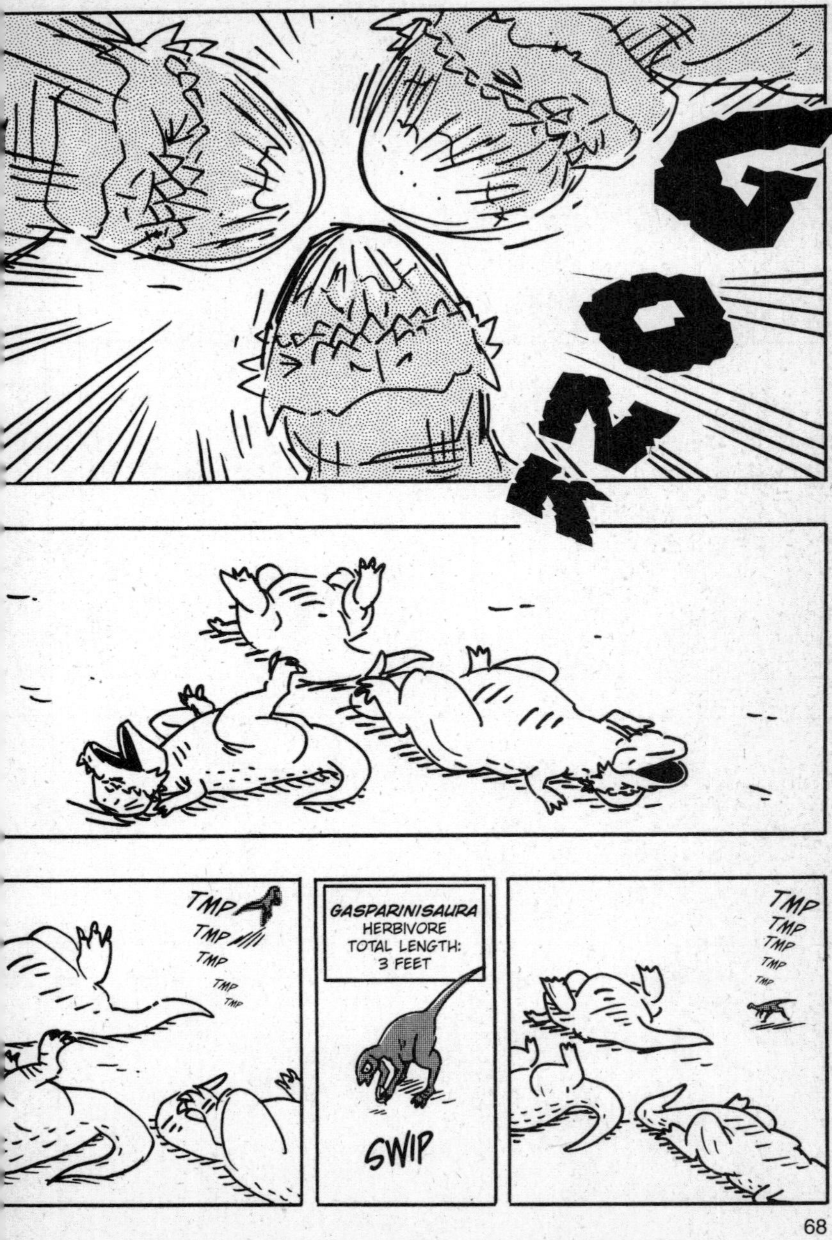
GONK
TMP
TMP
TMP
TMP
TMP
GASPARINISAURA
HERBIVORE
TOTAL LENGTH:
3 FEET
SWIP
TMP
TMP
TMP
TMP
TMP

BONE 9
Picky Dinosaurs

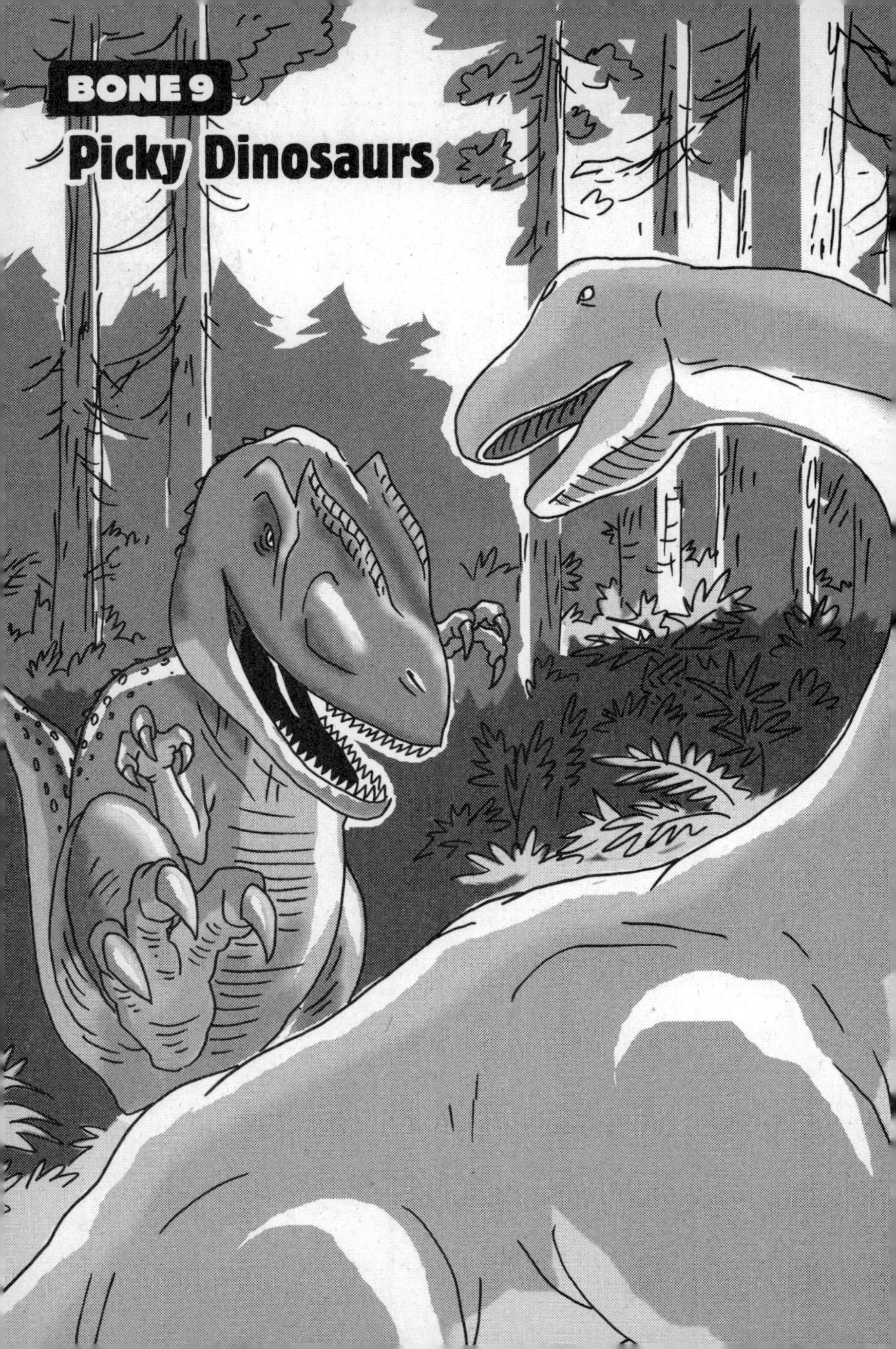

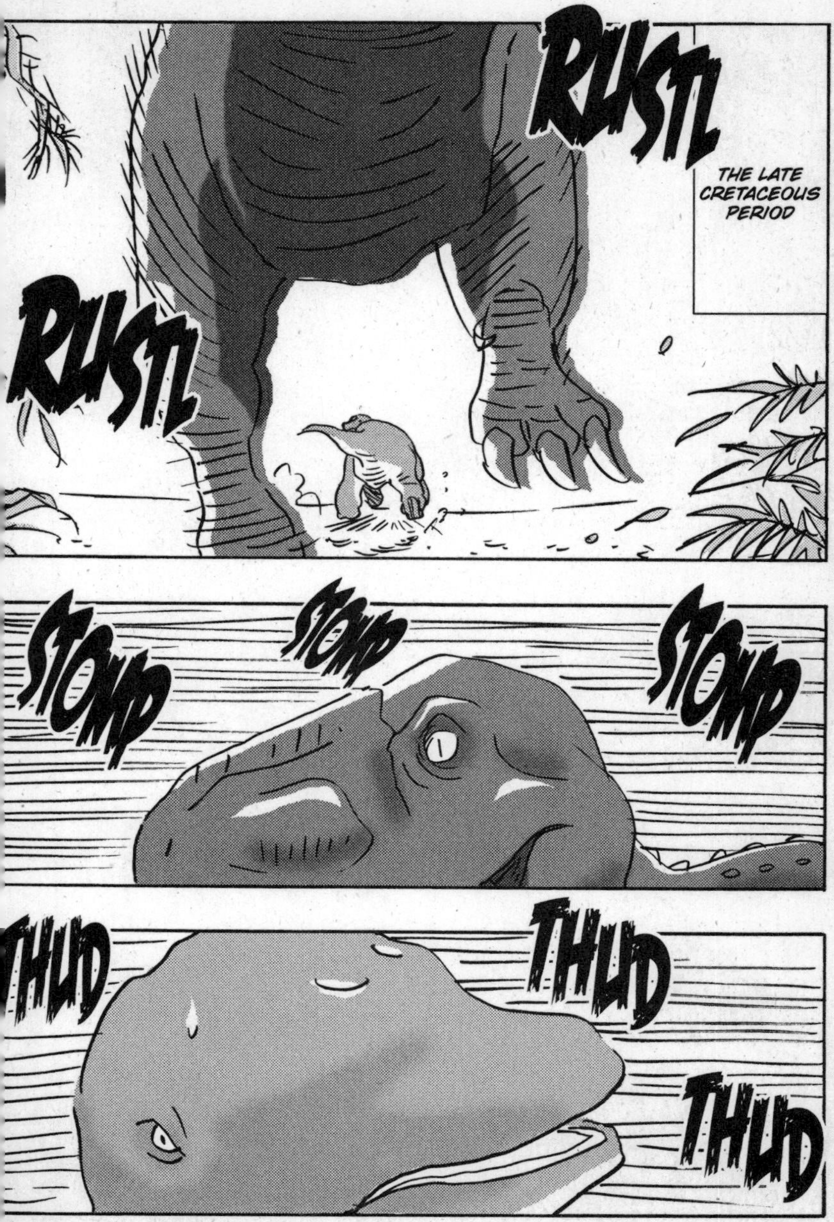
RUSTL
THE LATE CRETACEOUS PERIOD
RUSTL
STOMP
STOMP
STOMP
THUD
THUD
THUD

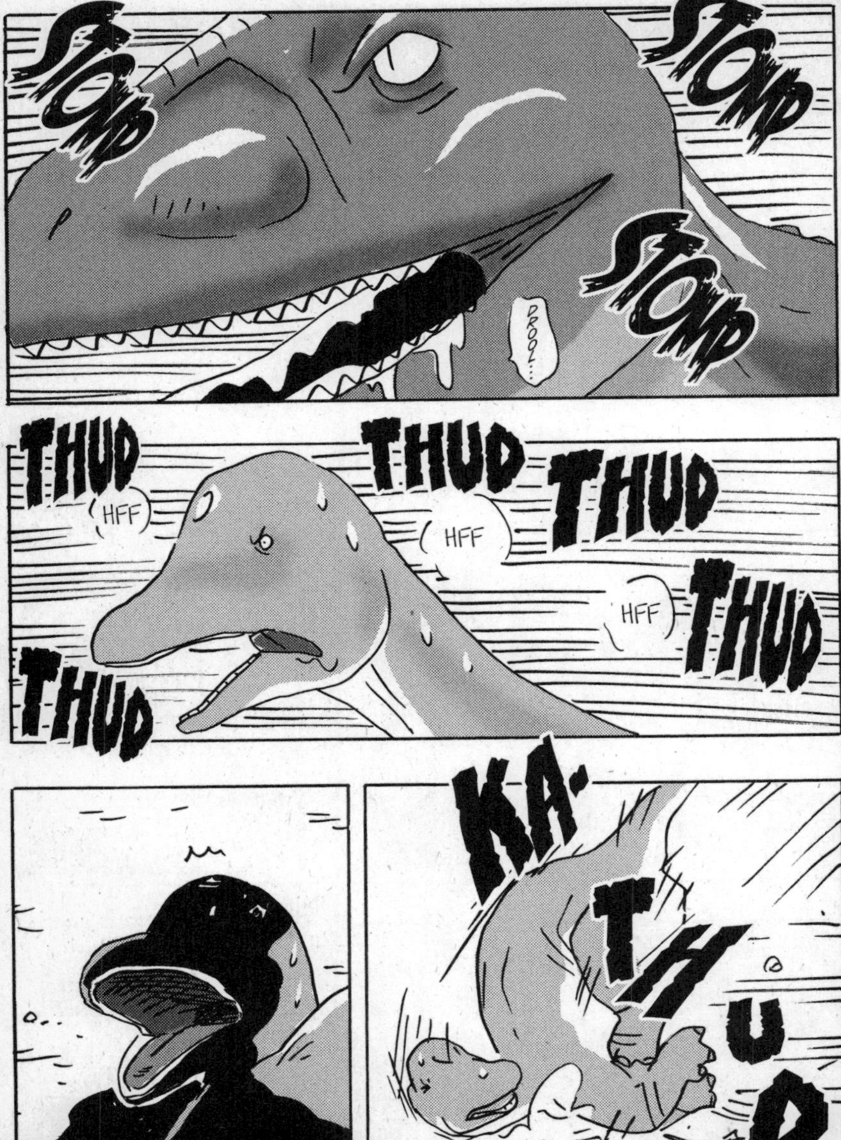
STOMP
STOMP
DROOL...
STOMP
THUD
THUD
THUD
HFF
HFF
HFF
THUD
THUD
KA-THUD

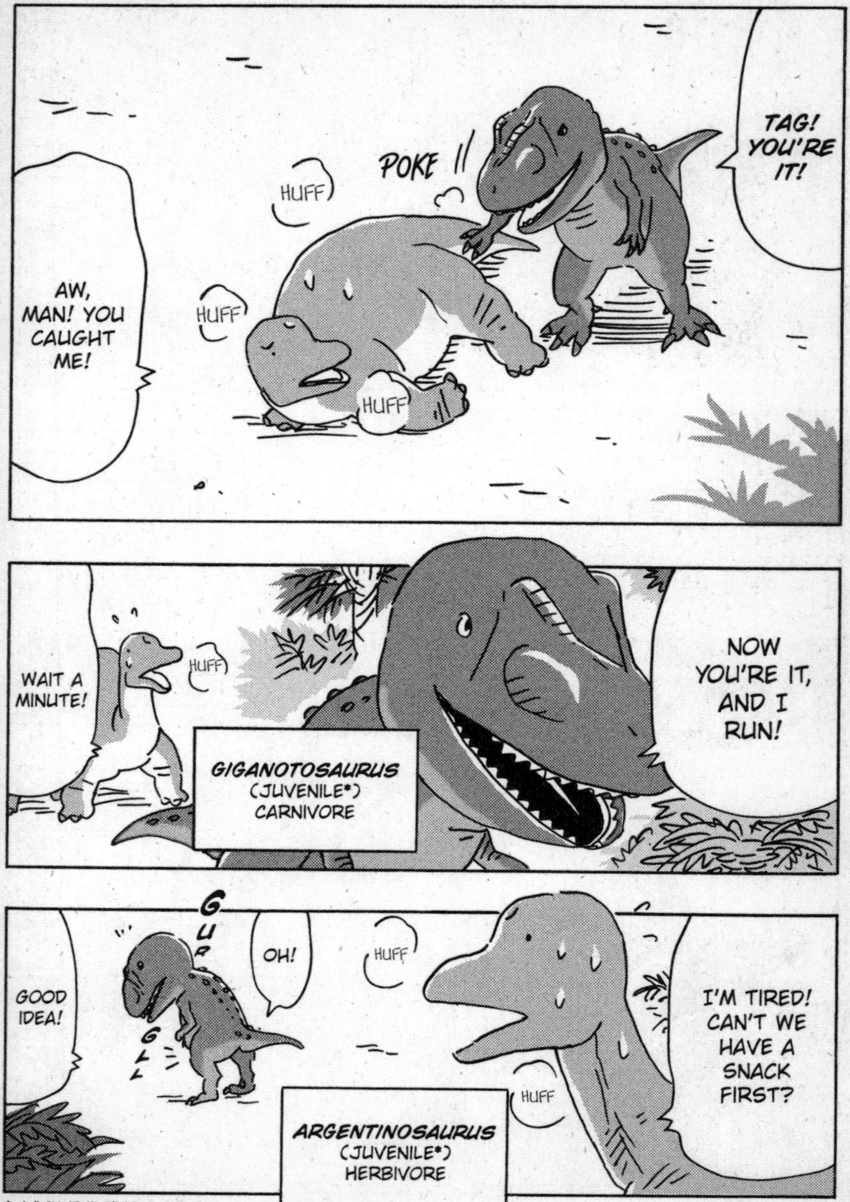
TAG! YOU'RE IT!
POKE
HUFF
HUFF
HUFF
AW, MAN! YOU CAUGHT ME!
NOW YOU'RE IT, AND I RUN!
GIGANOTOSAURUS (JUVENILE*) CARNIVORE
HUFF
WAIT A MINUTE!
I'M TIRED! CAN'T WE HAVE A SNACK FIRST?
HUFF
ARGENTINOSAURUS (JUVENILE*) HERBIVORE
HUFF
OH!
GURGLY
GOOD IDEA!

* A "JUVENILE" IS A CHILD.

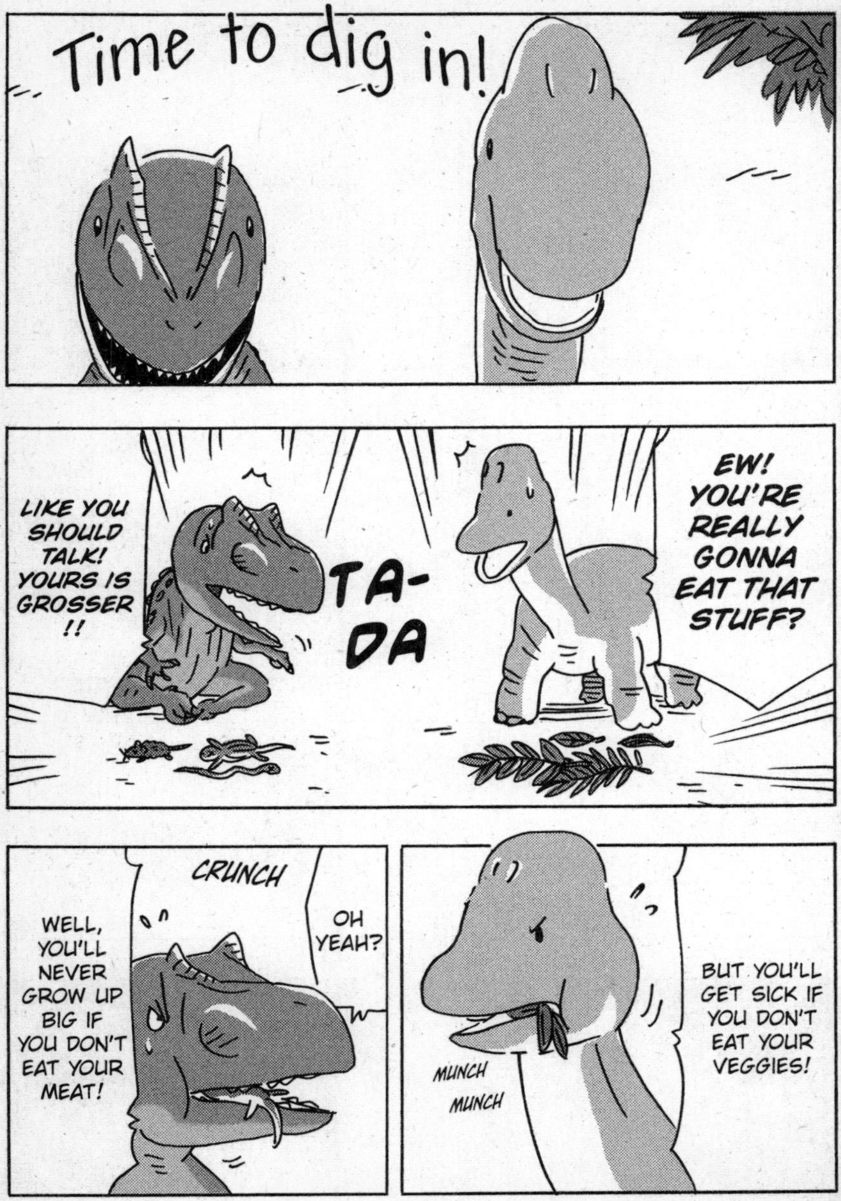
Time to dig in!
TA-DA
EW! YOU'RE REALLY GONNA EAT THAT STUFF?
LIKE YOU SHOULD TALK! YOURS IS GROSSER!!
BUT YOU'LL GET SICK IF YOU DON'T EAT YOUR VEGGIES!
MUNCH MUNCH
CRUNCH
OH YEAH?
WELL, YOU'LL NEVER GROW UP BIG IF YOU DON'T EAT YOUR MEAT!

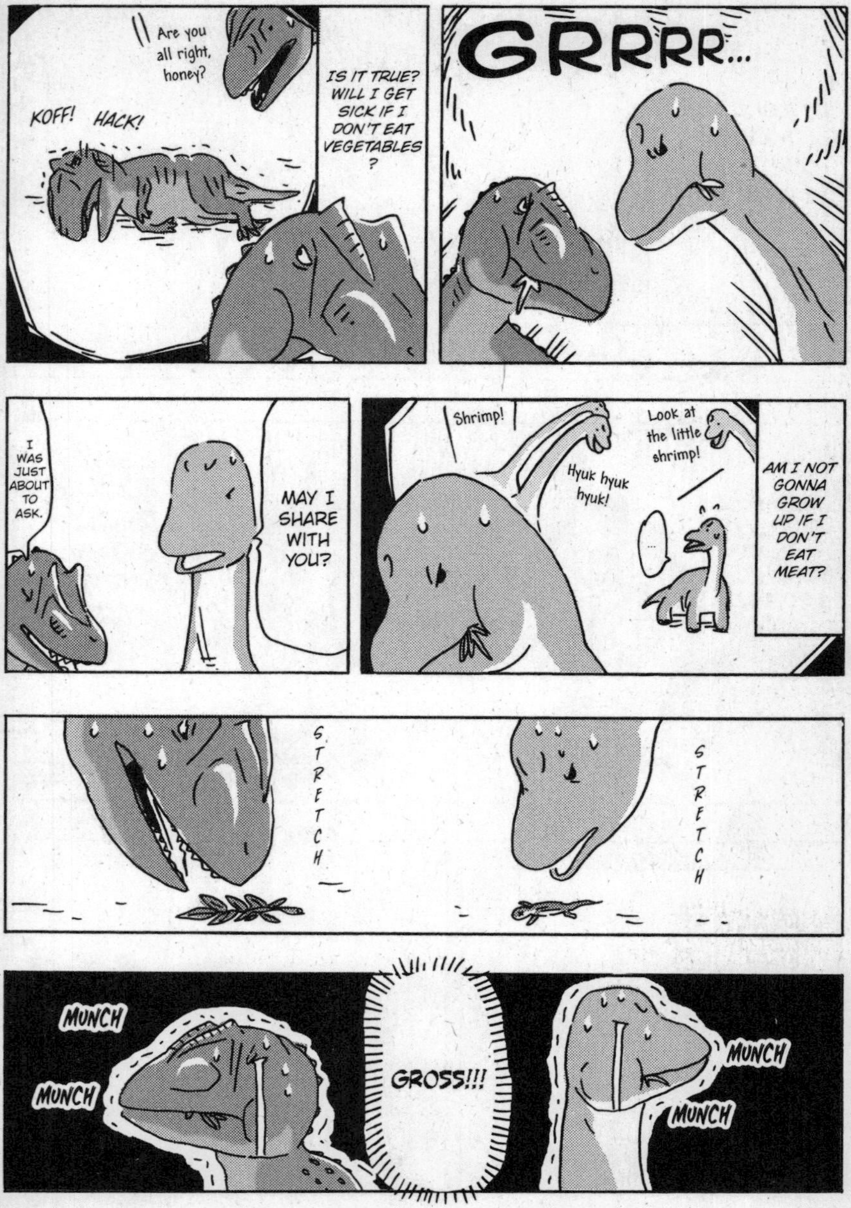
GRRRR...
IS IT TRUE? WILL I GET SICK IF I DON'T EAT VEGETABLES?
Are you all right, honey?
KOFF! HACK!
AM I NOT GONNA GROW UP IF I DON'T EAT MEAT?
Look at the little shrimp!
Shrimp!
Hyuk hyuk hyuk!
...
MAY I SHARE WITH YOU?
I WAS JUST ABOUT TO ASK.
STRETCH
STRETCH
MUNCH
MUNCH
GROSS!!!
MUNCH
MUNCH

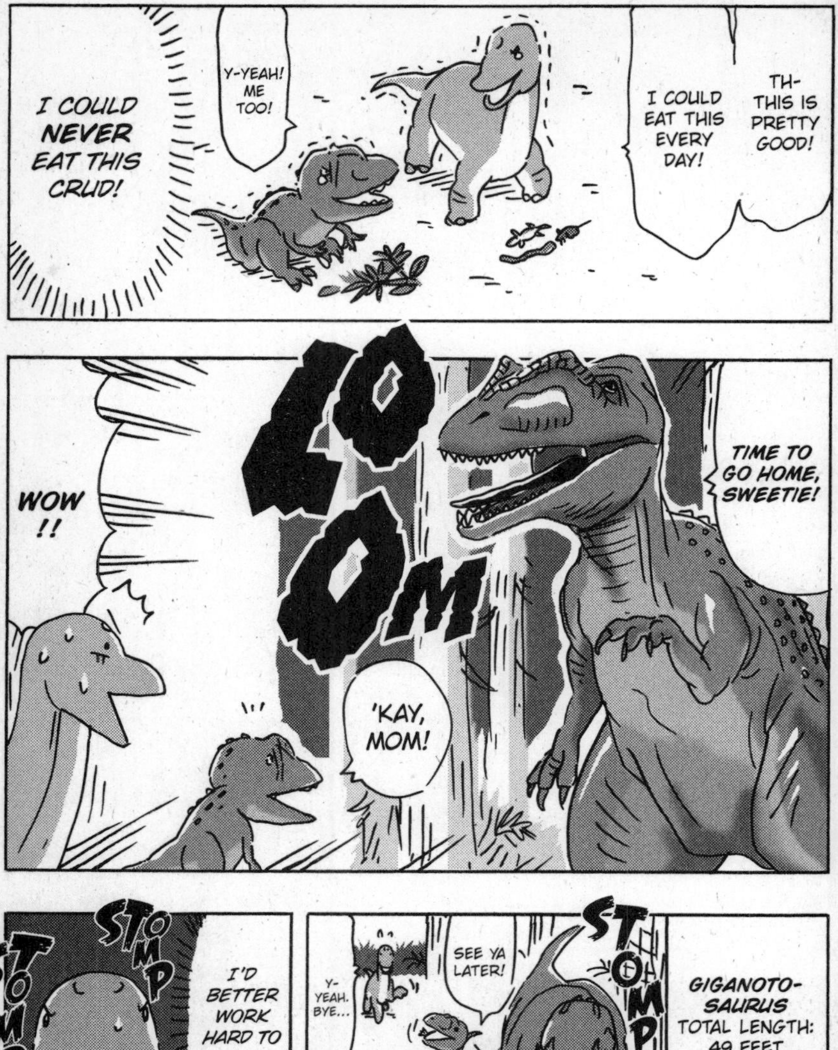
TH- THIS IS PRETTY GOOD!
I COULD EAT THIS EVERY DAY!
Y-YEAH! ME TOO!
I COULD NEVER EAT THIS CRUD!
TIME TO GO HOME, SWEETIE!
LOOM
'KAY, MOM!
WOW !!
GIGANOTO-SAURUS
TOTAL LENGTH: 49 FEET
ONE OF THE LARGEST MEAT-EATING DINOSAURS ON THE PLANET.
STOMP
SEE YA LATER!
Y- YEAH. BYE...
STOMP
STOMP
STOMP
I'D BETTER WORK HARD TO EAT SOME MEAT!
THOMP
THOMP
THOMP

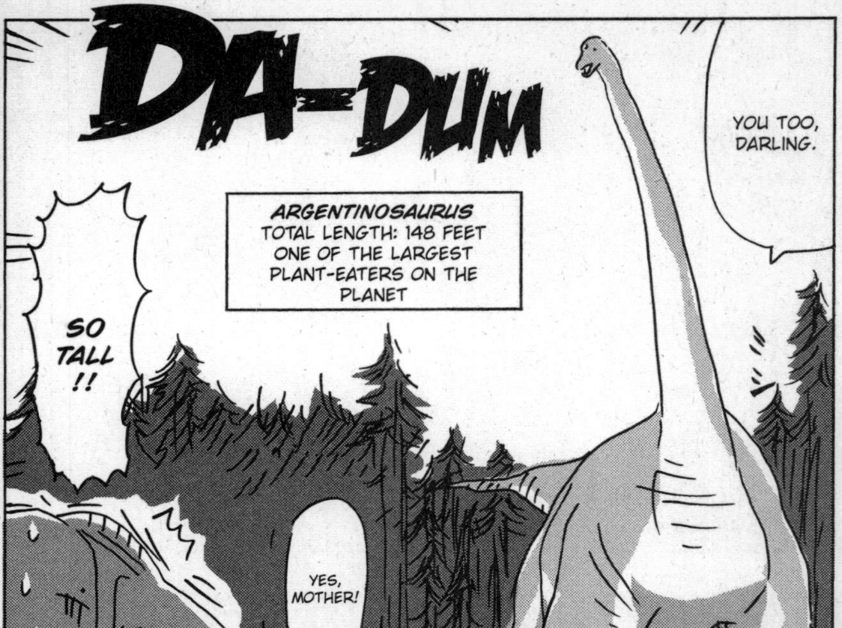
YOU TOO, DARLING.
DA-DUM
ARGENTINOSAURUS
TOTAL LENGTH: 148 FEET
ONE OF THE LARGEST PLANT-EATERS ON THE PLANET
SO TALL!!
YES, MOTHER!
SMUSH
SMUSH

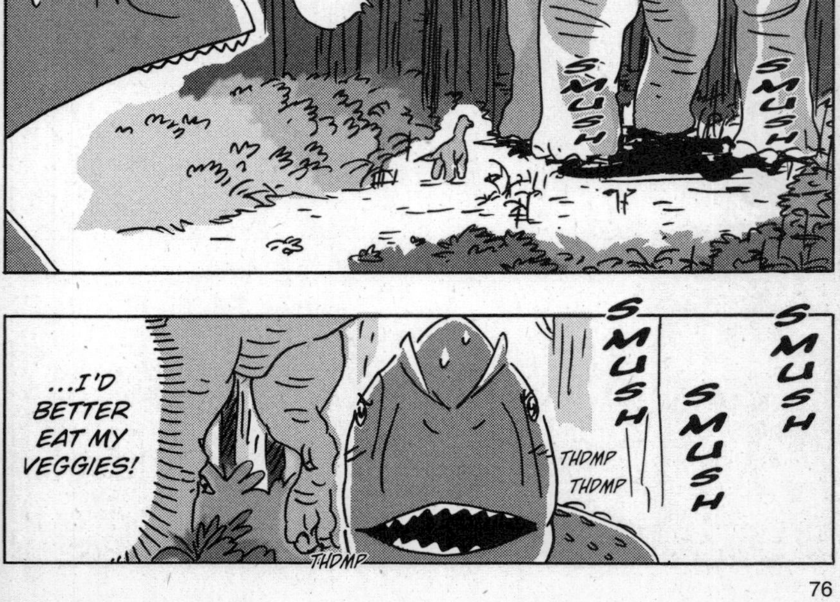
SMUSH
SMUSH
SMUSH
THDMP
THDMP
...I'D BETTER EAT MY VEGGIES!
THDMP

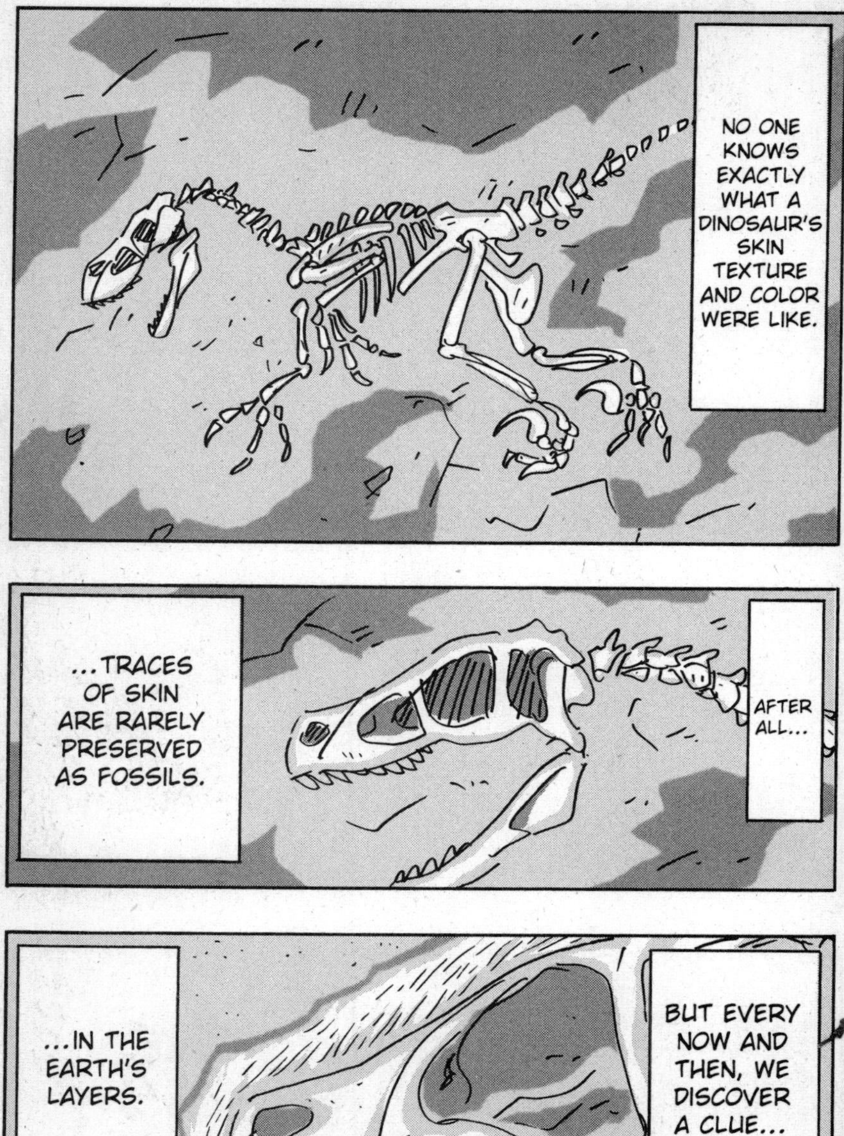
NO ONE KNOWS EXACTLY WHAT A DINOSAUR'S SKIN TEXTURE AND COLOR WERE LIKE.
AFTER ALL...
...TRACES OF SKIN ARE RARELY PRESERVED AS FOSSILS.
BUT EVERY NOW AND THEN, WE DISCOVER A CLUE...
...IN THE EARTH'S LAYERS.

BONE 10

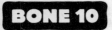

Mystery of the Feathered Dinos

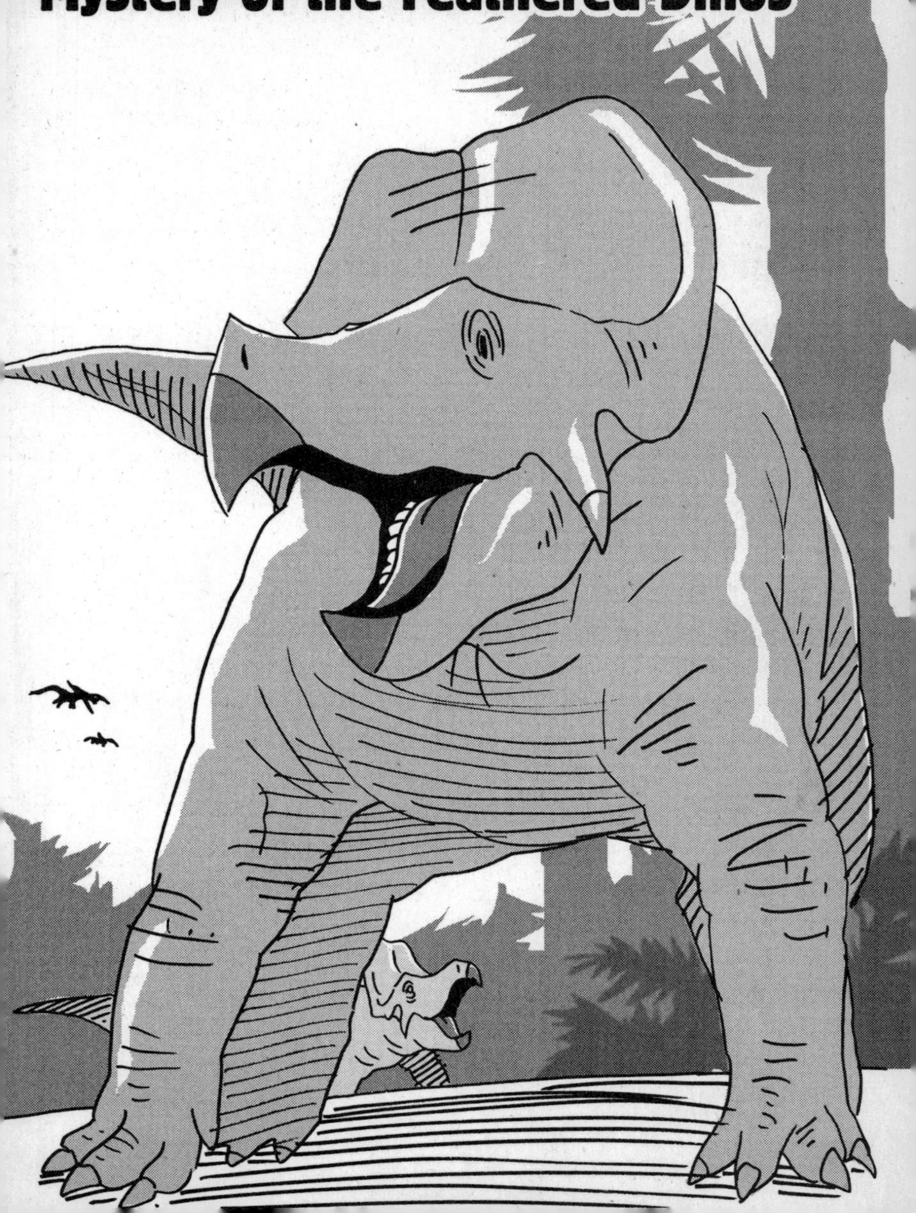

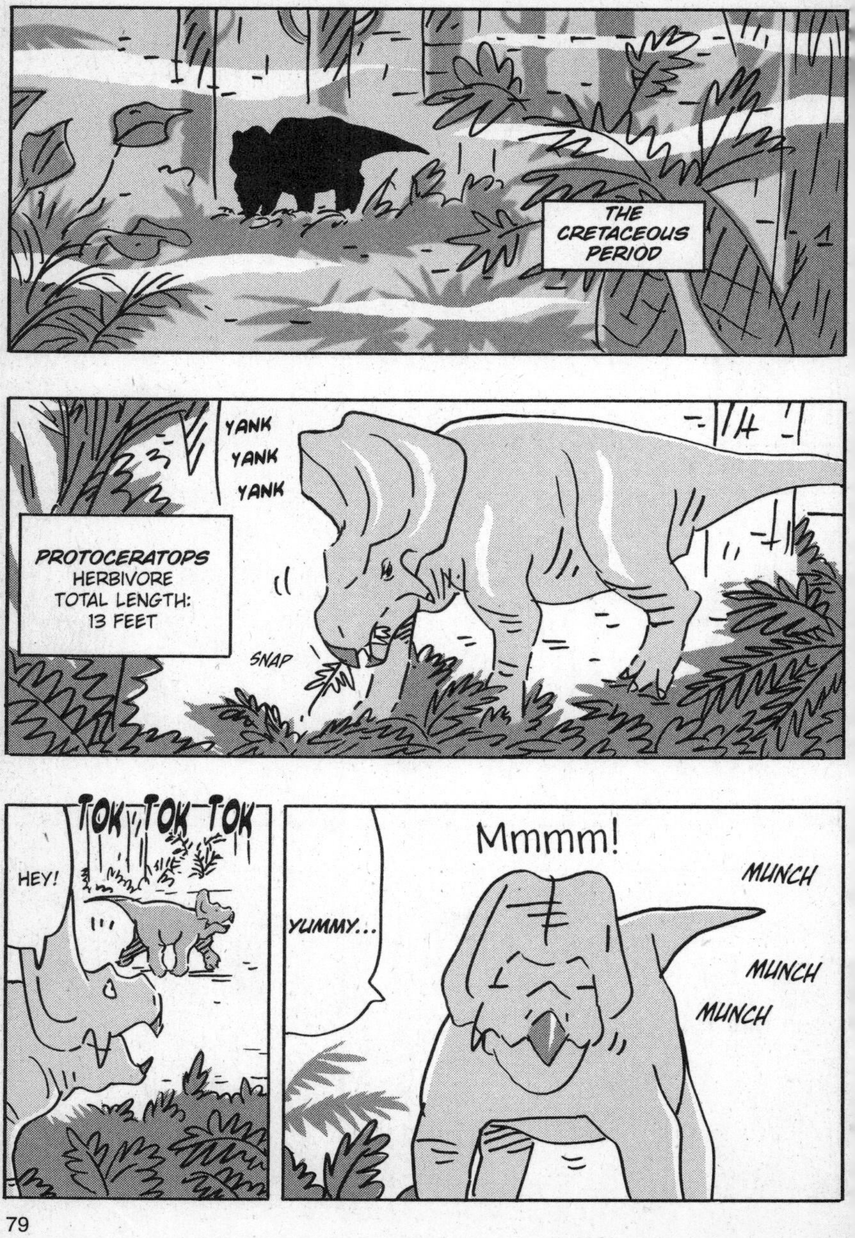
THE CRETACEOUS PERIOD
YANK
YANK
YANK
PROTOCERATOPS
HERBIVORE
TOTAL LENGTH:
13 FEET
SNAP
Mmmm!
MUNCH
MUNCH
MUNCH
YUMMY...
TOK TOK TOK
HEY!

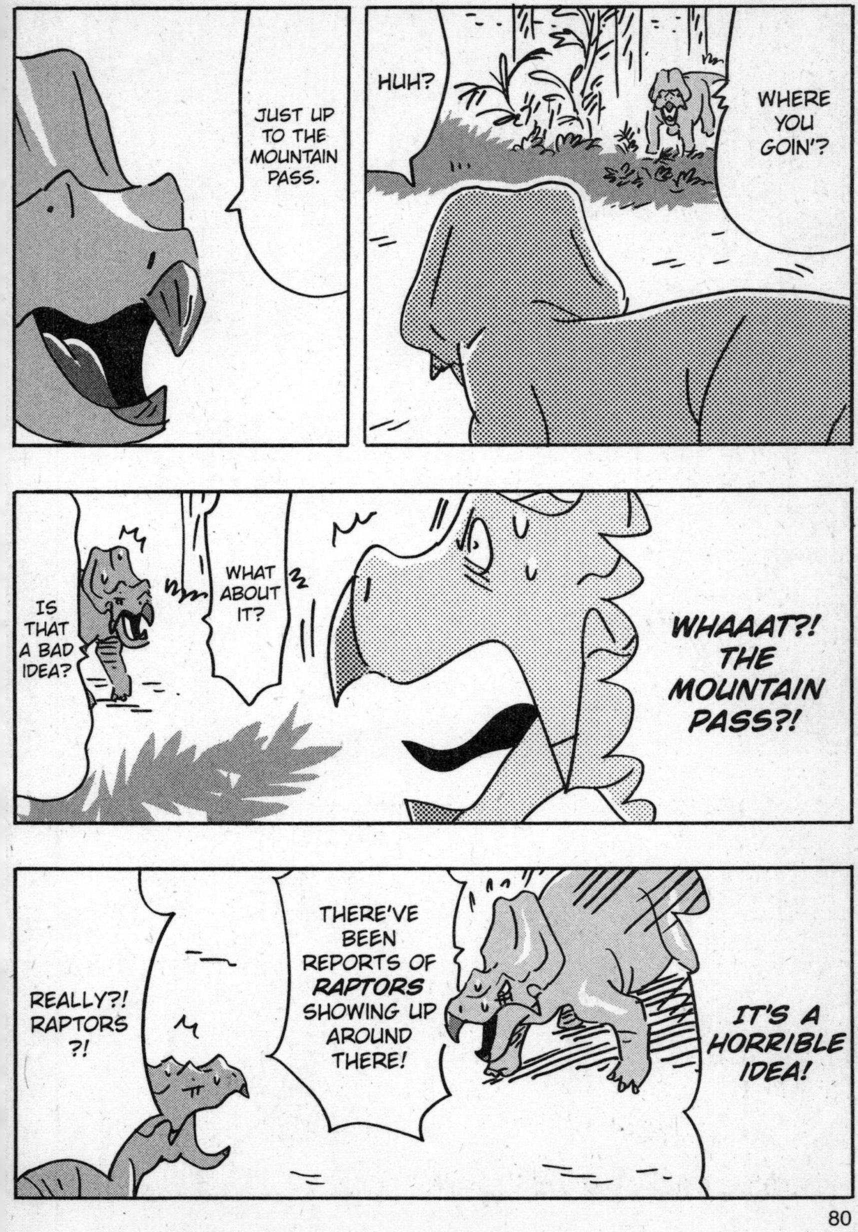
WHERE YOU GOIN'?
HUH?
JUST UP TO THE MOUNTAIN PASS.
WHAAAT?! THE MOUNTAIN PASS?!
WHAT ABOUT IT?
IS THAT A BAD IDEA?
IT'S A HORRIBLE IDEA!
THERE'VE BEEN REPORTS OF RAPTORS SHOWING UP AROUND THERE!
REALLY?! RAPTORS?!

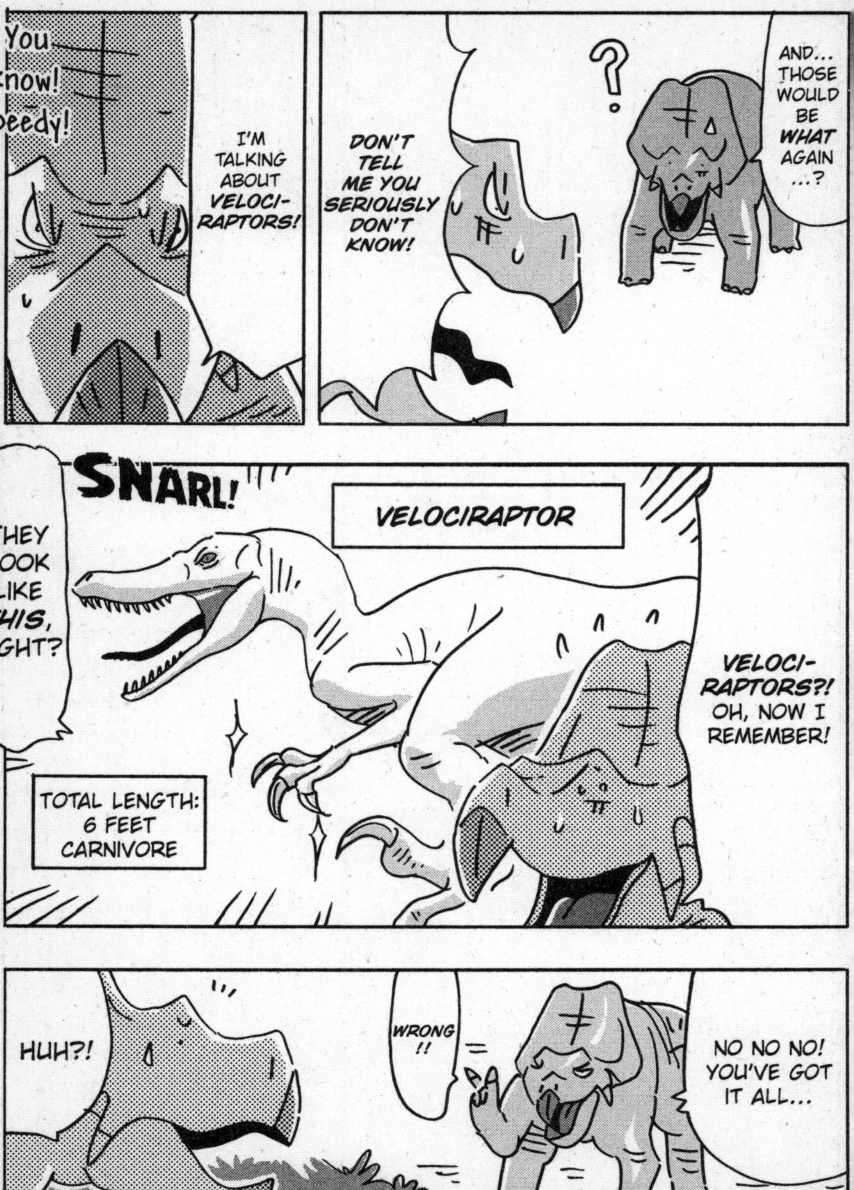
AND... THOSE WOULD BE WHAT AGAIN ...?
?
DON'T TELL ME YOU SERIOUSLY DON'T KNOW!
I'M TALKING ABOUT VELOCI-RAPTORS!
You know! Speedy!
VELOCI-RAPTORS?! OH, NOW I REMEMBER!
VELOCIRAPTOR
SNARL!
THEY LOOK LIKE THIS, RIGHT?
TOTAL LENGTH: 6 FEET CARNIVORE
NO NO NO! YOU'VE GOT IT ALL...
WRONG !!
HUH?!

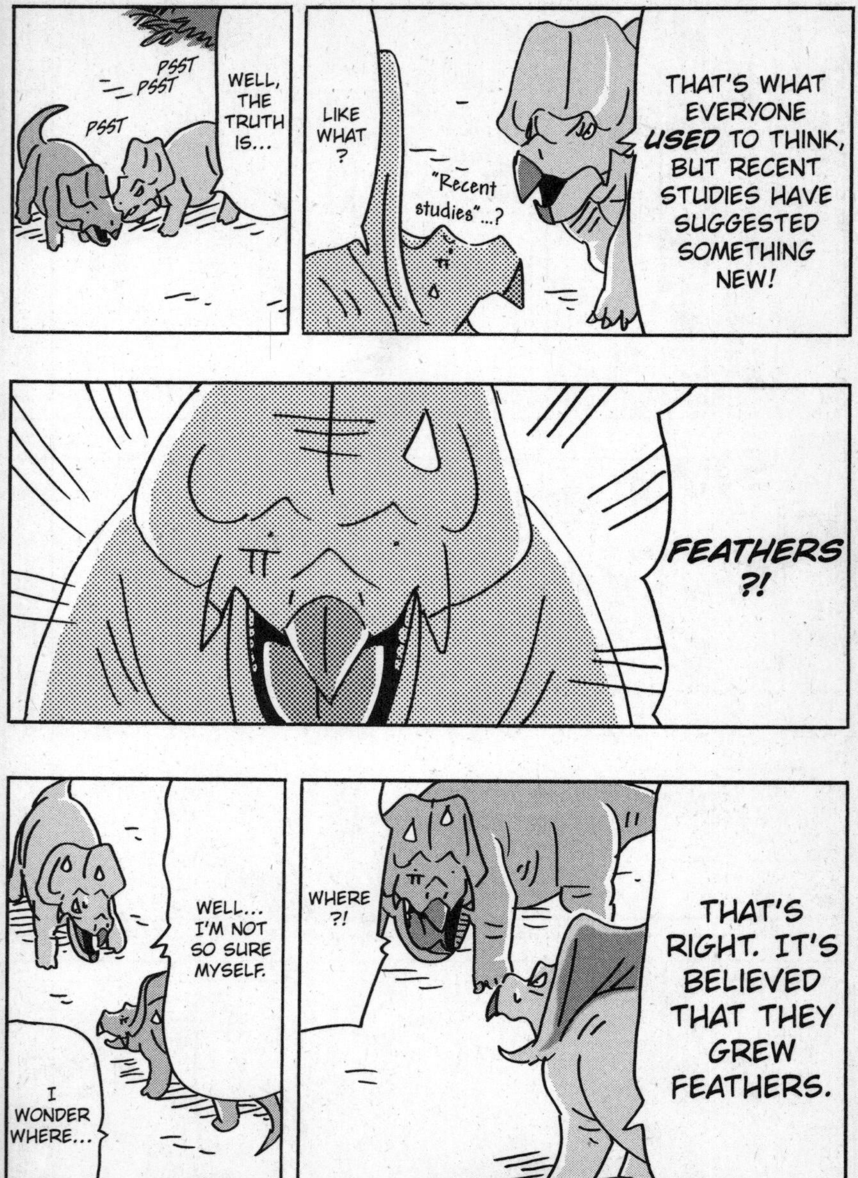
THAT'S WHAT EVERYONE USED TO THINK, BUT RECENT STUDIES HAVE SUGGESTED SOMETHING NEW!
LIKE WHAT ?
"Recent studies"...?
WELL, THE TRUTH IS...
PSST
PSST
PSST
FEATHERS ?!
THAT'S RIGHT. IT'S BELIEVED THAT THEY GREW FEATHERS.
WHERE ?!
WELL... I'M NOT SO SURE MYSELF.
I WONDER WHERE...

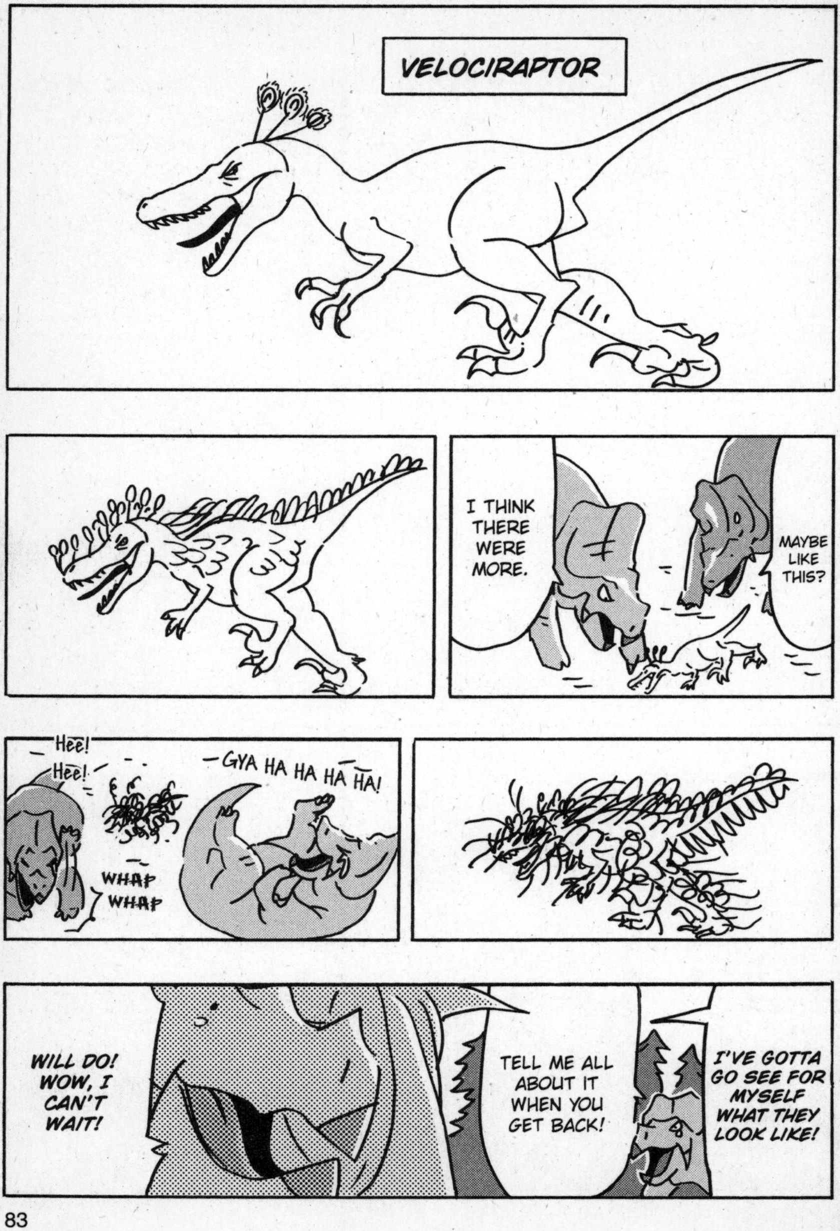

VELOCIRAPTOR
MAYBE LIKE THIS?
I THINK THERE WERE MORE.
GYA HA HA HA HA!
Hee! Hee!
WHAP WHAP
I'VE GOTTA GO SEE FOR MYSELF WHAT THEY LOOK LIKE!
TELL ME ALL ABOUT IT WHEN YOU GET BACK!
WILL DO! WOW, I CAN'T WAIT!

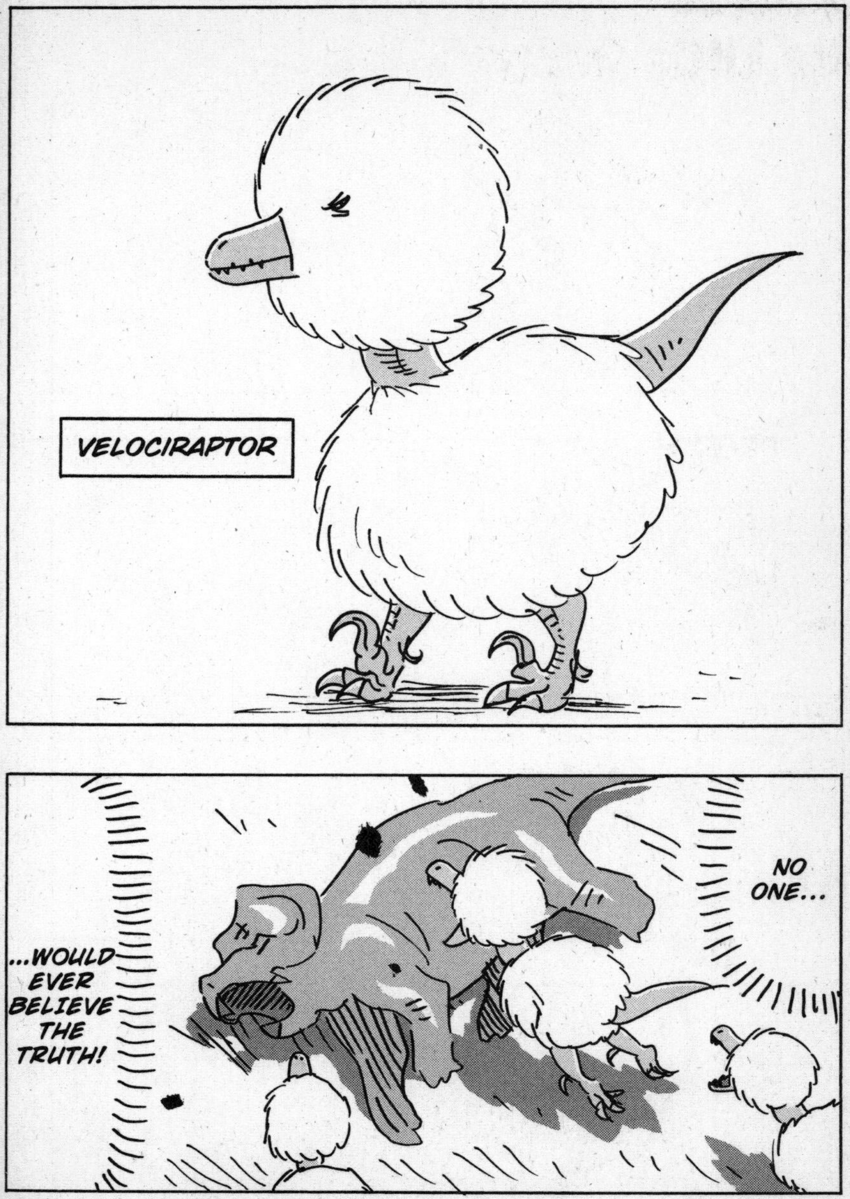
VELOCIRAPTOR
NO ONE...
...WOULD EVER BELIEVE THE TRUTH!

BONE 11

The Little Raptor's Test

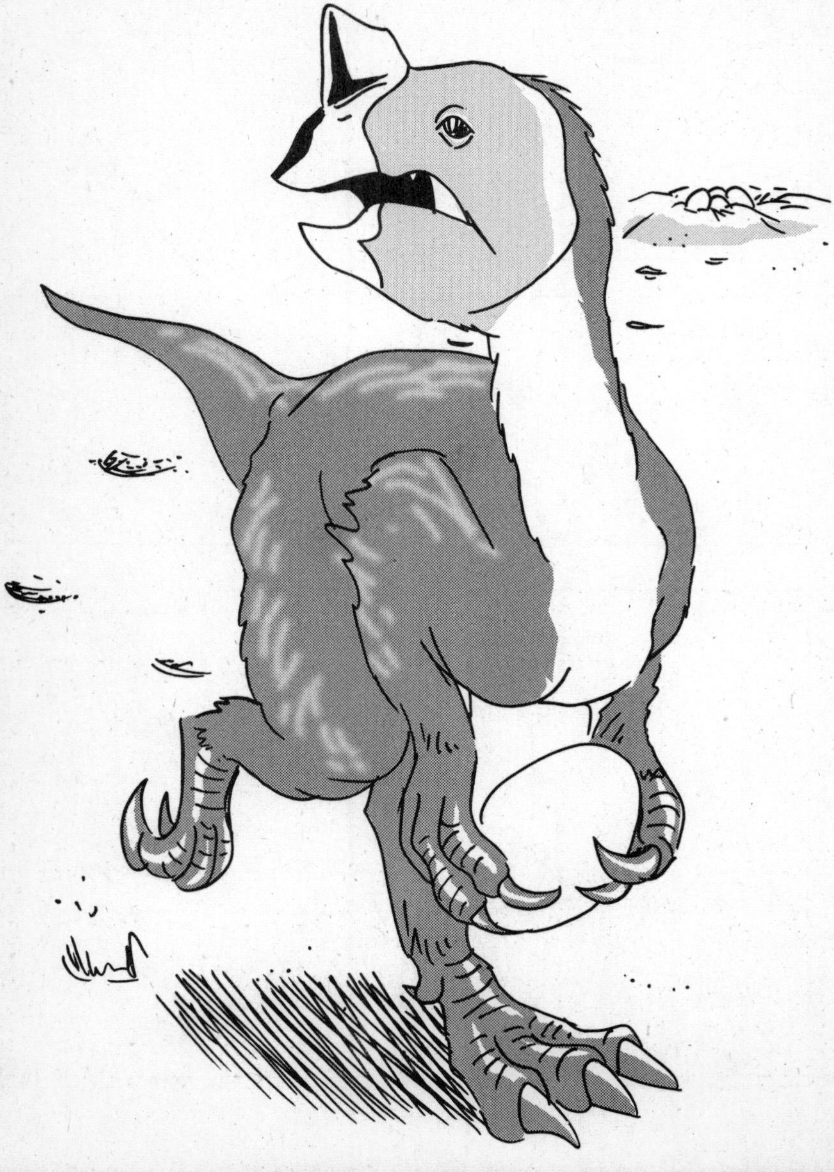

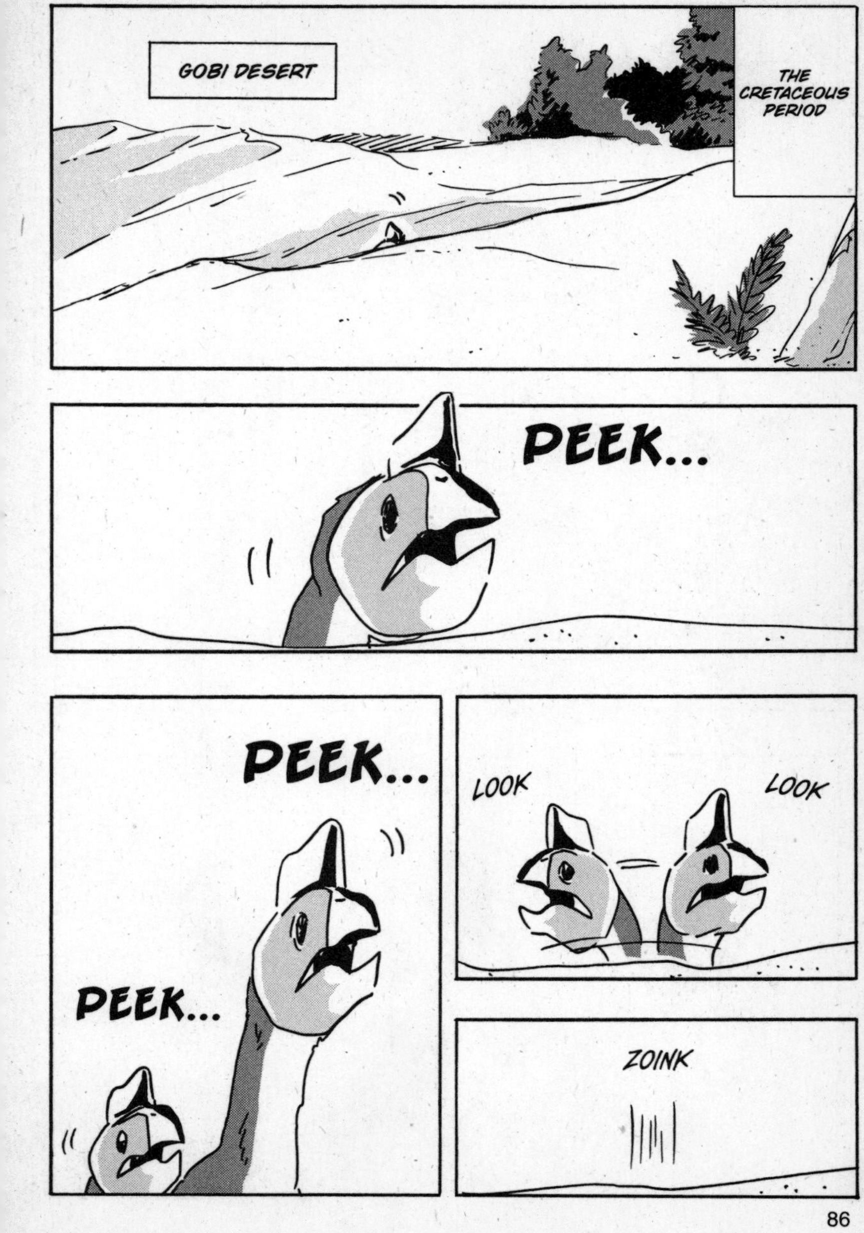
THE CRETACEOUS PERIOD
GOBI DESERT
PEEK...
LOOK
LOOK
ZOINK
PEEK...
PEEK...

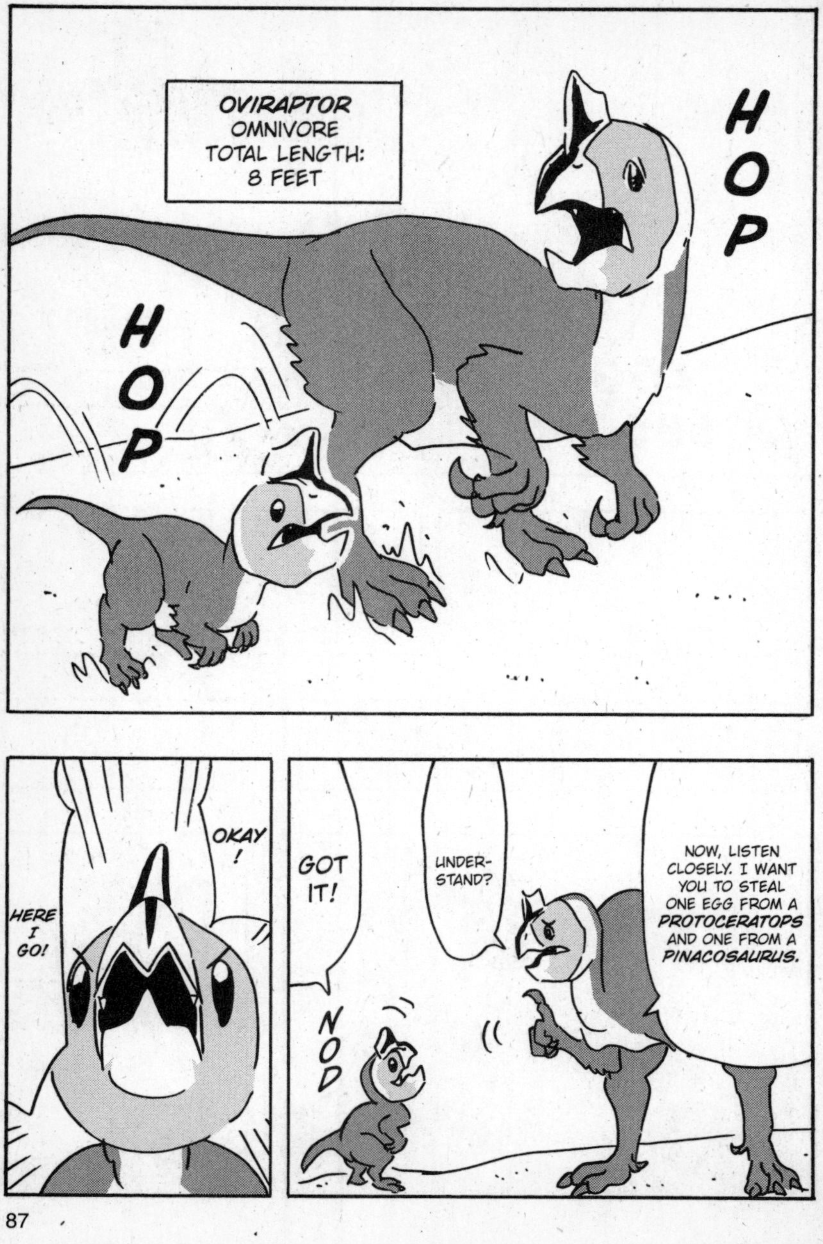
OVIRAPTOR
OMNIVORE
TOTAL LENGTH:
8 FEET
HOP
HOP
HOP
HOP
NOW, LISTEN CLOSELY. I WANT YOU TO STEAL ONE EGG FROM A PROTOCERATOPS AND ONE FROM A PINACOSAURUS.
UNDER-STAND?
GOT IT!
NOD
OKAY!
HERE I GO!

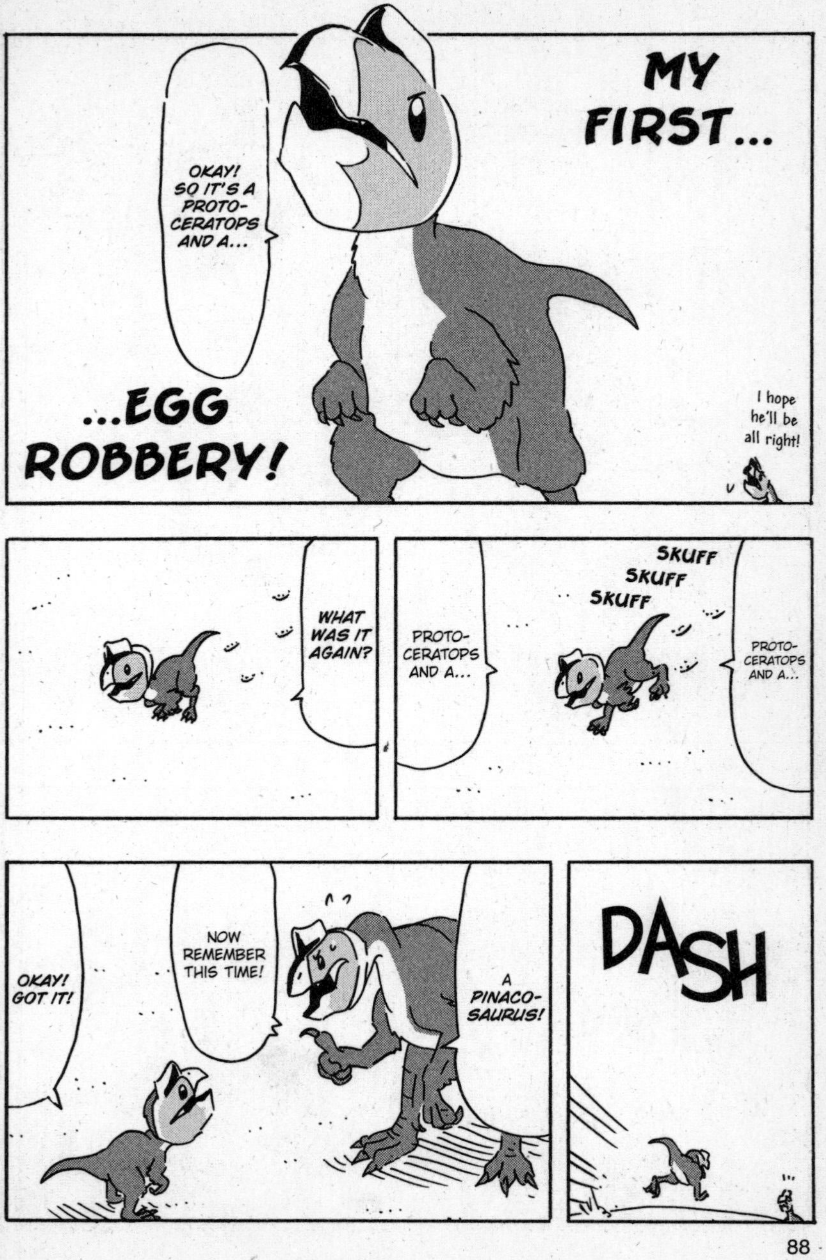
MY FIRST...
OKAY! SO IT'S A PROTO-CERATOPS AND A...
I hope he'll be all right!
...EGG ROBBERY!
PROTO-CERATOPS AND A...
SKUFF SKUFF SKUFF
PROTO-CERATOPS AND A...
WHAT WAS IT AGAIN?
DASH
A PINACO-SAURUS!
NOW REMEMBER THIS TIME!
OKAY! GOT IT!

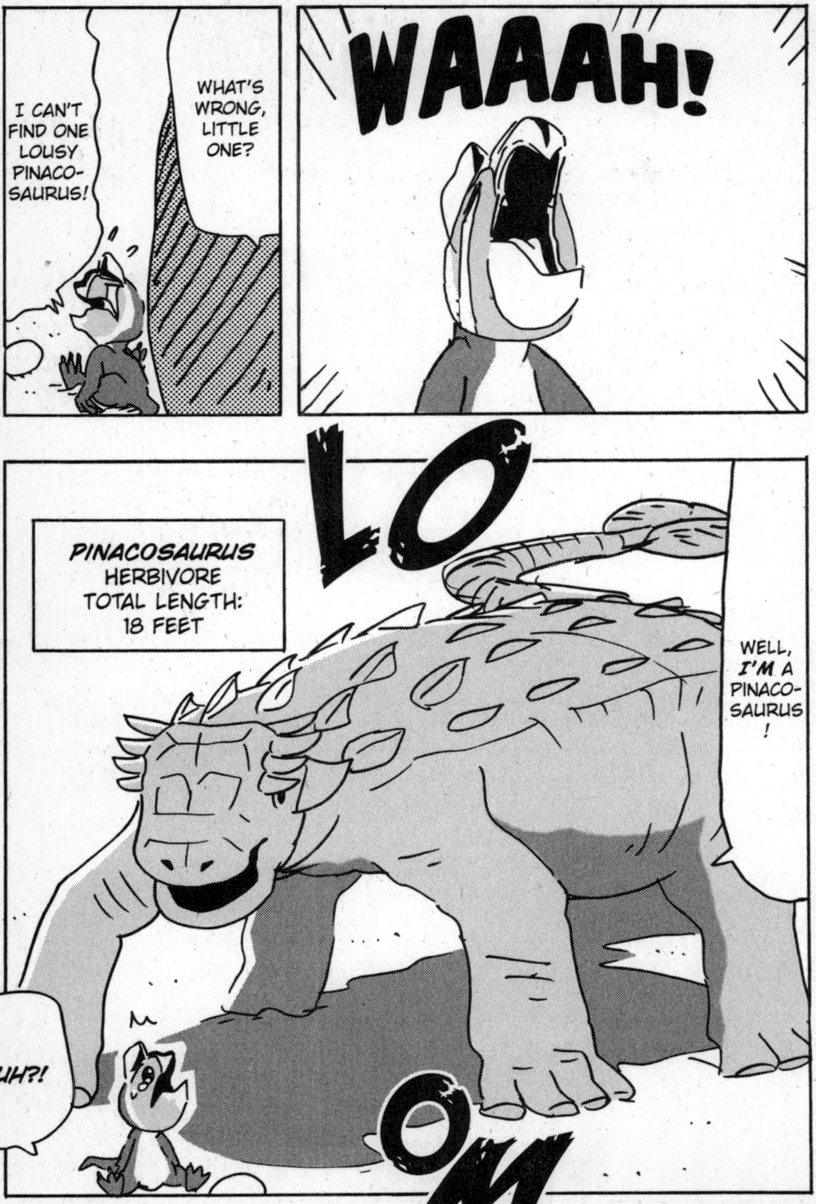
WAAAH!
WHAT'S WRONG, LITTLE ONE?
I CAN'T FIND ONE LOUSY PINACOSAURUS!
LO
WELL, I'M A PINACOSAURUS!
PINACOSAURUS
HERBIVORE
TOTAL LENGTH: 18 FEET
HUH?!
OM

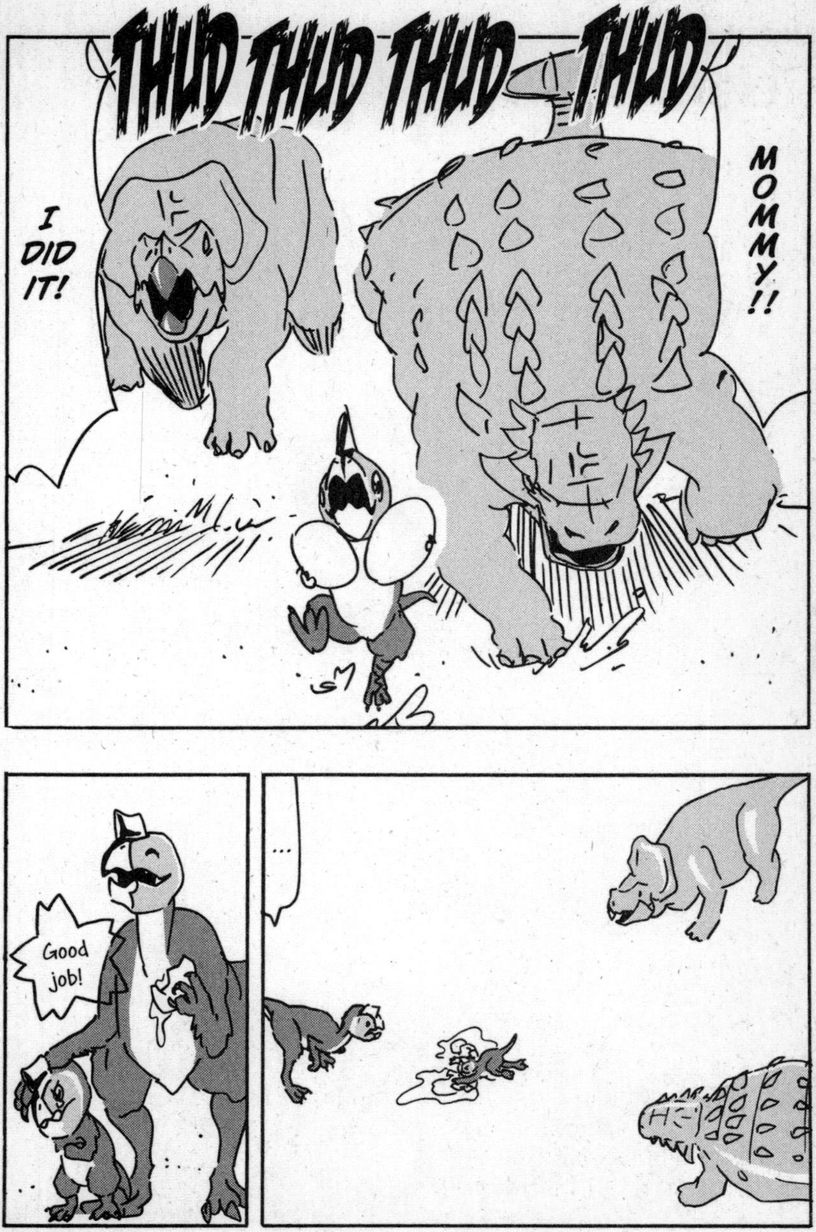
THUD THUD THUD THUD
MOMMY!!
I DID IT!
...
Good job!

BONE 12

Sleight of Fin

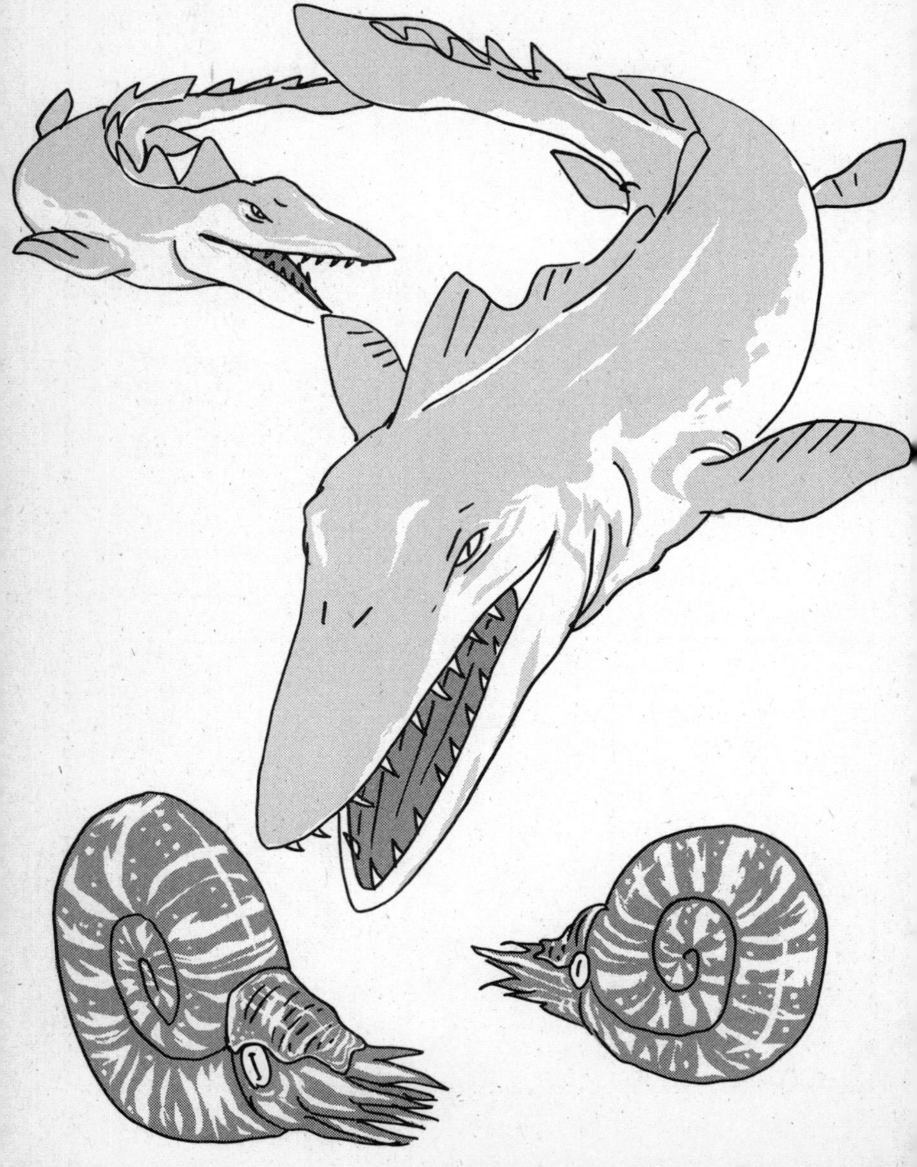

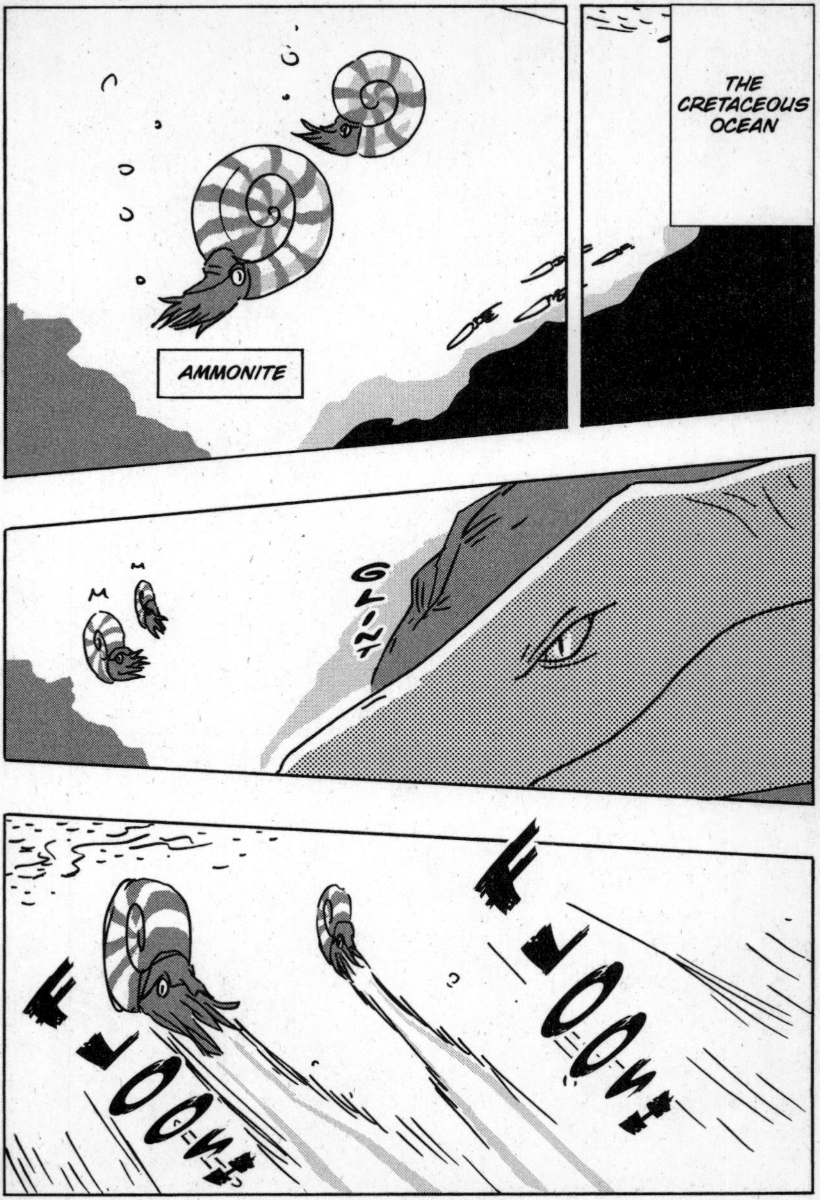
THE CRETACEOUS OCEAN
AMMONITE
M
M
GLINT
FLOOM!
FLOOM!

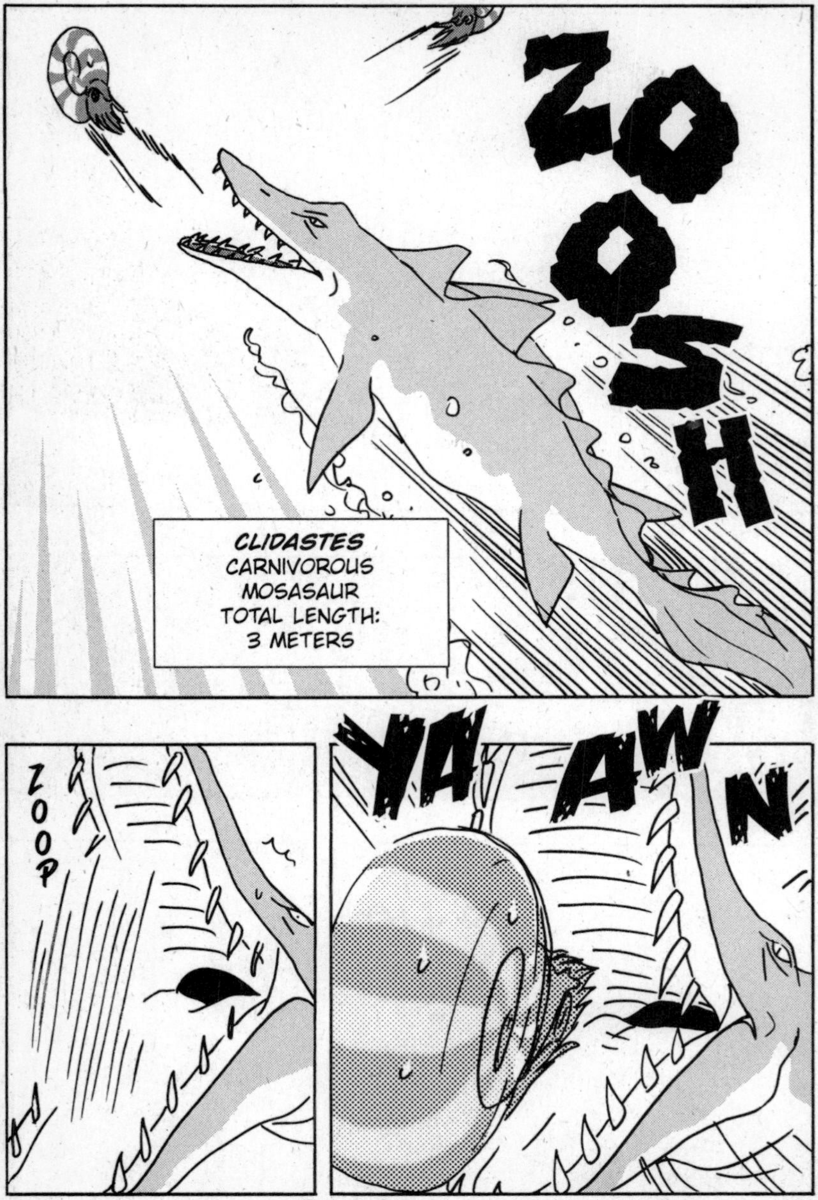
CLIDASTES
CARNIVOROUS MOSASAUR
TOTAL LENGTH: 3 METERS
ZOOSH
YAAWN
ZOOOP

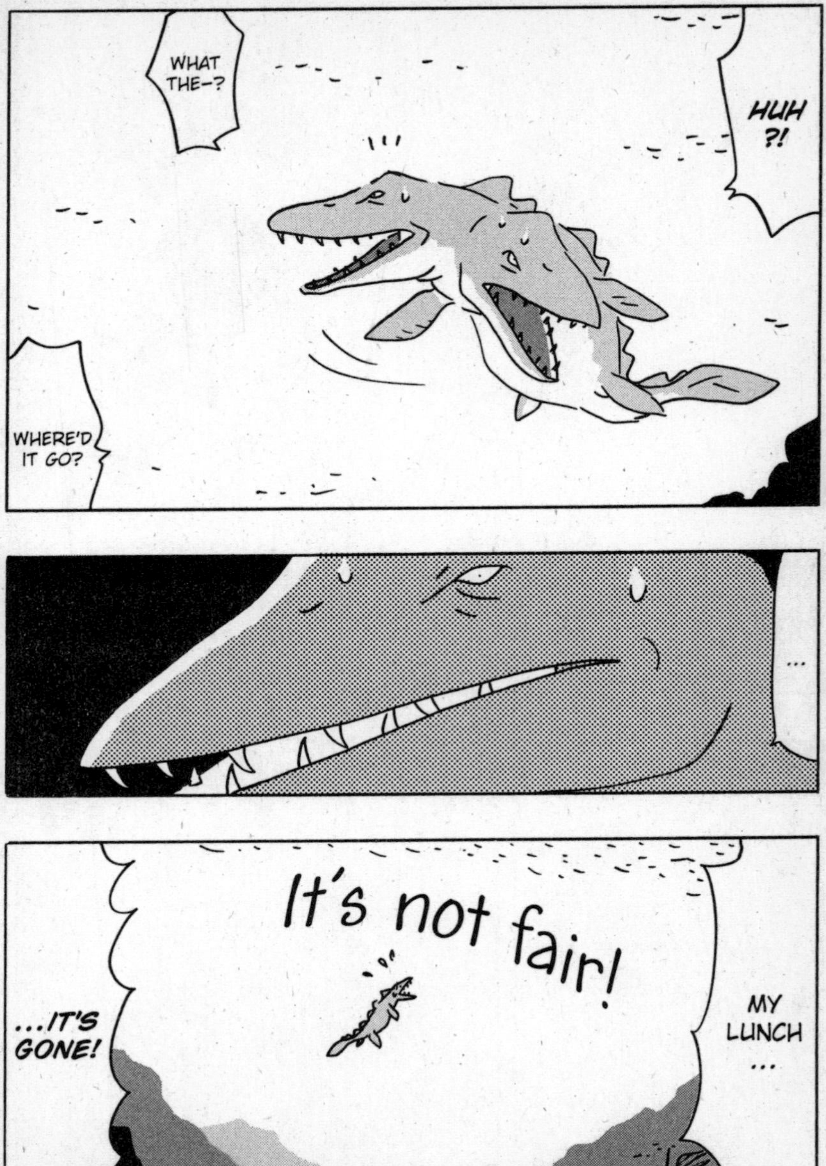

HUH ?!
WHAT THE-?
WHERE'D IT GO?
...
MY LUNCH ...
It's not fair!
...IT'S GONE!

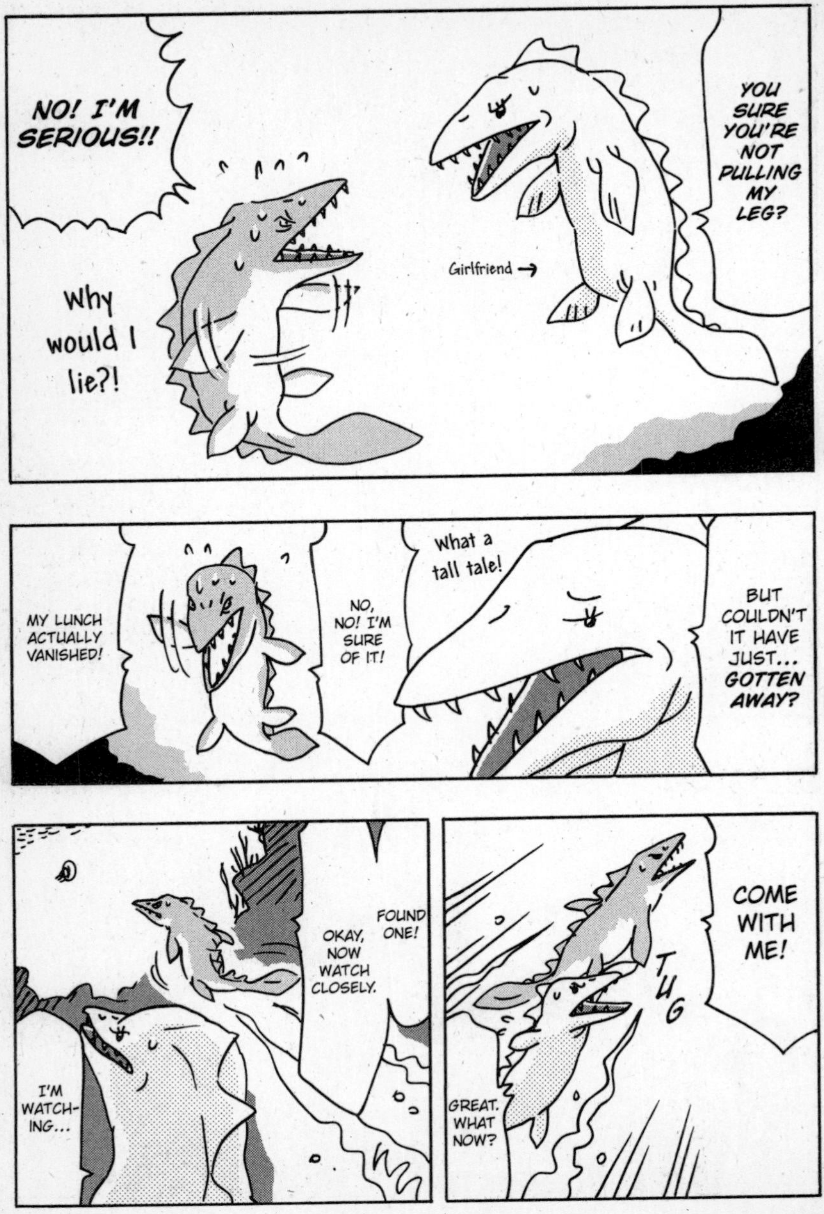

YOU SURE YOU'RE NOT PULLING MY LEG?
NO! I'M SERIOUS!!
Why would I lie?!
Girlfriend →
MY LUNCH ACTUALLY VANISHED!
NO, NO! I'M SURE OF IT!
What a tall tale!
BUT COULDN'T IT HAVE JUST... GOTTEN AWAY?
FOUND ONE!
OKAY, NOW WATCH CLOSELY.
I'M WATCH-ING...
COME WITH ME!
TUG
GREAT. WHAT NOW?

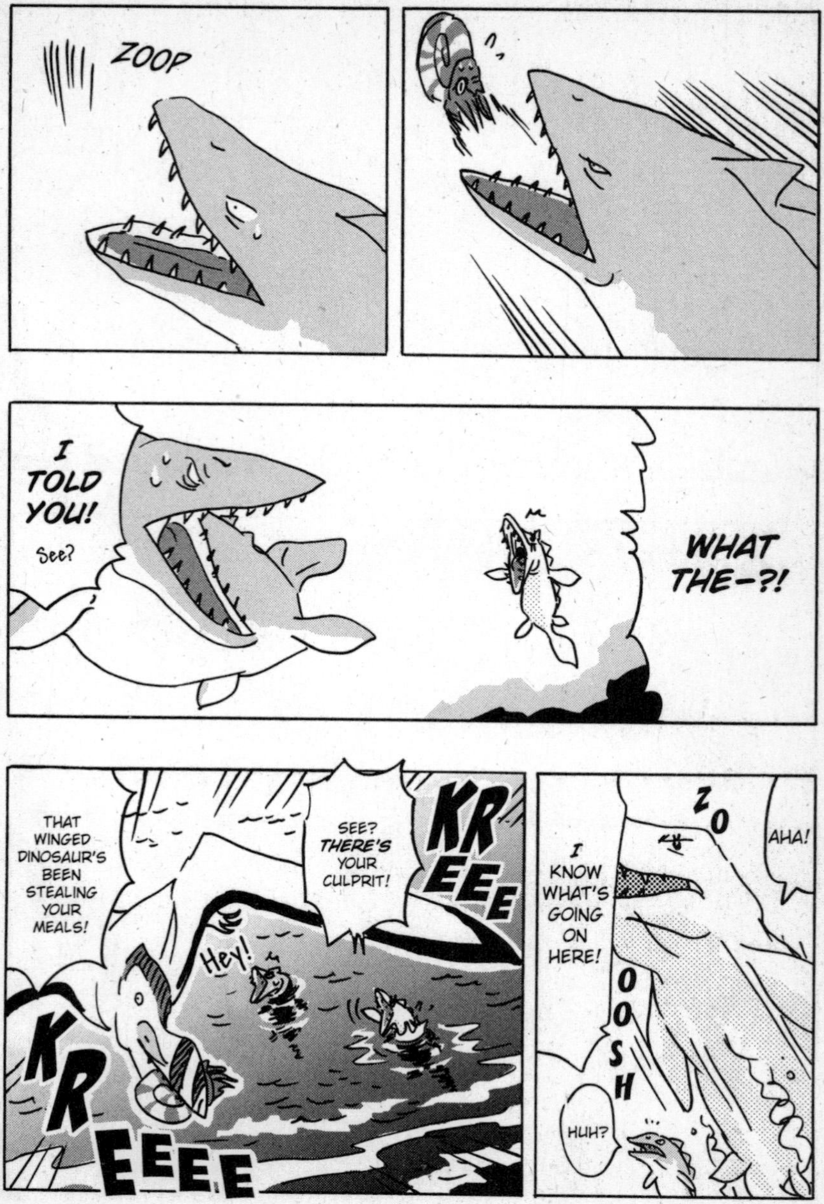
ZOOP
WHAT THE-?!
I TOLD YOU!
See?
AHA!
ZOOOOSH
I KNOW WHAT'S GOING ON HERE!
HUH?
SEE? THERE'S YOUR CULPRIT!
KREEEE
THAT WINGED DINOSAUR'S BEEN STEALING YOUR MEALS!
Hey!
KREEEEE

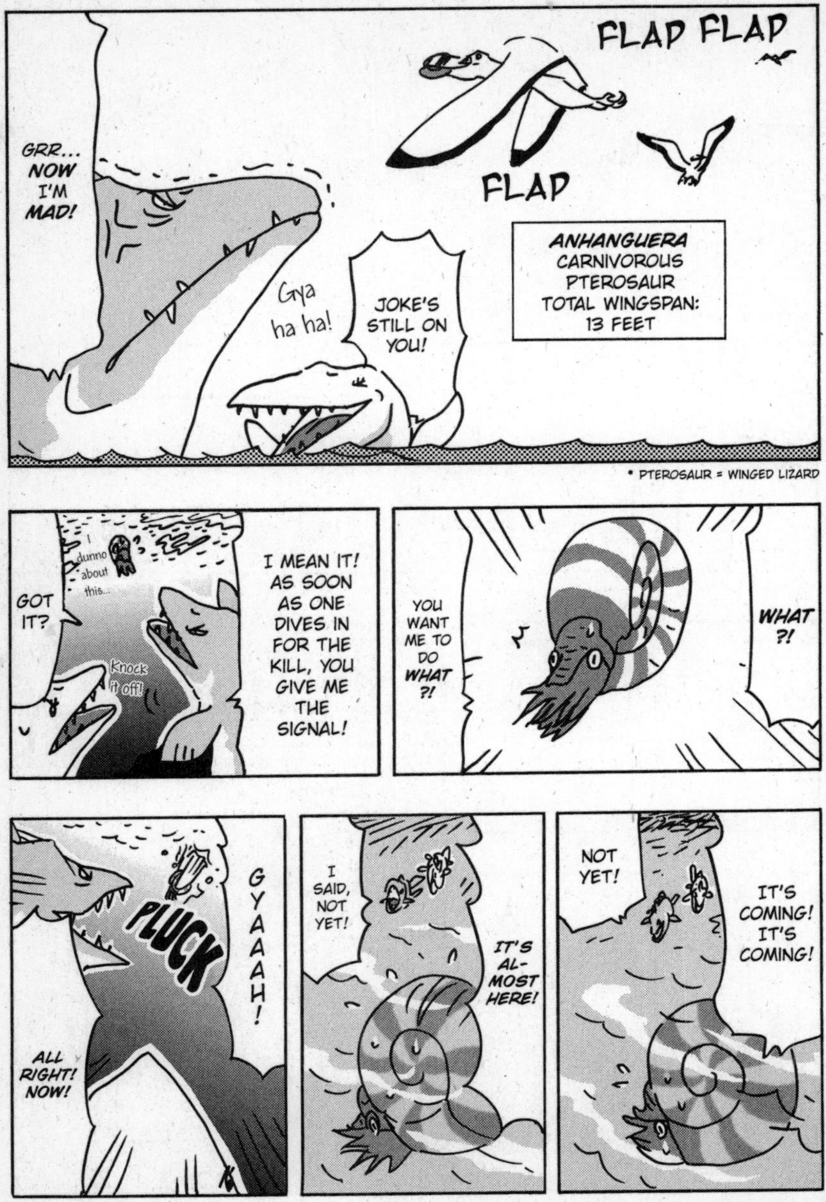
FLAP FLAP
FLAP
ANHANGUERA CARNIVOROUS PTEROSAUR TOTAL WINGSPAN: 13 FEET
JOKE'S STILL ON YOU!
Gya ha ha!
GRR... NOW I'M MAD!
* PTEROSAUR = WINGED LIZARD
WHAT?!
YOU WANT ME TO DO WHAT?!
I MEAN IT! AS SOON AS ONE DIVES IN FOR THE KILL, YOU GIVE ME THE SIGNAL!
GOT IT?
I dunno about this...
Knock it off!
IT'S COMING! IT'S COMING!
NOT YET!
IT'S AL-MOST HERE!
I SAID, NOT YET!
GYAAAAH!
PLUCK
ALL RIGHT! NOW!

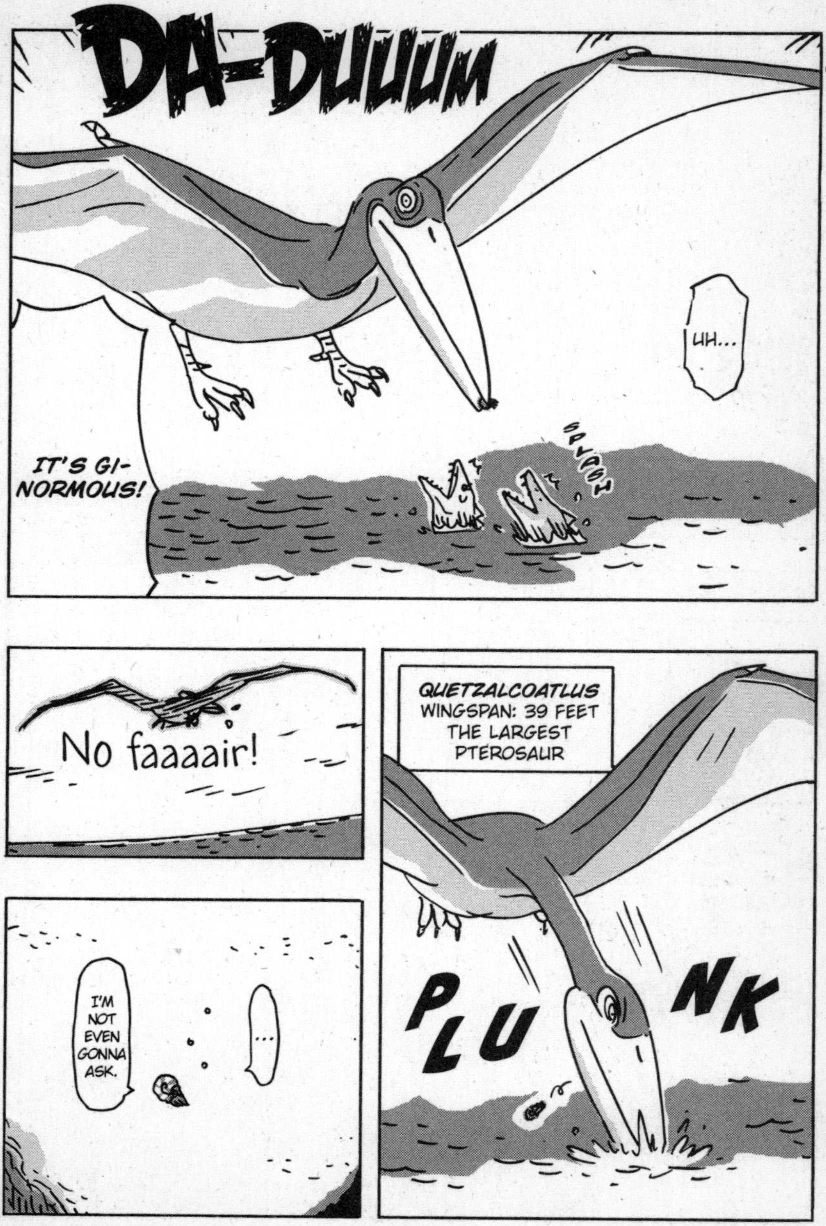
DA-DUUUM
UH...
SPLASH
IT'S GI-NORMOUS!
QUETZALCOATLUS WINGSPAN: 39 FEET THE LARGEST PTEROSAUR
PLUNK
No faaaair!
...
I'M NOT EVEN GONNA ASK.

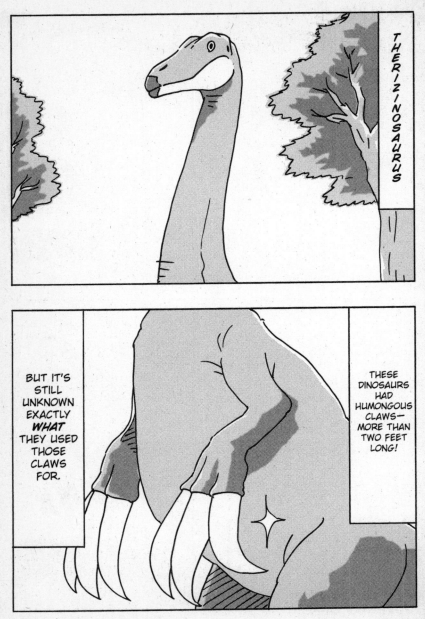

THERIZINOSAURUS

THESE DINOSAURS HAD HUMONGOUS CLAWS— MORE THAN TWO FEET LONG!

BUT IT'S STILL UNKNOWN EXACTLY *WHAT* THEY USED THOSE CLAWS FOR.

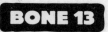

BONE 13

Secret of the Giant Claws

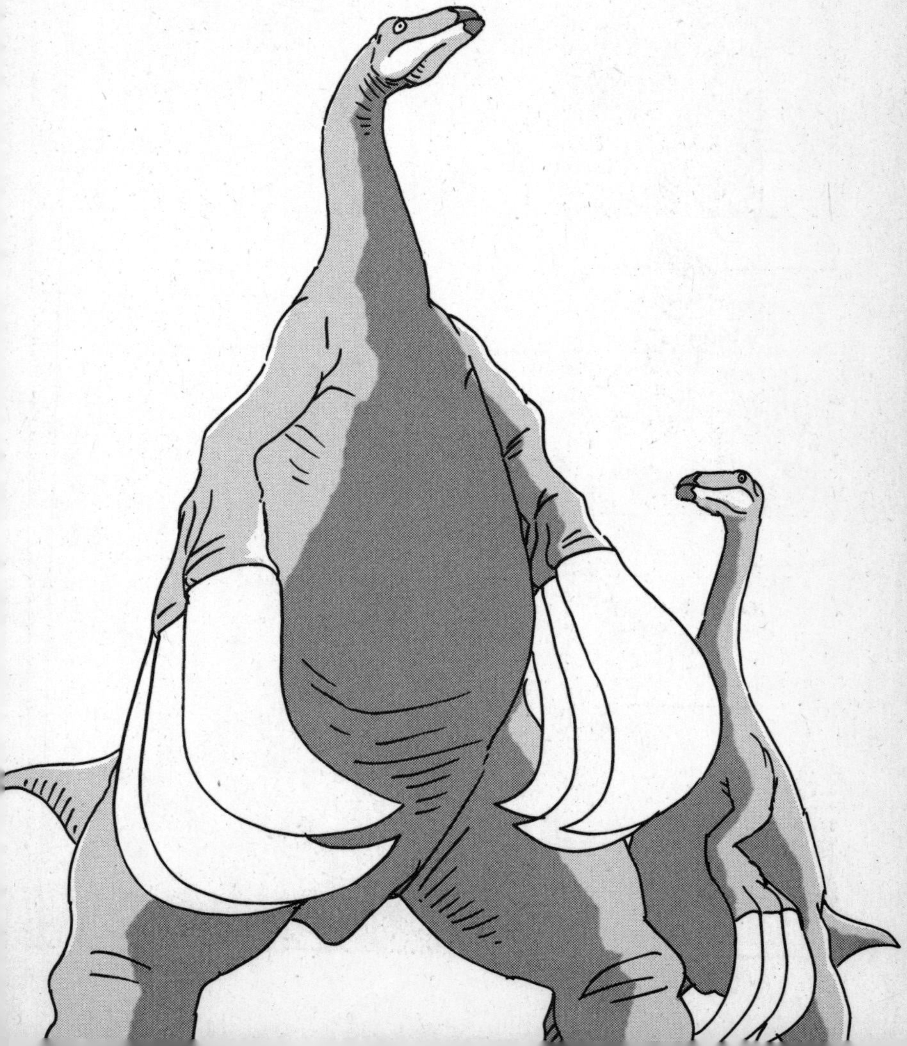

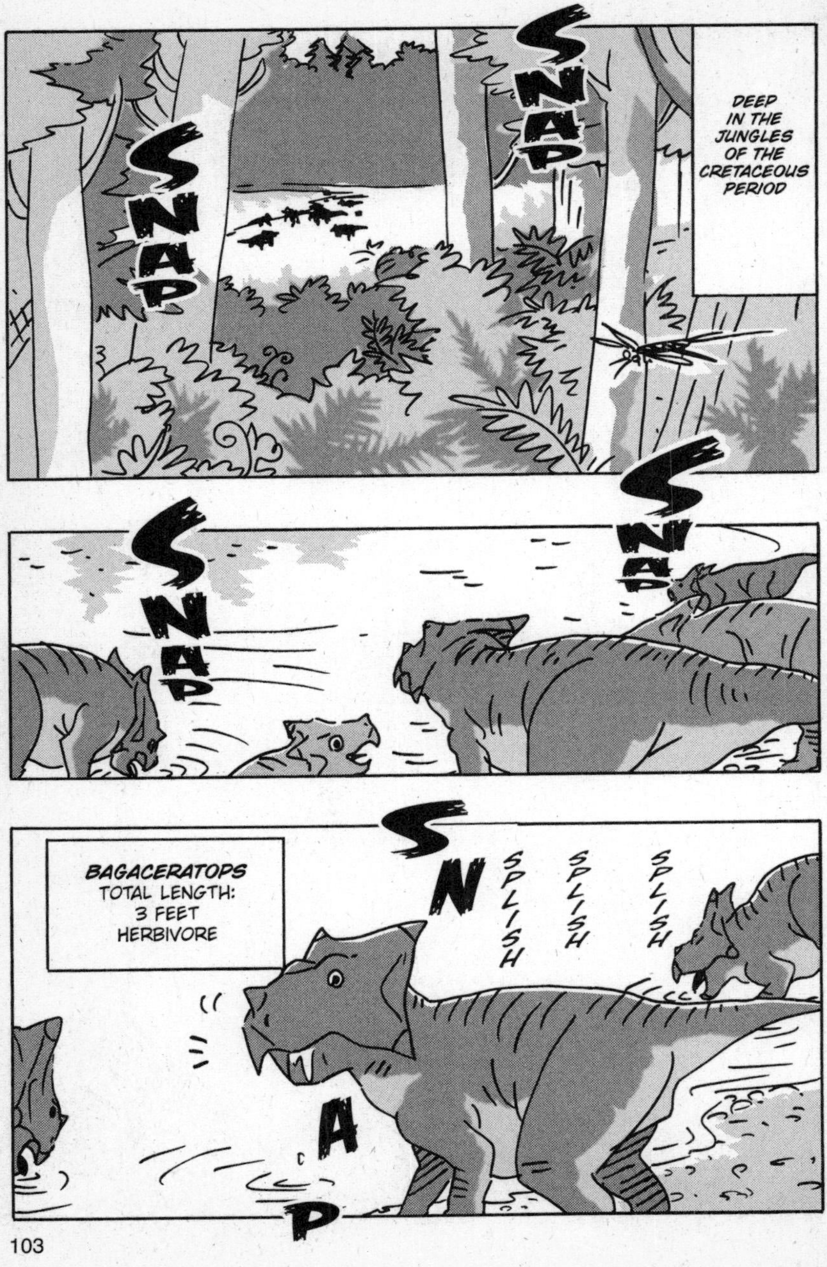
DEEP IN THE JUNGLES OF THE CRETACEOUS PERIOD
SNAP
SNAP
SNAP
SNAP
SPLISH
SPLISH
SPLISH
BAGACERATOPS
TOTAL LENGTH: 3 FEET
HERBIVORE
SNAP

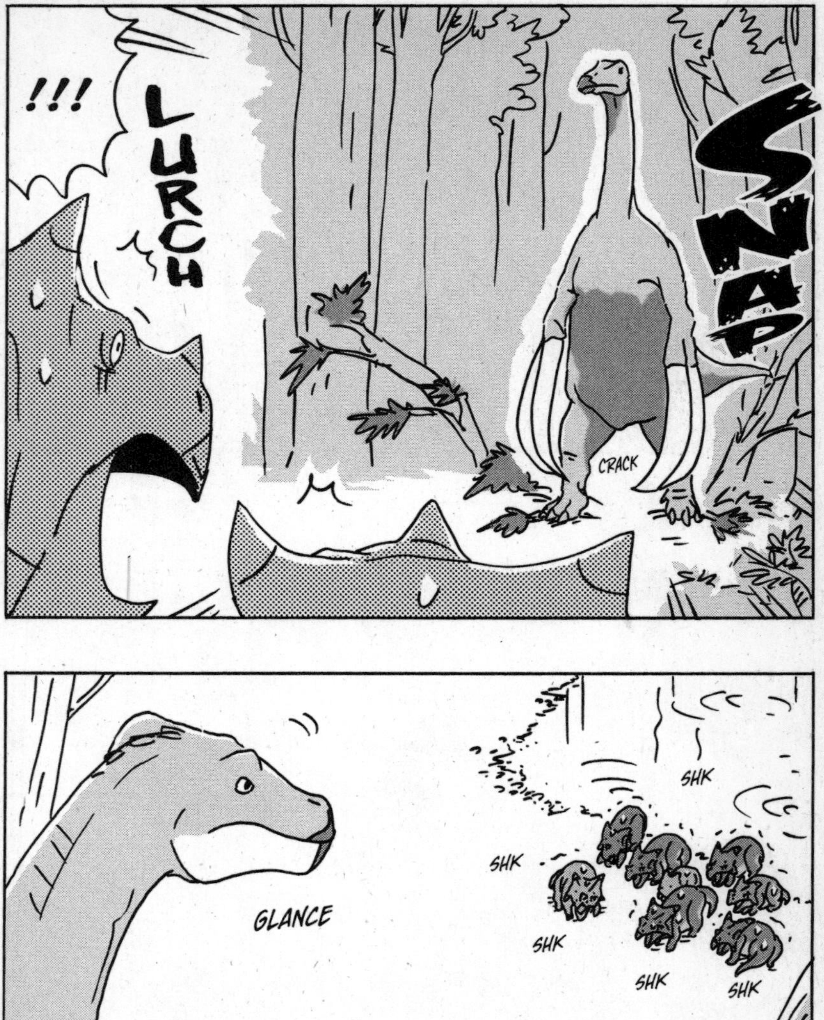
SNAP
CRACK
LURCH
!!!
SHK
SHK
SHK
SHK
SHK
GLANCE
THERIZINOSAURUS
HERBIVORE / CARNIVORE
STATUS: UNKNOWN
TOTAL LENGTH: 36 FEET

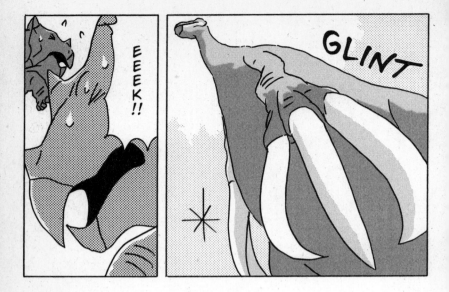

E E E K ! !

GLINT

MAY I HAVE A SIP OF WATER?

EXCUSE ME.

I'VE TRAVELED VERY FAR AND I'M QUITE THIRSTY.

HUH ?!

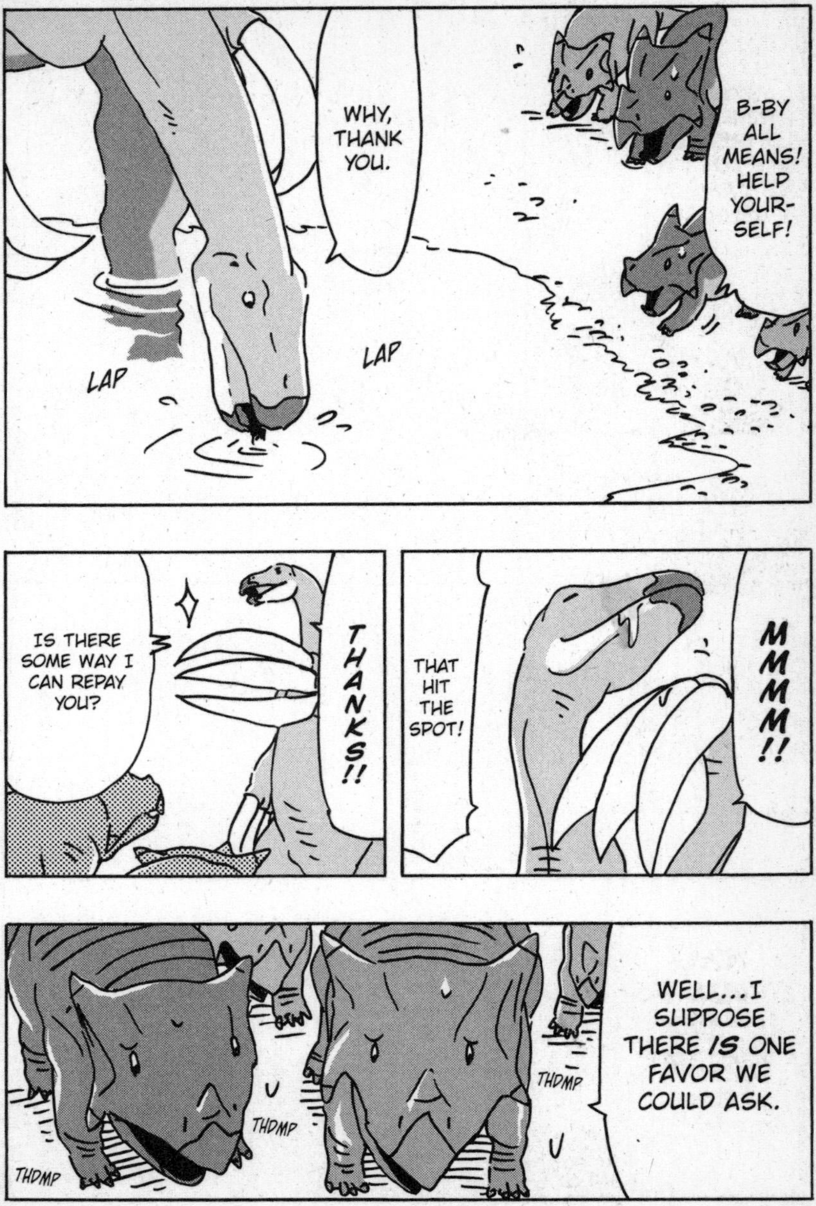
B-BY ALL MEANS! HELP YOURSELF!
WHY, THANK YOU.
LAP
LAP
MMMMM!!
THAT HIT THE SPOT!
THANKS!!
IS THERE SOME WAY I CAN REPAY YOU?
WELL...I SUPPOSE THERE IS ONE FAVOR WE COULD ASK.
THDMP
THDMP
THDMP

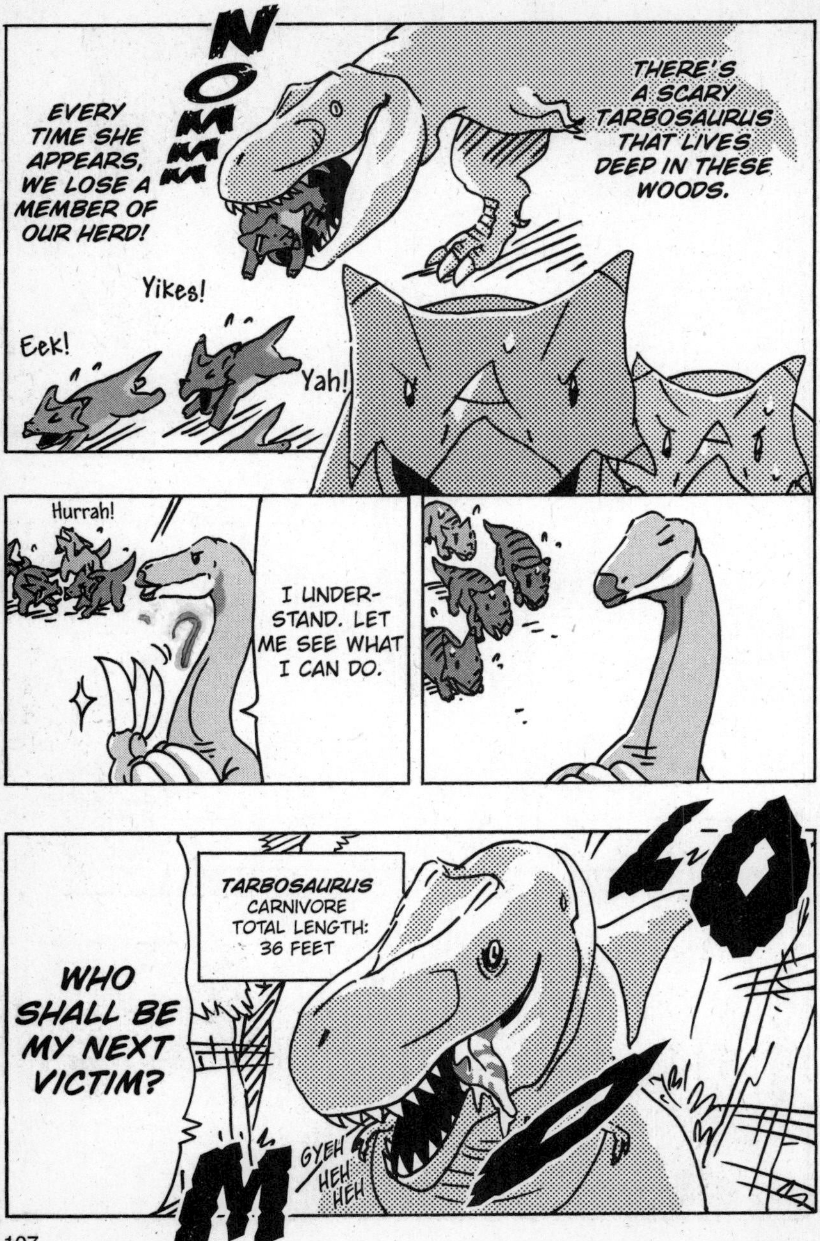
THERE'S A SCARY TARBOSAURUS THAT LIVES DEEP IN THESE WOODS.
NOMMMM
EVERY TIME SHE APPEARS, WE LOSE A MEMBER OF OUR HERD!
Yikes!
Yah!
Eek!
I UNDER-STAND. LET ME SEE WHAT I CAN DO.
Hurrah!
TARBOSAURUS
CARNIVORE
TOTAL LENGTH: 36 FEET
WHO SHALL BE MY NEXT VICTIM?
GYEH HEH HEH

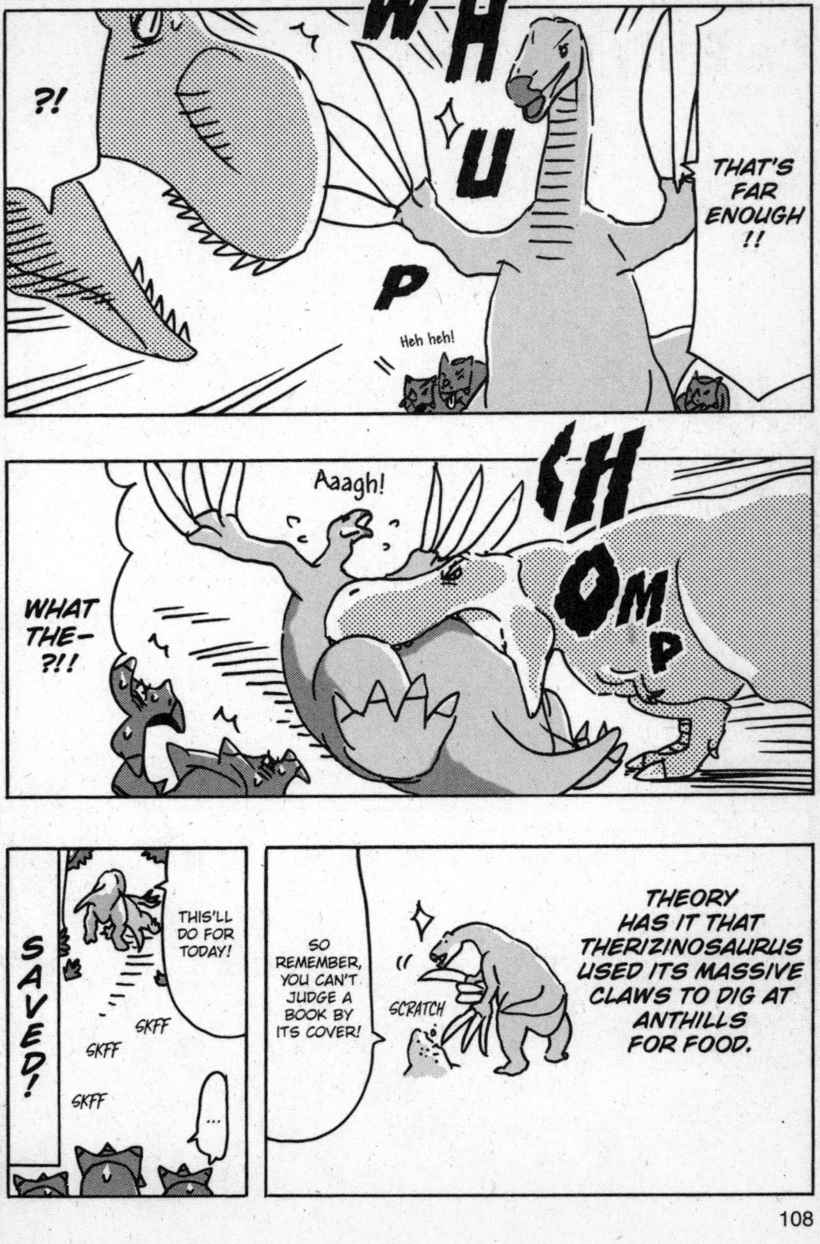
WHUP
THAT'S FAR ENOUGH!!
?!
Heh heh!
CHOMP
Aaagh!
WHAT THE-?!!
THEORY HAS IT THAT THERIZINOSAURUS USED ITS MASSIVE CLAWS TO DIG AT ANTHILLS FOR FOOD.
SO REMEMBER, YOU CAN'T JUDGE A BOOK BY ITS COVER!
SCRATCH
THIS'LL DO FOR TODAY!
SAVED!
SKFF
SKFF
SKFF
...

BONE 14

The Early Dinosaur

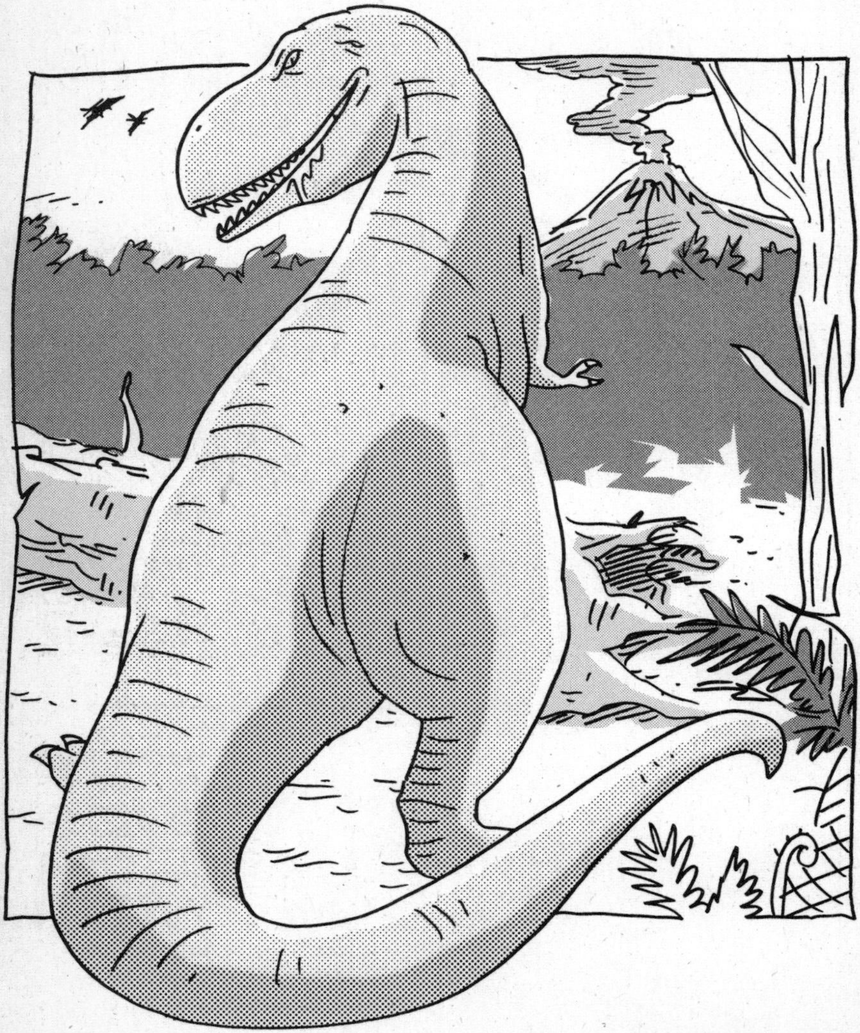

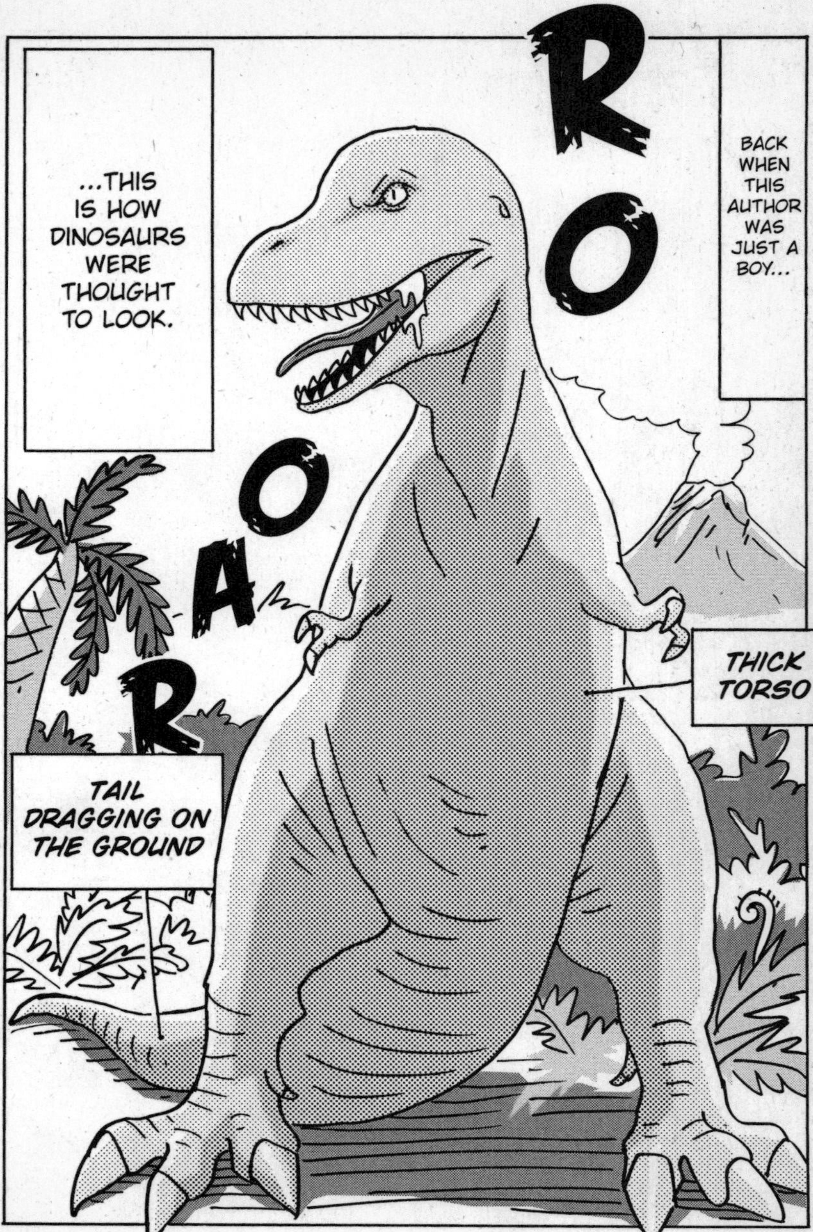
BACK WHEN THIS AUTHOR WAS JUST A BOY...
ROOAR
...THIS IS HOW DINOSAURS WERE THOUGHT TO LOOK.
THICK TORSO
TAIL DRAGGING ON THE GROUND

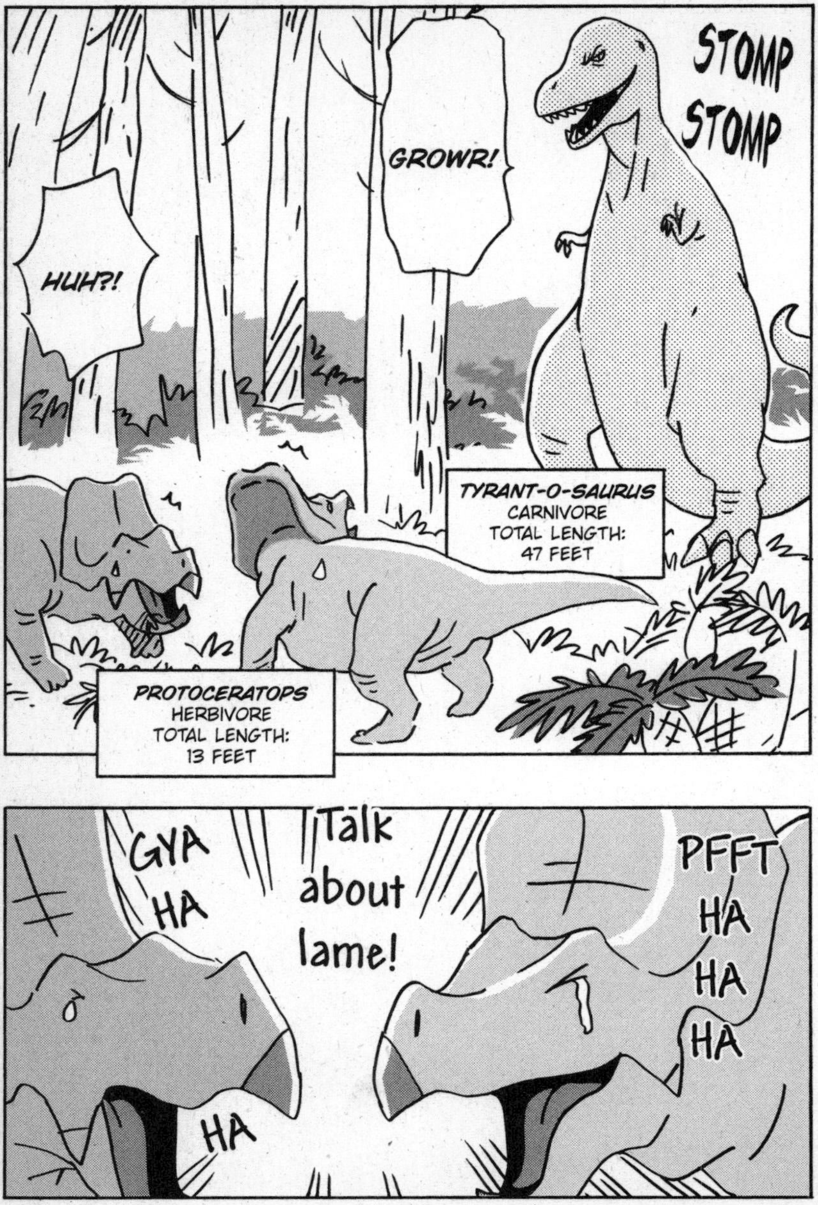
STOMP STOMP
GROWR!
HUH?!
TYRANT-O-SAURUS
CARNIVORE
TOTAL LENGTH:
47 FEET
PROTOCERATOPS
HERBIVORE
TOTAL LENGTH:
13 FEET
PFFT HA HA HA HA
Talk about lame!
GYA HA
HA

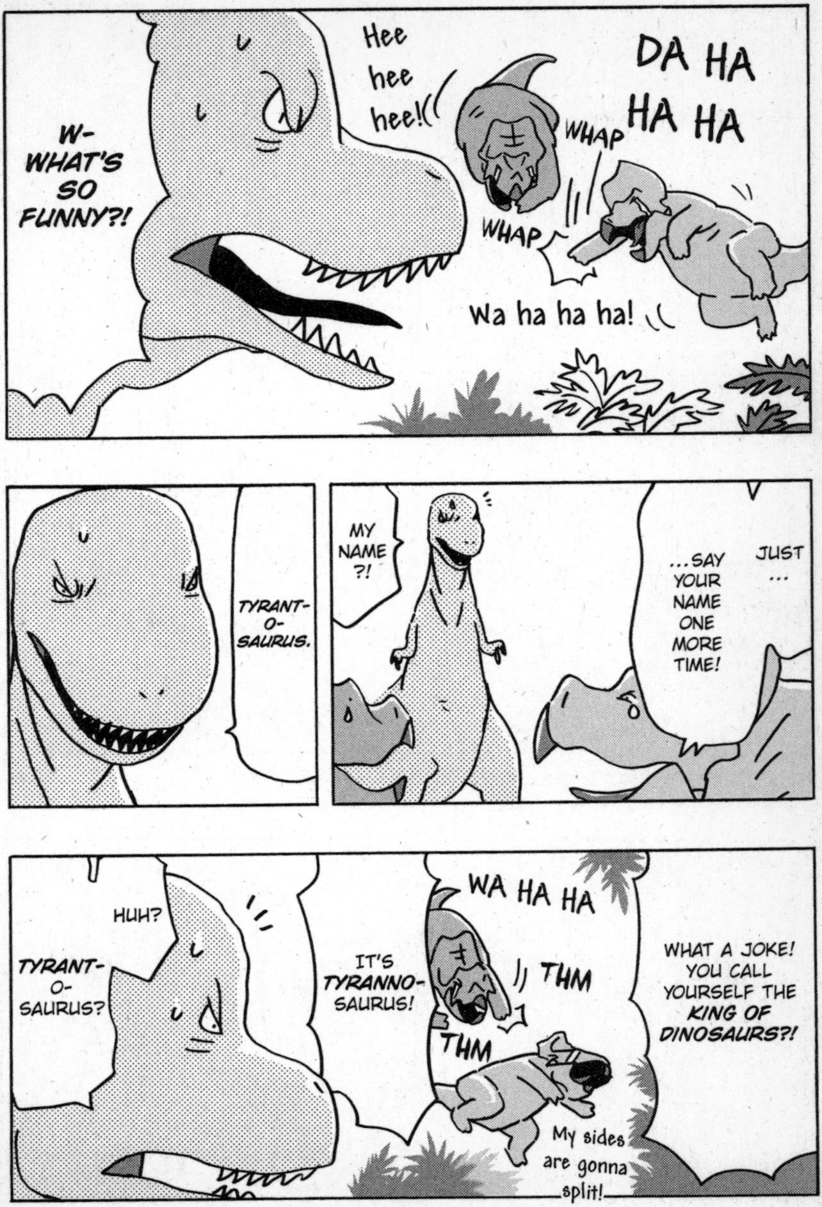
DA HA HA HA
WHAP
Hee hee hee!
WHAP
Wa ha ha ha!
W- WHAT'S SO FUNNY?!
JUST ...
...SAY YOUR NAME ONE MORE TIME!
MY NAME ?!
TYRANT-O-SAURUS.
WHAT A JOKE! YOU CALL YOURSELF THE *KING OF DINOSAURS?!*
WA HA HA
THM
THM
My sides are gonna split!
IT'S *TYRANNO-*SAURUS!
HUH?
*TYRANT-*O-SAURUS?

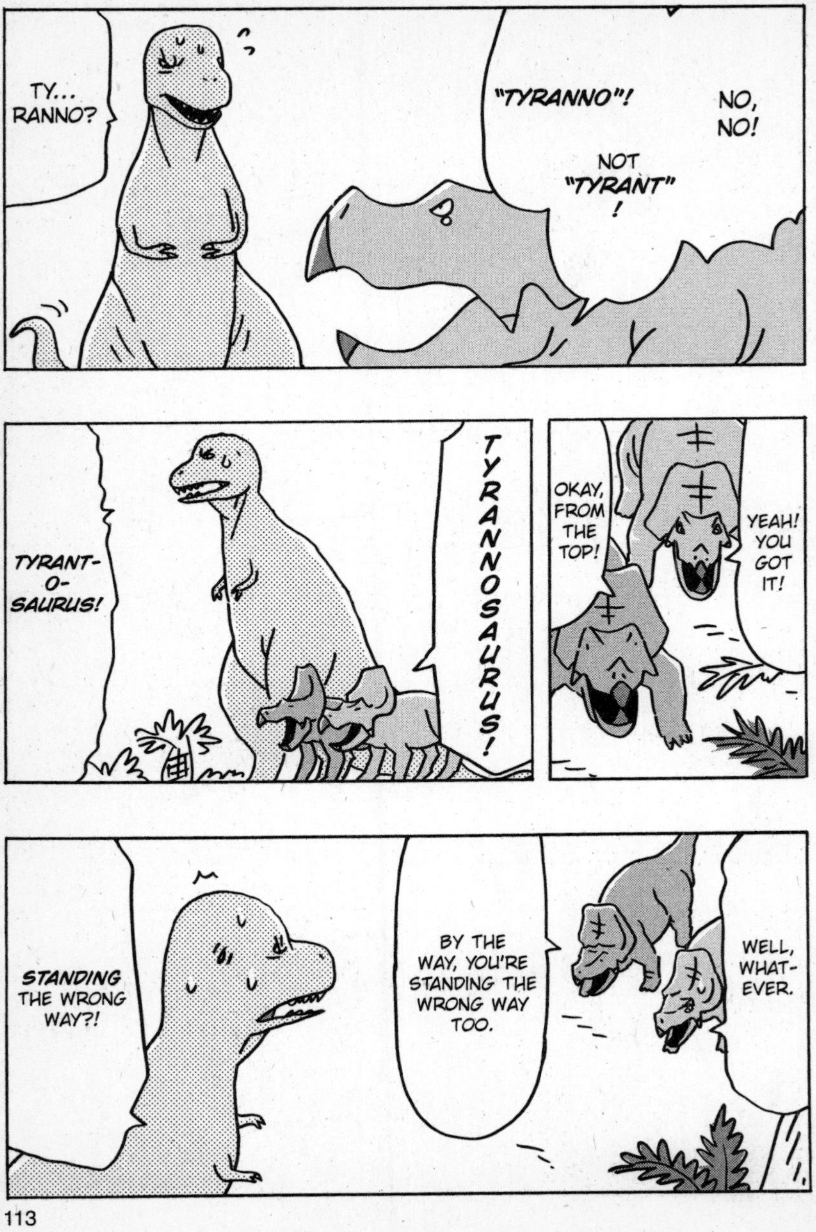
NO, NO!
"TYRANNO"!
NOT "TYRANT"!
TY... RANNO?
YEAH! YOU GOT IT!
OKAY, FROM THE TOP!
TYRANNOSAURUS!
TYRANT-O-SAURUS!
WELL, WHAT-EVER.
BY THE WAY, YOU'RE STANDING THE WRONG WAY TOO.
STANDING THE WRONG WAY?!

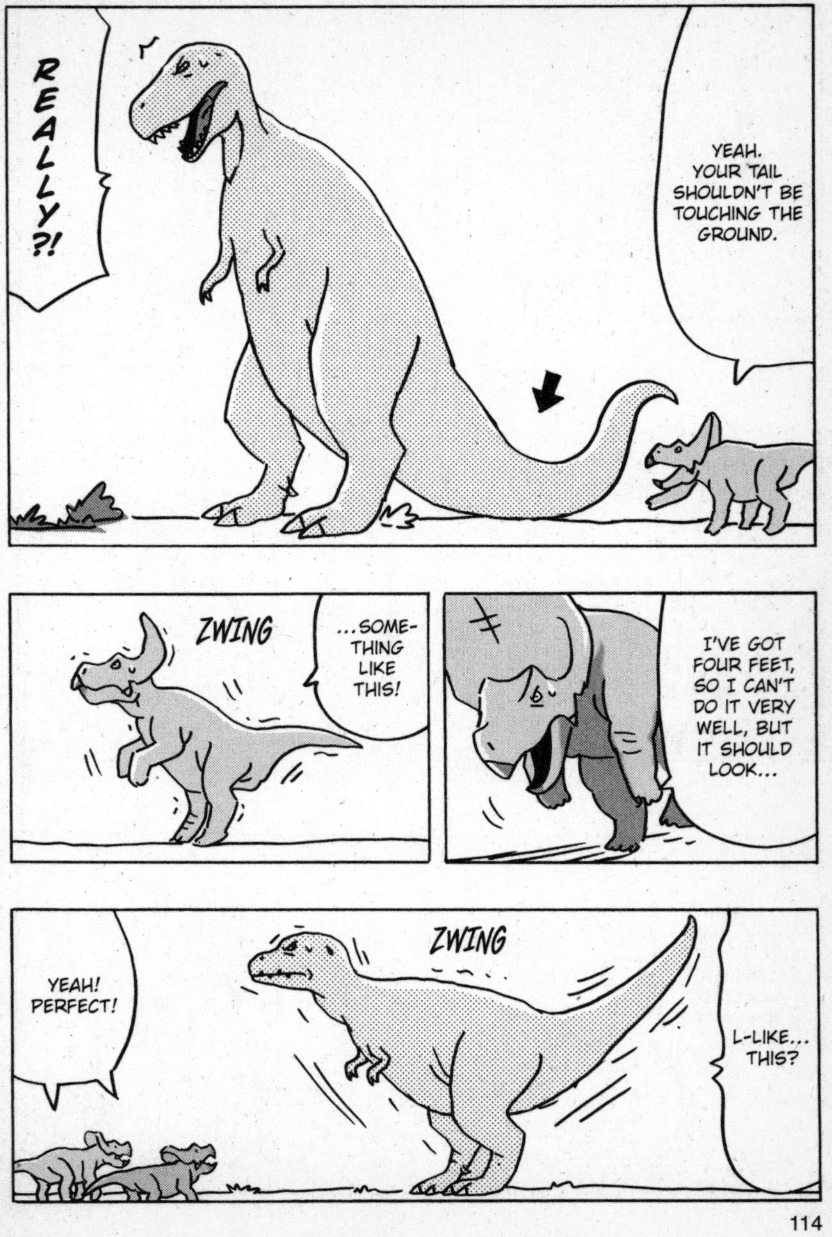
YEAH. YOUR TAIL SHOULDN'T BE TOUCHING THE GROUND.
REALLY?!
I'VE GOT FOUR FEET, SO I CAN'T DO IT VERY WELL, BUT IT SHOULD LOOK...
...SOME-THING LIKE THIS!
ZWING
L-LIKE... THIS?
ZWING
YEAH! PERFECT!

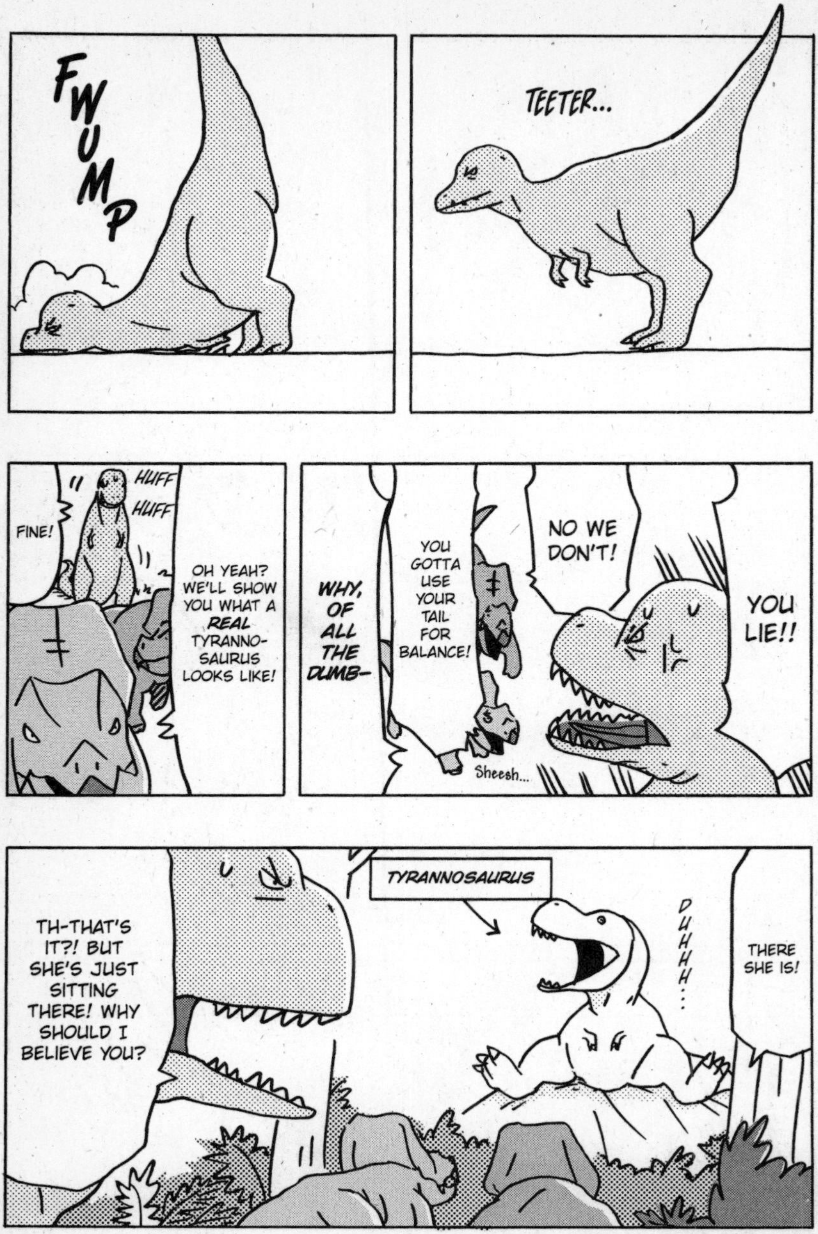
TEETER...
FWUMP
YOU LIE!!
NO WE DON'T!
YOU GOTTA USE YOUR TAIL FOR BALANCE!
WHY, OF ALL THE DUMB-
Sheesh...
OH YEAH? WE'LL SHOW YOU WHAT A *REAL* TYRANNOSAURUS LOOKS LIKE!
HUFF HUFF
FINE!
THERE SHE IS!
DUHHH...
TYRANNOSAURUS
TH-THAT'S IT?! BUT SHE'S JUST SITTING THERE! WHY SHOULD I BELIEVE YOU?

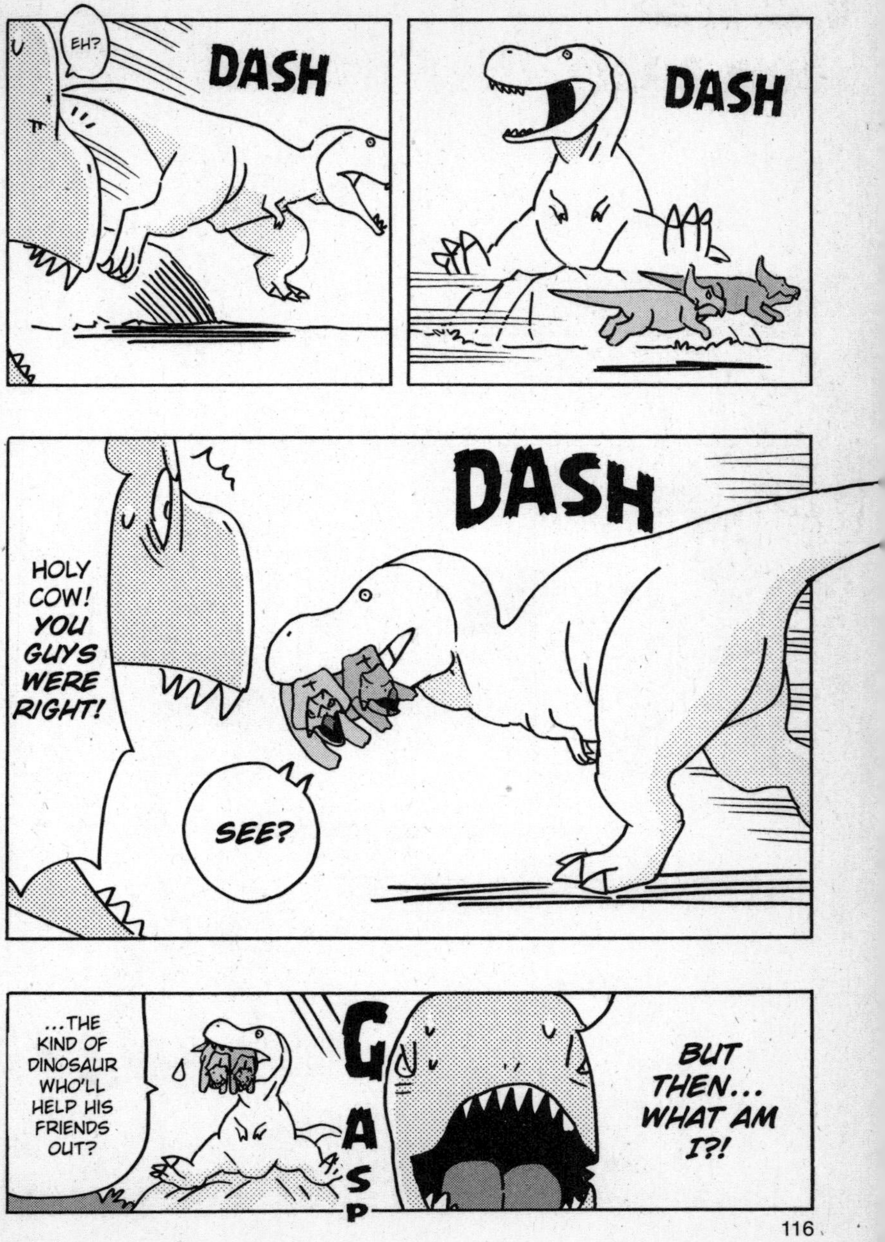

DASH
EH?
DASH
DASH
HOLY COW! YOU GUYS WERE RIGHT!
SEE?
BUT THEN... WHAT AM I?!
GASP
...THE KIND OF DINOSAUR WHO'LL HELP HIS FRIENDS OUT?

BONE 15

How a Dino Used Its Brain

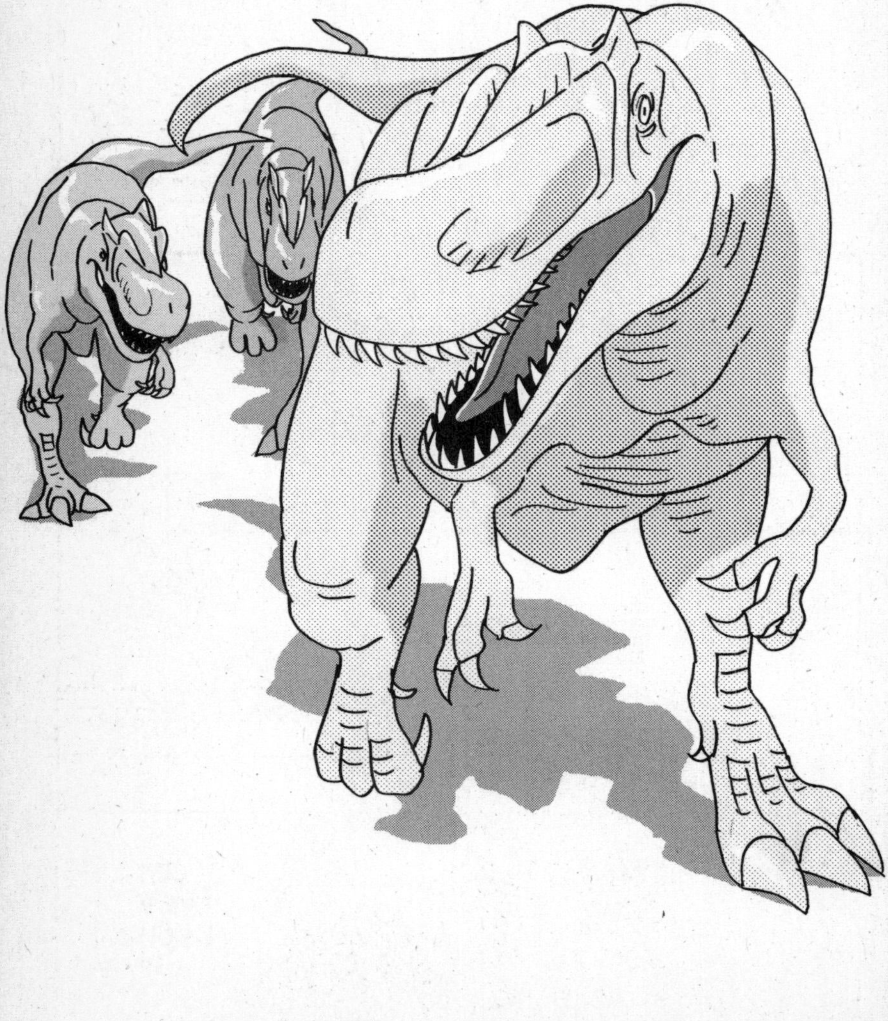

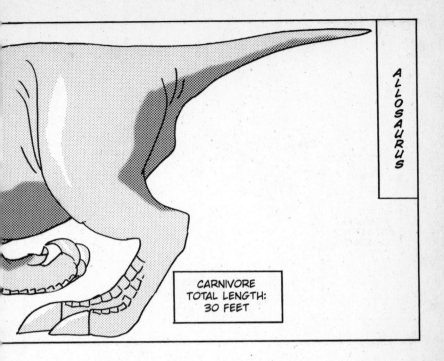

CARNIVORE
TOTAL LENGTH:
30 FEET

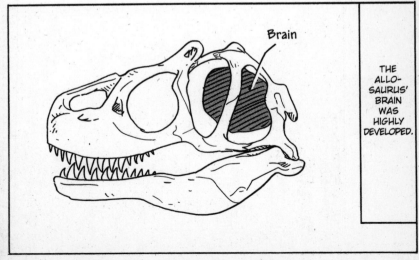

Brain

THE
ALLO-
SAURUS'
BRAIN
WAS
HIGHLY
DEVELOPED.

118

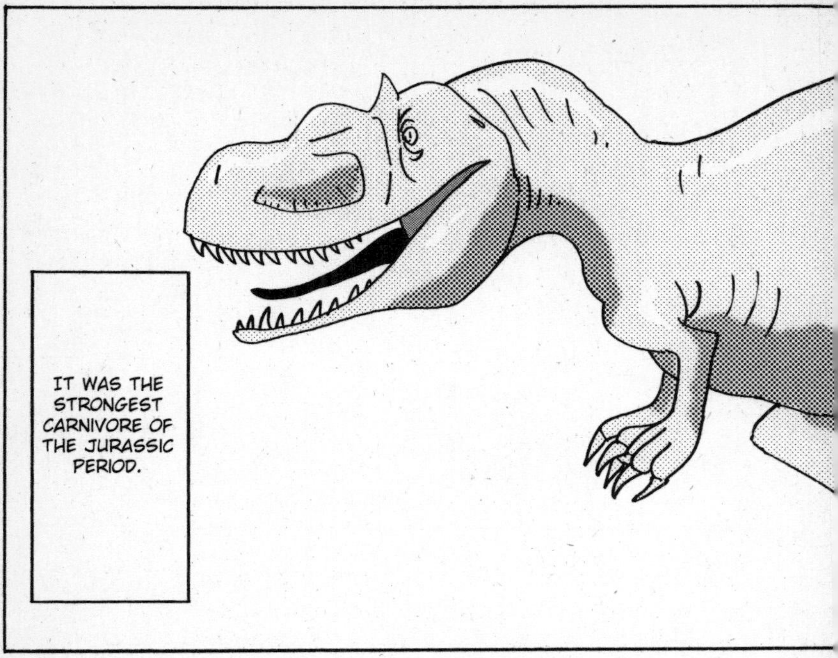
IT WAS THE STRONGEST CARNIVORE OF THE JURASSIC PERIOD.

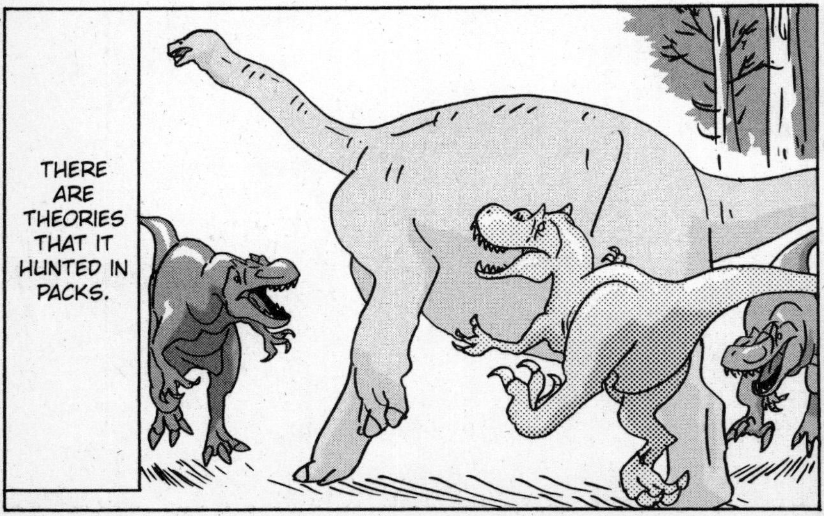
THERE ARE THEORIES THAT IT HUNTED IN PACKS.

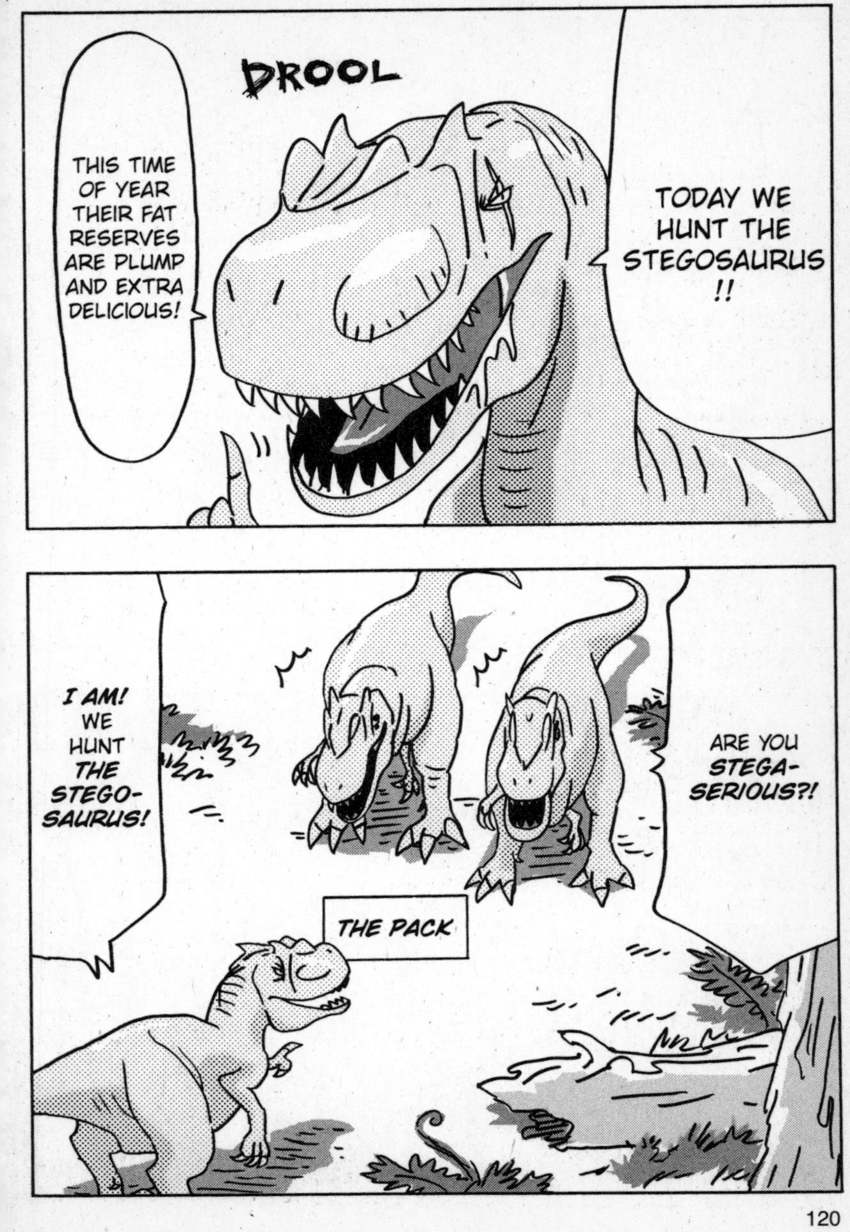
TODAY WE HUNT THE STEGOSAURUS !!
DROOL
THIS TIME OF YEAR THEIR FAT RESERVES ARE PLUMP AND EXTRA DELICIOUS!
ARE YOU STEGA-SERIOUS?!
I AM! WE HUNT THE STEGO-SAURUS!
THE PACK

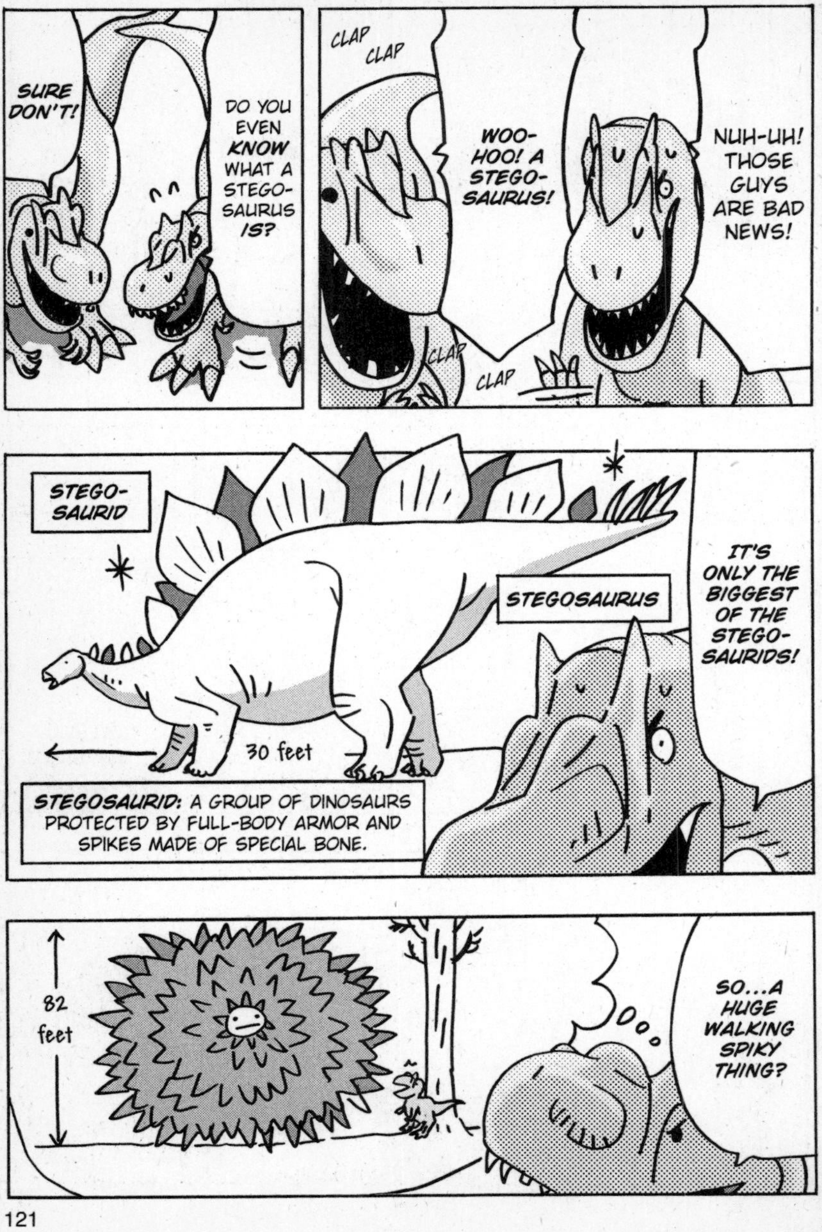
NUH-UH! THOSE GUYS ARE BAD NEWS!
CLAP CLAP
WOO-HOO! A STEGO-SAURUS!
CLAP CLAP
DO YOU EVEN KNOW WHAT A STEGO-SAURUS IS?
SURE DON'T!
IT'S ONLY THE BIGGEST OF THE STEGO-SAURIDS!
STEGOSAURUS
STEGO-SAURID
30 feet
STEGOSAURID: A GROUP OF DINOSAURS PROTECTED BY FULL-BODY ARMOR AND SPIKES MADE OF SPECIAL BONE.
SO...A HUGE WALKING SPIKY THING?
Ooo
82 feet

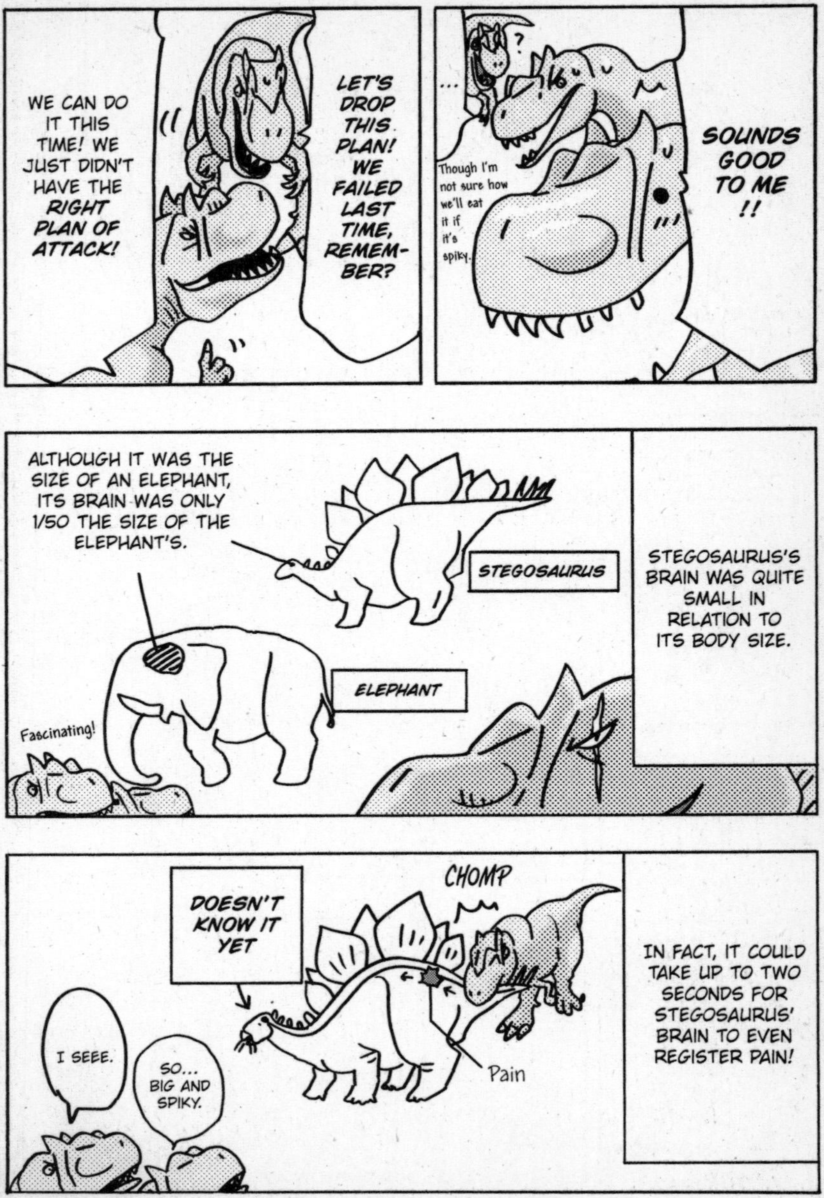
WE CAN DO IT THIS TIME! WE JUST DIDN'T HAVE THE RIGHT PLAN OF ATTACK!
LET'S DROP THIS PLAN! WE FAILED LAST TIME, REMEMBER?
...
?
Though I'm not sure how we'll eat it if it's spiky.
SOUNDS GOOD TO ME!!
STEGOSAURUS'S BRAIN WAS QUITE SMALL IN RELATION TO ITS BODY SIZE.
ALTHOUGH IT WAS THE SIZE OF AN ELEPHANT, ITS BRAIN WAS ONLY 1/50 THE SIZE OF THE ELEPHANT'S.
STEGOSAURUS
ELEPHANT
Fascinating!
IN FACT, IT COULD TAKE UP TO TWO SECONDS FOR STEGOSAURUS' BRAIN TO EVEN REGISTER PAIN!
CHOMP
DOESN'T KNOW IT YET
Pain
I SEEE.
SO... BIG AND SPIKY.

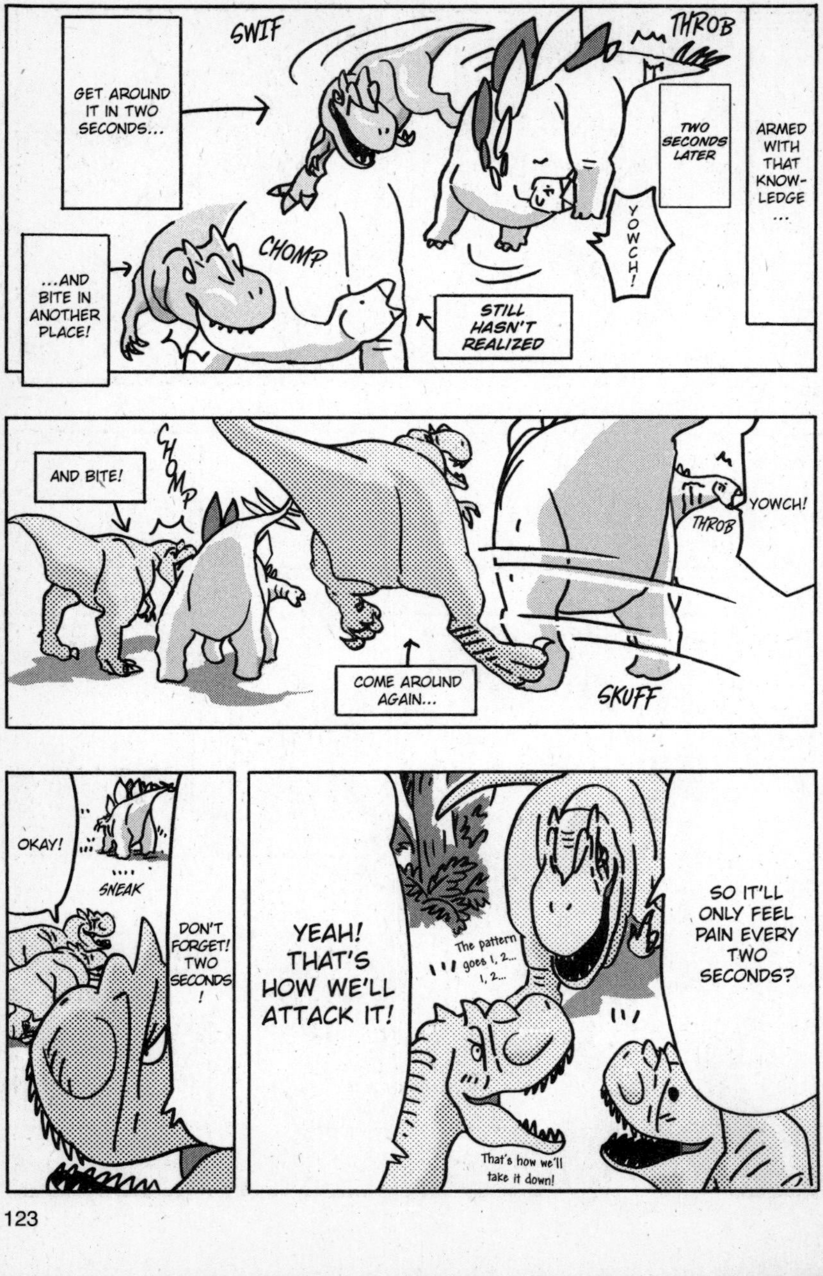
ARMED WITH THAT KNOW-LEDGE...
TWO SECONDS LATER
THROB
YOWCH!
STILL HASN'T REALIZED
SWIF
GET AROUND IT IN TWO SECONDS...
CHOMP
...AND BITE IN ANOTHER PLACE!
YOWCH!
THROB
SKUFF
COME AROUND AGAIN...
CHOMP
AND BITE!
SO IT'LL ONLY FEEL PAIN EVERY TWO SECONDS?
The pattern goes 1, 2... 1, 2...
YEAH! THAT'S HOW WE'LL ATTACK IT!
That's how we'll take it down!
DON'T FORGET! TWO SECONDS!
OKAY!
SNEAK

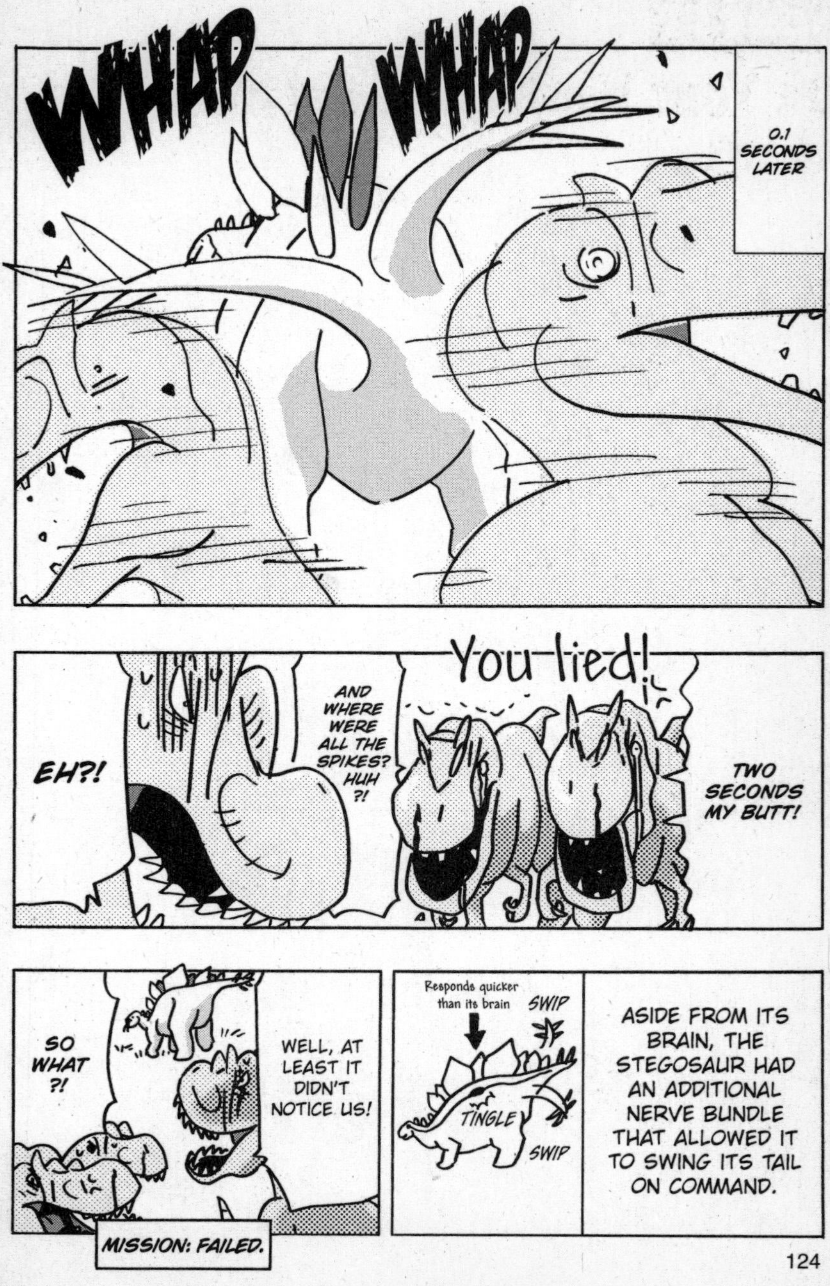
0.1 SECONDS LATER
WHAP
WHAP
TWO SECONDS MY BUTT!
You lied!
AND WHERE WERE ALL THE SPIKES? HUH ?!
EH?!
ASIDE FROM ITS BRAIN, THE STEGOSAUR HAD AN ADDITIONAL NERVE BUNDLE THAT ALLOWED IT TO SWING ITS TAIL ON COMMAND.
SWIP
Responds quicker than its brain
TINGLE
SWIP
WELL, AT LEAST IT DIDN'T NOTICE US!
SO WHAT ?!
MISSION: FAILED.

BONE 16

On Your Marks, Get Set, Dino-Go!

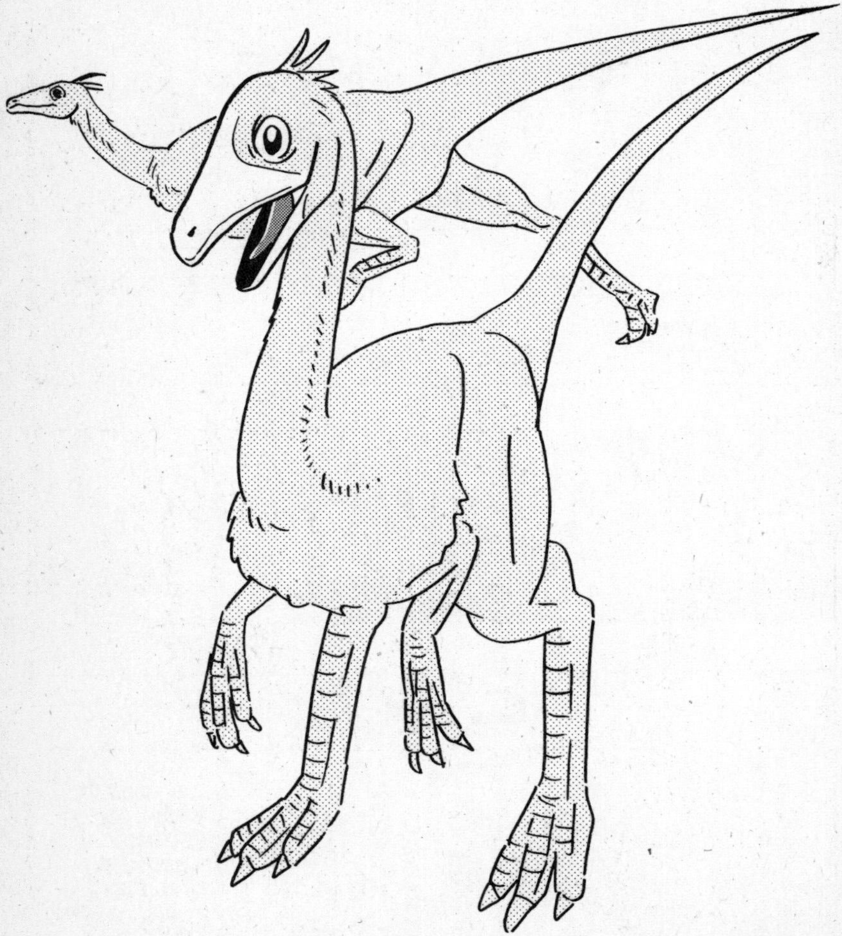

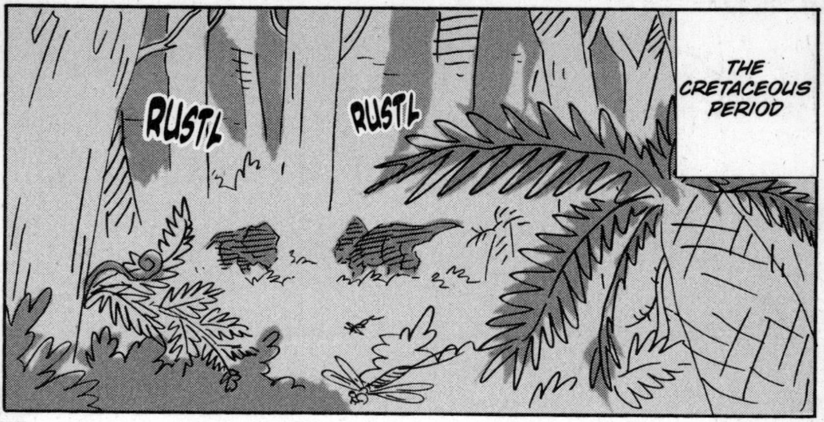
THE CRETACEOUS PERIOD
RUSTL
RUSTL

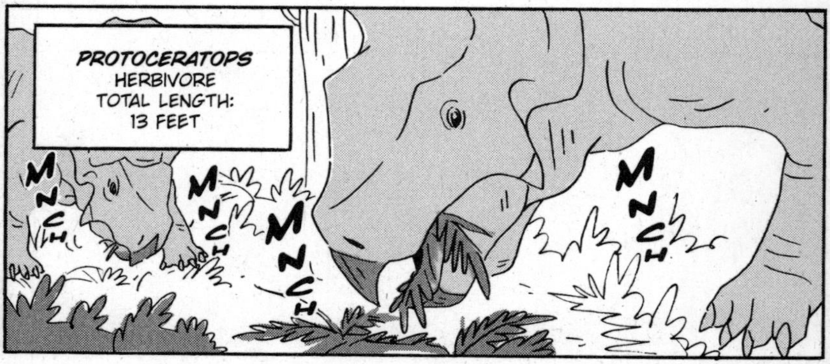
MNCH
PROTOCERATOPS
HERBIVORE
TOTAL LENGTH:
13 FEET
MNCH
MNCH
MNCH

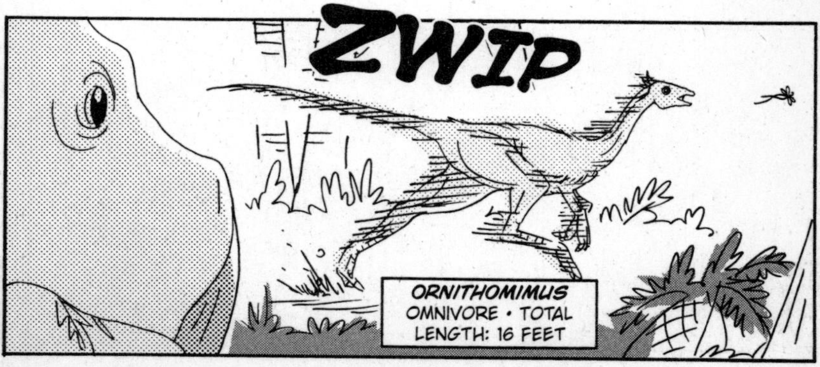
ZWIP
ORNITHOMIMUS
OMNIVORE • TOTAL
LENGTH: 16 FEET

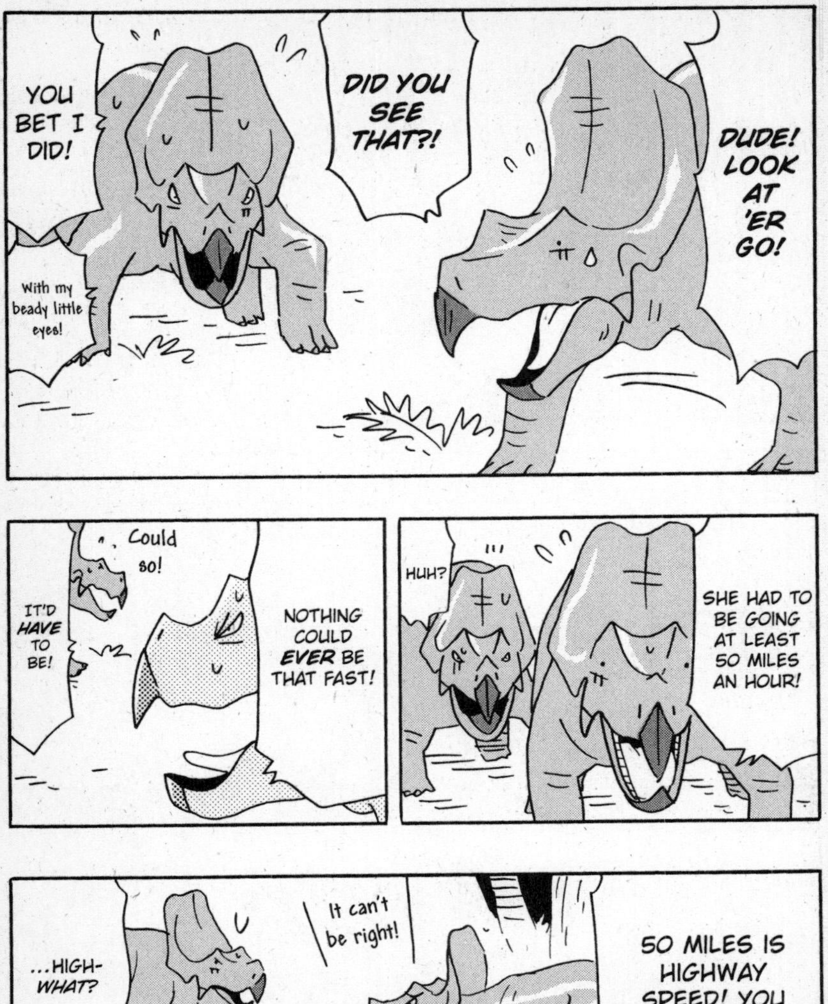
DUDE! LOOK AT 'ER GO!
DID YOU SEE THAT?!
YOU BET I DID!
With my beady little eyes!
SHE HAD TO BE GOING AT LEAST 50 MILES AN HOUR!
HUH?
NOTHING COULD *EVER* BE THAT FAST!
Could so!
IT'D *HAVE* TO BE!
50 MILES IS HIGHWAY SPEED! YOU CAN'T DO THAT IN A DENSE JUNGLE!
It can't be right!
...HIGH-WHAT?

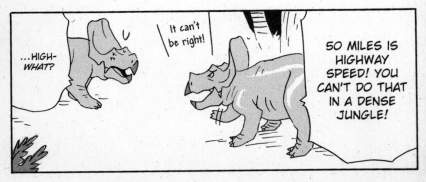

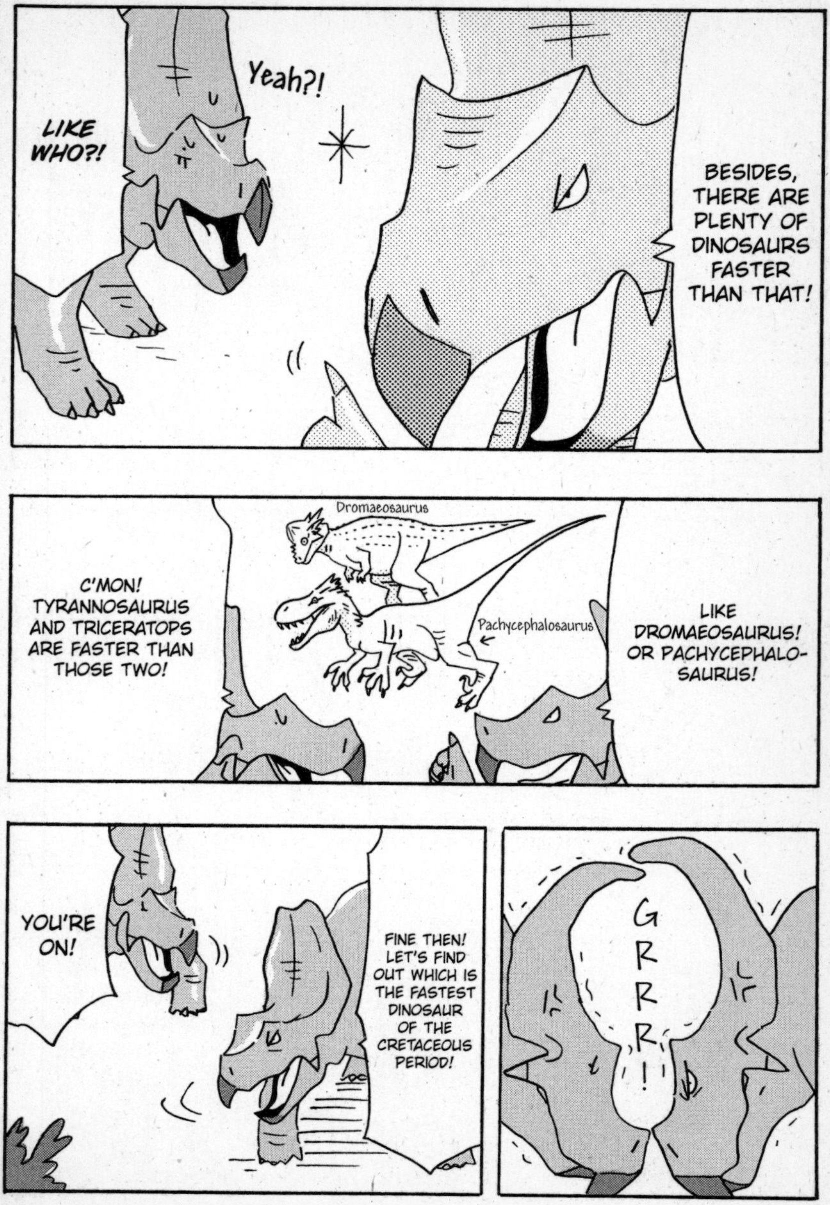
BESIDES, THERE ARE PLENTY OF DINOSAURS FASTER THAN THAT!
Yeah?!
LIKE WHO?!
LIKE DROMAEOSAURUS! OR PACHYCEPHALO-SAURUS!
Dromaeosaurus
Pachycephalosaurus
C'MON! TYRANNOSAURUS AND TRICERATOPS ARE FASTER THAN THOSE TWO!
GRRR!
FINE THEN! LET'S FIND OUT WHICH IS THE FASTEST DINOSAUR OF THE CRETACEOUS PERIOD!
YOU'RE ON!

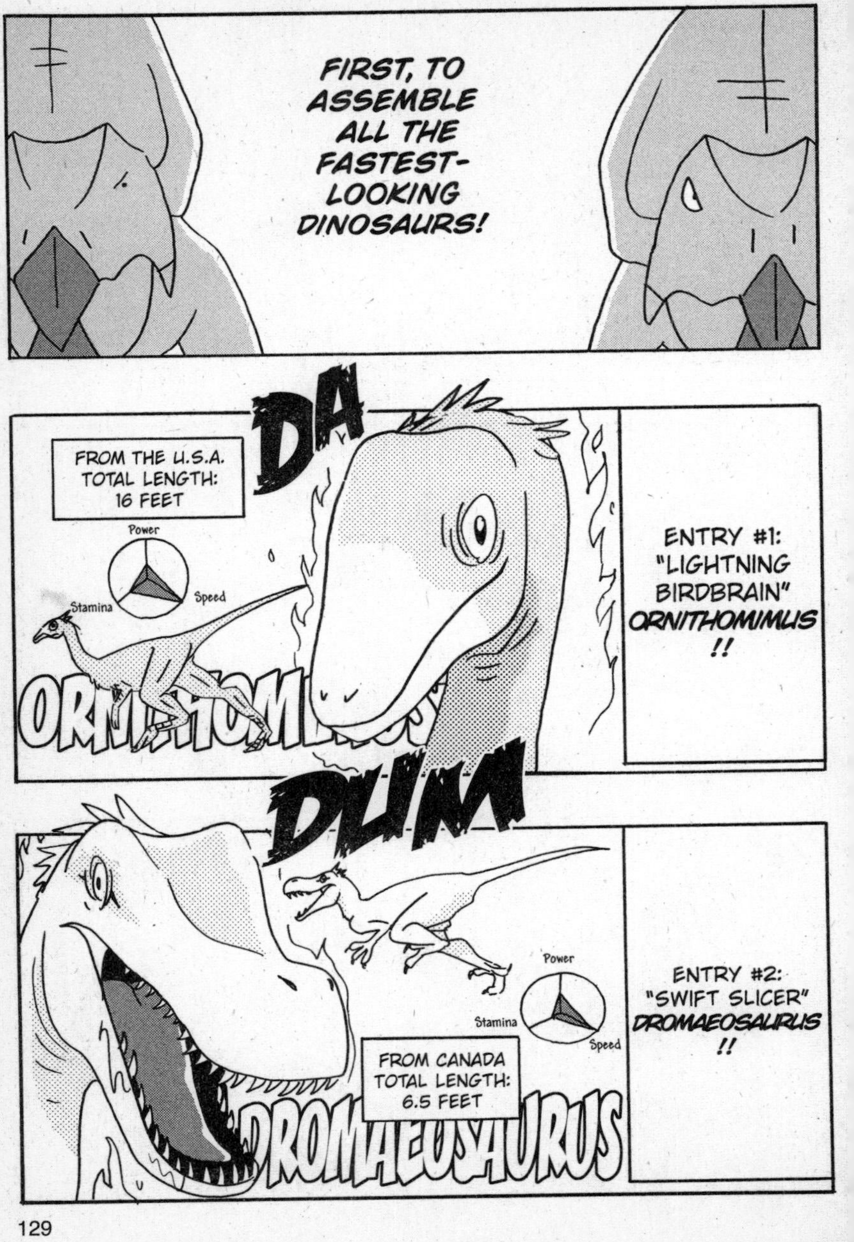
FIRST, TO ASSEMBLE ALL THE FASTEST-LOOKING DINOSAURS!
ENTRY #1: "LIGHTNING BIRDBRAIN" ORNITHOMIMUS !!
DA
FROM THE U.S.A. TOTAL LENGTH: 16 FEET
Power
Speed
Stamina
DUM
ENTRY #2: "SWIFT SLICER" DROMAEOSAURUS !!
Power
Stamina
Speed
FROM CANADA TOTAL LENGTH: 6.5 FEET
DROMAEOSAURUS

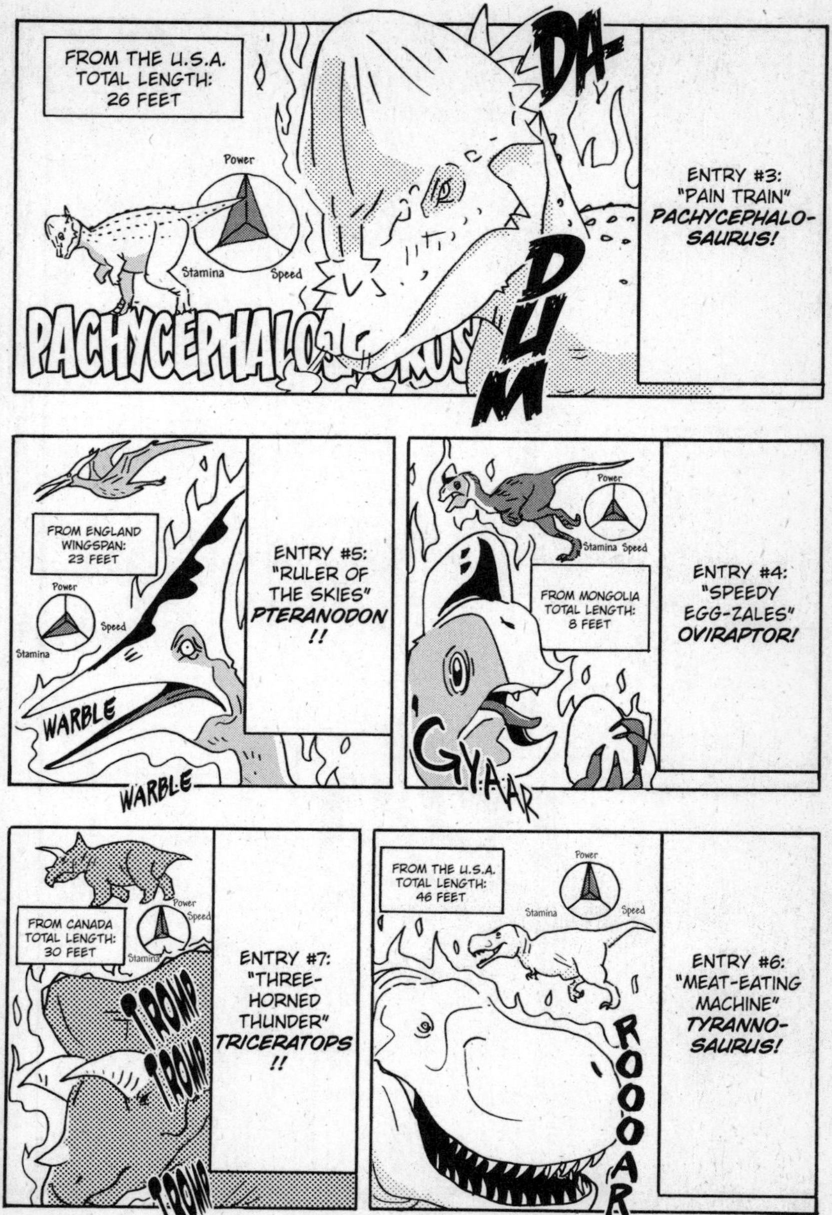

ENTRY #3: "PAIN TRAIN" PACHYCEPHALO-SAURUS!
DA-DUM
FROM THE U.S.A. TOTAL LENGTH: 26 FEET
Power
Stamina
Speed
PACHYCEPHALO
ENTRY #4: "SPEEDY EGG-ZALES" OVIRAPTOR!
Power
Stamina Speed
FROM MONGOLIA TOTAL LENGTH: 8 FEET
GYAAAR
ENTRY #5: "RULER OF THE SKIES" PTERANODON !!
FROM ENGLAND WINGSPAN: 23 FEET
Power
Speed
Stamina
WARBLE
WARBLE
ENTRY #6: "MEAT-EATING MACHINE" TYRANNO-SAURUS!
FROM THE U.S.A. TOTAL LENGTH: 46 FEET
Power
Stamina
Speed
ROOOAR
ENTRY #7: "THREE-HORNED THUNDER" TRICERATOPS !!
FROM CANADA TOTAL LENGTH: 30 FEET
Power
Speed
Stamina
TROMP
TROMP
TROMP

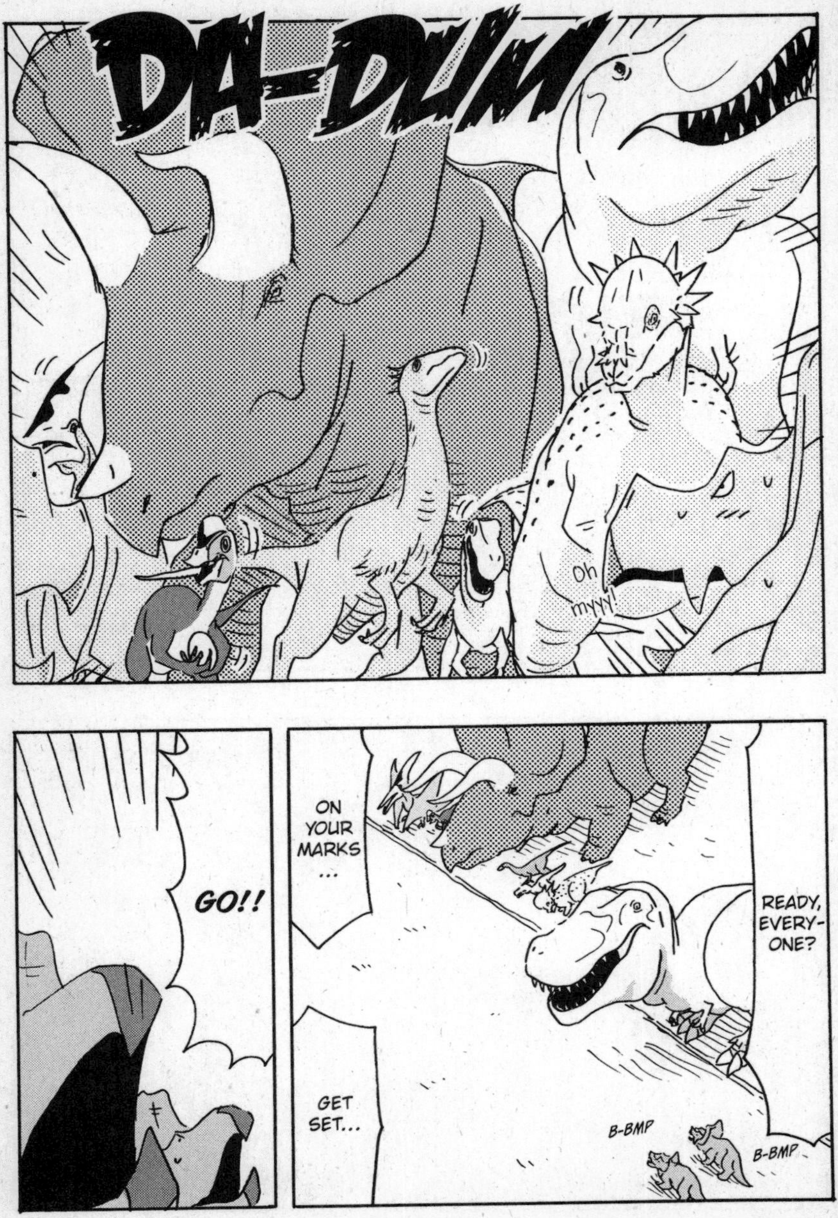
DA-DUM
Oh myyy!
READY, EVERY-ONE?
ON YOUR MARKS...
GET SET...
B-BMP
B-BMP
GO!!

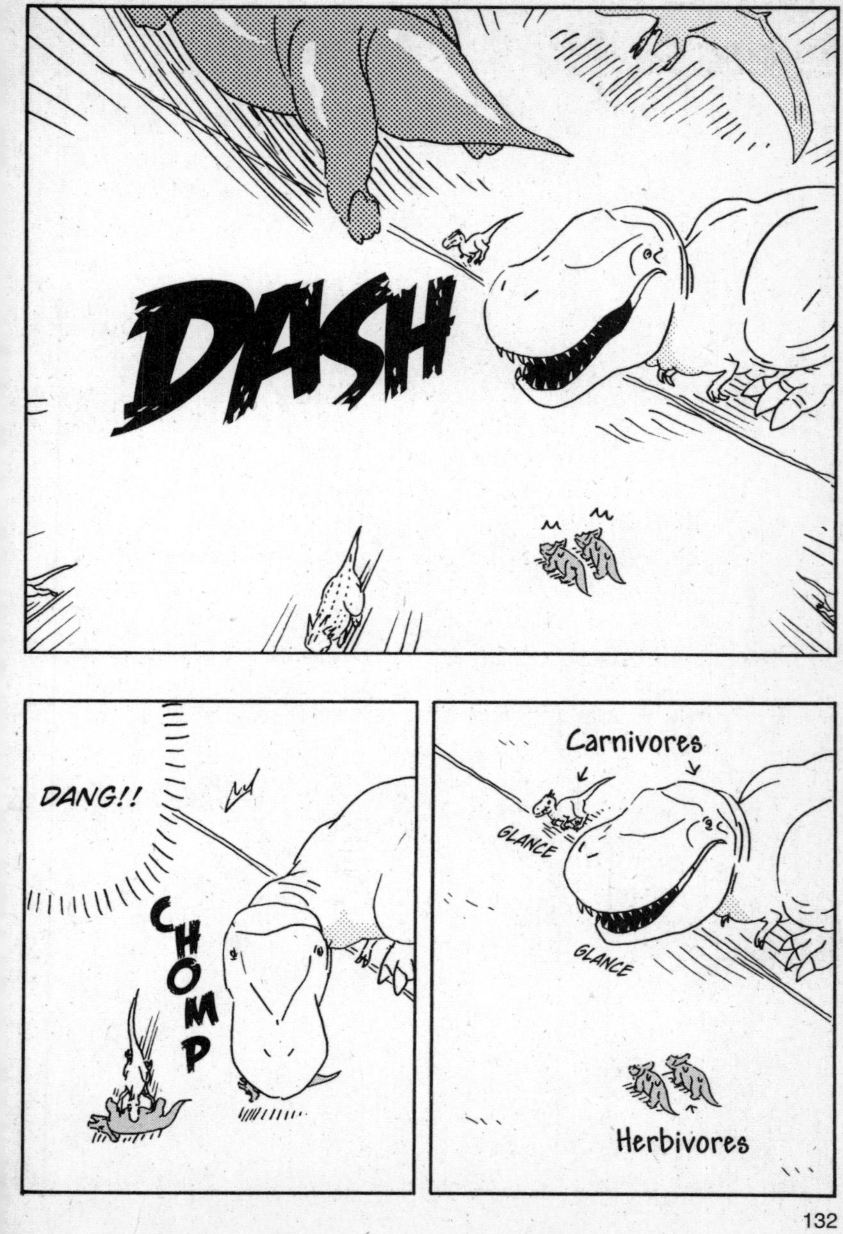
DASH
Carnivores
GLANCE
GLANCE
Herbivores
DANG!!
CHOMP

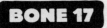

BONE 17

Paleozoic Era Solar Power

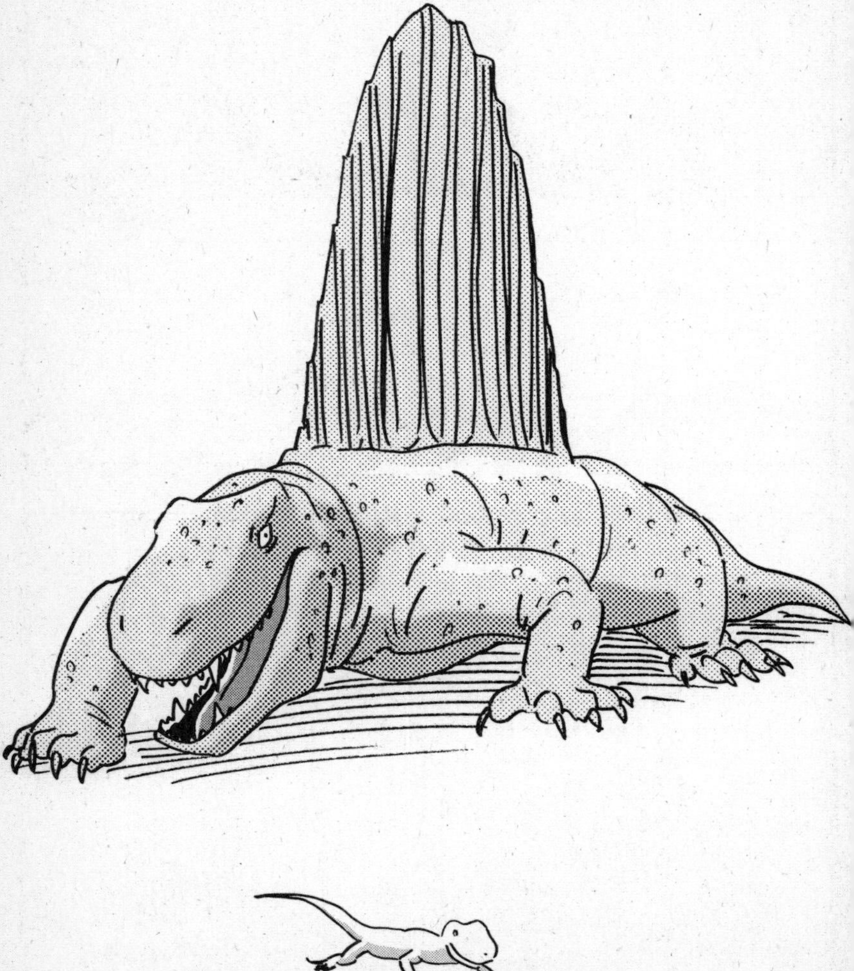

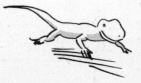

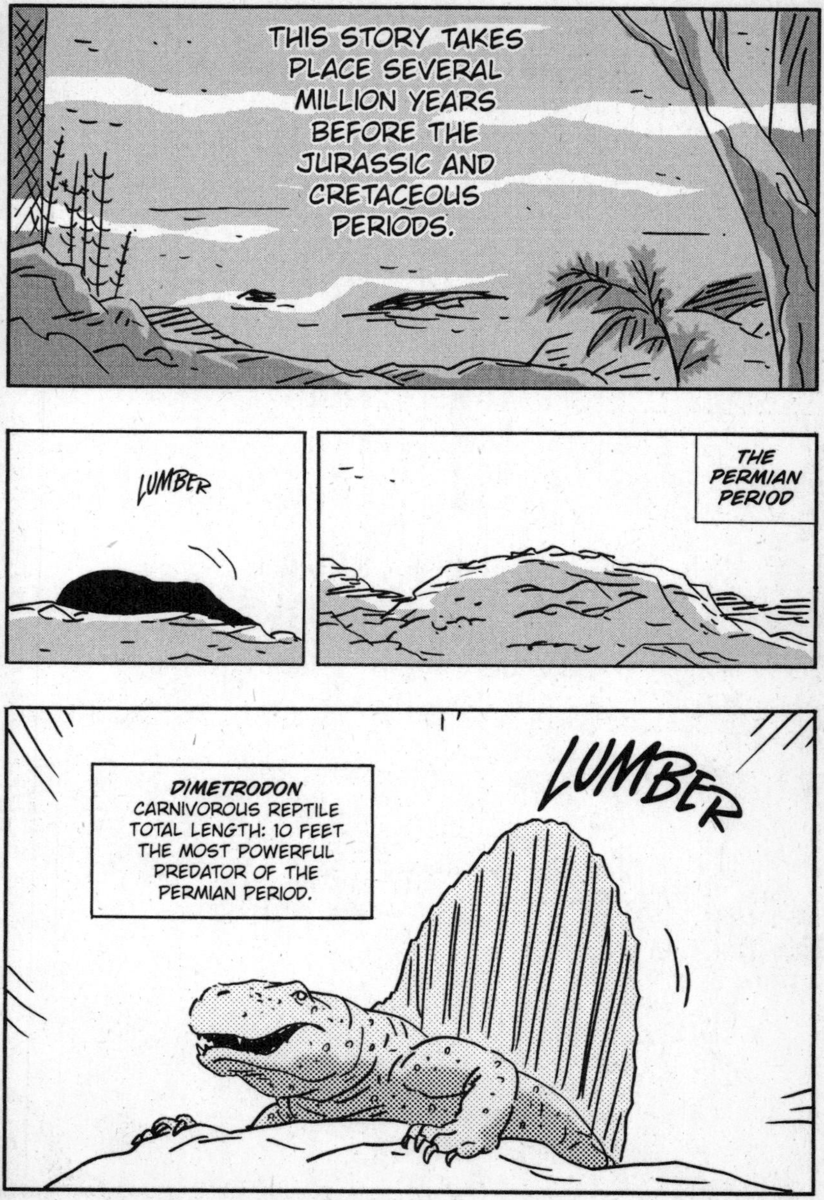
THIS STORY TAKES PLACE SEVERAL MILLION YEARS BEFORE THE JURASSIC AND CRETACEOUS PERIODS.
THE PERMIAN PERIOD
LUMBER
LUMBER
DIMETRODON
CARNIVOROUS REPTILE
TOTAL LENGTH: 10 FEET
THE MOST POWERFUL PREDATOR OF THE PERMIAN PERIOD.

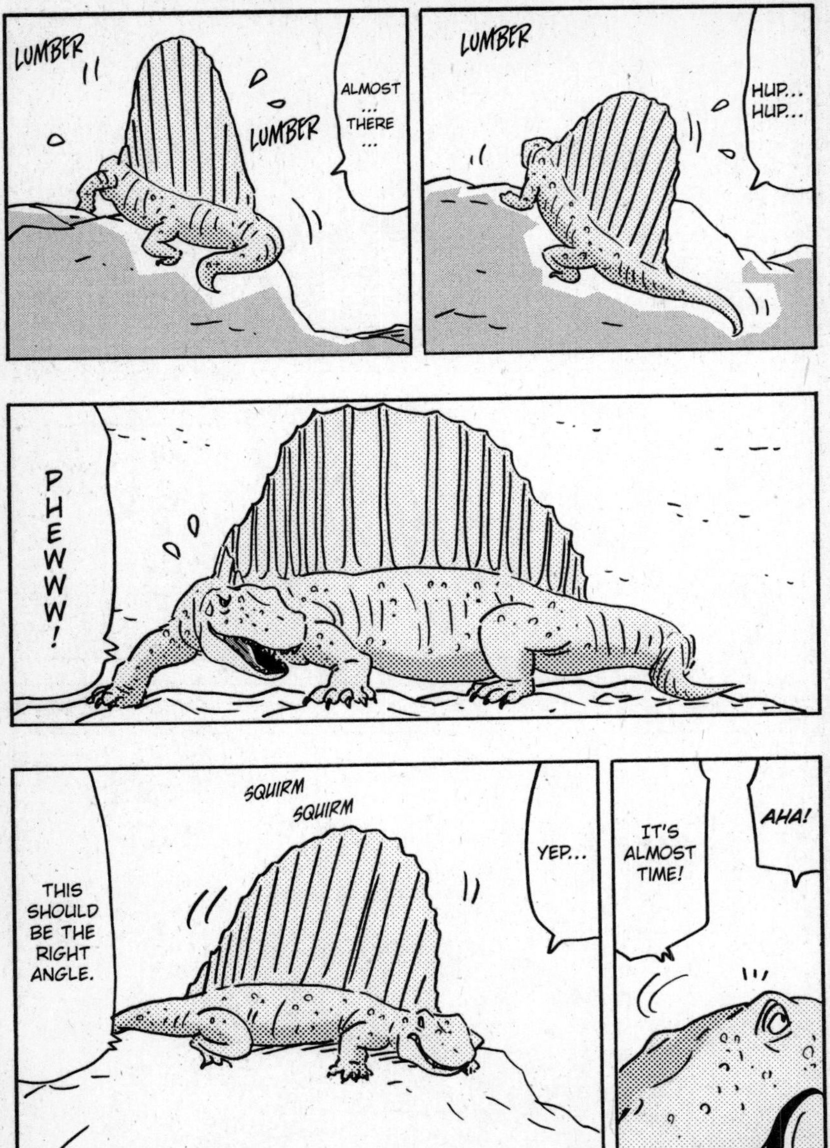
HUP... HUP...
LUMBER
ALMOST ... THERE ...
LUMBER
LUMBER
PHEWWW!
AHA!
IT'S ALMOST TIME!
YEP...
SQUIRM
SQUIRM
THIS SHOULD BE THE RIGHT ANGLE.

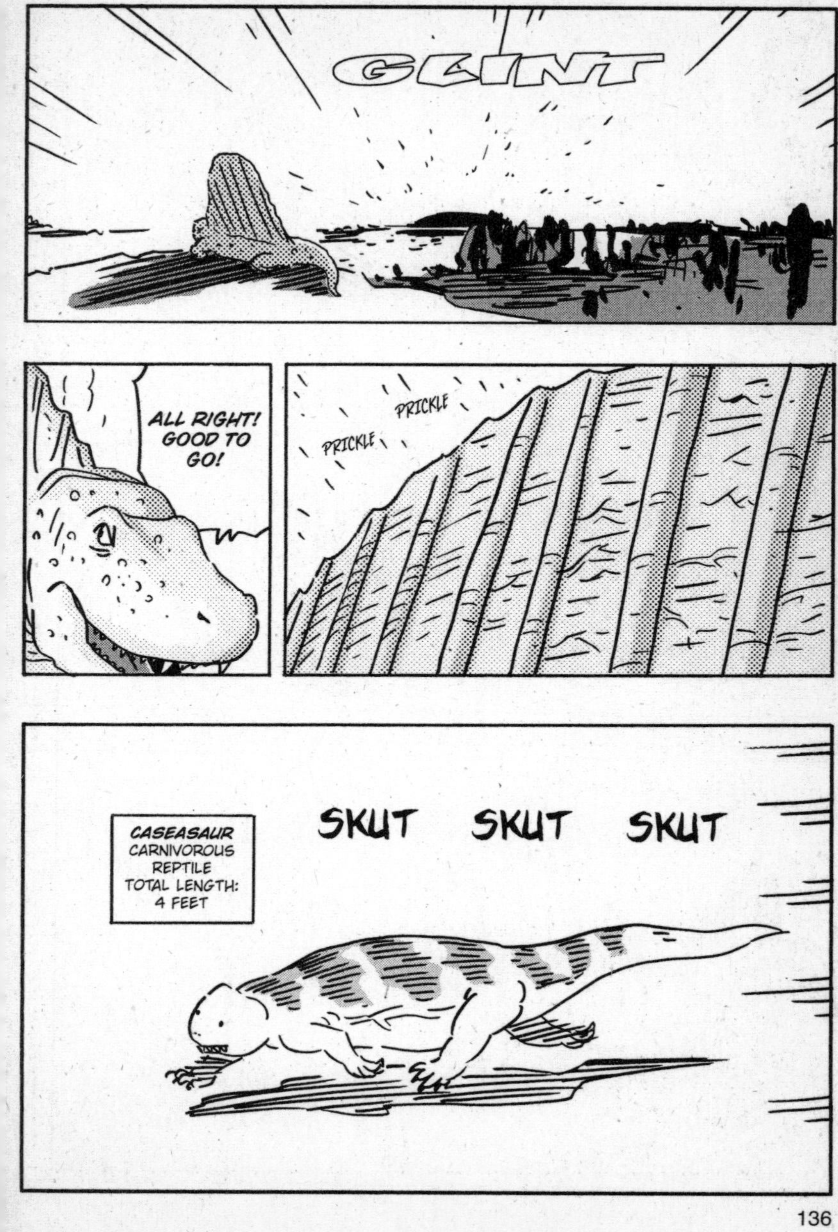
GLINT
PRICKLE
PRICKLE
ALL RIGHT! GOOD TO GO!
SKUT SKUT SKUT
CASEASAUR
CARNIVOROUS REPTILE
TOTAL LENGTH: 4 FEET

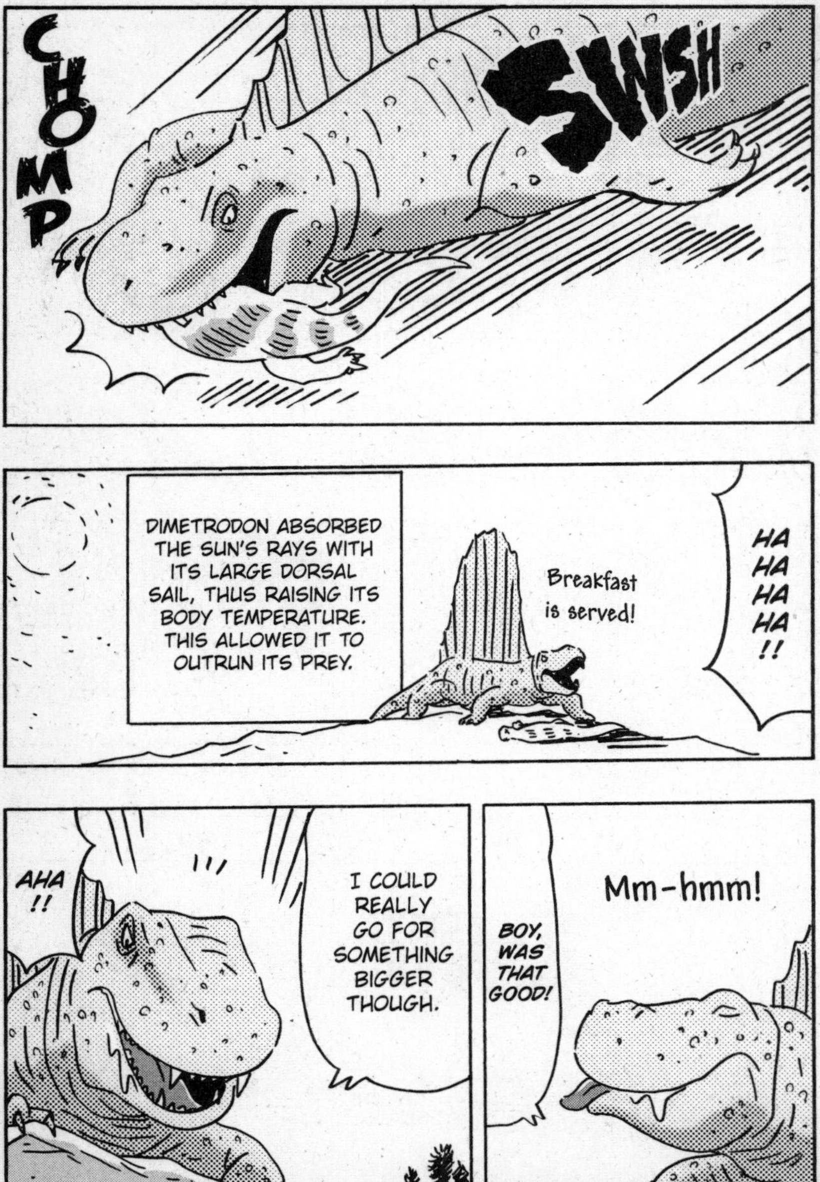
SWSH
CHOMP
HA HA HA HA!!
Breakfast is served!
DIMETRODON ABSORBED THE SUN'S RAYS WITH ITS LARGE DORSAL SAIL, THUS RAISING ITS BODY TEMPERATURE. THIS ALLOWED IT TO OUTRUN ITS PREY.
Mm-hmm!
BOY, WAS THAT GOOD!
I COULD REALLY GO FOR SOMETHING BIGGER THOUGH.
AHA!!

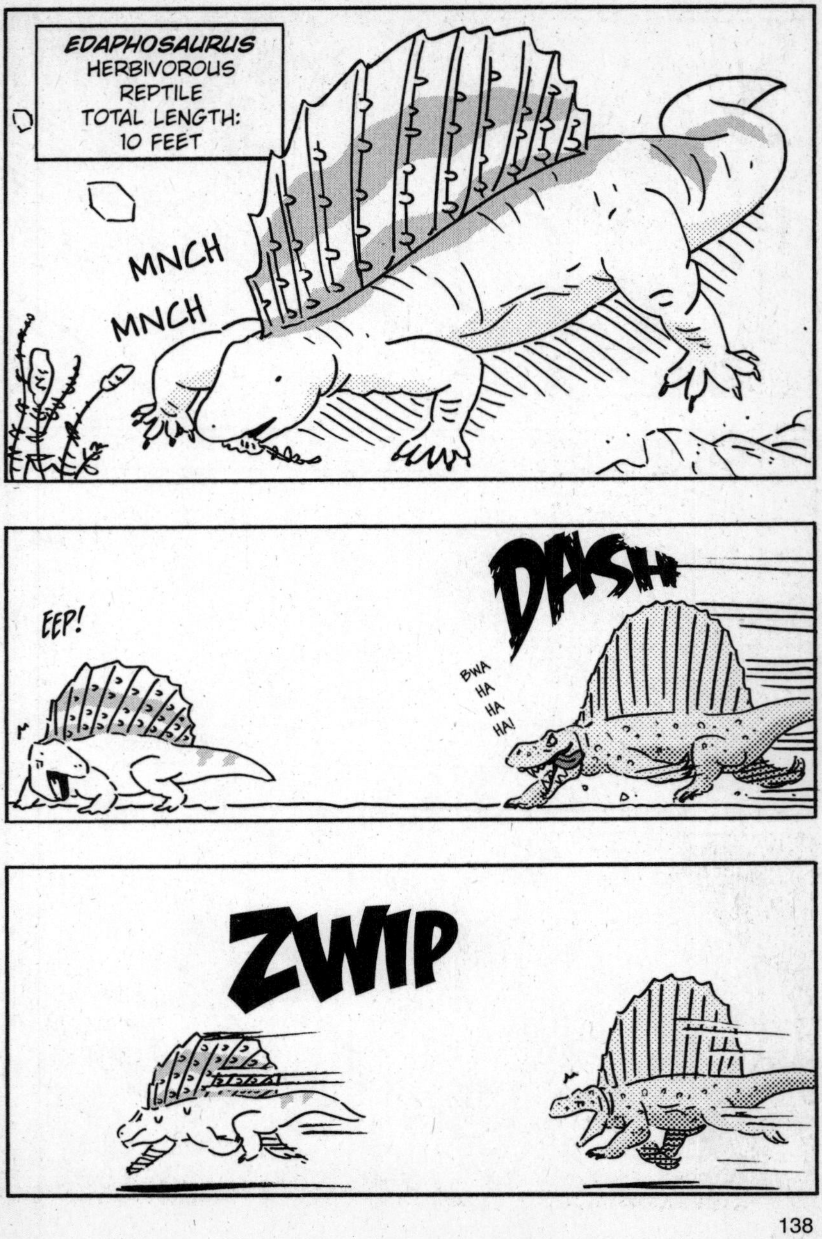
EDAPHOSAURUS
HERBIVOROUS
REPTILE
TOTAL LENGTH:
10 FEET
MNCH
MNCH
DASH
BWA HA HA HA!
EEP!
ZWIP

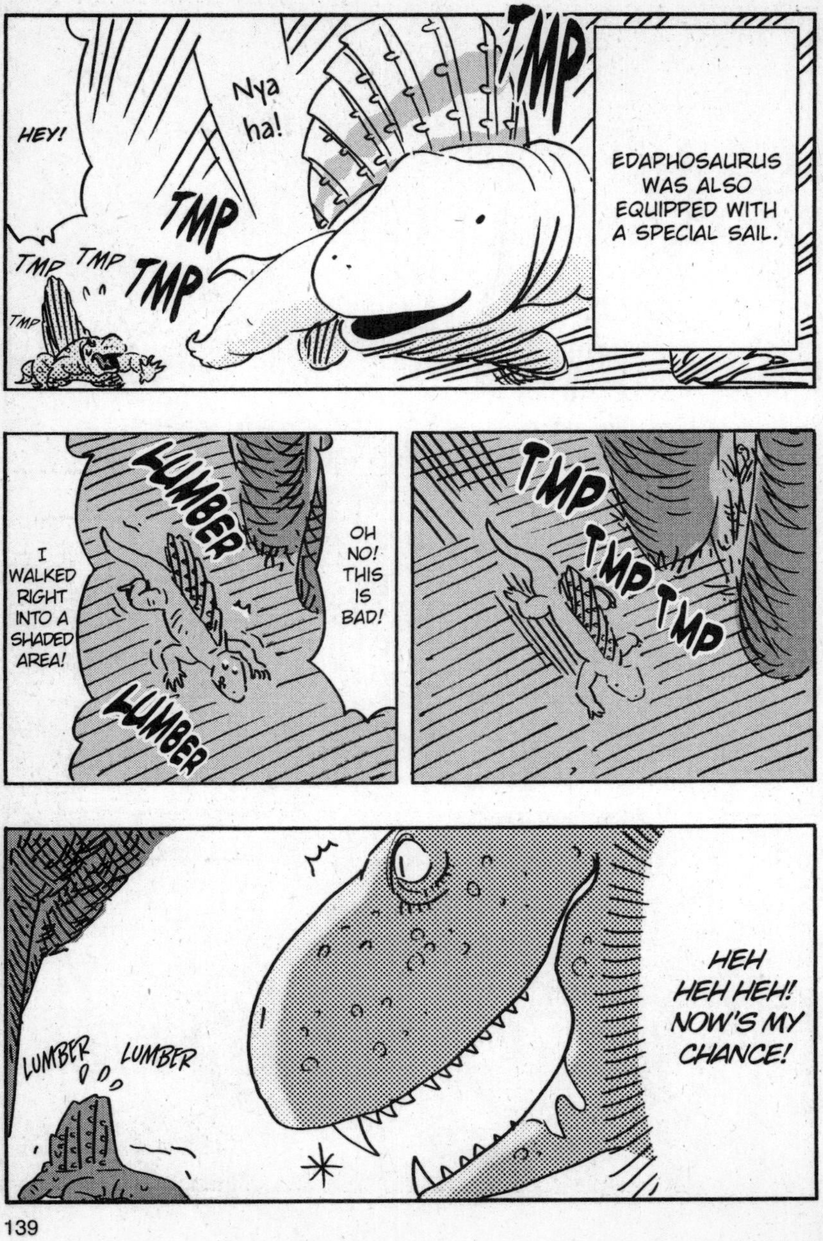
EDAPHOSAURUS WAS ALSO EQUIPPED WITH A SPECIAL SAIL.
TMP
Nya ha!
HEY!
TMP
TMP
TMP
TMP
TMP
TMP
TMP
TMP
TMP
OH NO! THIS IS BAD!
LUMBER
I WALKED RIGHT INTO A SHADED AREA!
LUMBER
HEH HEH HEH! NOW'S MY CHANCE!
LUMBER
LUMBER

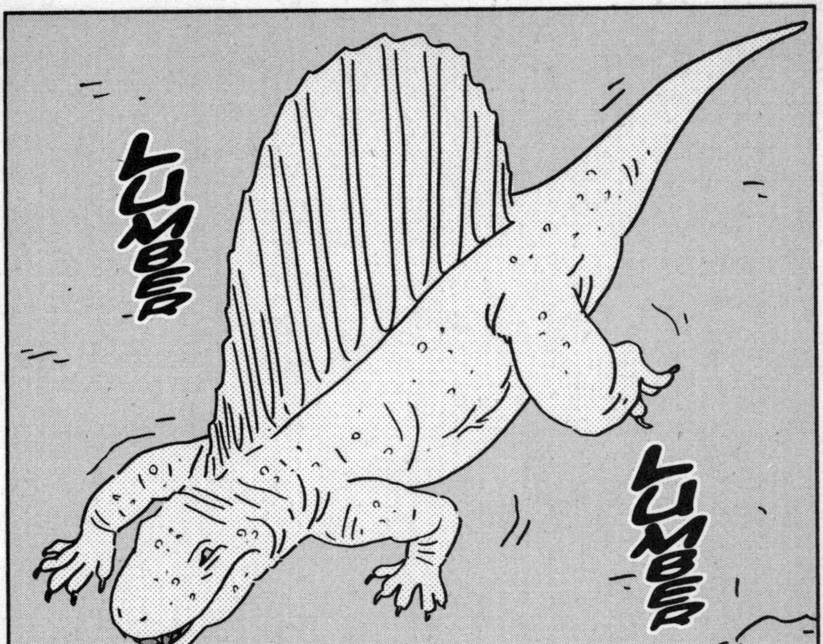
LUMBER
LUMBER

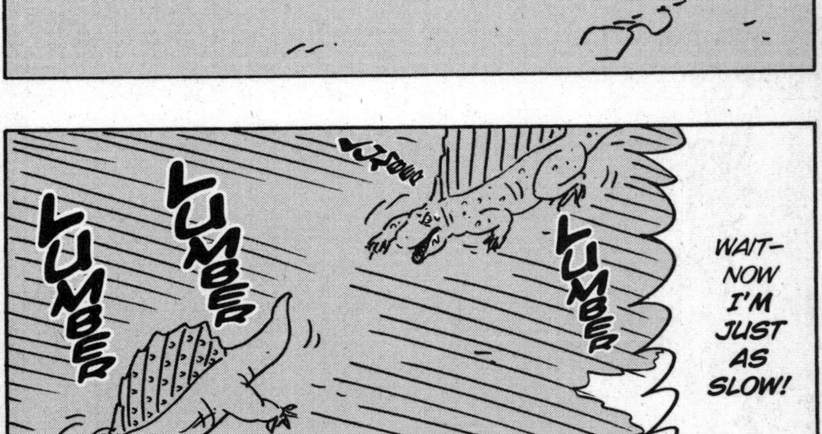
WAIT—NOW I'M JUST AS SLOW!
LUMBER
LUMBER
LUMBER

BONE 18

Hook, Line and Neck

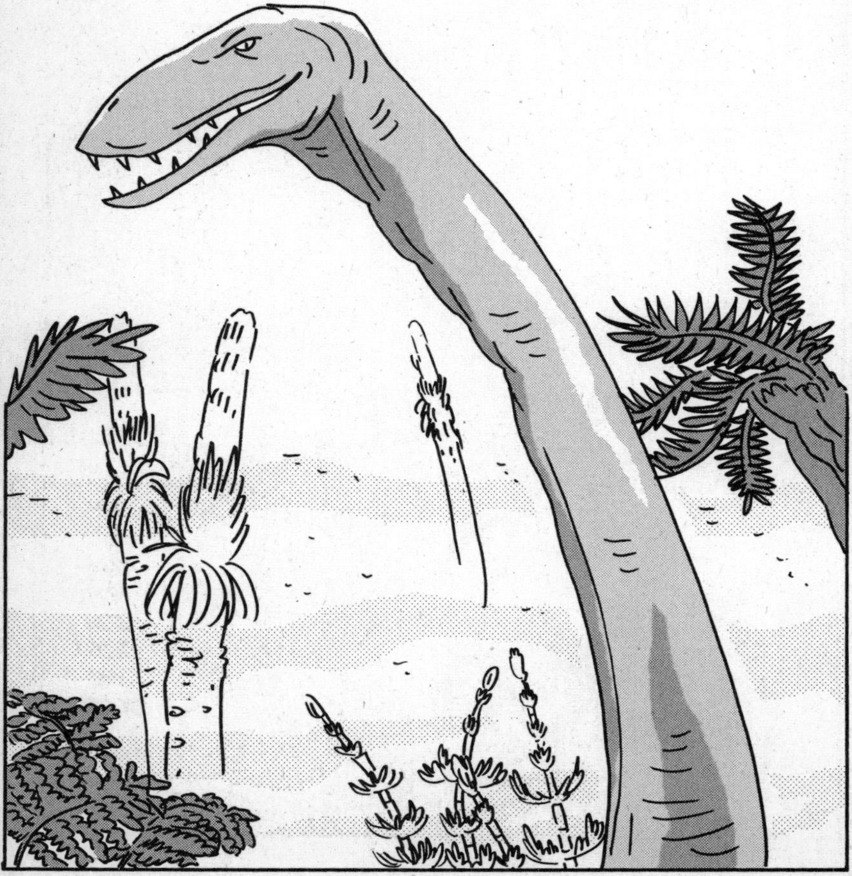

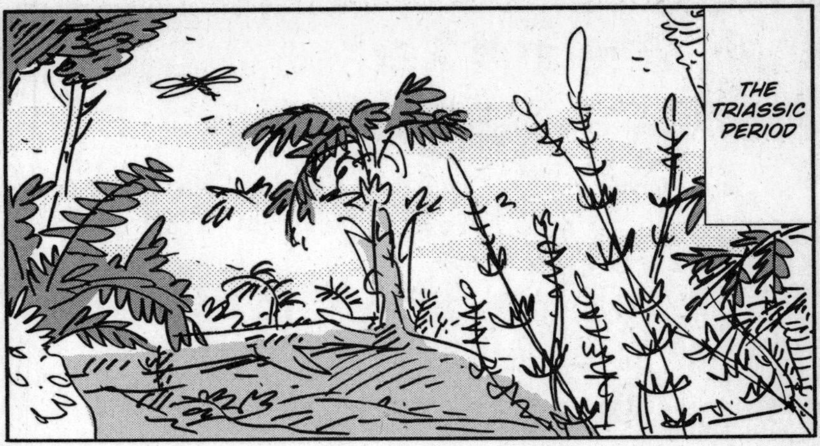
THE TRIASSIC PERIOD

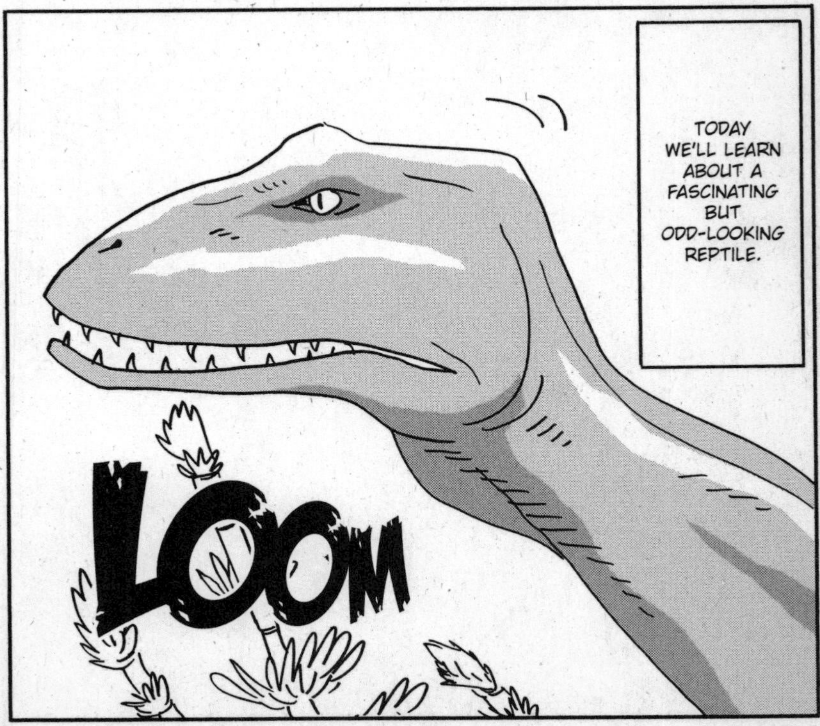
TODAY WE'LL LEARN ABOUT A FASCINATING BUT ODD-LOOKING REPTILE.
LOOM

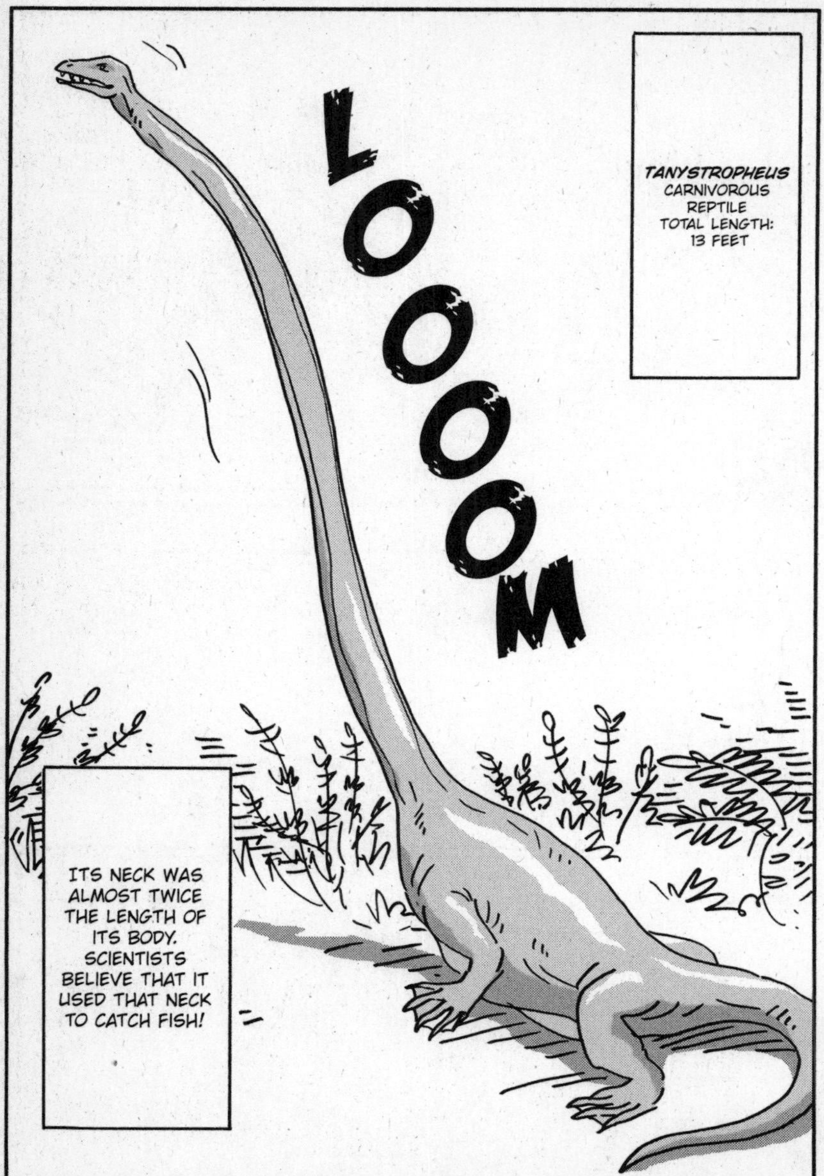
TANYSTROPHEUS
CARNIVOROUS REPTILE
TOTAL LENGTH: 13 FEET
LOOOOM
ITS NECK WAS ALMOST TWICE THE LENGTH OF ITS BODY. SCIENTISTS BELIEVE THAT IT USED THAT NECK TO CATCH FISH!

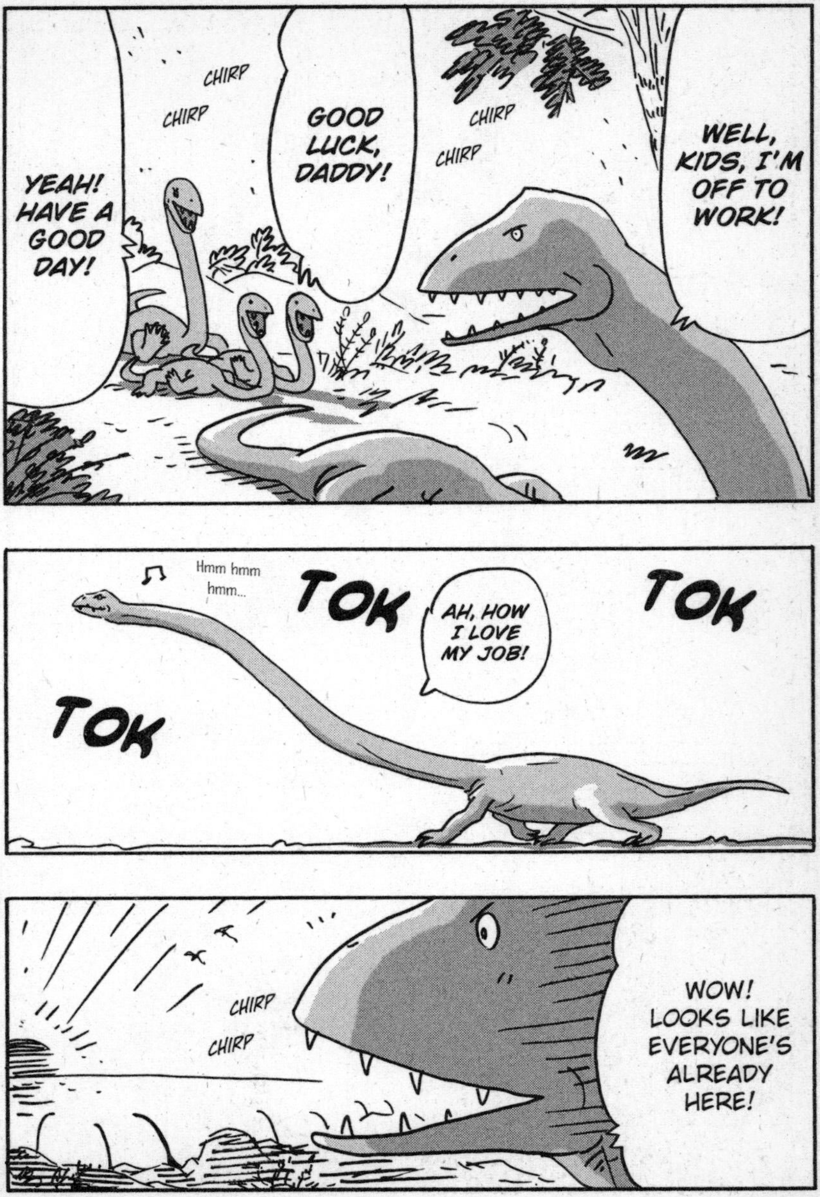
WELL, KIDS, I'M OFF TO WORK!
CHIRP
CHIRP
GOOD LUCK, DADDY!
CHIRP
CHIRP
YEAH! HAVE A GOOD DAY!
TOK
AH, HOW I LOVE MY JOB!
TOK
Hmm hmm hmm...
TOK
WOW! LOOKS LIKE EVERYONE'S ALREADY HERE!
CHIRP
CHIRP

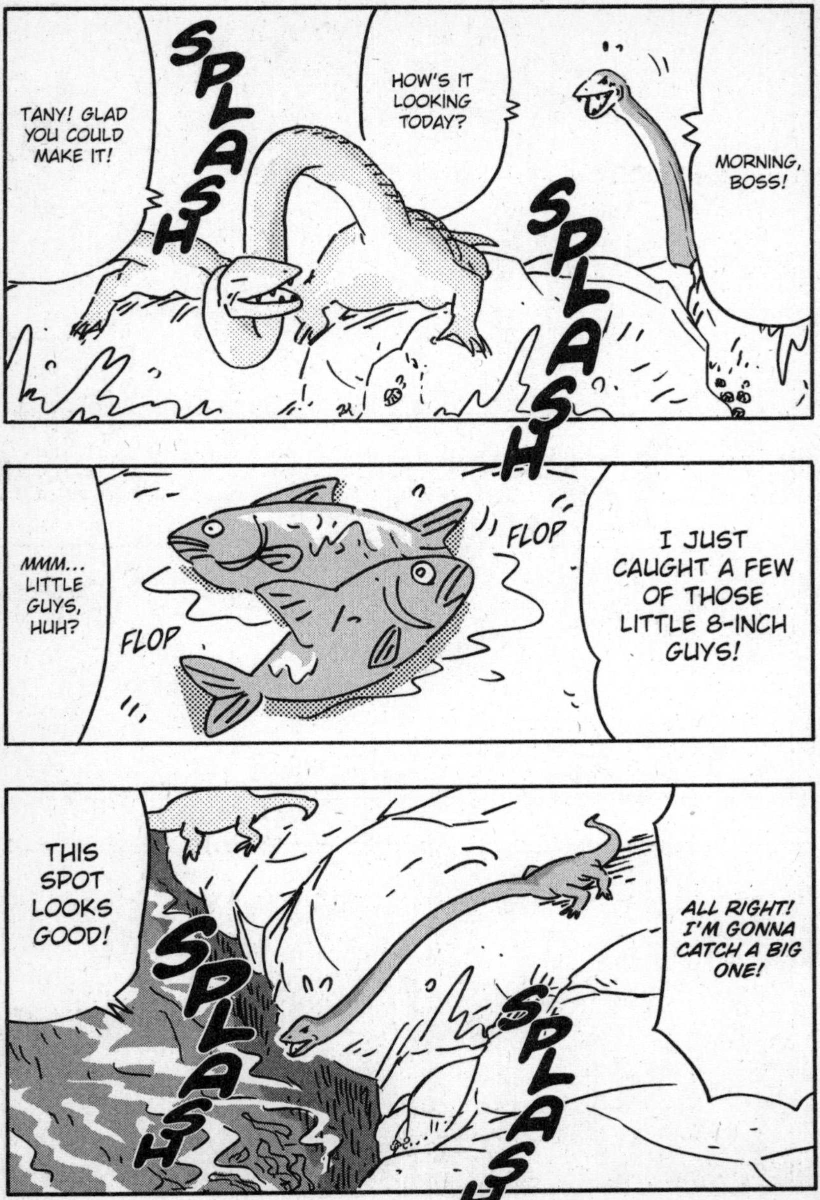
MORNING, BOSS!
SPLASH
HOW'S IT LOOKING TODAY?
SPLASH
TANY! GLAD YOU COULD MAKE IT!
I JUST CAUGHT A FEW OF THOSE LITTLE 8-INCH GUYS!
FLOP
FLOP
MMM... LITTLE GUYS, HUH?
ALL RIGHT! I'M GONNA CATCH A BIG ONE!
SPLASH
SPLASH
THIS SPOT LOOKS GOOD!

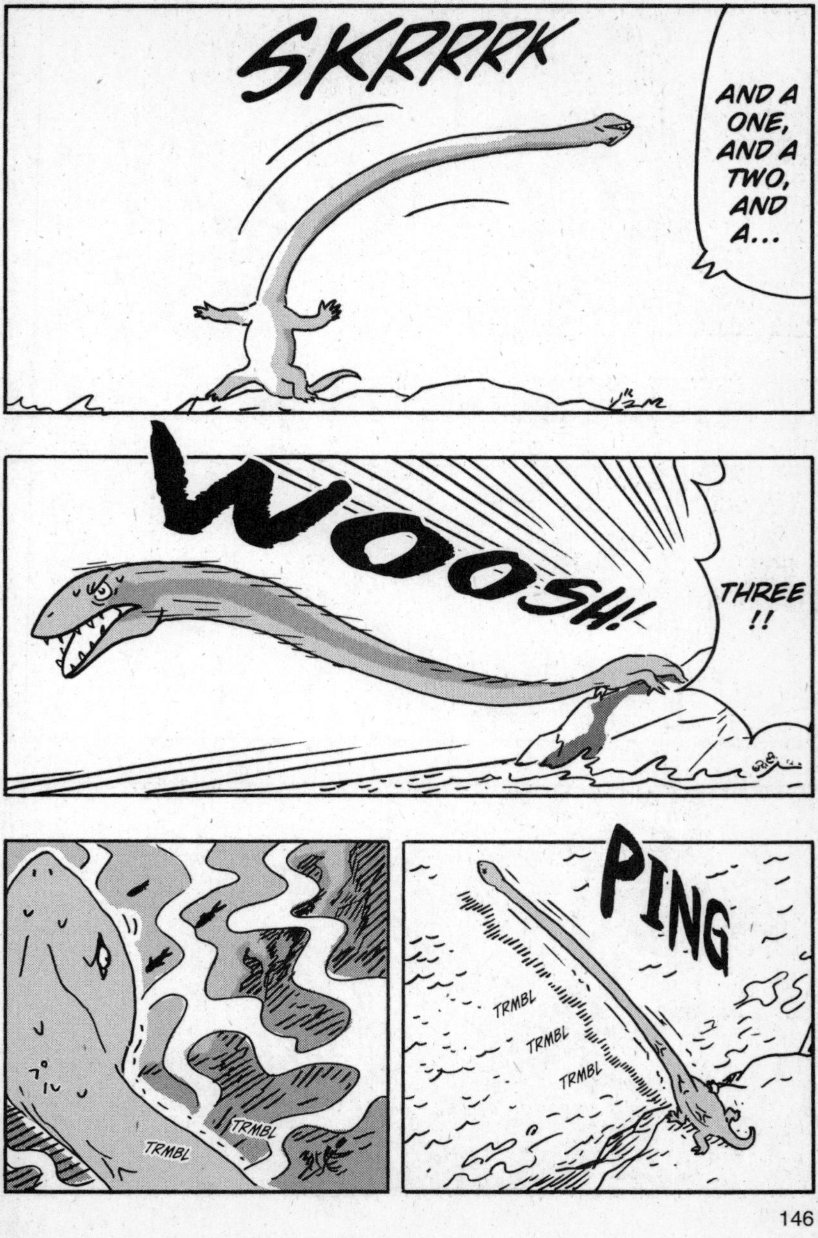
AND A ONE, AND A TWO, AND A...
SKRRRK
THREE !!
WOOSH!
PING
TRMBL
TRMBL
TRMBL
TRMBL
TRMBL

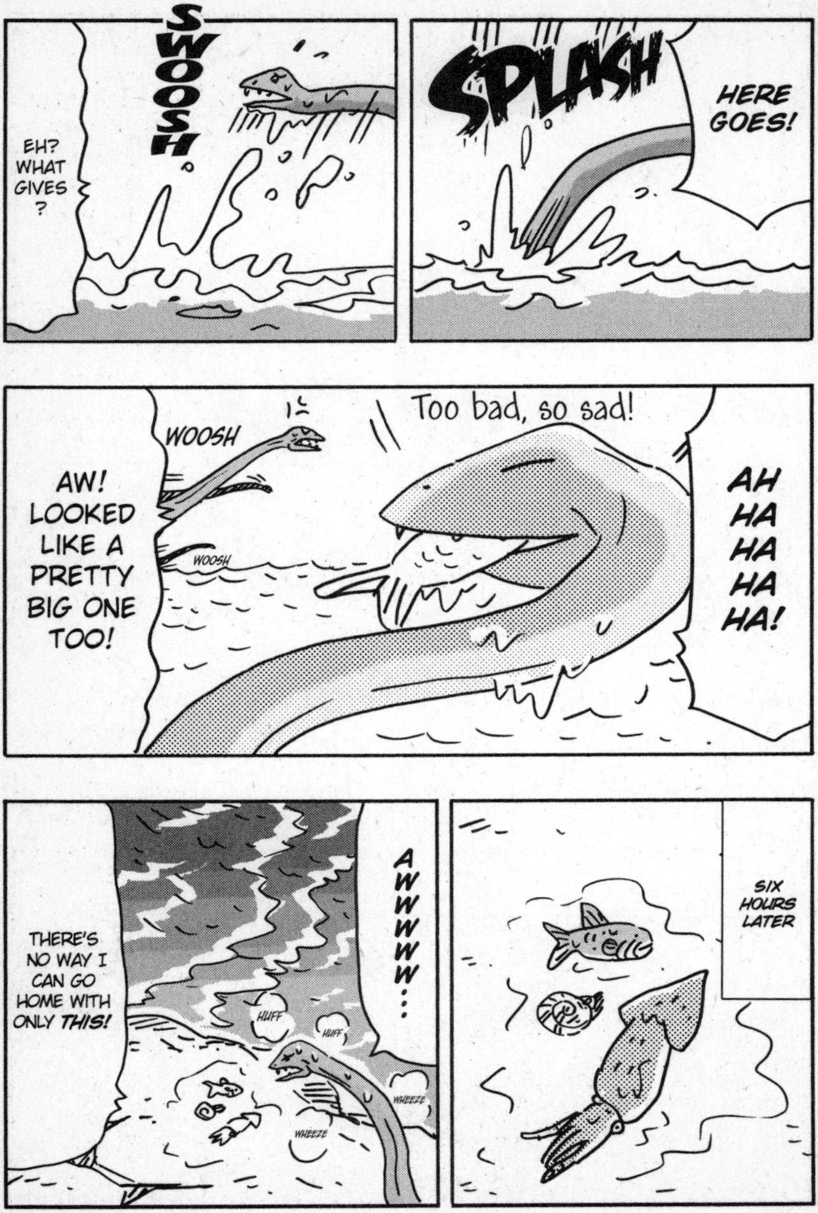
SPLASH
HERE GOES!
SWOOSH
EH? WHAT GIVES?
AH HA HA HA HA!
Too bad, so sad!
WOOSH
AW! LOOKED LIKE A PRETTY BIG ONE TOO!
WOOSH
SIX HOURS LATER
AWWWWWW...
HUFF
HUFF
WHEEZE
WHEEZE
THERE'S NO WAY I CAN GO HOME WITH ONLY THIS!

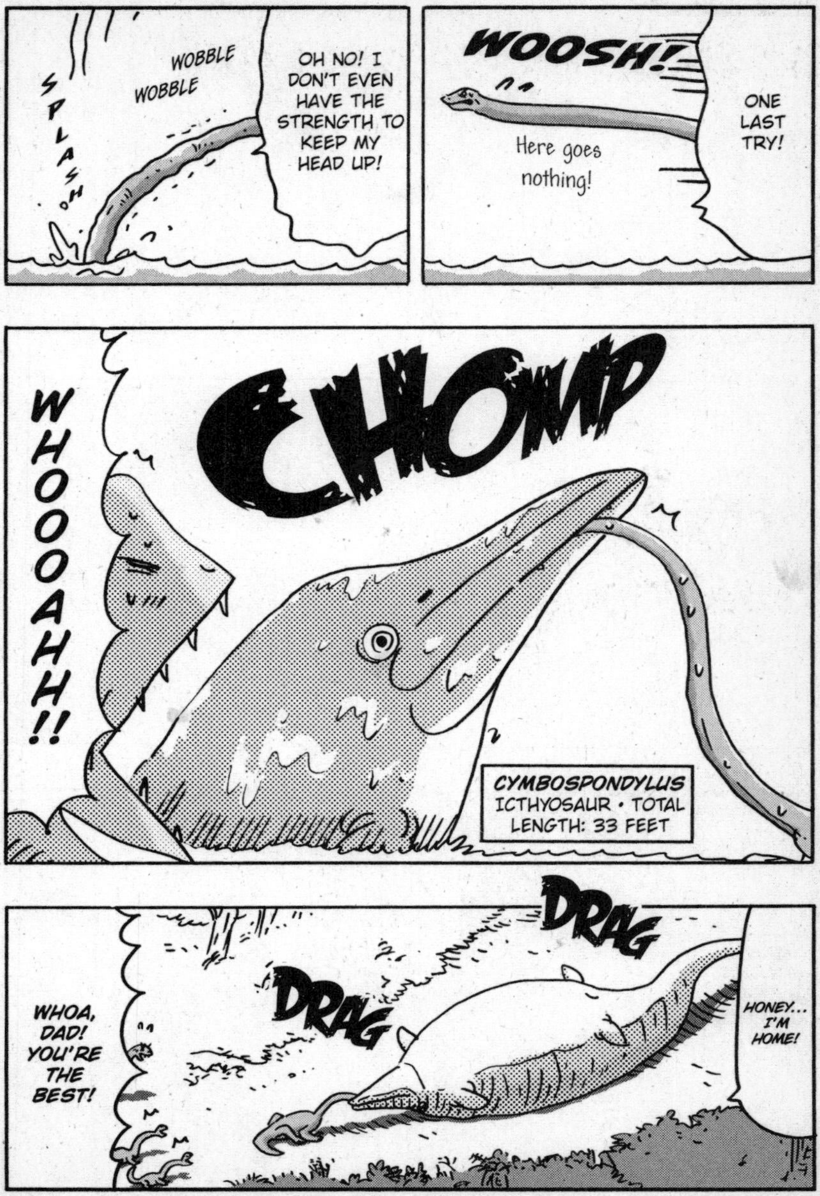
ONE LAST TRY!
WOOSH!
Here goes nothing!
OH NO! I DON'T EVEN HAVE THE STRENGTH TO KEEP MY HEAD UP!
WOBBLE
WOBBLE
SPLASH
CHOMP
WHOOOOAHH!!
CYMBOSPONDYLUS
ICTHYOSAUR • TOTAL LENGTH: 33 FEET
HONEY... I'M HOME!
DRAG
DRAG
WHOA, DAD! YOU'RE THE BEST!

BONE 19

The Three Triceratops Gruff

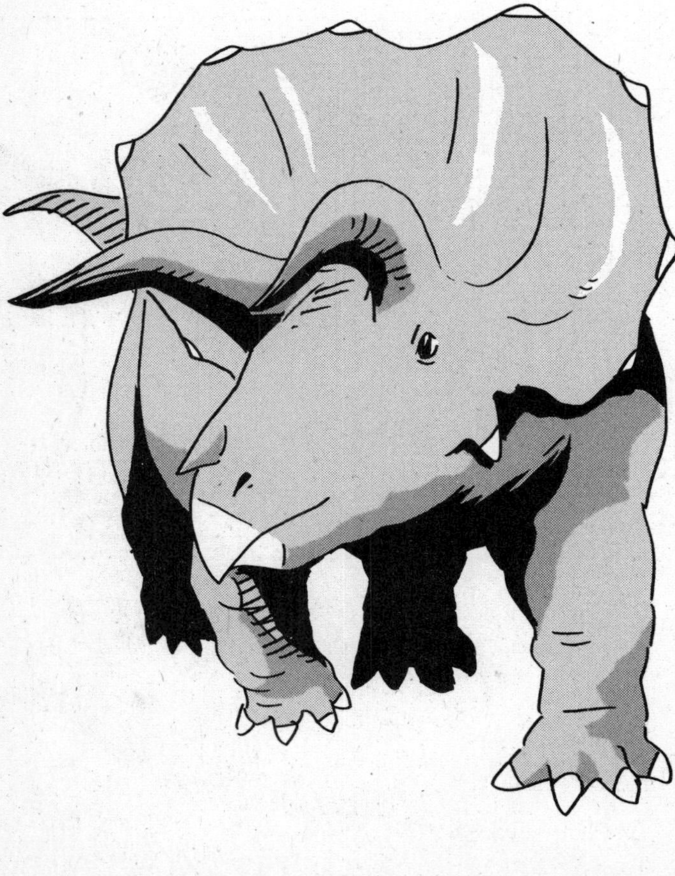

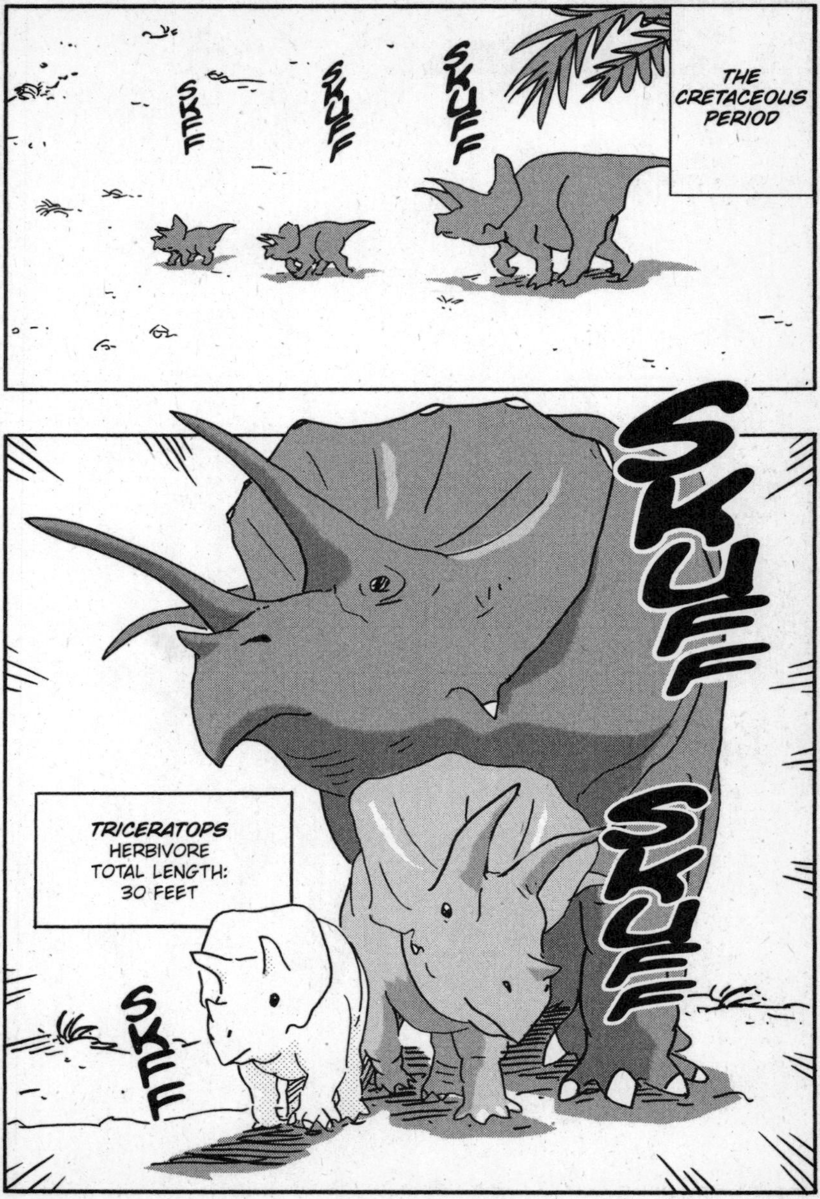
THE CRETACEOUS PERIOD
SKUFF
SKUFF
SKFF
SKUFF
SKUFF
TRICERATOPS
HERBIVORE
TOTAL LENGTH: 30 FEET
SKFF

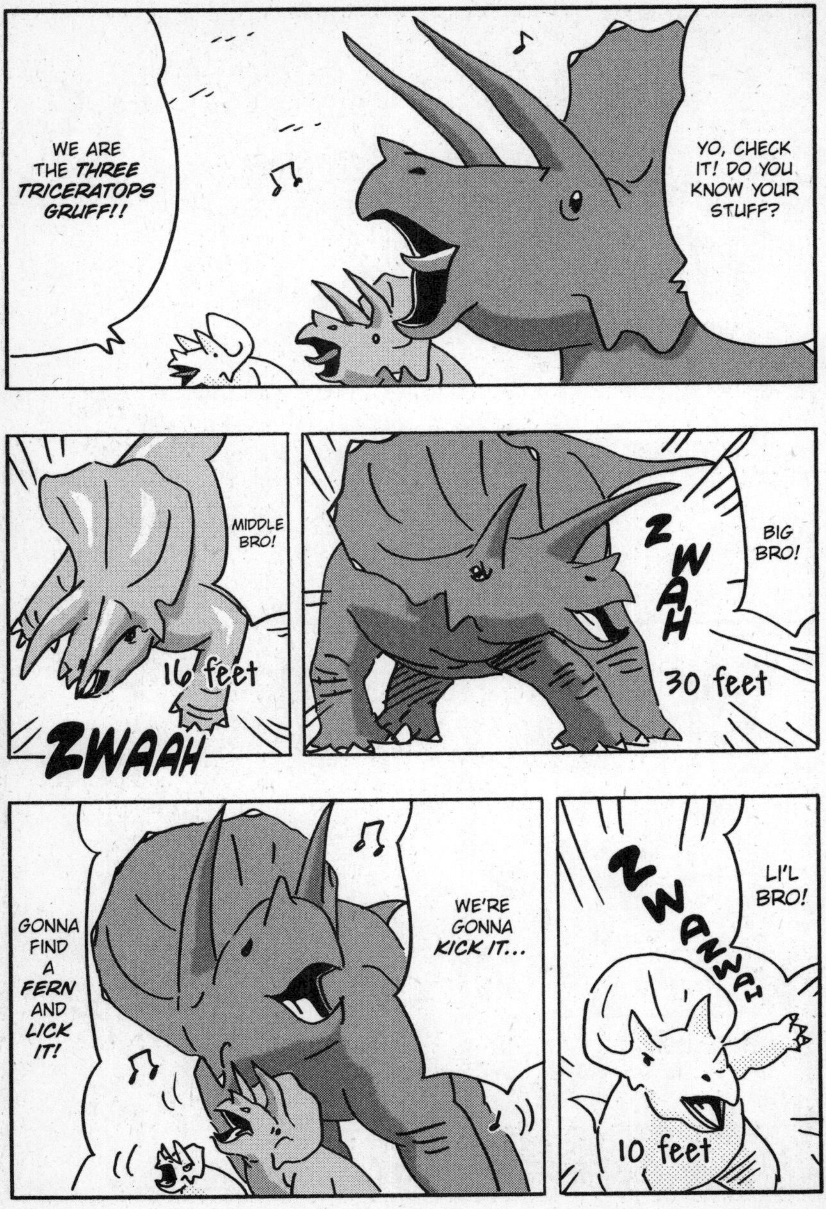

YO, CHECK IT! DO YOU KNOW YOUR STUFF?
WE ARE THE *THREE TRICERATOPS GRUFF!!*
BIG BRO!
ZWAAH
30 feet
MIDDLE BRO!
16 feet
ZWAAH
LI'L BRO!
ZWANWAH
10 feet
WE'RE GONNA *KICK IT...*
GONNA FIND A *FERN* AND *LICK IT!*

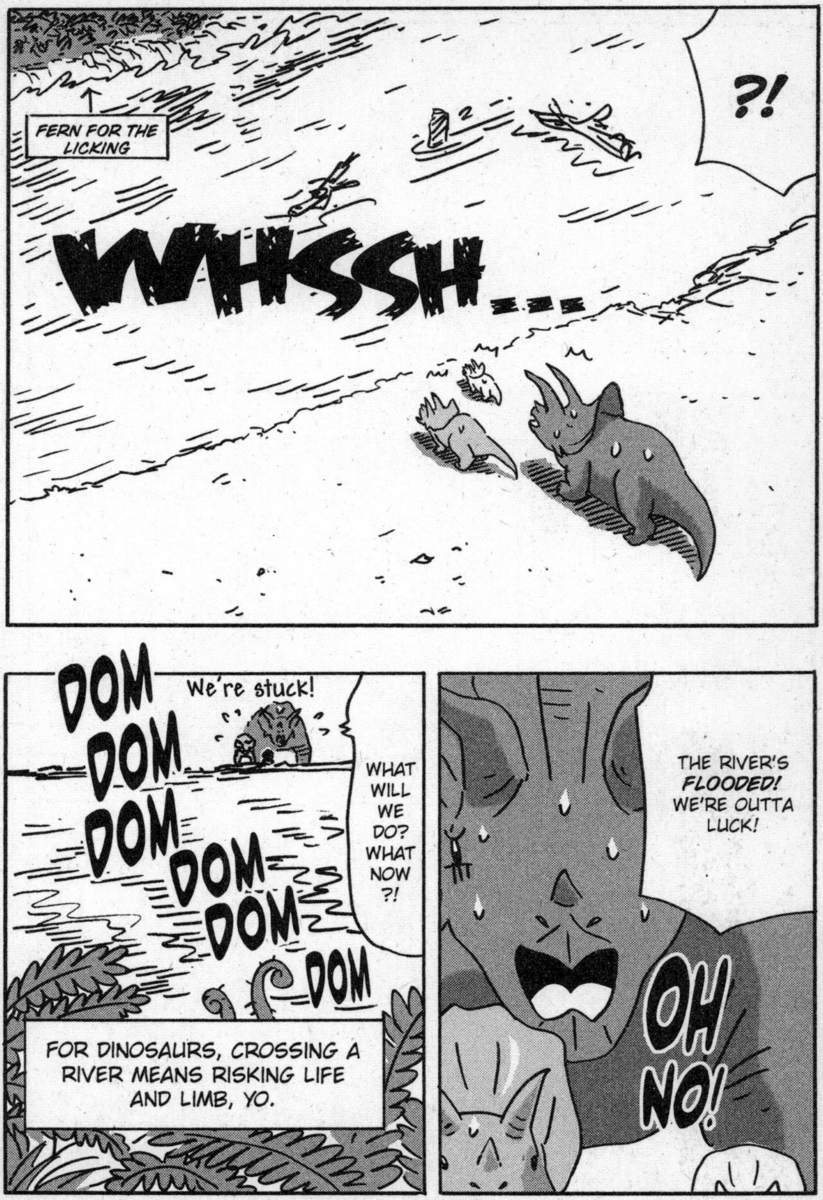
?!
FERN FOR THE LICKING
WHSSH...
THE RIVER'S *FLOODED!* WE'RE OUTTA LUCK!
OH NO!
WHAT WILL WE DO? WHAT NOW ?!
We're stuck!
DOM DOM DOM DOM DOM DOM
FOR DINOSAURS, CROSSING A RIVER MEANS RISKING LIFE AND LIMB, YO.

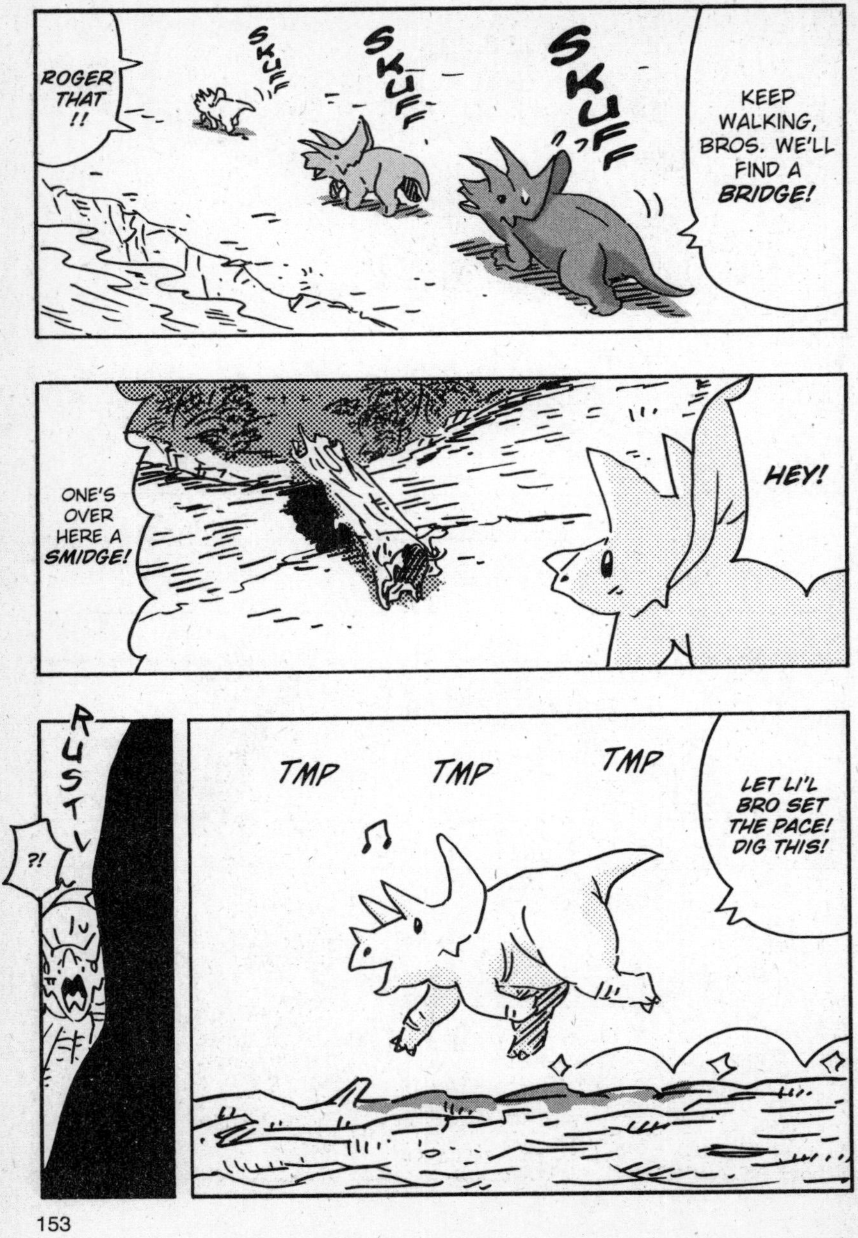

KEEP WALKING, BROS. WE'LL FIND A BRIDGE!
SKUFF
SKUFF
SKUFF
ROGER THAT!!
HEY!
ONE'S OVER HERE A SMIDGE!
LET LI'L BRO SET THE PACE! DIG THIS!
TMP
TMP
TMP
RUSTL
?!

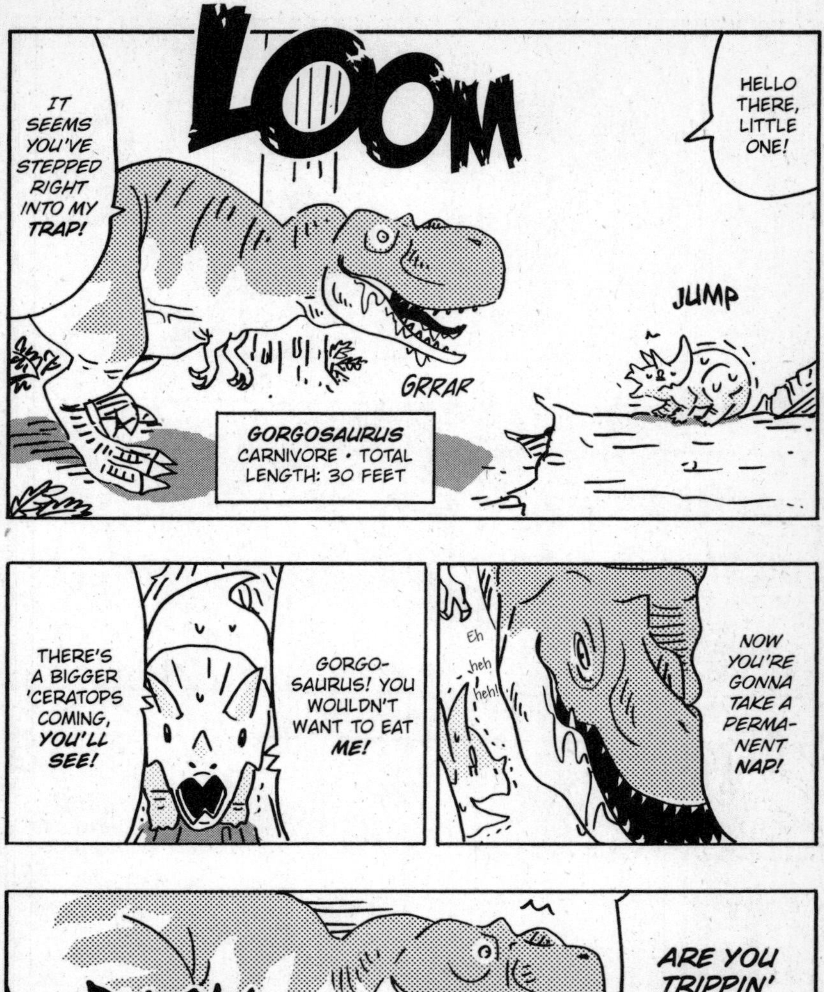
HELLO THERE, LITTLE ONE!
JUMP
LOOM
IT SEEMS YOU'VE STEPPED RIGHT INTO MY TRAP!
GRRAR
GORGOSAURUS CARNIVORE • TOTAL LENGTH: 30 FEET
NOW YOU'RE GONNA TAKE A PERMA-NENT NAP!
Eh heh heh!
GORGO-SAURUS! YOU WOULDN'T WANT TO EAT ME!
THERE'S A BIGGER 'CERATOPS COMING, YOU'LL SEE!
ARE YOU TRIPPIN' ?!!
DASH!

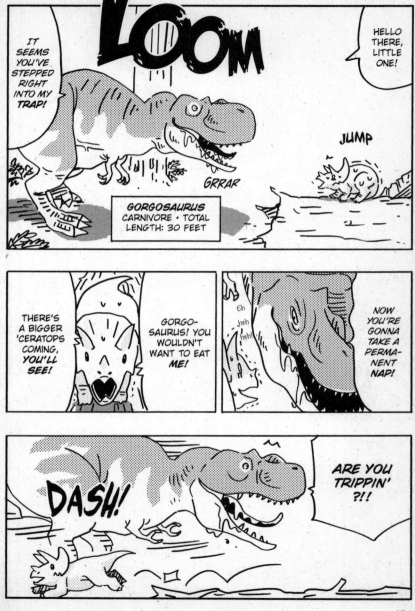

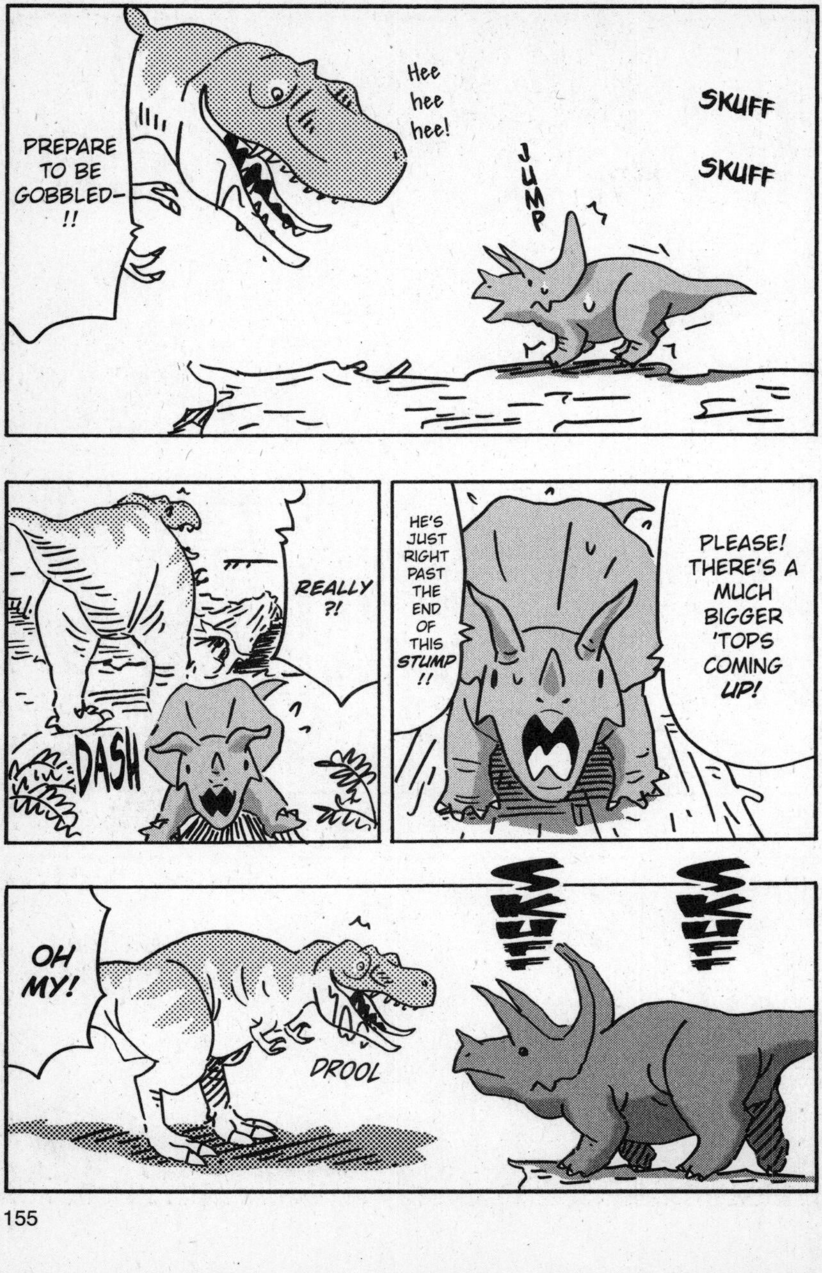
SKUFF
SKUFF
JUMP
Hee hee hee!
PREPARE TO BE GOBBLED-!!
PLEASE! THERE'S A MUCH BIGGER 'TOPS COMING UP!
HE'S JUST RIGHT PAST THE END OF THIS STUMP!!
REALLY?!
DASH
SKUFF
SKUFF
DROOL
OH MY!

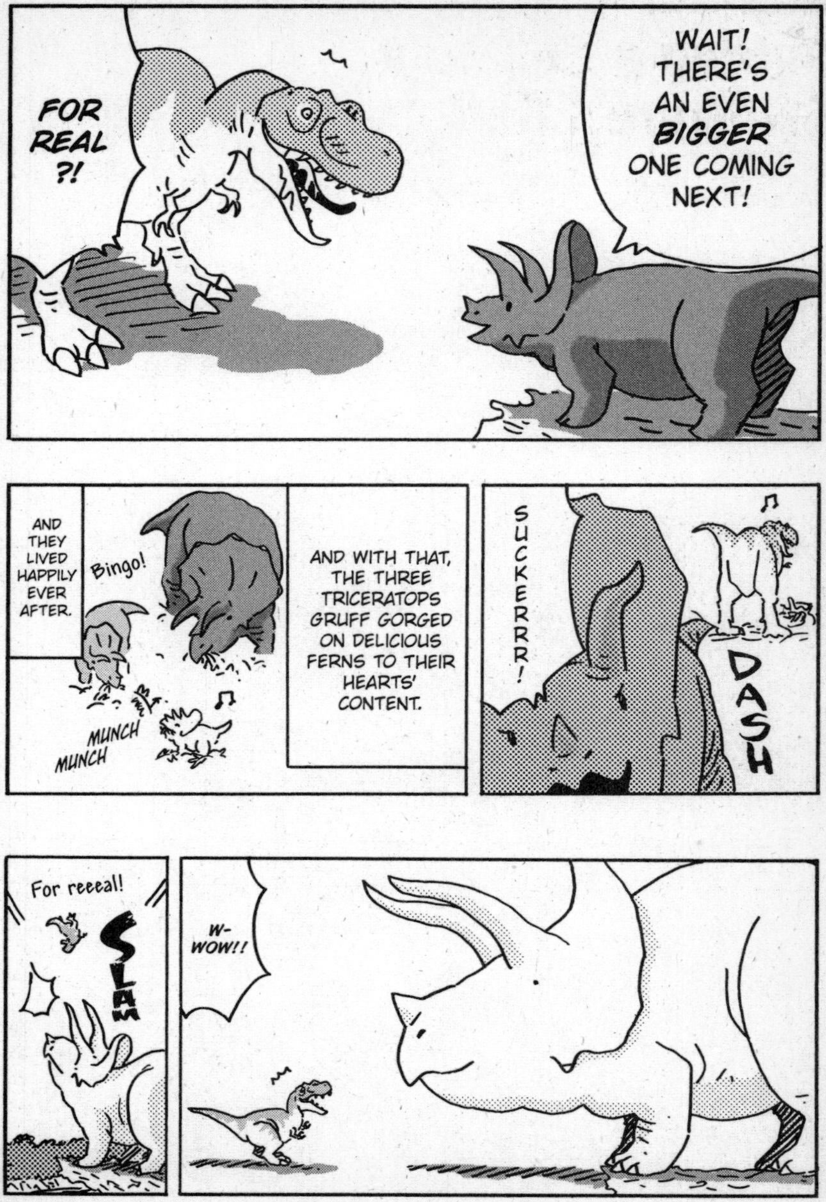
WAIT! THERE'S AN EVEN BIGGER ONE COMING NEXT!
FOR REAL ?!
SUCKERRR!
DASH
AND WITH THAT, THE THREE TRICERATOPS GRUFF GORGED ON DELICIOUS FERNS TO THEIR HEARTS' CONTENT.
Bingo!
AND THEY LIVED HAPPILY EVER AFTER.
MUNCH MUNCH
W-WOW!!
For reeeal!
SLAM

BONE 20

Putting a Bell on a Carnivore's Neck

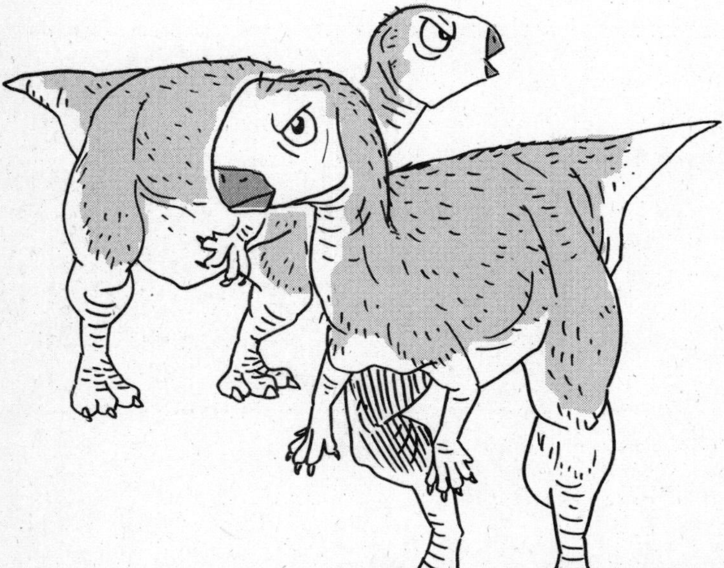

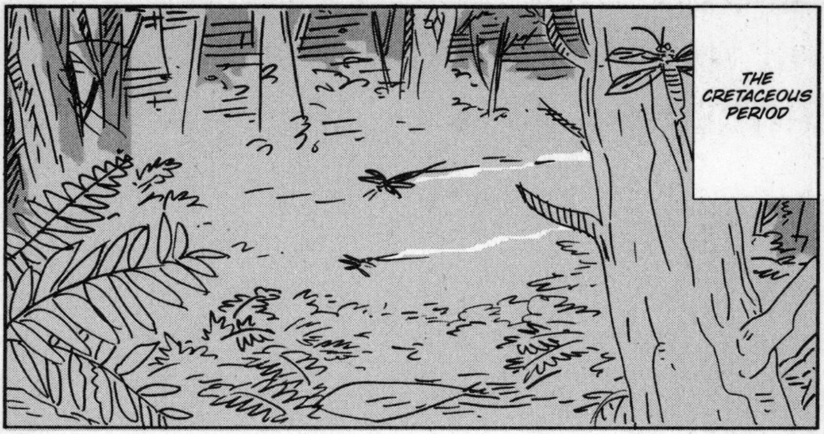
THE CRETACEOUS PERIOD

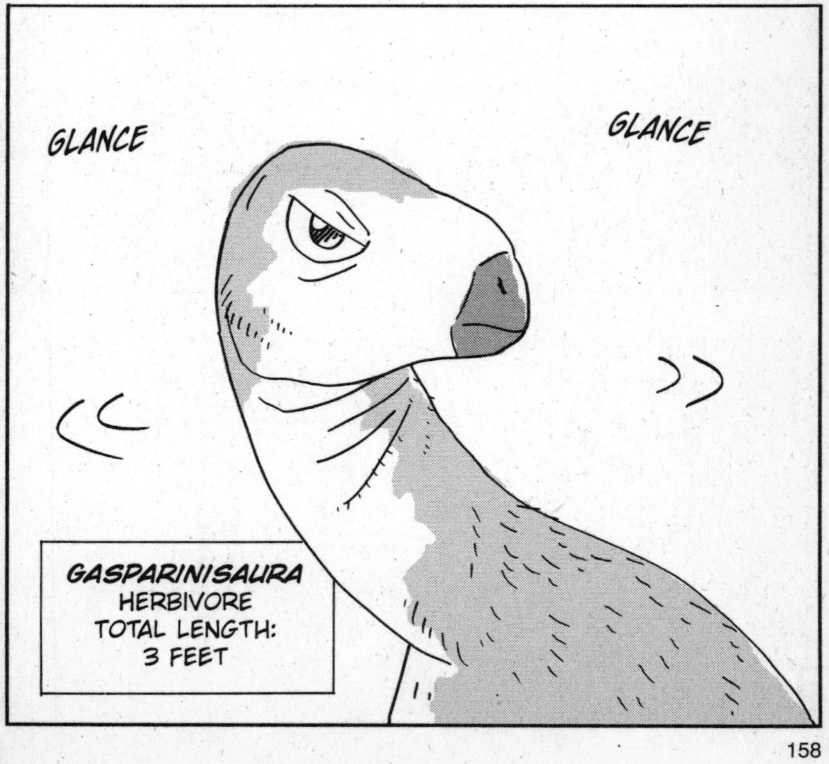
GLANCE
GLANCE
GASPARINISAURA
HERBIVORE
TOTAL LENGTH:
3 FEET

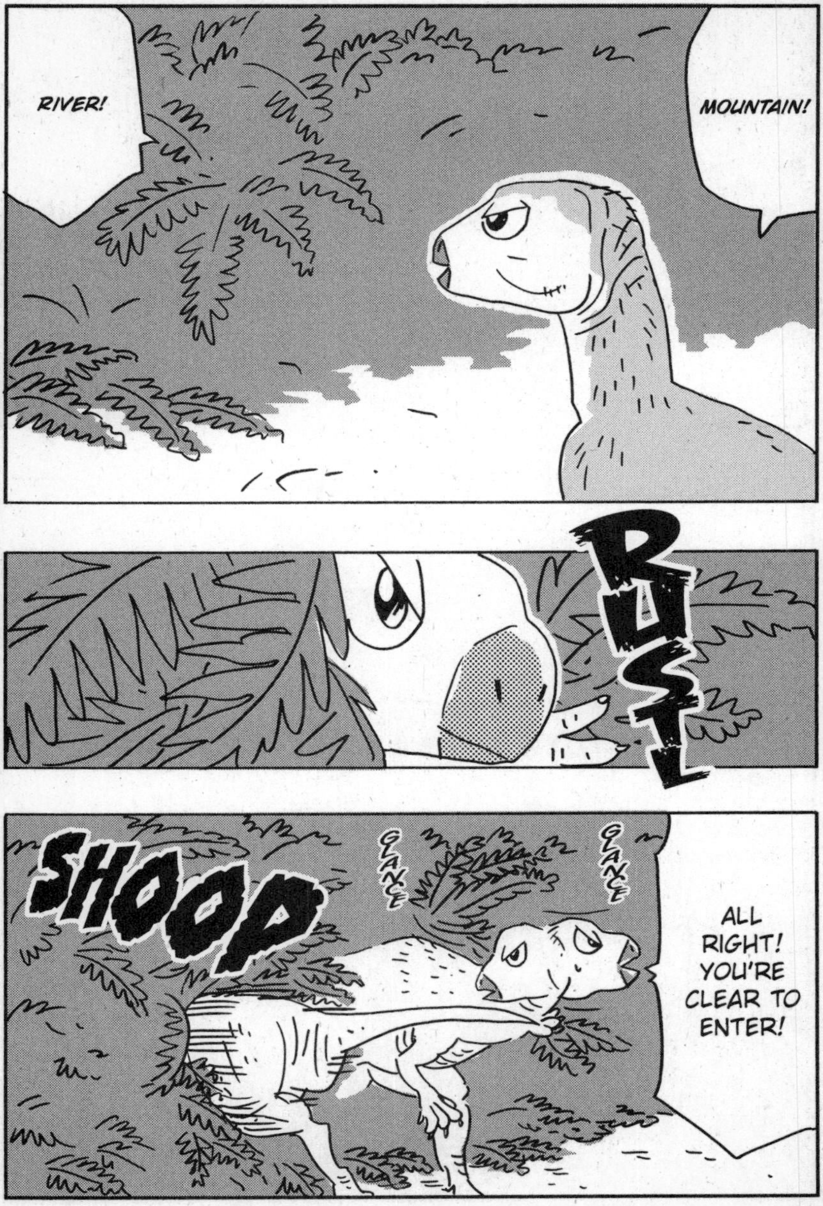
MOUNTAIN!
RIVER!
RUSTL
ALL RIGHT! YOU'RE CLEAR TO ENTER!
GLANCE
GLANCE
SHOOP

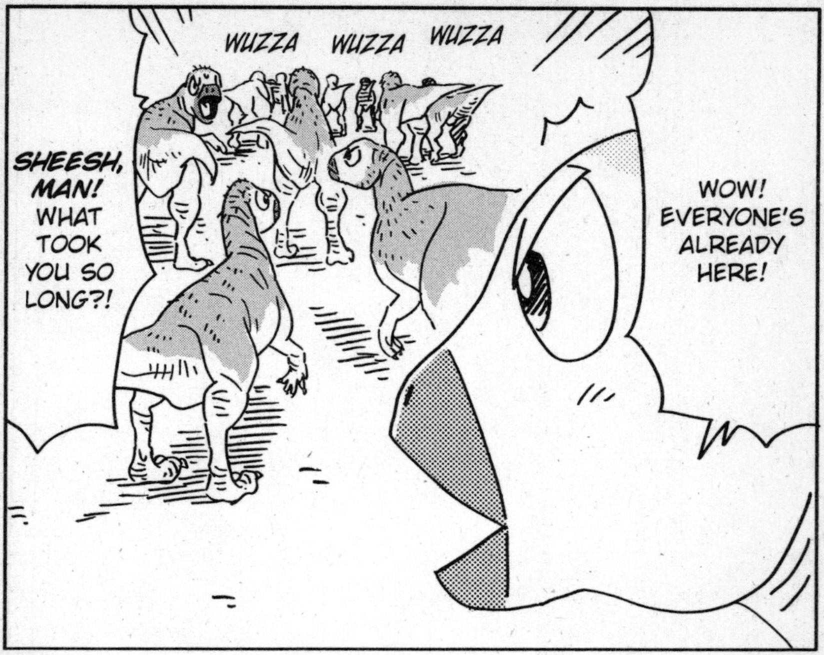
WUZZA WUZZA WUZZA
WOW! EVERYONE'S ALREADY HERE!
SHEESH, MAN! WHAT TOOK YOU SO LONG?!

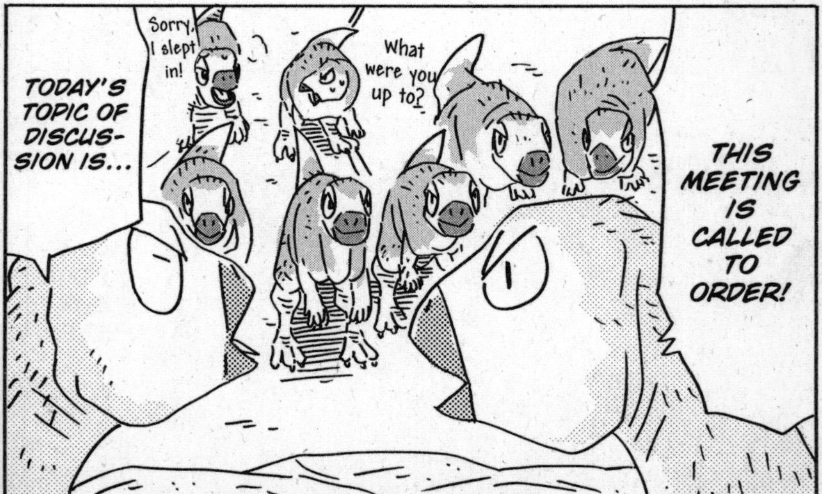
What were you up to?
Sorry, I slept in!
THIS MEETING IS CALLED TO ORDER!
TODAY'S TOPIC OF DISCUSSION IS...

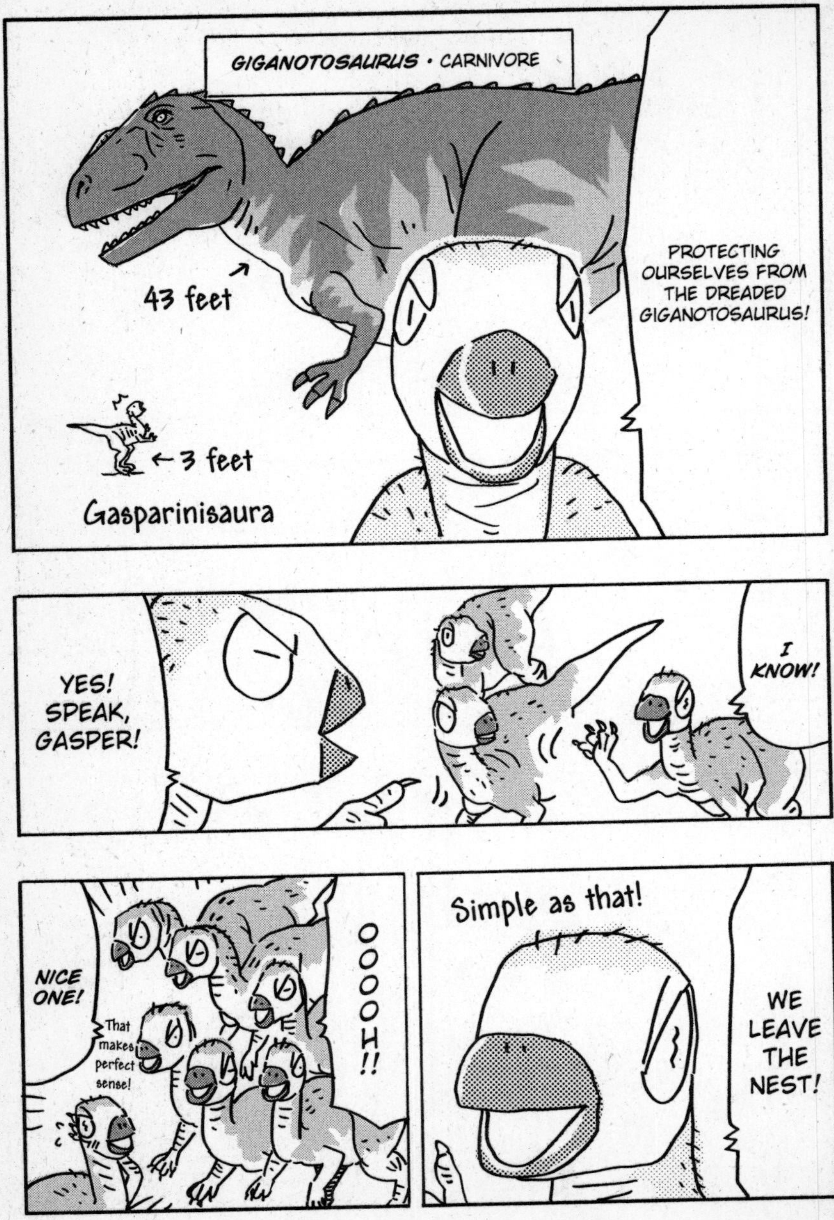
GIGANOTOSAURUS • CARNIVORE
PROTECTING OURSELVES FROM THE DREADED GIGANOTOSAURUS!
43 feet
3 feet
Gasparinisaura
I KNOW!
YES! SPEAK, GASPER!
Simple as that!
WE LEAVE THE NEST!
OOOOOH!!
NICE ONE!
That makes perfect sense!

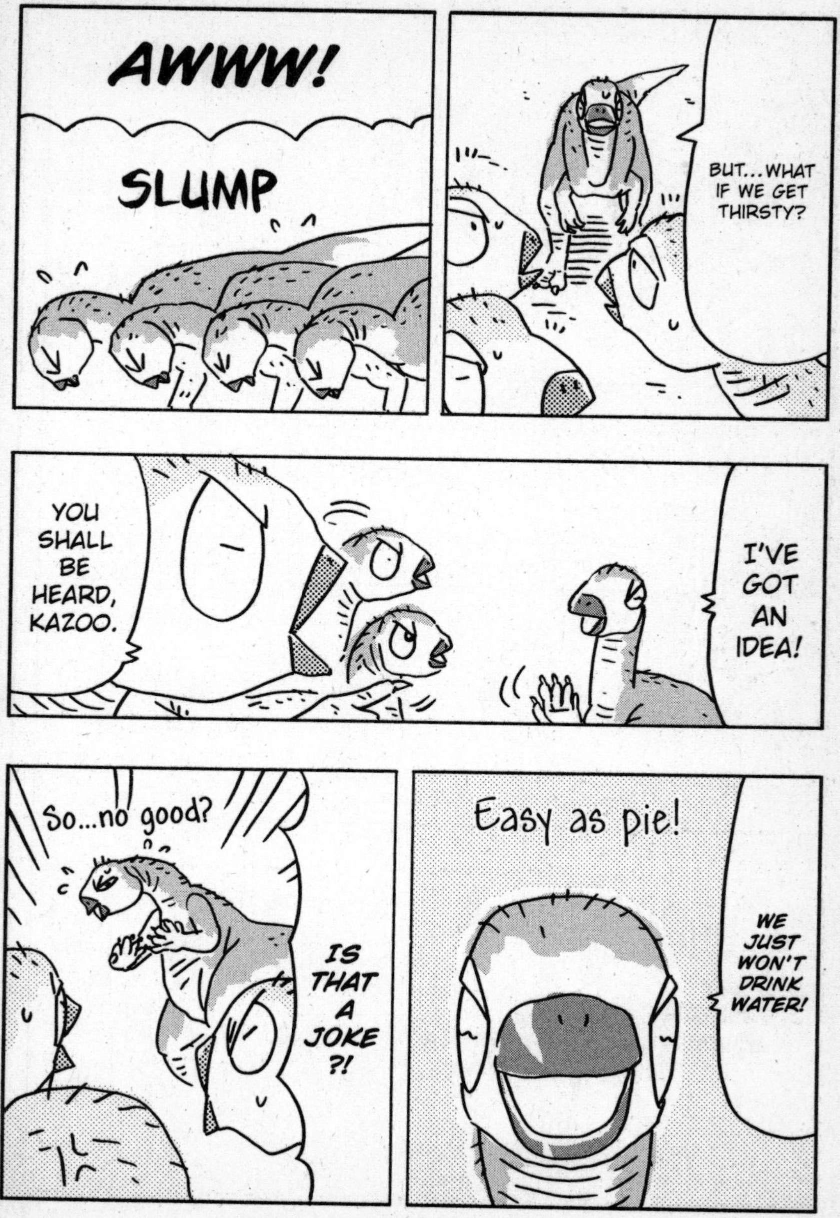
BUT...WHAT IF WE GET THIRSTY?
AWWW!
SLUMP
I'VE GOT AN IDEA!
YOU SHALL BE HEARD, KAZOO.
WE JUST WON'T DRINK WATER!
Easy as pie!
IS THAT A JOKE?!
So...no good?

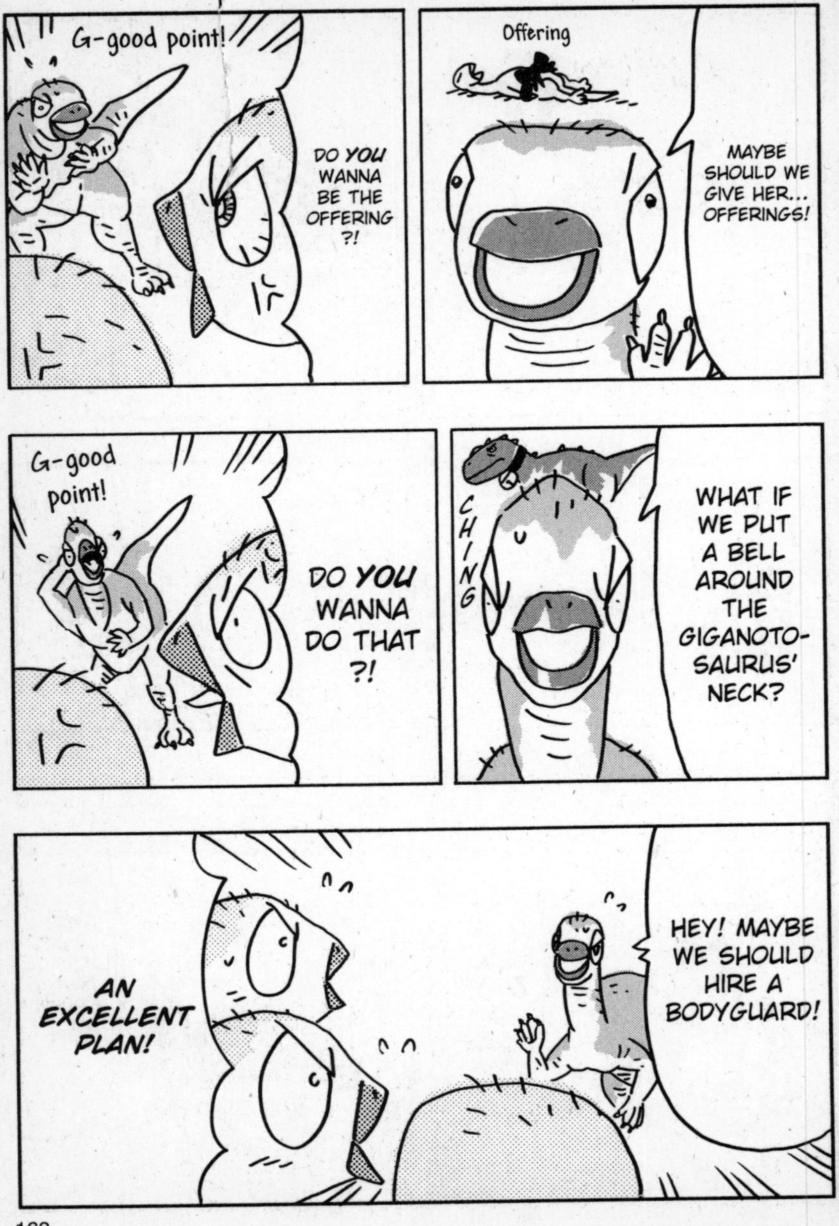
MAYBE SHOULD WE GIVE HER... OFFERINGS!
Offering
DO YOU WANNA BE THE OFFERING ?!
G-good point!
WHAT IF WE PUT A BELL AROUND THE GIGANOTO-SAURUS' NECK?
CHING
DO YOU WANNA DO THAT ?!
G-good point!
HEY! MAYBE WE SHOULD HIRE A BODYGUARD!
AN EXCELLENT PLAN!

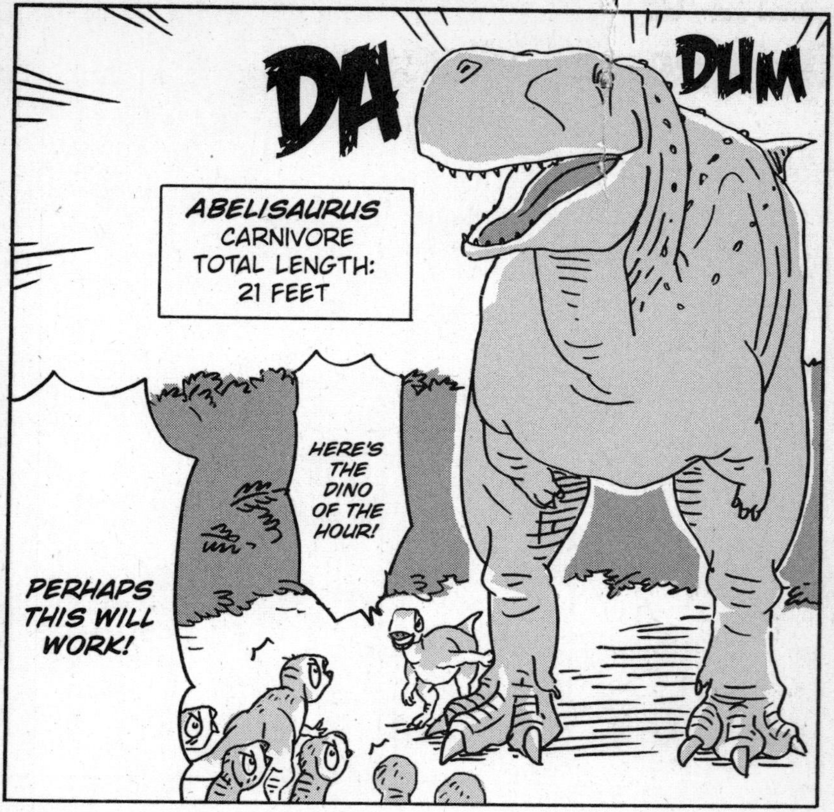
DA DUM
ABELISAURUS
CARNIVORE
TOTAL LENGTH:
21 FEET
HERE'S THE DINO OF THE HOUR!
PERHAPS THIS WILL WORK!

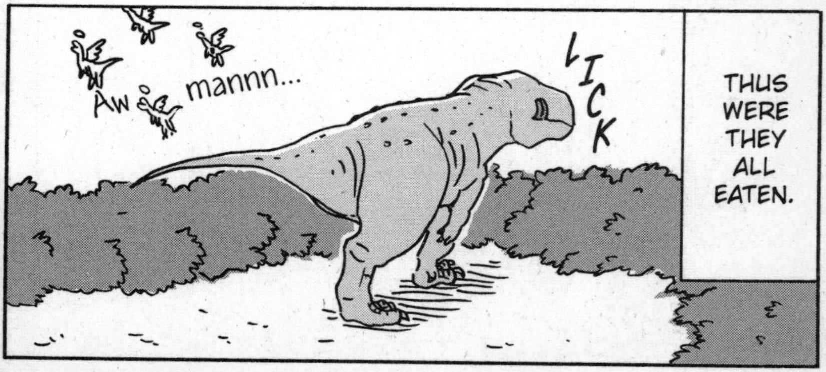
THUS WERE THEY ALL EATEN.
LICK
Aw mannn...

BONE 21

Dino Rescue Mission

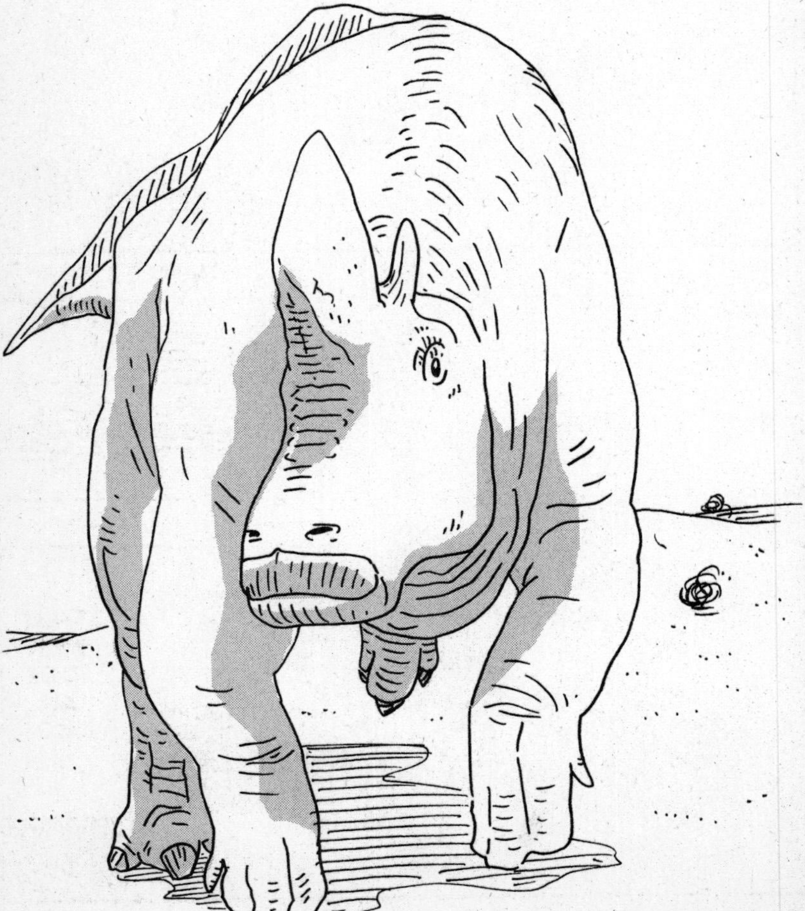

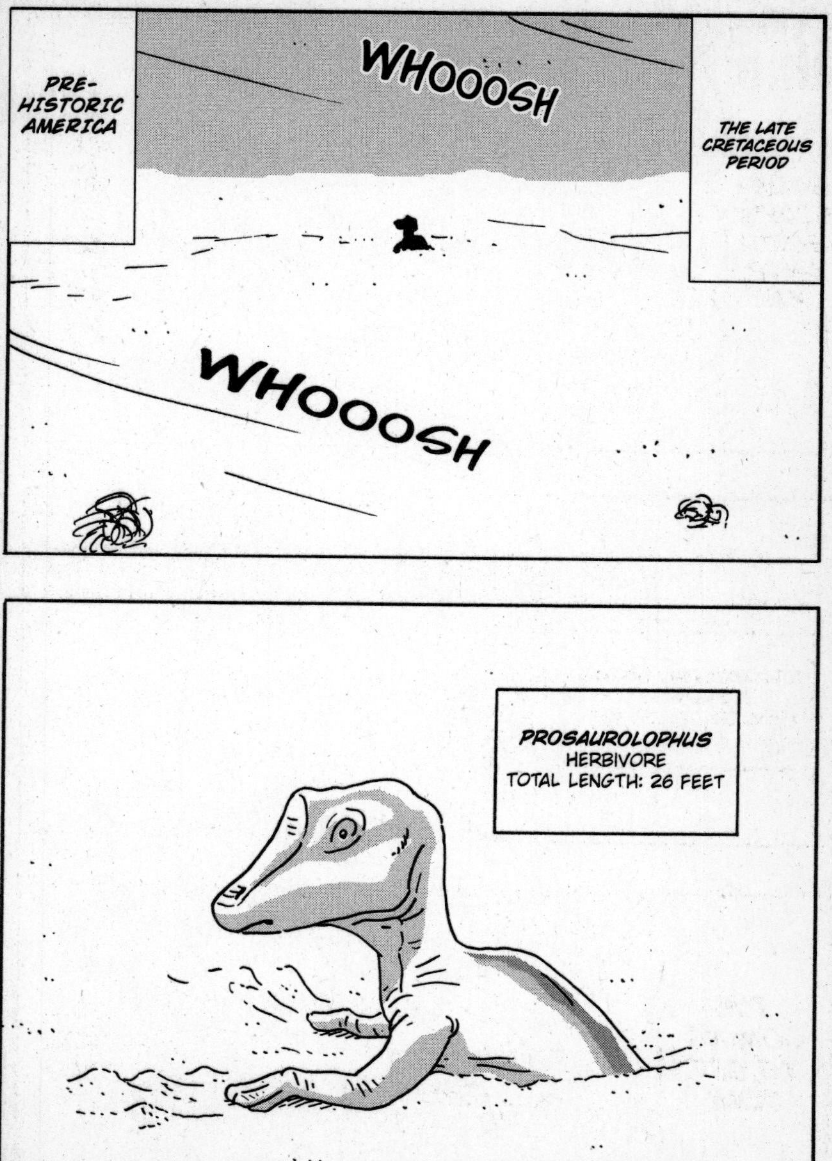
THE LATE CRETACEOUS PERIOD
WHOOOSH
PRE-HISTORIC AMERICA
WHOOOSH
PROSAUROLOPHUS
HERBIVORE
TOTAL LENGTH: 26 FEET

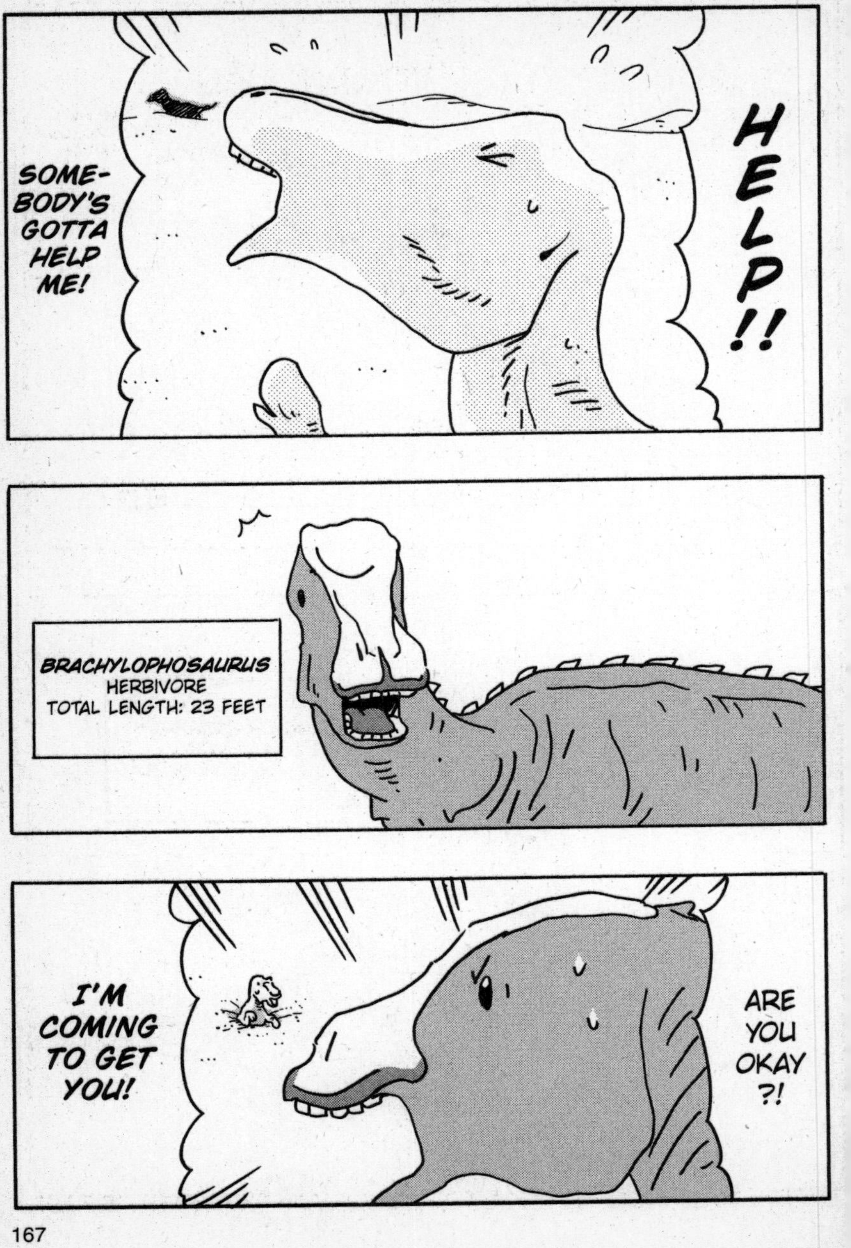
HELP!!
SOME-BODY'S GOTTA HELP ME!
BRACHYLOPHOSAURUS
HERBIVORE
TOTAL LENGTH: 23 FEET
ARE YOU OKAY ?!
I'M COMING TO GET YOU!

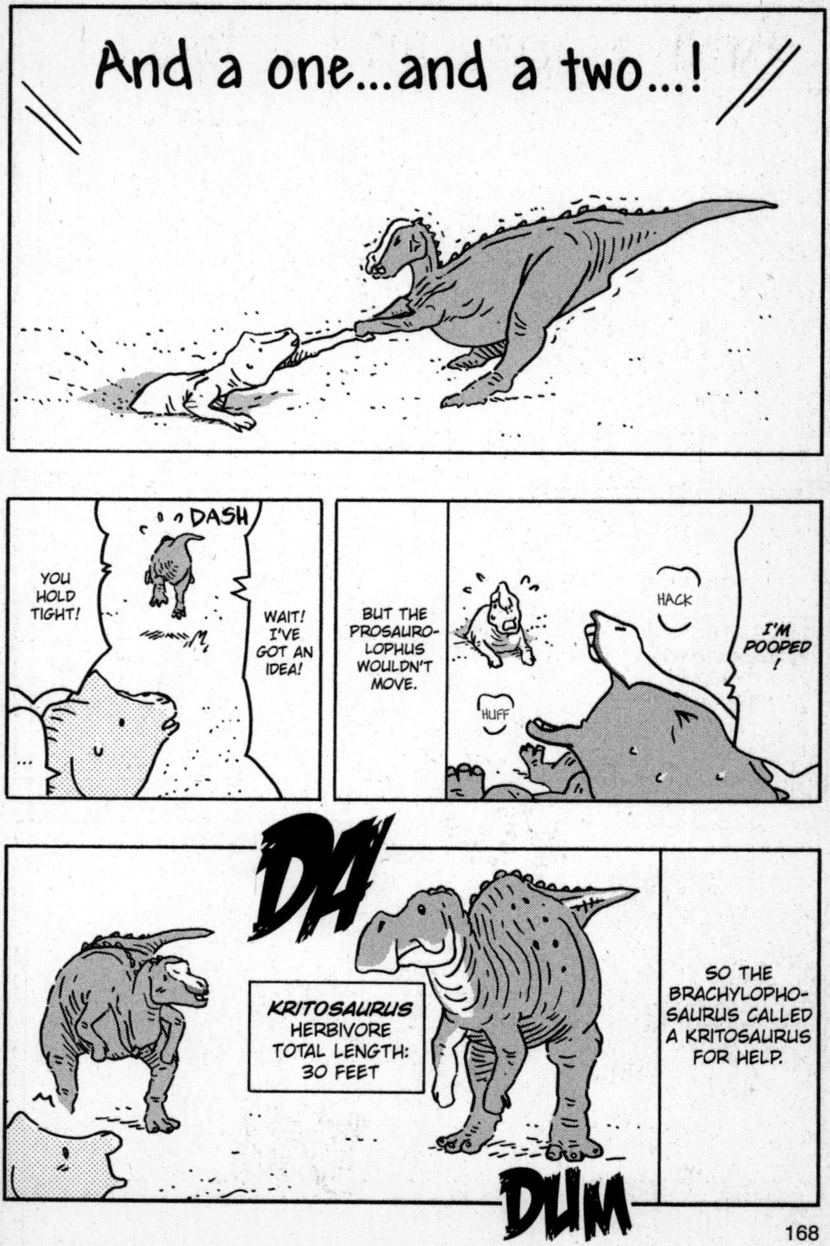
And a one...and a two...!
I'M POOPED!
HACK
BUT THE PROSAUROLOPHUS WOULDN'T MOVE.
HUFF
DASH
WAIT! I'VE GOT AN IDEA!
YOU HOLD TIGHT!
...
SO THE BRACHYLOPHOSAURUS CALLED A KRITOSAURUS FOR HELP.
DA
KRITOSAURUS HERBIVORE TOTAL LENGTH: 30 FEET
DUM

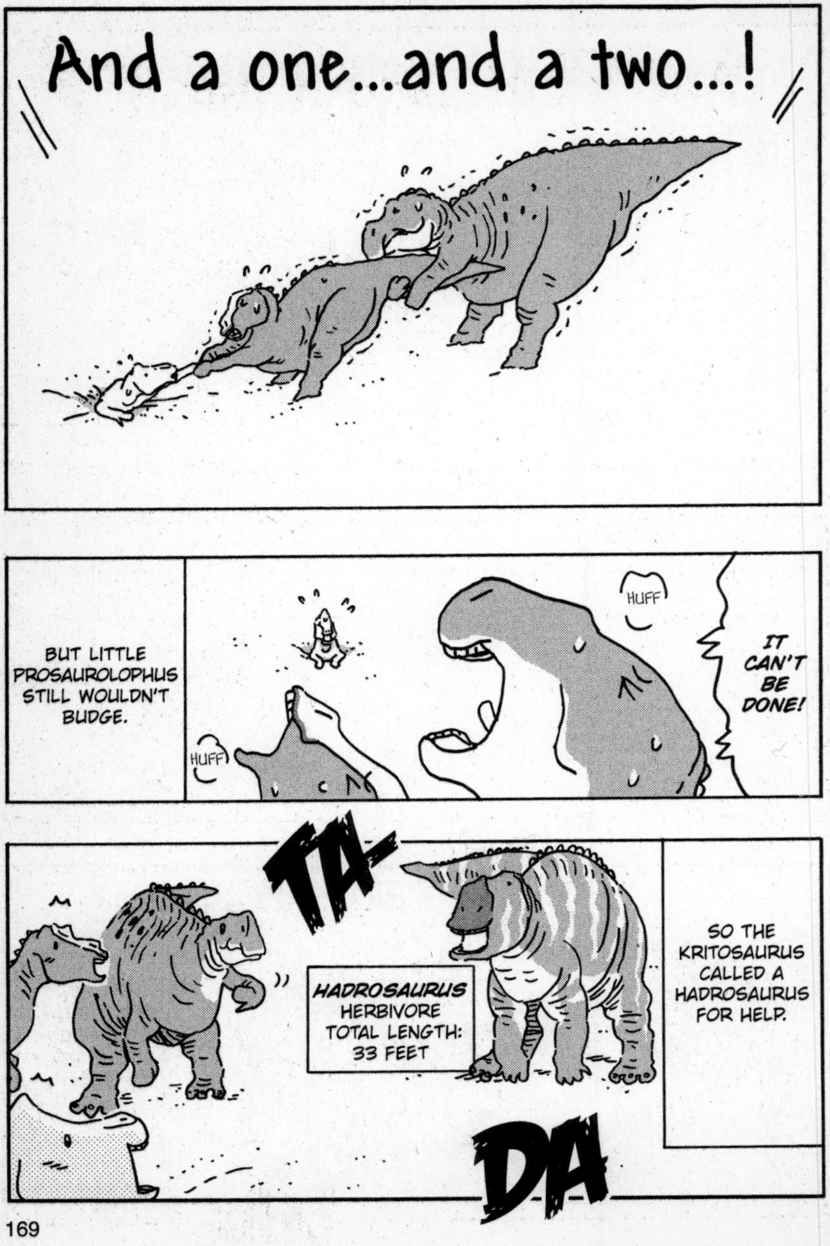
And a one...and a two...!
HUFF
IT CAN'T BE DONE!
HUFF
BUT LITTLE PROSAUROLOPHUS STILL WOULDN'T BUDGE.
SO THE KRITOSAURUS CALLED A HADROSAURUS FOR HELP.
TA-
HADROSAURUS HERBIVORE TOTAL LENGTH: 33 FEET
DA

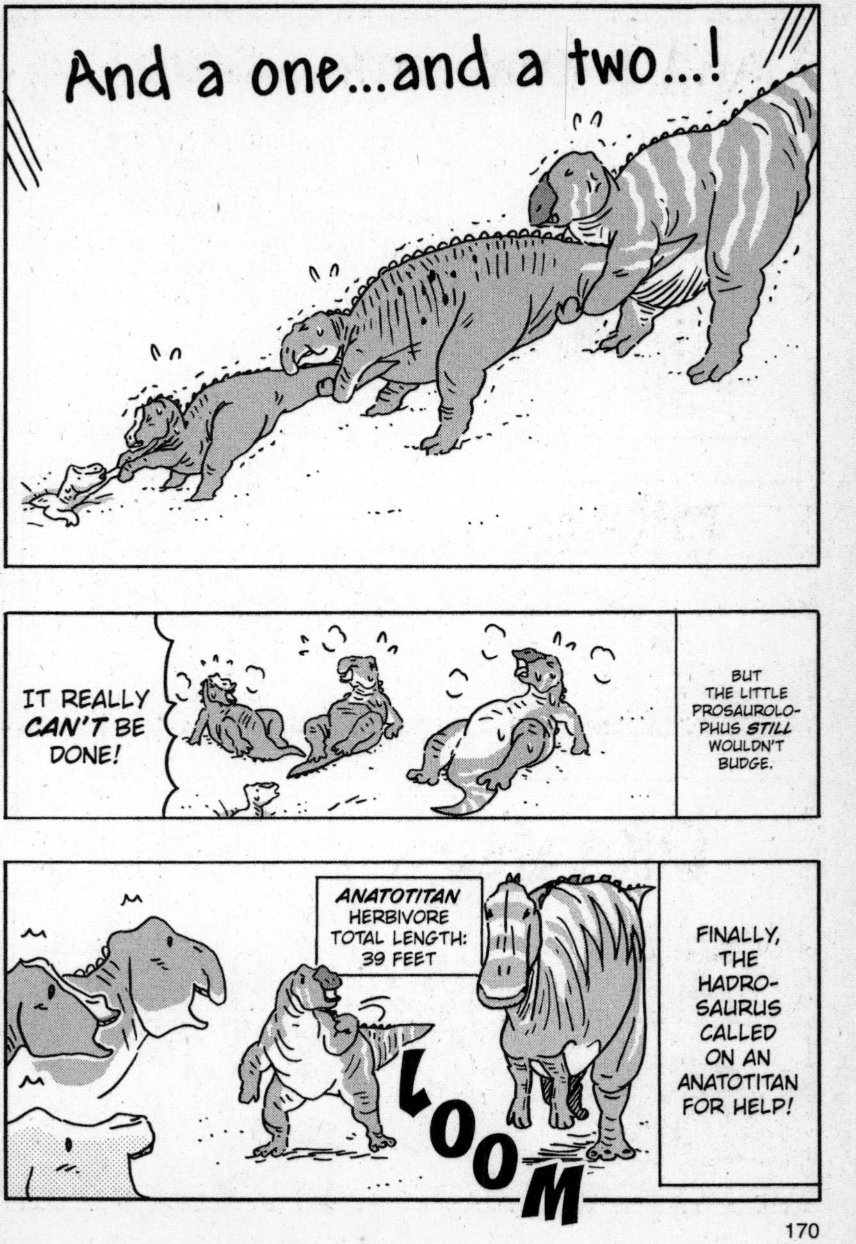
And a one...and a two...!
BUT THE LITTLE PROSAUROLOPHUS *STILL* WOULDN'T BUDGE.
IT REALLY *CAN'T* BE DONE!
FINALLY, THE HADROSAURUS CALLED ON AN ANATOTITAN FOR HELP!
ANATOTITAN HERBIVORE TOTAL LENGTH: 39 FEET
LOOM

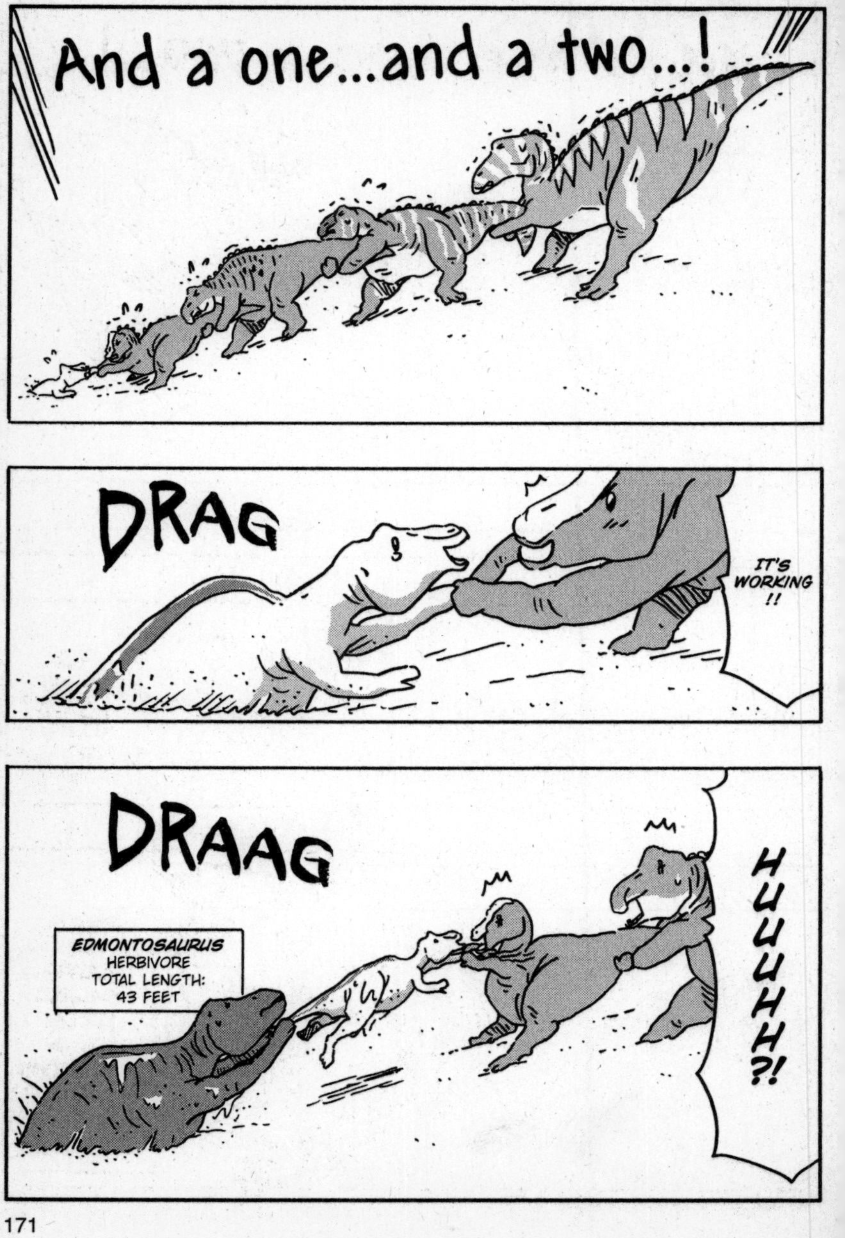
And a one...and a two...!
IT'S WORKING !!
DRAG
HUUUHH?!
DRAAG
EDMONTOSAURUS
HERBIVORE
TOTAL LENGTH:
43 FEET

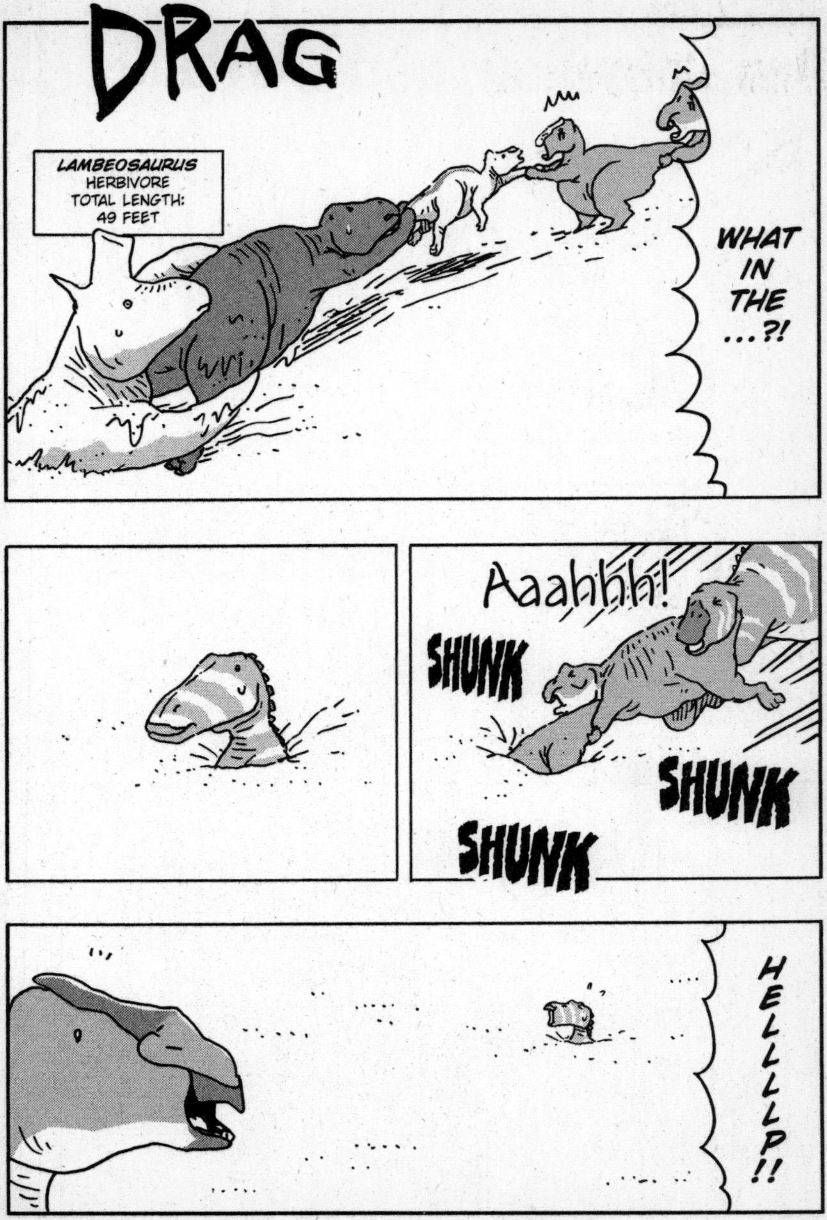

DRAG
LAMBEOSAURUS
HERBIVORE
TOTAL LENGTH:
49 FEET
WHAT IN THE ...?!
Aaahhh!
SHUNK
SHUNK
SHUNK
HELLLLP!!

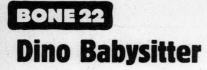

BONE 22

Dino Babysitter

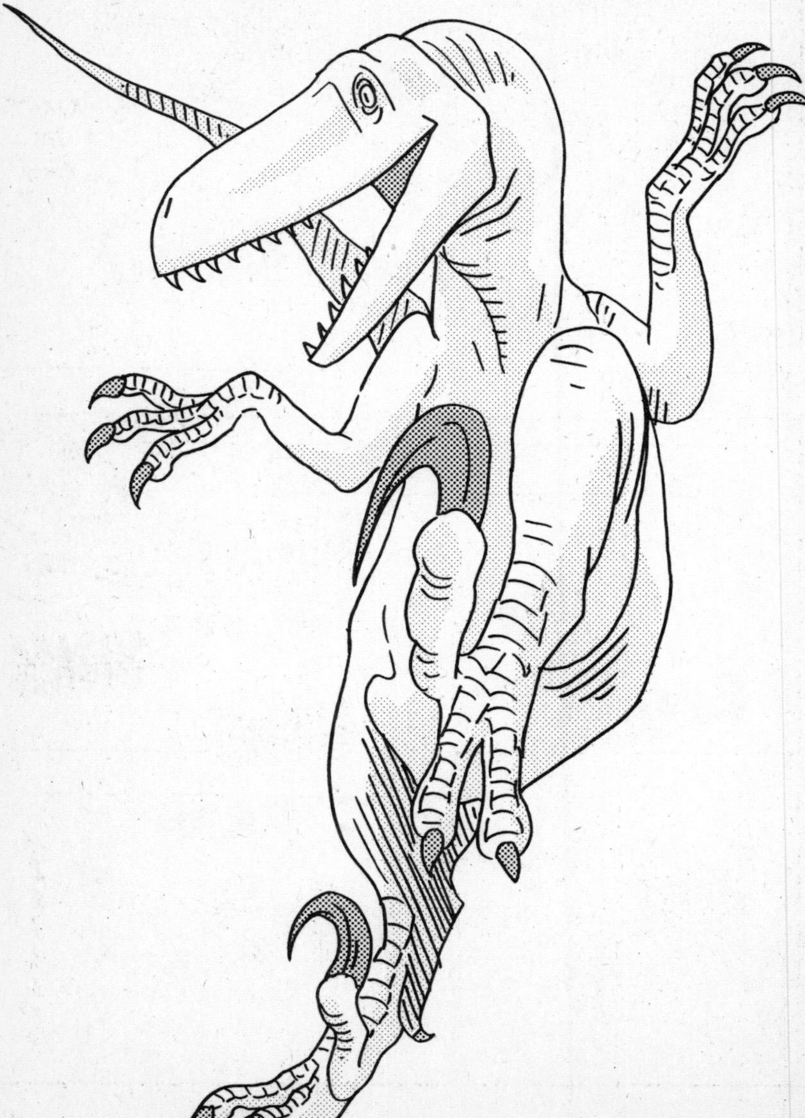

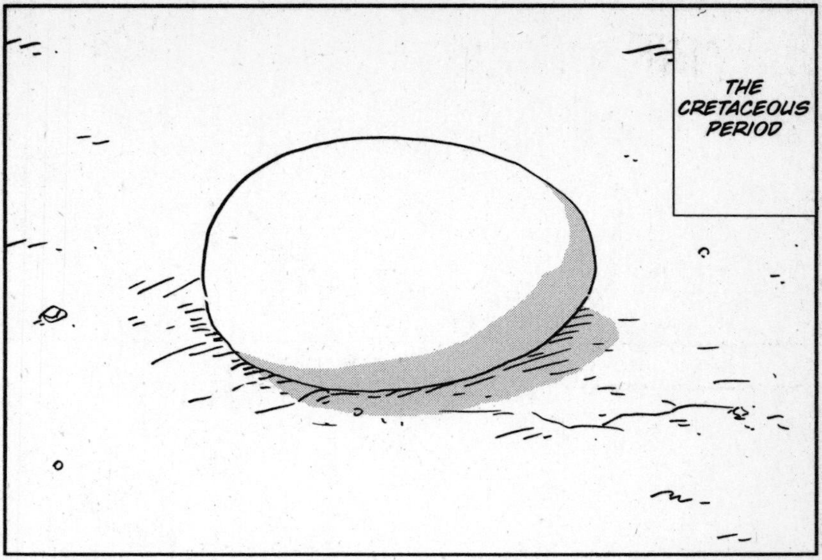
THE CRETACEOUS PERIOD

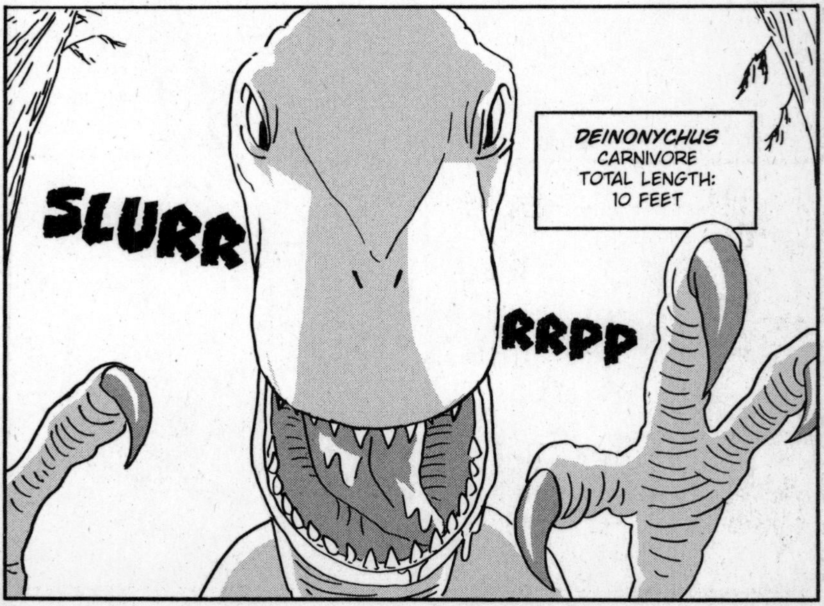
DEINONYCHUS
CARNIVORE
TOTAL LENGTH:
10 FEET
SLURR
RRPP

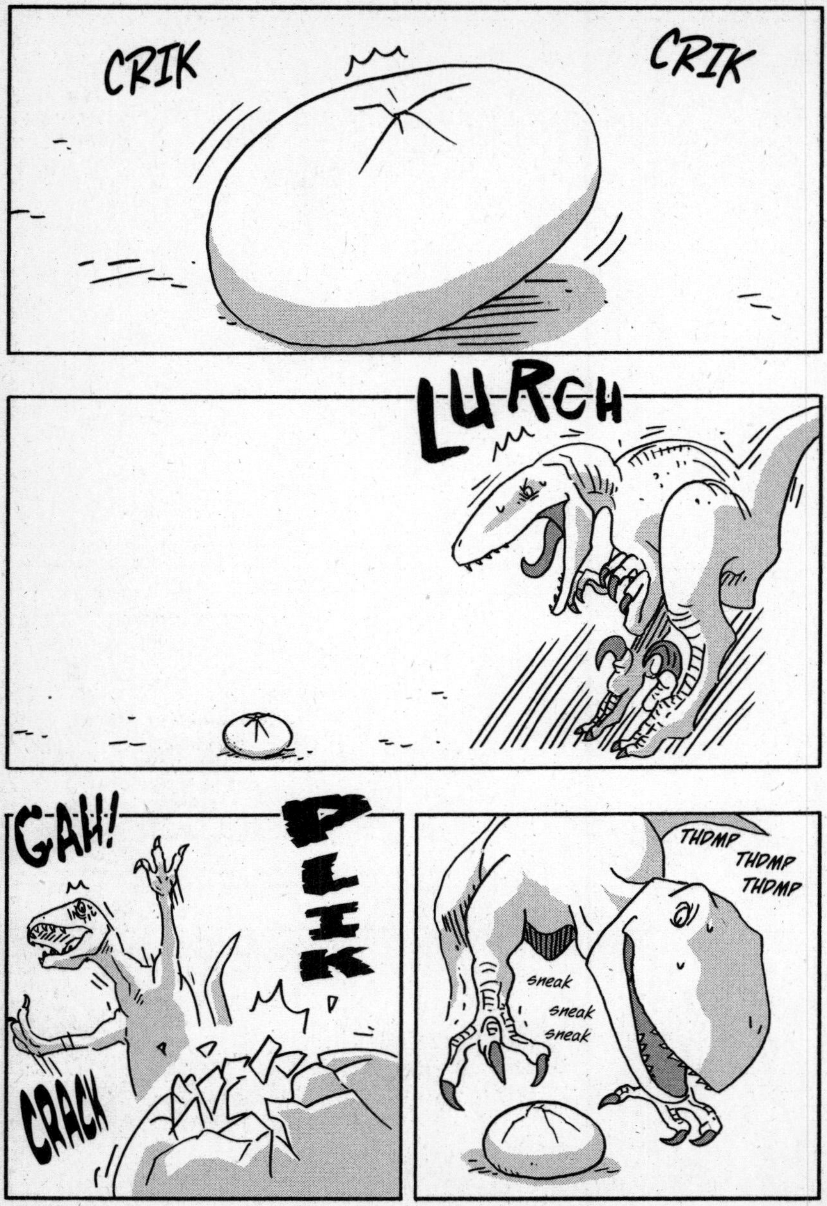
CRIK
CRIK
LURCH
THDMP
THDMP
THDMP
sneak
sneak
sneak
PLIK
GAH!
CRACK

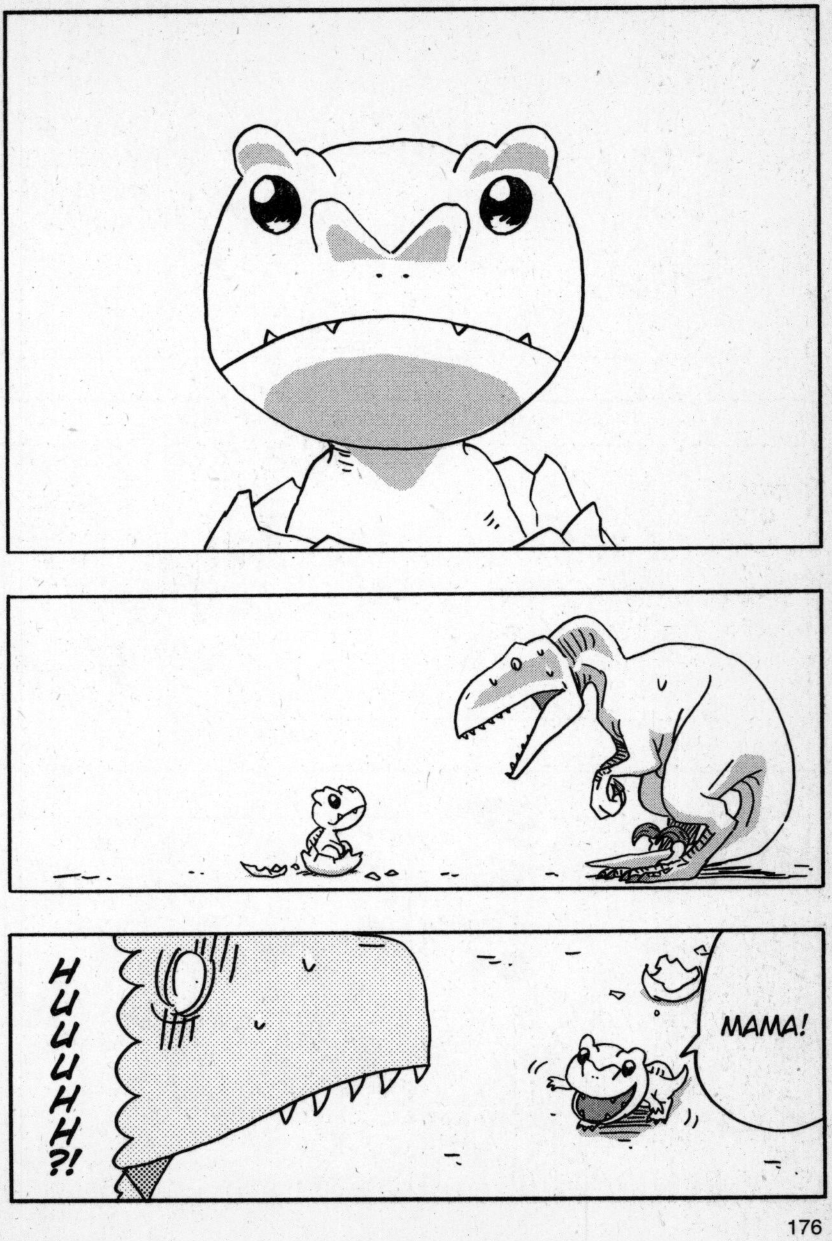
MAMA!
HUUUUHH?!

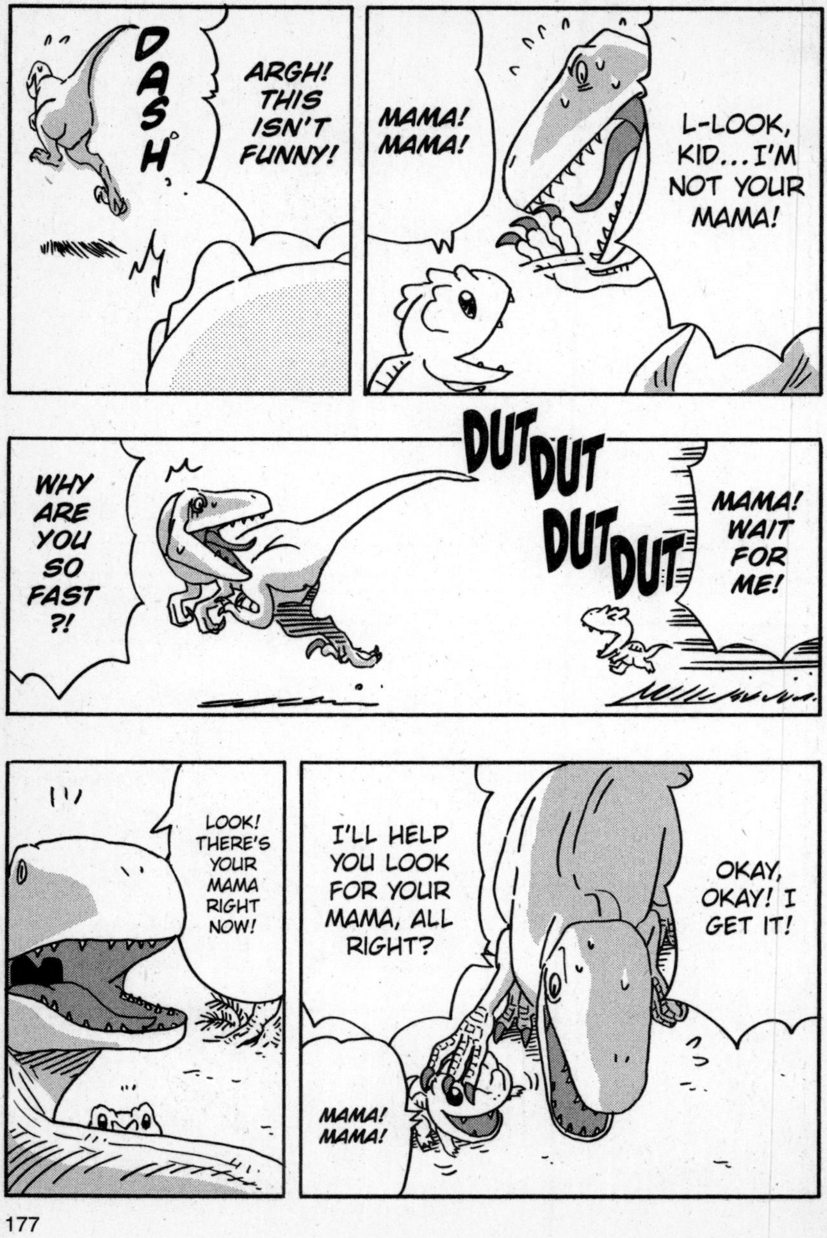
L-LOOK, KID...I'M NOT YOUR MAMA!
MAMA! MAMA!
ARGH! THIS ISN'T FUNNY!
DASH
MAMA! WAIT FOR ME!
DUT DUT DUT DUT
WHY ARE YOU SO FAST?!
OKAY, OKAY! I GET IT!
I'LL HELP YOU LOOK FOR YOUR MAMA, ALL RIGHT?
MAMA! MAMA!
LOOK! THERE'S YOUR MAMA RIGHT NOW!

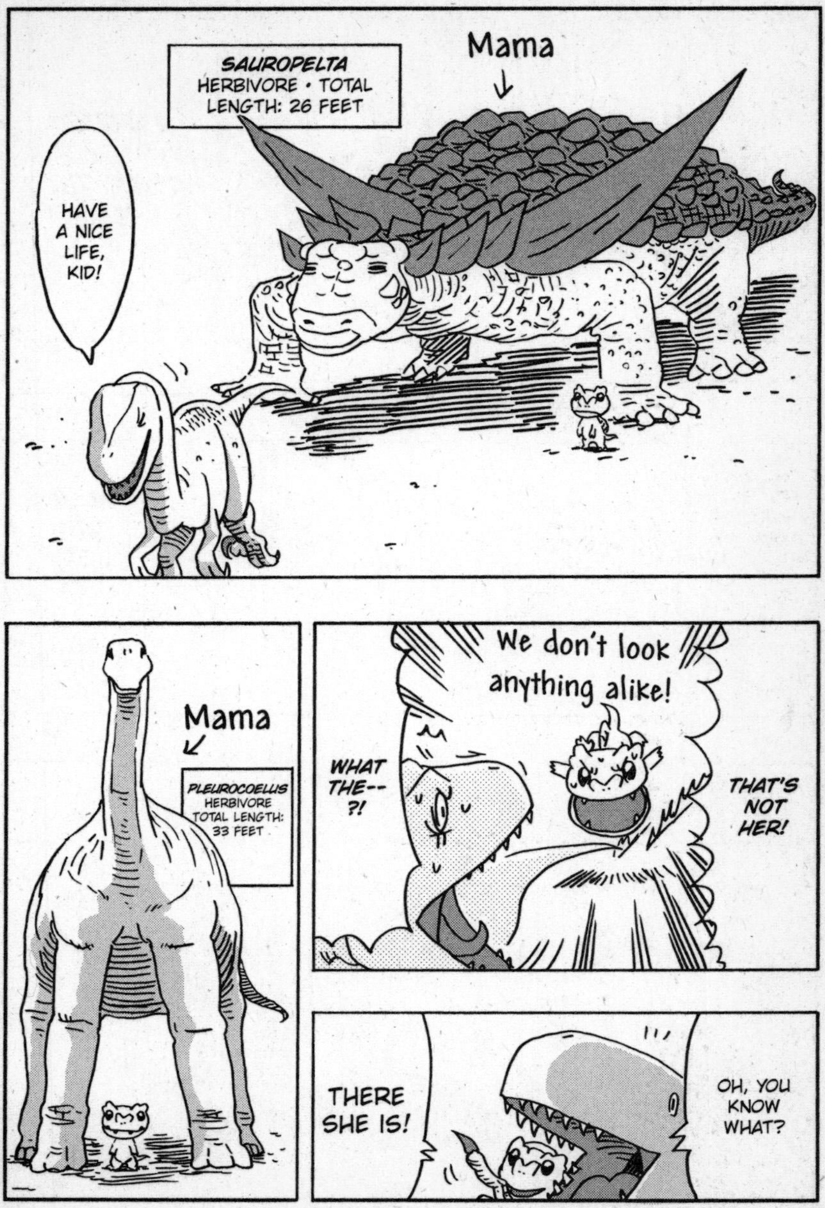
Mama
SAUROPELTA HERBIVORE • TOTAL LENGTH: 26 FEET
HAVE A NICE LIFE, KID!
We don't look anything alike!
THAT'S NOT HER!
WHAT THE-- ?!
OH, YOU KNOW WHAT?
THERE SHE IS!
Mama
PLEUROCOELUS HERBIVORE TOTAL LENGTH: 33 FEET

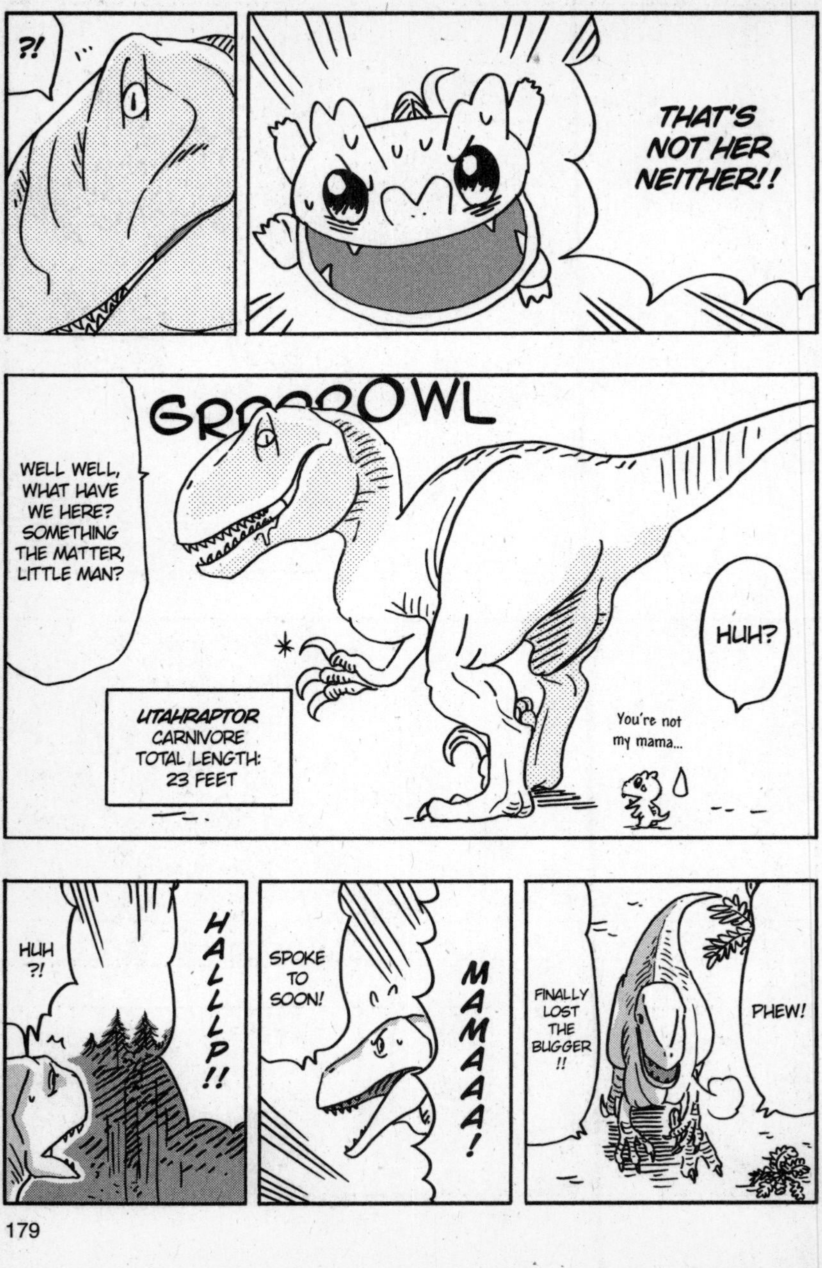
THAT'S NOT HER NEITHER!!
?!
...
GRRRROWL
HUH?
WELL WELL, WHAT HAVE WE HERE? SOMETHING THE MATTER, LITTLE MAN?
You're not my mama...
UTAHRAPTOR
CARNIVORE
TOTAL LENGTH: 23 FEET
PHEW!
FINALLY LOST THE BUGGER!!
MAMAAAA!
SPOKE TO SOON!
HALLLP!!
HUH?!

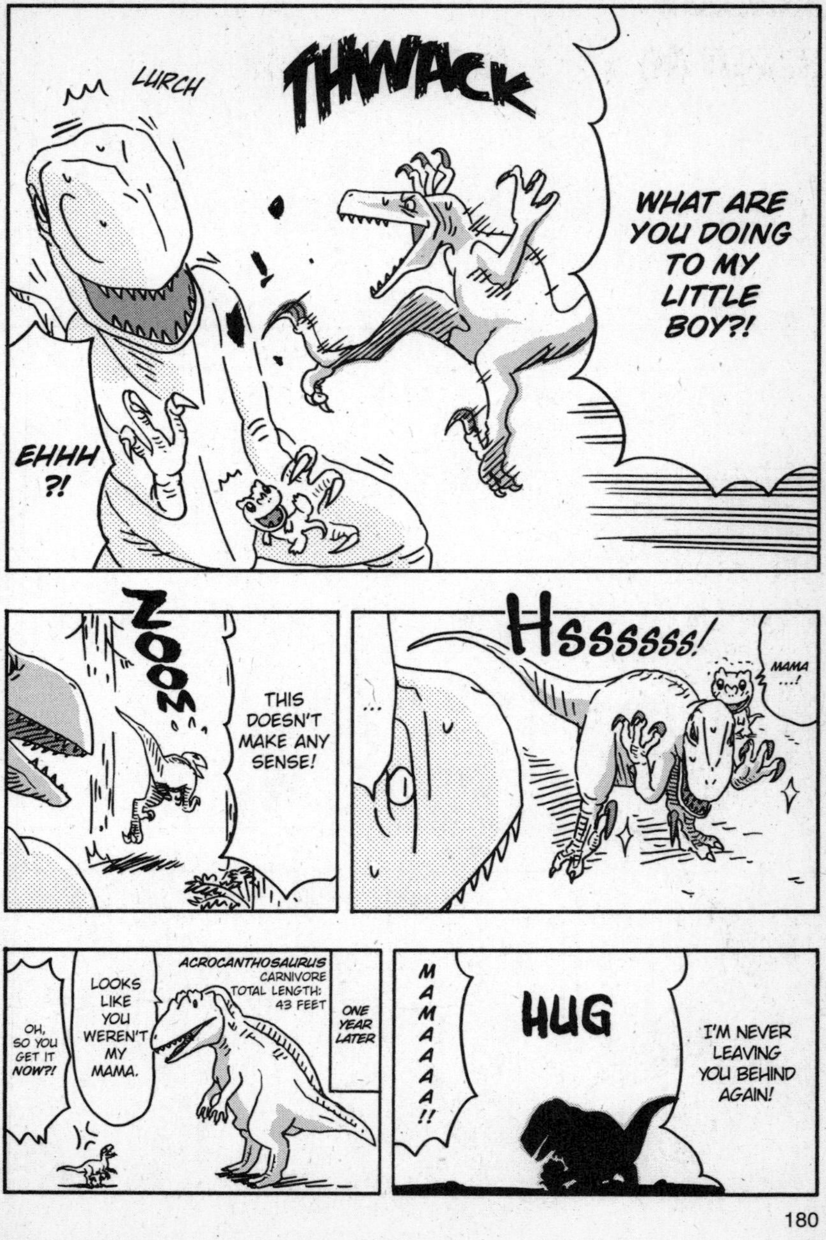
THWACK
WHAT ARE YOU DOING TO MY LITTLE BOY?!
LURCH
EHHH ?!
Hssssss!
MAMA ...!
...
ZOOM
THIS DOESN'T MAKE ANY SENSE!
MAMAAAAA!!
HUG
I'M NEVER LEAVING YOU BEHIND AGAIN!
ONE YEAR LATER
ACROCANTHOSAURUS CARNIVORE TOTAL LENGTH: 43 FEET
LOOKS LIKE YOU WEREN'T MY MAMA.
OH, SO YOU GET IT NOW?!

BONE 23

Airborne M-1 Grand Prix

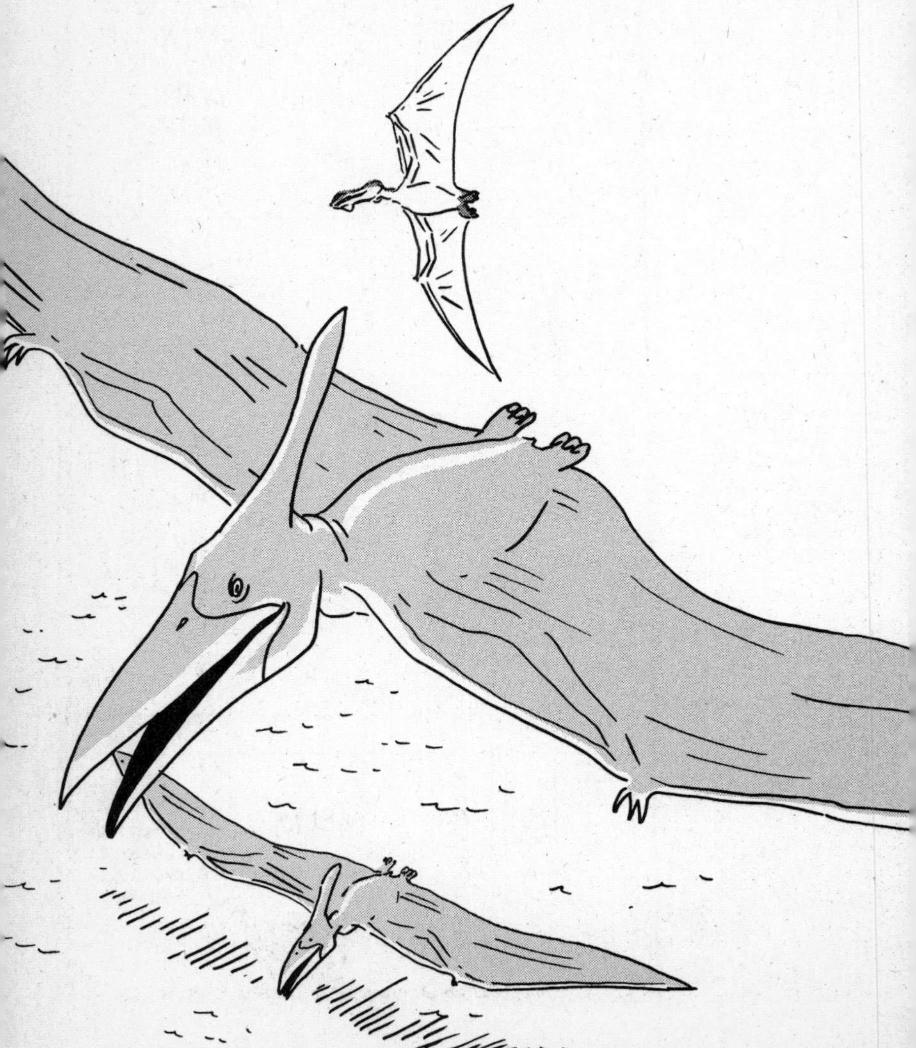

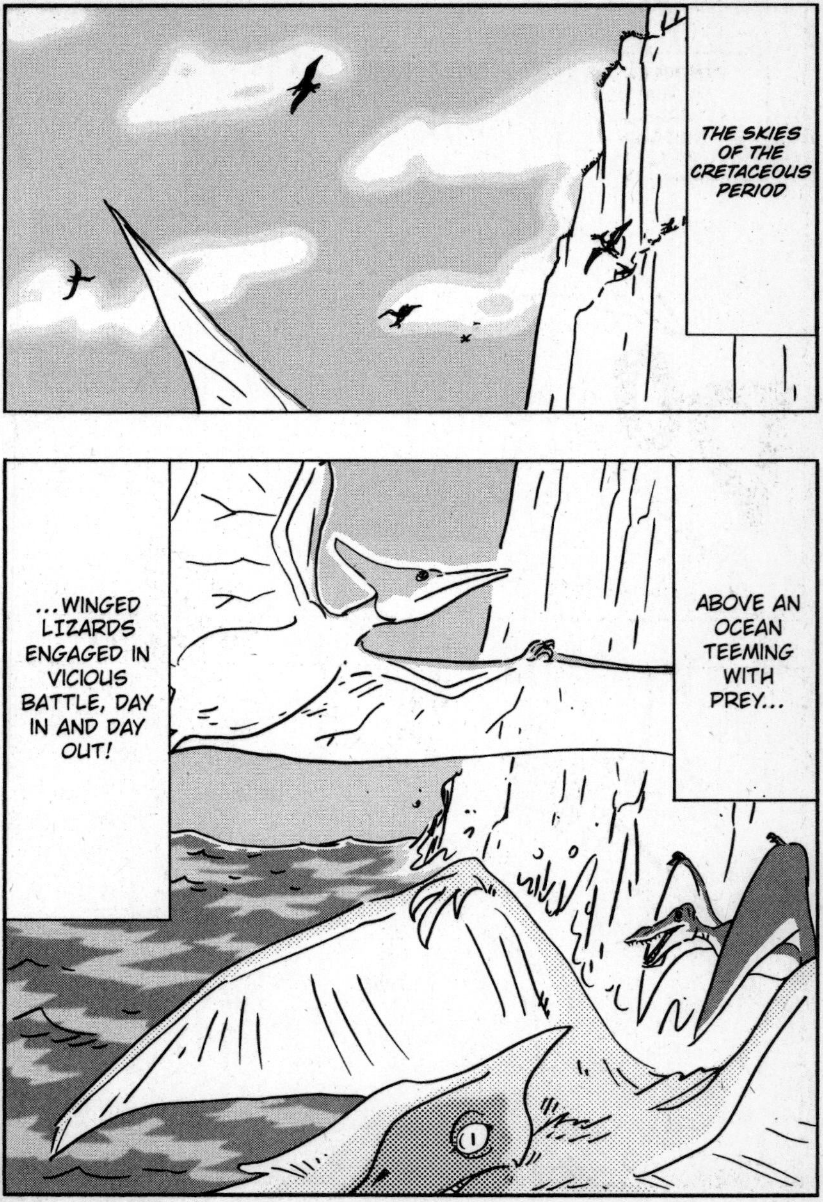
THE SKIES OF THE CRETACEOUS PERIOD
ABOVE AN OCEAN TEEMING WITH PREY...
...WINGED LIZARDS ENGAGED IN VICIOUS BATTLE, DAY IN AND DAY OUT!

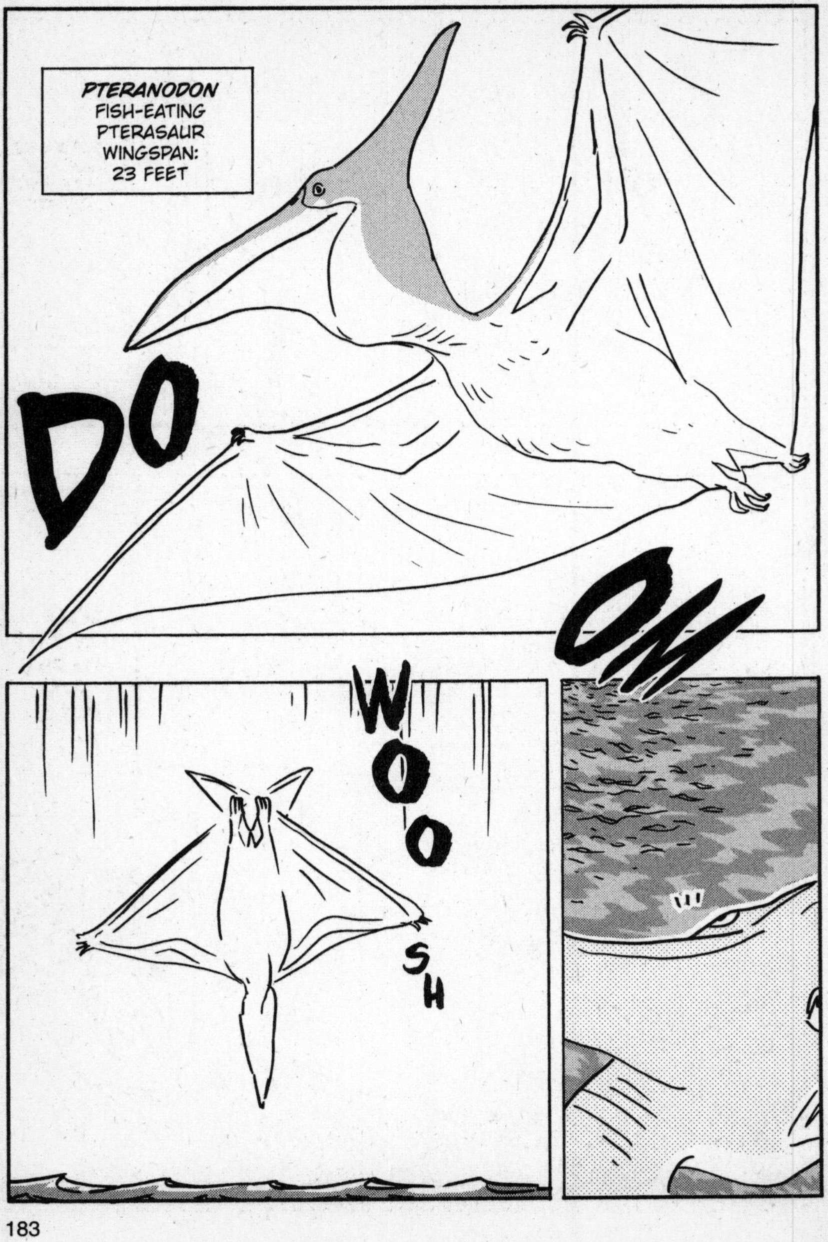
PTERANODON
FISH-EATING
PTERASAUR
WINGSPAN:
23 FEET
DO
OM
WOOO
SH

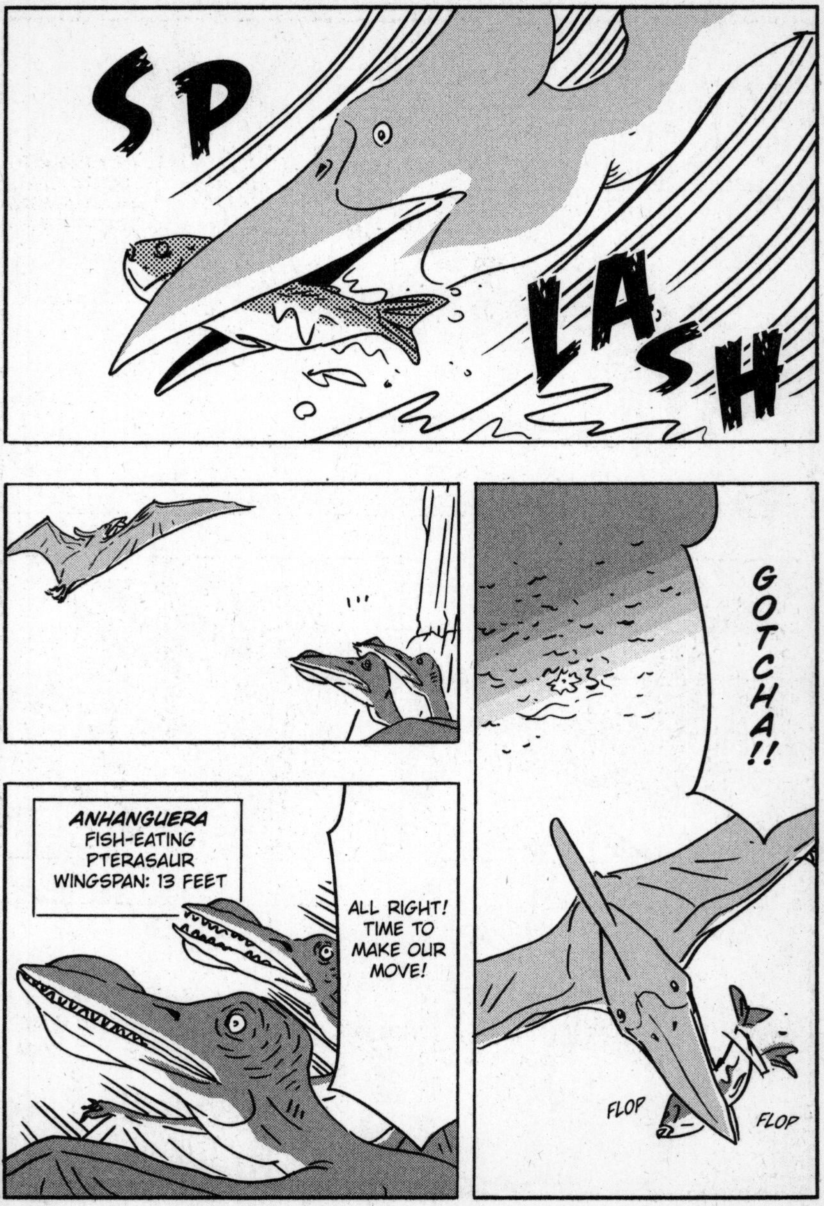
SPLASH
GOTCHA!!
FLOP
FLOP
...
ANHANGUERA
FISH-EATING
PTERASAUR
WINGSPAN: 13 FEET
ALL RIGHT! TIME TO MAKE OUR MOVE!

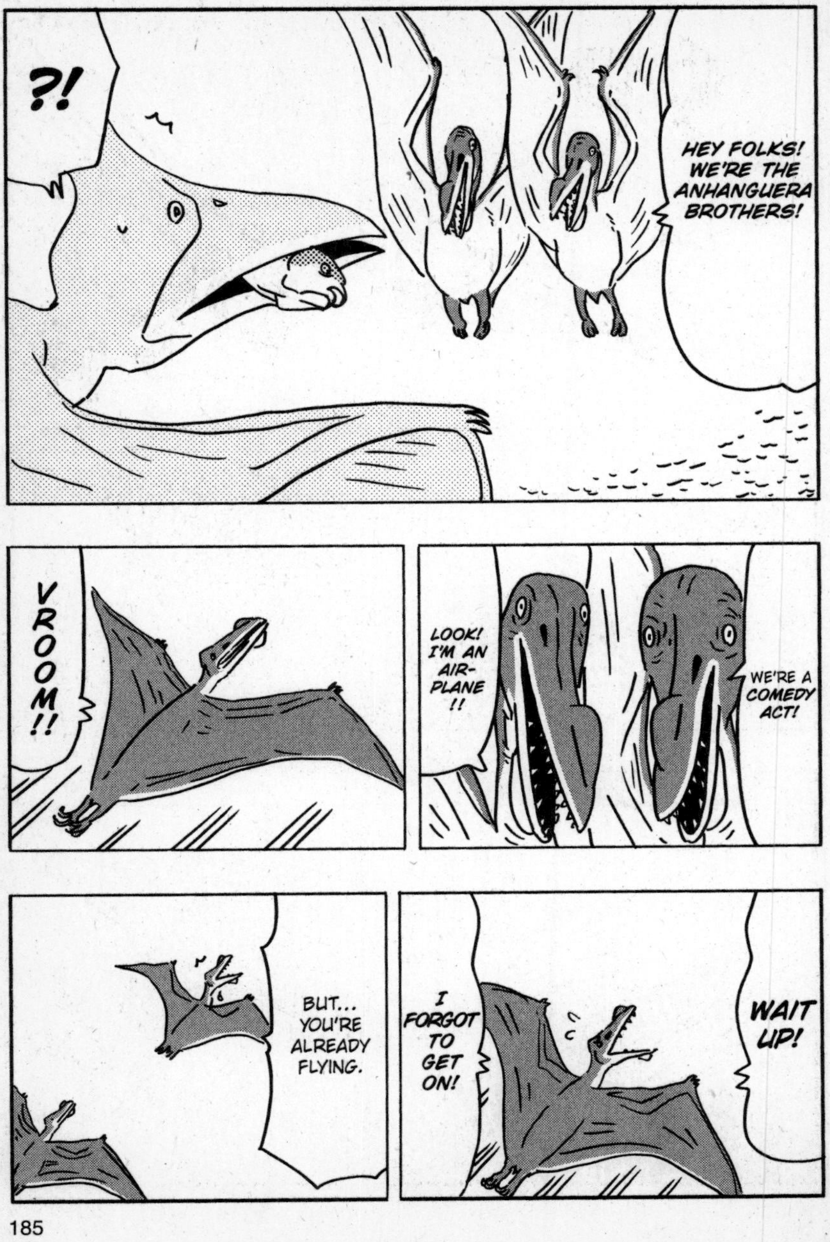
HEY FOLKS! WE'RE THE ANHANGUERA BROTHERS!
?!
WE'RE A COMEDY ACT!
LOOK! I'M AN AIR-PLANE !!
VROOM!!
WAIT UP!
I FORGOT TO GET ON!
BUT... YOU'RE ALREADY FLYING.

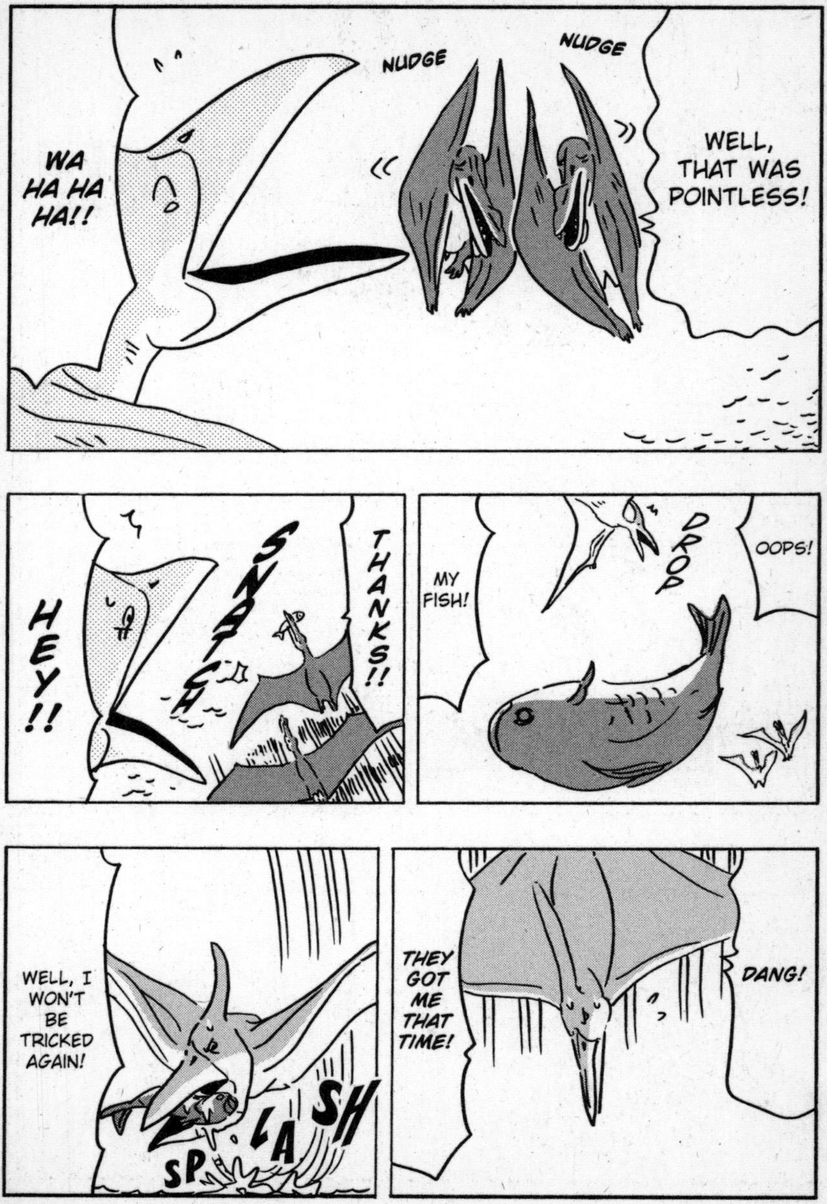
WELL, THAT WAS POINTLESS!
NUDGE
NUDGE
WA HA HA HA!!
OOPS!
DROP
MY FISH!
THANKS!!
SNATCH
HEY!!
DANG!
THEY GOT ME THAT TIME!
WELL, I WON'T BE TRICKED AGAIN!
SPLASH

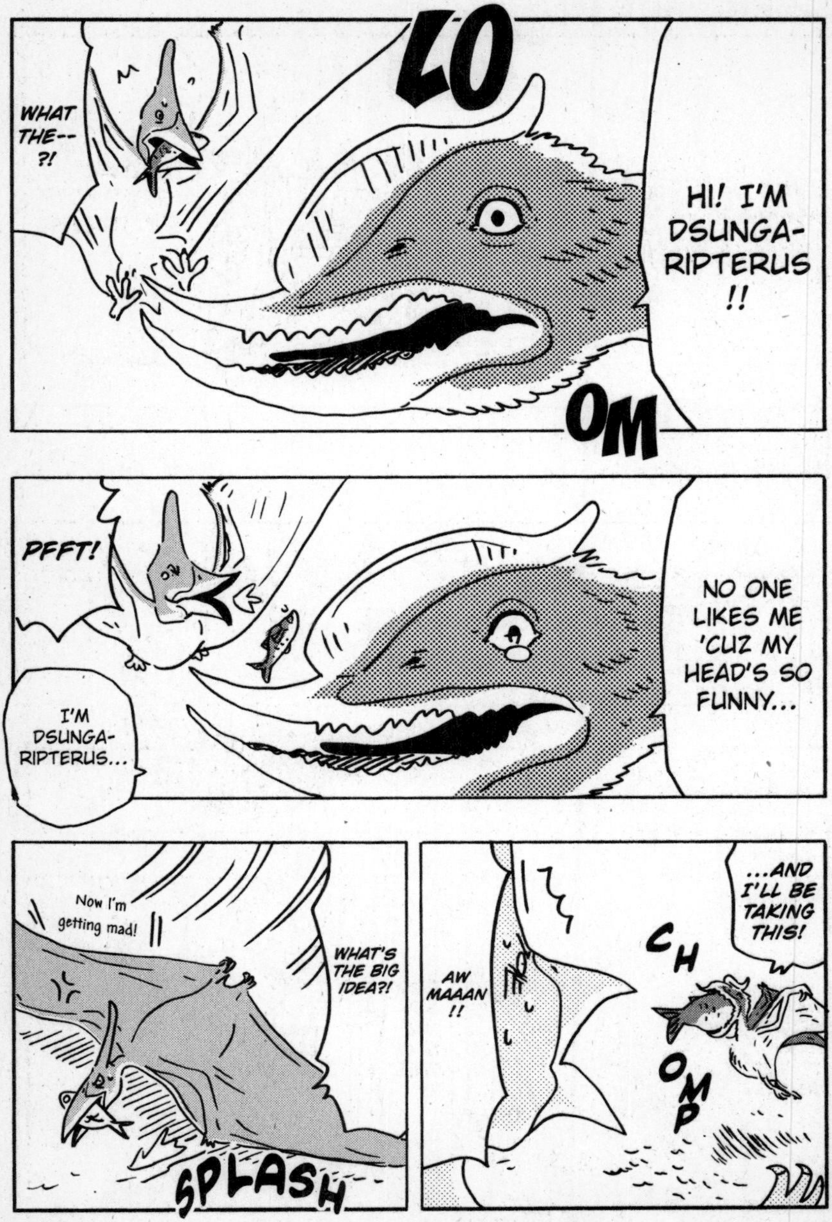
LO
HI! I'M DSUNGARIPTERUS!!
WHAT THE--?!
OM
NO ONE LIKES ME 'CUZ MY HEAD'S SO FUNNY...
PFFT!
I'M DSUNGARIPTERUS...
...AND I'LL BE TAKING THIS!
CH
OMP
AW MAAAN!!
WHAT'S THE BIG IDEA?!
Now I'm getting mad!
SPLASH

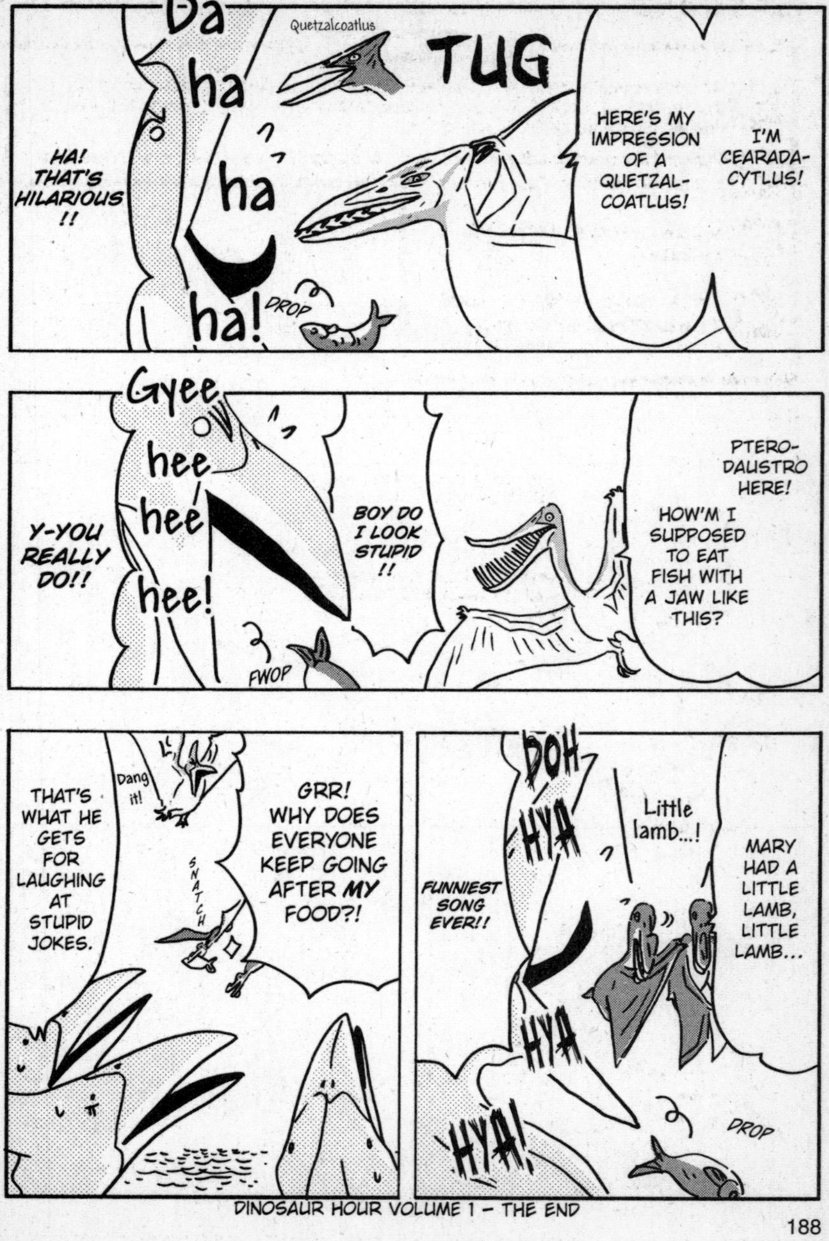
I'M CEARADACYTLUS!
HERE'S MY IMPRESSION OF A QUETZALCOATLUS!
TUG
Quetzalcoatlus
Da ha ha ha!
HA! THAT'S HILARIOUS!!
DROP
PTERODAUSTRO HERE!
HOW'M I SUPPOSED TO EAT FISH WITH A JAW LIKE THIS?
BOY DO I LOOK STUPID!!
Gyee hee hee hee!
Y-YOU REALLY DO!!
FWOP
MARY HAD A LITTLE LAMB, LITTLE LAMB...
Little lamb...!
DOH HYA HYA HYA!
FUNNIEST SONG EVER!!
DROP
GRR! WHY DOES EVERYONE KEEP GOING AFTER *MY* FOOD?!
Dang it!
SNATCH
THAT'S WHAT HE GETS FOR LAUGHING AT STUPID JOKES.

DINOSAUR HOUR VOLUME 1 – THE END

Dino Sumo Wrestlers

Rules for Play

1 Cut along the dotted lines, then prop your dinosaur up by folding the paper down the middle. For best results (and lots of dinosaurs!) photocopy these pages onto heavy paper, then cut out figures along the dotted lines.

2 Position your dinosaur and a friend's on top of an empty box or other shaky surface. Each dinosaur will stand a little differently.

3 Tap either end of the box to begin the battle!

4 The first dinosaur to fall down loses! (Referee dinosaur doesn't count!)

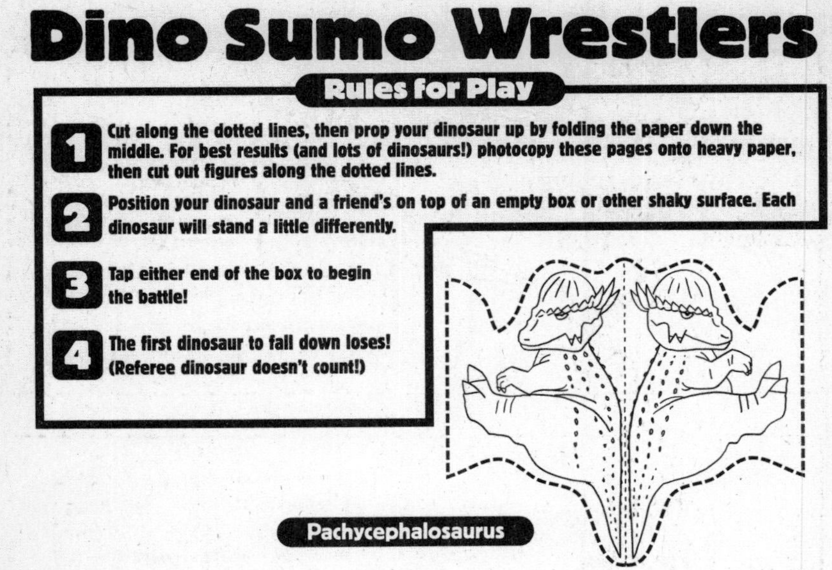

Pachycephalosaurus

Tyrannosaurus

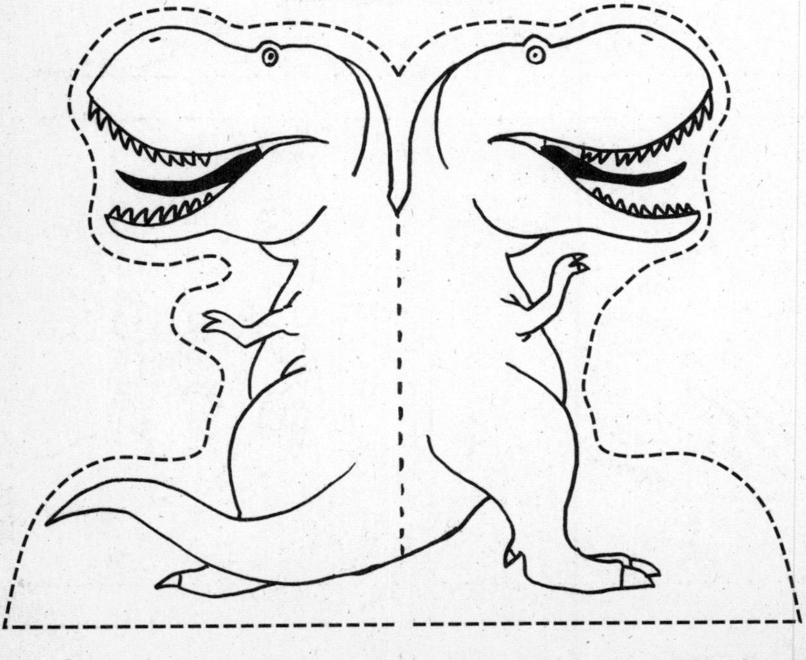

- Color in your dinosaur with crayons or colored pencils!
- Use two Pachycephalosaurus to go head-to-head in battle!
- Be careful when handling scissors. Ask a grown-up to help you.

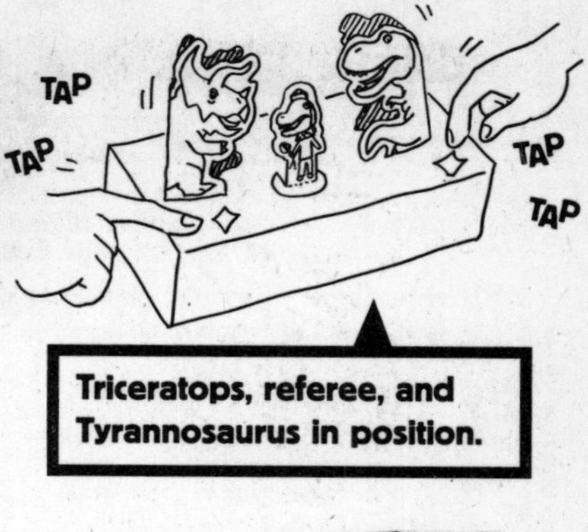
TAP
TAP
TAP
TAP

Triceratops, referee, and Tyrannosaurus in position.

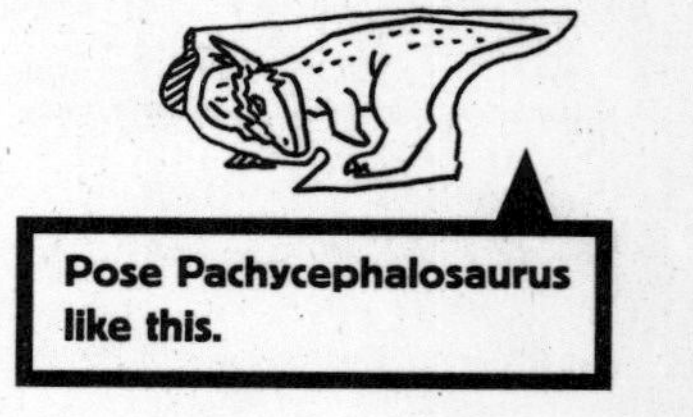

Pose Pachycephalosaurus like this.

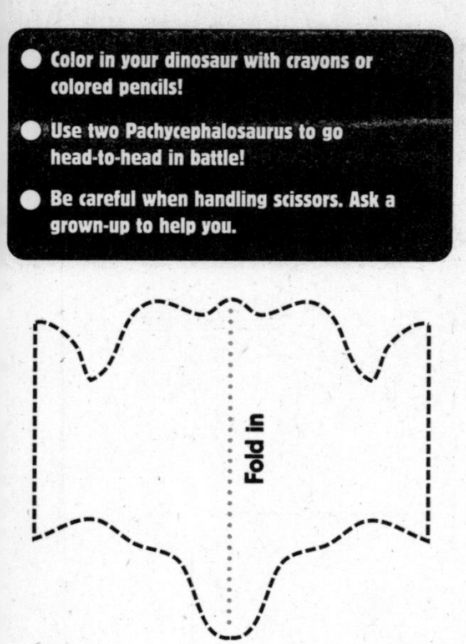
Fold in

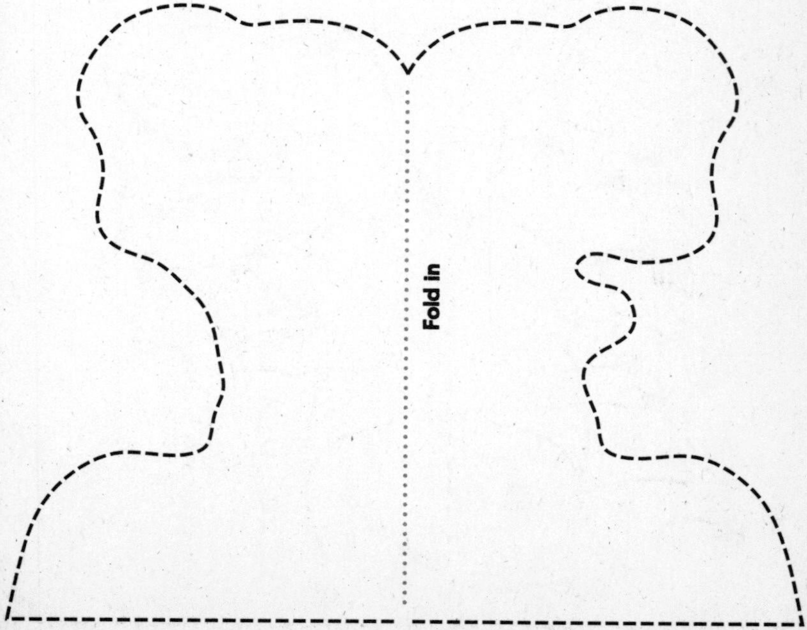
Fold in

Referee

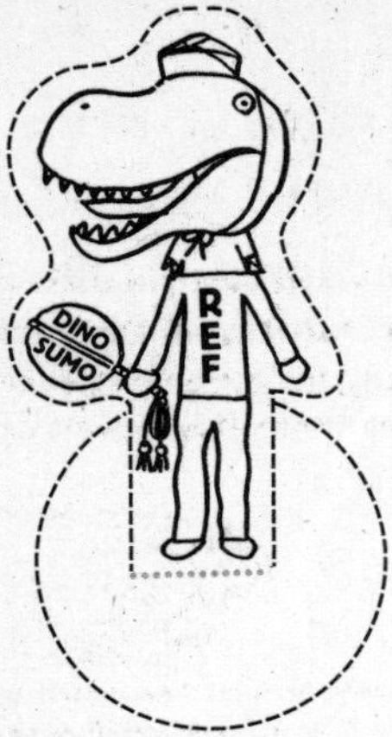
DINO
SUMO
REF

Pachycephalosaurus

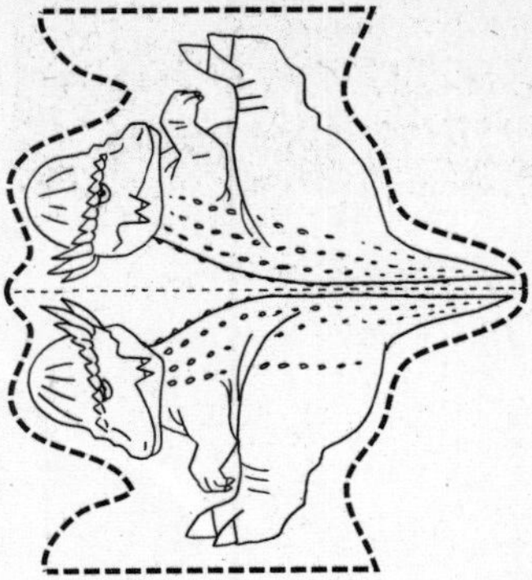

Triceratops

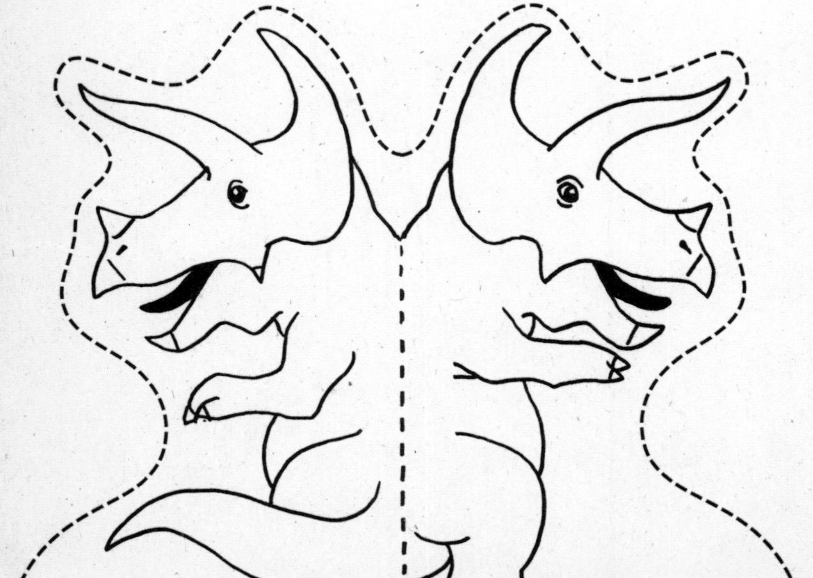

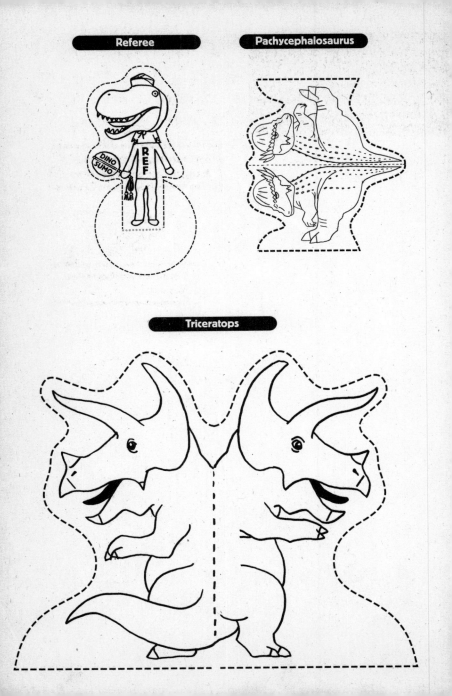

ABOUT THE AUTHOR

Hitoshi Shioya was born in 1969 in Sapporo, Japan. He likes rugby, loves soda pop, and owns a very fierce...cat.